I0572542

The Best of Abyss & Apex

Volume One

The Best of Abyss & Apex

Volume One

Edited by Wendy S. Delmater

HADLEY
RILLE
BOOKS

The stories contained within this book are works of fiction. Any resemblance, unless noted by the author, to actual persons, living or dead, is purely coincidental.

ISBN-13 978-0-9819243-0-4

Published by: Hadley Rille Books
Attention: Eric T. Reynolds
PO Box 25466
Overland Park, KS 66225
USA

www.hadleyrillebooks.com
contact@hadleyrillebooks.com

For Eleanor Grace Good (1925-2003), the toughest editor and best critique partner I ever worked with. My mother was perhaps the one exception to "never show a relative your work." She was my harshest critic, and she believed in my ability to improve back when I was still learning the craft. We should all be graced with someone in this life that encourages us to work hard and follow our dreams.

Copyright Acknowledgments

"The Night The Stars Sang Out My Name" appeared in *Abyss & Apex*, Issue 27, 3rd Quarter 2008, copyright © 2008 by Ken Scholes, reprinted by permission of the author.

"Interfaith" appeared in *Abyss & Apex*, Issue 19, 3rd Quarter 2006, copyright © 2006 by Lisa Mantchev, reprinted by permission of the author.

"Lament for Titan" appeared in *Abyss & Apex*, Issue 24, 4th Quarter 2007, copyright © 2007 by Robin M. Mayhall, reprinted by permission of the author.

"Godspeed, Inc." appeared in *Abyss & Apex*, Issue 20, 4th Quarter 2006, copyright © 2006 by Vincent Miskell, reprinted by permission of the author.

"Night is My House" appeared in *Abyss & Apex*, Issue 21, 1st Quarter 2007, copyright © 2007 by Christopher Vera, reprinted by permission of the author.

"Metamorphoses in Amber" appeared in *Abyss & Apex*, Issue 24, 4th Quarter 2007, copyright © 2007 by Tony Pi, reprinted by permission of the author.

"City of Beautiful Nonsense" appeared in *Abyss & Apex*, Issue 25, 1st Quarter 2008, copyright © 2008 by Justin Howe, reprinted by permission of the author.

"New Spectacles" appeared in *Abyss & Apex*, Issue 19, 3rd Quarter 2006, copyright © 2006 by Will McIntosh, reprinted by permission of the author.

"The Devil You Know" appeared in *Abyss & Apex*, Issue 22, 2nd Quarter 2007, copyright © 2006 by Heidi Wessman Kneale, reprinted by permission of the author.

"Dear Yourself" appeared in *Abyss & Apex*, Issue 16, 4th Quarter 2005, copyright © 2005 by Yoon ha Lee, reprinted by permission of the author.

"Nomad" appeared in *Abyss & Apex*, Issue 20, 4th Quarter 2006, copyright © 2006 by Karl Bunker, reprinted by permission of the author.

"Stories of the Alien Invasion" appeared in *Abyss & Apex*, Issue 21, 1st Quarter 2007, copyright © 2007 by Manek Mistry, reprinted by permission of the author.

Acknowledgments

I hardly know where to start in praise of *Abyss & Apex*'s all-volunteer staff. They've all done marvelous work over the years, and helped make the magazine what it is today.

Our publisher Carol Burrell deserves full credit for getting us all off the ground: it was her vision that birthed the publication. Other managing editors before me—such as Elizabeth Bear, Leah Bobet, Kathryn Allen and Robin Mayhall—found their own story gems in the slush pile, some of which are printed here.

From those who coded the HTML (*thank you* Rebecca and Kelly!) to those who ran the poetry shop—Robyn Mayhall, Trent Walters, and more recently Samantha Henderson—undying thanks. And to all the slush readers who've endured anything from Hugo-worthy writing to badly written westerns and worse pron . . . bless you. I raise a spork[*] in your honor. Thank you Trent, Aleta, Kathryn, Camille, Deirdre, Kelly, Bill, Ilona, Jon, Bill, Rob, Will, Elizabeth, Benjamin, David, and any others might have missed over the years. Some of you even took it upon yourselves to assist with rewrites, polishing nearly perfect stories into gems. Special thanks to Rob Campbell, J.D. Paradise, and others for hard work with authors to rewrite stories that often went on to garner Locus nods and honorable mentions in YBSF anthologies.

Kenn Brown and Chris Wren of Mondolithic Studios made my vision for the cover art a reality—I am in awe. They never cease to amaze me with their talent. And Eric T. Reynolds of Hadley Rille Books is a joy to work with. I thank my sons for their patience when—instead of visiting them—I spent vacation time working on this book and related work at genre conventions. But the chief person I want to single out is Jude-Marie (Kelly) Green. I may have the artistic vision and deep pockets to keep the magazine going and growing but she is the workhorse that makes things tick. You would not be reading *Abyss & Apex* if it were not for her love of the magazine, the genre and her deep friendship with me. She's one of the universe's most wonderful people. You keep conquering the West Coast, Kelly; I will keep trying to conquer the East Coast.

Here is a word of appreciation for all of the authors who sent us their

[*] The customary way for genre editors to remove their eyeballs after reading truly painful stories is via spork.

stories. Although we have good relationships with established writers big names are not our focus—our focus is the writing. But established writers often keep coming back after they've made it. This is because we pay pro rates for flash and sometimes publish their pesky novellas and novelettes (by request) and then submit them for genre awards. We've been able to provide a very high proportion of "first sales" to new writers, too, and are always glad when you think of A&A. It's frightening to send your story out into the world, especially when you are new at submitting to markets. We value our reputation for being writer-friendly and hope to live up to that in the future.

Last but not least, undying thanks has to go to all of you, our readers. Thank you for enjoying the unique vision of Speculative Fiction that A&A offers. Drop us an email at signup@abyssandapex.com to have a link to our quarterly issues to be delivered straight to your email box.

We hope to continue to entertain and amaze you for years to come.

Wendy S. Delmater, Managing Editor
Abyss & Apex Magazine of Speculative Fiction

Contents

Introduction

Writers are artists who paint a picture on your mind and heart. Some of them burn their images deep inside, sculpting who you are. Others play with light shows and illuminate the corners of your soul. May you, the reader, find the music of words, the colors of foreign worlds and the thrill of adventure in these pages.

Science fiction and fantasy have something in common at their core: a sense of wonder. In these tales you will be touched by how human beings might react to powers and technologies, principalities and powers, circumstances and fate.

It's all here. Some writing is indistinguishable from magic.

Wendy S. Delmater
King Park, New York
October 2008

The Night the Stars Sang Out My Name
by Ken Scholes

I should have been a runner.

Of course I'm naked. Naked and running full-on. Suit seized up three weeks back. Then captured. So now I'm naked and running under stars that steal my words and warp my sense of size in the vastness of Everything. Using a stolen charstick to burn my way out. A flash. A scream. A smell of burning meat.

I should have been a chef.

CHIB-CHILI, CHIB-PUREE, CHIB-KABOB—That's my jiminy. He chatters endlessly when nervous. His name is Eddie.

My stomach lurches. I haven't eaten in days. Even chib sounds good.

Speak of the devil, one appears. I burn out its face. Chibby Chibby Burning Bright—

I should have been a poet.

My jiminy agrees with this and launches into a litany of children's verse. *Find our way out of here,* I send.

A trisket a—WORKING ON IT, BOSSMAN—a trasket a green and yellow—

Another chib breaks through the foliage to my west. I sweep the charstick over it. Another flash. Another scream. More meat.

Hey diddle diddle, my son John—WEST FIVE LEAGUES, ROVING PACK SEVEN—went to bed with his stockings—

I adjust my course. Good work, Eddie.

DON'T MENTION IT.

And he's back at it with the verses. Five leagues more of Eddie's manic sing-song. I tell myself I'm going to have him removed. Upgraded. I tell myself he's been a real pain in the you-know-what for the past thirty years. I tell myself that he's not my friend and I don't need him.

But I do. I really *should* have been a poet. Then I wouldn't need this extra personality piggy-backing my own, watching my six. Then all I'd need is words.

WORDS—BIRDS—TURDS—CURDS—

A moment's peace is all I ask.

A teacher. I should have been a teacher. An academic, stuffy and proud and (most important of all) without a jiminy.

The whoop-whoop of a Finder goes off somewhere to my left. The moss gives way to ankle-deep swamp-water. Something slimy and soft moves over my foot. God knows what else lives on these far-flung planets. We thought the chibs were bad enough.

THE INNER C'HIBORYAL SYSTEMS ARE HOME TO THOUSANDS OF DISTINCT SPECIES OF FLORA AND FAUNA, LENDING SUPPORT TO FELORIAN'S THEORUM OF—

Enough, Eddie. You left me, you fucker.

The jiminy finally, finally shuts up. Lights squeeze past me hissing into the water. Behind me, chib-talk warbles in panting shouts. I spin-drop to one knee, the foul water splashing up into my face. I level the charstick and sweep it left and right. More screams. One of them is mine. A near passing beam opens a welt on my side.

I'm not gonna make it. I'm going back to the camp, I think. That stinking hole where'd they'd taken me. Where they'd hurt me into talking even though I knew absolutely nothing about the battleboats.

I should have been a—

SOLDIER! SOLDIER! ON YOUR FEET, SOLDIER!

And he sounds like my Drilly back Home. Like two hundred fifteen pounds of midnight black meanness poured into a man and force-fed to a brigade of eager young bucks. Drilly's dead, I know, but that voice. That—

MOVE! MOVE! MOVE!

I'm up and running. Somewhere, Eddie is ticking away the long list of what's wrong with me. Chib unbending drugs. Head injury. Dehydration. Exhaustion. All good reasons for me to falter but piss-poor excuses. Did they used to say piss-poor back in the old days?

The things you wonder.

A pop somewhere way back behind. Another Finder? Or maybe a Seeker? Something tangles around my foot. It tightens and pulls. I fall face first and the charstick hisses and sparks out when it hits the water. I lose it, scramble for it and find nothing. I'm being dragged backwards now, my fingers digging into the muck to find some kind of grip. Somewhere behind me a chib is reeling me in and I remember fishing with my father back before the bug-bombs fell. I was eight. It took six months to figure out that we were being poisoned by something other than evolution.

He held up a trout. My Dad, I mean. Held it up and grinned. "Look, Billy!"

I smile back. "Nice one, Dad."

CHIB PATROL EIGHT CUBITS TO THE SIX, Eddie says.

I push off from the bottom. I flip myself over so that my shoulders and arms leave a wake behind me. Overhead, stars like scattered new pennies glint and shimmer in a thick field of sky punctuated by skeletal trees.

I'm afraid now. My nose is in the wash of rotten water. I escaped once, I tell myself. I could do it again.

NOW THEY KNOW ABOUT ME. YOU'LL BE ON YOUR OWN THIS TIME.

I snarl. *Like before.*

TEMPORARY DISASSOCIATIVE MALFUNCTION.

I know he's right. He came back when he could. Came back and got me the hell out of there.

I see them now. They huddle, hunched over, piles of stinking meat on too many legs with too many arms. One of them works the Seeker and reminds me of my Dad and that trout again. My bladder's dry or I'd have cut loose right then. My body is remembering those arms, those long fingers, the weird tools and needles that made me scream and talk and sob.

PREPARE FOR COGNITIVE OVERRIDE. I've heard of it happening before. I've also heard of it going very wrong. There's a reason why the AI's aren't allowed to drive. Unhinged minds. Atrocities.

No, Eddie, I send. *Terminate override.*

SORRY BOSSMAN.

The chib pain was nothing compared to this. Head squeezed in a vice and popping. Fire underneath the skin spreading. But I do not scream. Roar of water rushing by.

My roar.

And somehow, I am on my feet. Every limb is lashing out and I spin and spin like those gypsies in Mom's shake and whirl dervish glass.

I should have been a dancer.

I yank the reel from the fisher-chib's hands and beat him with it. My foot caves in a soft chib jaw. My other hand finds well-hidden but unprotected genitalia and squeezes out the howls. It's not me. It's Eddie. My jiminy. Raging.

In moments, they are all down. Eddie has another charstick now. He thumbs it to life and burns them into the bloody, boiling swamp-water. Chib-stew. Now I'm the rider in the backseat watching him do something I've done a hundred times on twenty worlds.

LET'S GO, I say.

He doesn't answer. He turns in the direction of Roving Pack Seven and we set out. No more chibs find us and somewhere in the mesh-cap beneath my own scalp I go to sleep.

When I wake up, it's my world again and I think for a moment that I am alone for the first time since I woke up in the chib camp. Before *that* terrible day, I'd spent thirty years with a voice inside my head keeping me safe, alive.

But I am not alone. Hulking suits move sluggishly around me, patrolling the fringe of my vision. I hear the hum of their biomechs. I hear each tiny pebble beneath their feet as it crushes to powder.

"Eddie?" It took a second to realize I'd said it aloud.

One of the suits stops, turns, moves toward me. There is a hiss as the voicemitter engages. "Sorry, Sarge. We've uploaded your jiminy for evaluation. It was pinging pretty high on the stress-check." The PFC pauses, probably wondering where my face went. I want to tell him that it's slid off me and into the dirt of this chib world hell. "I'm sure they'll get him back to you soon."

I swallow back a lump. I try to fight tears. Something breaks in me like one of those pebbles underneath massive metal boots. I am naked and alone in this place.

And I hear my name and look up. Overhead, the stars are moving in a dance like Eddie's dance. Overhead, deep space pushes down on me like a warm blanket. Overhead, a solitary speck of light moves at a different pace than all the others. A transport, full-up, off to find another chib world and punish it for the near extinction of the human race.

I miss the voice inside my head.

I should have been a—

No. I am a soldier.

I miss my friend.

Interfaith
by Lisa Mantchev

I found the box of angels in the attic when I went looking for the harvest wreathes. They were under the Christmas tree stand and alongside a stack of old suitcases, in one of His cardboard bins marked 'Winter Clothes, 1985.'

"Hallelujah! Hallelujah!" they sang as they swirled like celestial hummingbirds in the slanting golden light.

I shoved the box away and wiped my dusty palms on the seat of my robe.

"Damn it all."

The tiny creatures disapproved and smote me with flaming swords the size of toothpicks. I batted them away and went downstairs to get the Raid.

Justine was supposed to be doing her homework at the kitchen counter, but her notebook was covered with doodles of the Virgin Mary. This new bout of divinity was hitting her hard.

"I thought you were looking for the harvest decorations."

"I was." I stood on tiptoe and reached unsuccessfully for the bright red can. Justine shook her head and went back to her scribbles.

"It's a heathen holiday anyway, Mum. We shouldn't even celebrate the cutting of the wheat, or whatever it is."

"Spare me the pagan holiday lecture, Justine. You sound just like—" I bit the words off and swallowed them.

She gave me her Suffering Martyr look. "Just like who? Just like my Father?"

The separation was too fresh, the wound too raw. I needed a distraction. Besides, my little saint-in-training was never going to let me exterminate a holy infestation.

"There are seraphim in the attic. You want to round them up?"

"How wonderful!" Justine dropped her pen and clasped her hands together to give thanks.

"You have to the count of three, and then I'm setting off a bug bomb."

She ran, scattering beneficence and glory in her wake. I swept up the trail and emptied the glittery mess in the dustbin. The bits of silver and gold sparkled like stars and I swallowed. I should have ascended to my place in the heavens eons ago. But I hadn't been ready then, and I certainly wasn't ready now.

"Where are you going with those?"

Justine dragged the battered canary cage across the kitchen and dumped it next to her backpack.

"To school. They're a visual aid in my presentation."

The angels rattled the bars and protested their captivity in dulcet tones. I wrinkled my nose at the smell.

"You haven't cleaned that lately." I put six wafers and a bottle of grape juice in a brown paper bag for her. "I seem to recall a lot of noble promises you made."

"The bathroom font is empty. I'll stop at the chapel before first period." She sipped from a glass of water while I puttered around the kitchen. "What are you doing?"

"Cooking breakfast." I rediscovered the smell of honey and almonds in the morning and smiled.

"Whatever for?"

"Because I can. Because it's fun."

"You never ate in the morning *before*."

"Change isn't always a bad thing," I said, keeping my tone light.

She wrinkled her nose at me. "The smell is nauseating. Like a buttered beehive in high summer."

"Just have a bite," I urged, my mouth full of flaky pastry and nuts. "You might like it."

"Moth-er." She gave it a long look, even went so far as to poke it with her finger. Then she folded her hands together and prayed for my immortal soul.

I shrugged and took another bite. "Even the dedicated eat, Justine."

"Shush. I'm counting." Worn wooden beads clicked together. The angels smirked and stuck out their tongues. I threatened the cage with a spatula and they invoked the Almighty's wrath in pixie chirps.

"Oh, shut up," I muttered.

Justine finished her prayer, rescued her charges and kissed my cheek.

"I'll see you tonight!" she called over her shoulder as she ran for the bus. "Love you!"

"Love you more!" I shouted back. Then silence descended and even the angels would have been welcome company.

I dumped the dishes in the sink (*who's here to see?* I thought with a certain amount of grim glee.) Then I paced through the house and stood before the hearth. My touchstone. I built up the fire and took comfort in its steady warmth.

The doorbell rang and I started at the unfamiliar chime.

Amazing Grace? I need to change that.

I padded into the hall and unbolted the heavy oak door; a young woman stood on the stoop, heavy with pregnancy and worries.

"Please. Please help me," she cried, and staggered into my arms.

Apparently my return to my "heathen" roots had not gone unnoticed.

"Mother?" Justine hovered in the kitchen doorway as though she could sense the traces of alien worship. She set the birdcage on the floor and took a hesitant step inside. The angels—which I expected to launch into a full air raid—didn't make a peep.

"How did your presentation go?" I swiped a few crumbs off the counter then attacked the breakfast dishes with gusto.

"Fine." She peeked over my shoulder. "Why are you doing those now?"

"Didn't feel like doing them this morning. Is that a crime?" Energy hummed through me; if I wasn't careful, I was going to melt the plates.

"What's for dinner?" She set her backpack on a barstool as though it might explode.

"Dinner?" I blinked. "Um."

Both her eyebrows skidded up. "Um what? You didn't make dinner?"

"Calm down. It's not a sign of the apocalypse." I jerked open the freezer door, scanned the contents and gave up. "Why don't we order a pizza?"

"Pizza?" Her voice scaled two octaves. "Do you even know how to do that?"

"I'm not a moron, Justine. I know how to order a pizza."

"But—" she sputtered. "We never ordered pizza before."

I located the number in the directory and dialed before she could protest further.

"Change is good. Especially change covered in pepperoni and mushrooms."

She crossed her arms. "Just tell me why you didn't make dinner. Something happened. I can tell."

"Yes. Delivery please," I told the bored, teenaged voice on the other end of the line.

"Moth-er!"

I covered the receiver. "I had a visitor, all right? Now behave yourself. I'm on the damn phone."

Justine's mouth worked. Then she snapped it shut and stomped off to sprinkle holy water in every corner of the ground floor. A miniature exorcism/protest, I imagine. She finished just as the pizza arrived. The cardboard box sagged under the weight of crust and toppings; the aroma when I opened the lid was heavenly.

"Are you going to eat?"

Her stomach growled. She plopped down at the table and helped herself to a slice. We chewed in silence and I thought the storm was over. But in the middle of her third piece, she burst into tears.

"Honey, it's all right." I stroked the top of her head and left a smear of sauce in her hair. "Really."

"He'll never come back if you go wild like this."

"Oh, Justine." My sigh came from the very heart of me. "He wasn't going to come back anyway."

"He doesn't love me."

"Of course He does."

"Not any more than any of the other little children."

I grit my teeth. "You mustn't doubt. Have faith."

"I have. More faith than anyone!"

It was true. I couldn't argue.

"Maybe—maybe He'll come for Christmas."

"Maybe."

She heard the doubt in my voice and there were more tears. The rest of the pizza floated away on a sea of salt water and grief.

After I tucked her into bed, I went downstairs and picked up the phone. Set it down. Up. Down. I pounded the counter with the receiver, took a deep breath and dialed. Got His voicemail, of course.

"You fell out of love with me, and that was fine. But your daughter needs you—"

"Hello?" He'd picked up the phone. I stuttered with surprise.

"Um, hi."

Neither of us spoke for a moment. I tried to set my resentment on the back burner. For Justine's sake.

"Your daughter hasn't seen you for ages."

He sighed. "You got custody. I got visitations."

"She misses you. Only you know why."

"Tell her I love her."

"She doesn't need me to tell her." I slammed down the phone, but His voice followed me into the living room.

"I told you a long time ago that this is how it would have to be. That I have responsibilities. You're being unreasonable."

"This isn't about me." I swept the hearth clean with a look.

"How many times do we have to go through this?" The lights flickered.

I stood my ground. "Don't you get all High-And-Mighty with me."

"You sound just like the rest of your ilk."

I laughed. I couldn't help myself. "You met my family. Knew what you were letting yourself in for."

"You were supposed to be the quiet one," He answered.

"And I should never have married the Catholic God. All that incense . . . Ugh!" I flopped on the sofa and plugged my fingers pointedly in my ears, but His voice was in my head now.

"I've missed you."

"Oh, I don't believe in you."

"A likely story."

The angels chattered and flapped in their gilded prison.

"I wondered where I left those," he said as he materialized. The bars dissolved and they were free. They settled on the mantelpiece, unusually quiet. He sat next to me, wearing the skin I always liked the best. "It smells different in here. You had visitors."

"Visitor singular. Just a woman in need of—" I trailed off, unable to complete the thought.

"Her goddess," He finished for me. "You must have wanted the company, or she never would have been able to find the house."

"I suppose I did."

"Have you thought of ascending now that—"

"Give me a break. It was only one visitor." I stared at the hearth, into the blue twisting flames of the fire. "It's been a long time. I thought I might have forgotten the way of it."

"It's who you are." He gave me a rueful smile filled with a thousand questions. "Just don't start spilling goat entrails on the rug, all right?"

Justine hovered around Him the next morning. She chattered about her schoolwork and her visions while He nodded and looked wise. He ate toast and eggs, so she did too. They bent their heads together and whispered in tongues.

He soon grew distracted, pausing mid-sentence to listen very carefully to nothing I could hear. I scrubbed a frying pan until I scoured a hole through the Teflon. It didn't take divine insight to know He wouldn't stay much longer.

After a particularly long silence, He got to his feet and hugged Justine to Him.

"I need to go."

Justine's face puckered. "But you just got here."

He detached himself very carefully from her grasp. "I've neglected things to stay this long. You'll come see me soon, though, baby girl."

In the time it took me to turn around, He was halfway down the hall.

"Daddy!" Justine chased after him. "You forgot the angels!"

But the door was ajar and He was gone.

A much-subdued Justine caught the angels with infinite patience and love but had nowhere to put them. She let them go in the backyard, her eyes filled with tears. They followed her as far as the porch and batted at the windows.

"Go on, get out of here!" she yelled.

They hovered, fearful. I'd never seen her angry before and my skin prickled. I could protect the house, but the sky was no realm of mine. Clouds gathered overhead, as dark as my little girl's eyes. Thunder rattled the window and lightning bolts rained down. They squeaked with impotent wrath and I smelled burning feathers through the glass.

Justine stomped up the stairs and slammed her bedroom door. I could hear her kicking things.

The next morning, she dumped a large box on the floor.

"I don't want these anymore." The expression behind her water glass was sulky.

I picked through the plaid of her uniform. Her rosary beads. A bible worn thin with frequent readings.

"You sure?" I wiped the counter and tried not to dance.

"Yeah. I'm tired of all that sanctimonious bullshit."

I met her gaze. "Oh come on. It wasn't all bullshit."

She flounced to the counter and stuck a fork in a plate of ambrosia. She talked with her mouth full of marshmallows.

"Whatever, Mother. . ."

The doorbell rang. She jumped up.

"I'll get it."

"It's probably another petitioner here to see me." No use sugarcoating it. They'd probably be queuing up on the lawn by the end of the week.

"I figured as much." The set of her jaw looked very familiar. "After I let her in, I want to you show me how to set out the altar. I saw it in the attic."

The angels batted madly at the window. She heaved her fork at the glass and turned her back on them.

"What in the name of all that is Holy is going on?"

We'd shooed the last worshipper out of the living room temple a mere hour before and I was exhausted. The last thing I needed was an irate call from Him. I cradled the phone in the crook of my neck while Justine cooed and pecked crumbs off the counter.

"She's trying something new."

"So I gathered. And you're encouraging this behavior?"

Snap! The dove was gone. Justine stood naked in the middle of the tiled floor for a split second. Then she was a birch tree, slim and white in the pale sunrise.

"She's missed a week of school," He thundered.

"She's taking a little break."

Snap! The tree was gone, and wriggling golden puppy was in its place. I laughed. She'd always wanted a dog, but He was allergic.

"I don't know what you're trying to pull—"

"I'm not pulling anything. I let her worship you for years without saying a word against it. You could at least show me the same courtesy."

"She's one of the chosen—"

"You forget she's also my child. A child of *two* immortals. I know you thought that your half was stronger, but that doesn't appear to be the case." Justine squatted to pee on the floor and I yelped. "I've got to go!"

I whisked her outside. This time, the line stayed dead.

The angels circled Justine-the-puppy with concerned interest and disapproval. She leapt at them and barked, then caught one between flashing white teeth and shook it viciously.

She chewed on it for a bit then left it in the grass. It twitched back to life, sodden and disoriented, its wings punctured with teeth holes.

Justine grew her hair long and plaited it with beads. Flowers bloomed in unexpected corners of the house. Animals congregated on the porch and mingled with waiting petitioners. I watched her blossom, and I hummed while listened to prayers. By the end of the week, she could sweep the hearth clean with a look and grant simple appeals.

The pride of it nearly killed me. I knew that someday soon she'd be strong enough, old enough, that maybe I could take my place in the sky without worry or guilt. Until then, I contented myself with her and the temple.

He sent gifts, hoping to resurrect her affections. She returned two or three and gleefully destroyed a few others. But even I didn't approve when she broke the halo into pieces and constructed a fabulous, glittering swag to hang around her throat.

"He's going to be angry," I warned.

"Well, duh."

But even indefatigable youth was disconcerted when she began to bleed from her hands and her feet. I placed an angry phone call as she sobbed behind the locked bathroom door.

"Maybe you should call Him, tell Him you're sorry—"

"If He wants an apology, He's got a long wait coming."

"Honey, you are double damned for stubbornness. You got it from both of us." She didn't say anything. "I think He's more hurt than angry."

"He can just get bent."

"That's enough of that."

She jerked the door open and I took a step back.

"Stop defending him. I'm sick of listening to you defend him. He's not always right. And neither are you." She brushed past me and stormed down the hall.

"What's that supposed to mean?" Prickles of unease snaked over me. She didn't answer, just grabbed her jacket off the chair and slammed the door behind her.

"What's that supposed to mean?" I repeated to the empty room.

It was past midnight when she got home. I sat at the kitchen table, staring at food I'd prepared but not eaten. Wine I'd poured but not drunk.

"I think you're a bit young to stay out so late," I said after a moment.

"Why haven't you ascended?" The words tumbled out of her.

"I wasn't aware that you even knew that word, Justine." I took a sip from my wine glass, hand shaking.

"I heard it at school. The kids were all asking me about the temple . . . why you haven't ascended. They said it was because of Daddy. Because of me."

"That's partially true, I guess. I didn't want to leave either of you behind. I didn't want to forget, to go while you are still so young."

"Don't use me as an excuse Mother." Her hands clenched over and over. "You're afraid. You hid behind Daddy and now that he's gone you're hiding behind me."

"I'm happy here with you, with the temple."

"But you're not a priestess, you're a *goddess*. You belong up there." She stabbed a finger at the sky. "It's your destiny."

"I can't." The tears poured down my face now. "It's too late, Justine. I waited too long. I'm bound here, to you, to this house. You *need* me."

"Maybe I still need you. But I don't need a mother that's a coward." Justine put her chin in the air. "Just let go of him, Mom. We have to let go."

"Her anger is disconcerting, isn't it?" His voice slid in my ear and I almost welcomed His company. "How long do you suppose she'll be mad this time?"

"You're the omnipotent one. You tell me."

He shook His head. "I can't read her as I used to. What are we going to do about this?"

"Damned if I know. What are you doing here anyway? She doesn't want to speak to you either."

He didn't answer.

"You've been keeping tabs on me." I had no hope of reconciliation; part of me had died when He left. But it was nice to know He cared, even a little.

"Yeah. It's what I do." He faded around the edges and was gone.

I let him go.

I stood again in the attic. Moonlight danced over the detritus of a broken marriage and memories of a child grown. I unlocked a trunk of leather and hammered gold and opened it with a twist of my hand. Silver folds embroidered with brilliant threads of star shine glinted in the late afternoon light.

I'd left Olympus in this gown.

It slithered over my skin and settled on my curves, the fit perfect from memory. I added a parure of flame. Curls tumbled free to the backs of my knees.

Then I tiptoed downstairs and opened her bedroom door.

"Honey?"

She raised her tousled head from the pillow with an incoherent mumble. I knelt by the bed, stroked the hair off her brow.

"You're dressed. Why are you dressed?" she asked. I took her by the hand and offered her a gown of sunlight and dryad tears.

"Try this on. We're going on a little vacation."

Only a few minutes later, we mounted the stairs to the widow's walk, accompanied only by the murmur of silk on the floorboards. The door stuck—no one ever came up here—but I wrenched it open and took my first step outside since I'd crossed the threshold as a bride. Justine took a deep breath of cold night air and laughed. And I held her hand, and lifted the other to the sky.

Stars tumbled from the sky in benediction as I willed the two of us upwards. The heavens rushed around us and the house fell away. The space between Justine and I was an umbilicus, stretched but not snapped.

My family called their greetings. Zeus himself crowned me with stars.

"Welcome Hestia. We have waited a long time for you."

I wrapped myself in blue velvet, wiped the glittering constellations of my eyes. Justine stood at my side, shining with her own special light.

My greatest believer.

I hugged her close, and patted the pocket that held the last remaining angel. When the time came, he could show her the way home.

Lament For Titan

I lost my mind to rational thought.
I lost my heart to fundamental truth.
I just gave in to faith in the rightness of the place.
As soon as I saw those first grainy, greyscale images,
I knew I had found home.
The fog-shrouded landscape called to me
From eight hundred twenty million miles away.
From across most of our solar system,
That sullen orange siren was singing me home.
The other colonists used to ask me,
Joking, how I got born on Earth.
I couldn't explain why a recycled mixture
Was the air my lungs
Were meant to breathe.
I couldn't explain why our purified water
Tasted like mother's milk to me.

I know it hurt my parents to see me board
The settlement ship with such evident longing.
Like a black sheep, I strayed far from the herd.
But there were no green pastures on that world
Of methane rivers and acetylene ice. So
Now I'm back. For three long years
I've lived once more on the world where I was born.
My family is happy to have me "home" again.

But for almost fourteen years I was home, and home was Titan.
—Robin M. Mayhall

Godspeed, Inc.

Vincent Miskell

When you're making sweeps close to Pluto's orbit—okay, where Pluto's orbit *used to be*—the first thing you do when you're conscious is check voice, holovid, and text mail. No matter how much the techs compress a transmission, it still takes 5-6 hours to reach this far Out West after they get it all together. So news wise, you're always at least a half-day behind everybody else. But a few sports and news holovids, a perky or sultry hello from an old lover ("I miss you, Naomi"), even some bureaucratic smoke from the bubble heads at Godspeed Inc. help you feel less like Disembodied Ghost in Space.

So first thing, I check mail.

NOTHING. And no incoming either.

In fact, all the log files show empty as though an emergency system wipe blanked them. I figure a memory gelpak went overload, cascading through all the other gelpaks—something that's not supposed to happen. But most sweepers experience this kind of gel crash enough times to know that it's not "user error."

That is, when there used to be other sweepers.

Until just a few years ago, this was a two-person job. And before that, right after planetoid Pluto got sucked through a rift in the spacetime fabric to dimensions unknown, Godspeed had a half dozen sweeper ships deployed here Out West, mending spacetime with special particle beams. A few even had faster-than-light Q-drives of their own—not that they were ever used.

Now, there's just me in Sweeper Two, with the Q-drive removed, of course.

Even after almost twenty years, some of the space environmentalists, especially on Mars, are still pissed about losing Pluto and Charon. Still jittery about Godspeed's FTL Q-drive punching holes in the universe, which is why they affectionately refer to my employer as "God Peed." Officially, of course, Godspeed doesn't admit direct responsibility for rifts—they just sometimes appear after a Q-drive launch.

Could Mars go missing in a spacetime rift? Sure, if some faster-than-light submoron pilot powered up near Mars orbit. But that isn't likely—not with UN Security Units on board every active Q-drive ship. And not with their hot little fingers on the remote control of the pilot's brain implant. One push and *KA-BOOM*: the inside of the pilot's skull is applesauce.

Fortunately, there's nothing but the usual pack of neurons inside my head. And nothing but some nutrient implants in my body. In fact, I had to lose some parts for medical reasons for this job, like my breasts and uterus, which I'll get put back when I retire in about ten months at 32, with a big Godspeed Inc. pension and bonus. As a googol-buck corporation though, Godspeed can afford full body and organ restoration, plus whatever genetically engineered cosmetics my seductive little heart desires. Just less than a year more cocooned as a Godspeed tomboy caterpillar—then I emerge on Earth or Luna as the Femme Fatale Butterfly Goddess of Endless Fertility and Love. I've got all my bodily specs and a three-world tour worked out, especially Mars—which is still 100 percent retrovirus free.

That's the plan anyway. The exact same one that my former partner, Bonnie Perez, is supposed to be enjoying.

Anyway, I'm not really worried about the gelpaks because anything quasi-electronic or mechanical eventually yields to my touch. Computers, particle drives, environmental control systems—all succumb to what others have called my "magic hands."

Before I go to work on the mail problem though, I check for rifts on the spacetime monitoring screens. Eleven standard days ago from this sector, Godspeed slammed its most expensive luxury liner, Pegasus IV, on a 30-light-year journey to what sweepers call the Wild, Wild West. But, so far, no rifts.

Then I see something suddenly burst behind me.

The whole aft monitor is strobing scarlet and probably screaming a siren too—but I disconnected the audio a year ago. Interfered too much with my sleep cycle—every piece of debris and dust set the damn thing off.

The aft holovid cameras look offline now, unless a giant swirling Kandinsky painting has decided to join me for breakfast. Quickly, I switch everything aft over to my main screen. Graviton wave readings pop on and off like multi-colored ballooning fireworks.

The first thing I think is *Pluto's back*!

But I'm wrong. The wave readings should be periodic—not idiotic. Now X-ray squiggles jumble all over the screen in a dancing frenzy. This is *something else. Something really big*, and it's right on my ass. Maybe a whole alternative universe is trying to squeeze through a Godspeed spacetime rift.

An hour more dozing and I would have slept forever.

Instantly, I fire the aft particle gun at the *something really big*, and almost simultaneously I activate the magsail to catch any blow-back. Both should give me a little distance. I feel the dampening field rapidly turn up a few notches as I accelerate with a lot more kick than I expect. The magsail is billowing with all kinds of energy, and even through the damper, I can almost feel the ligament-ripping slam of hard acceleration.

Like the good Godspeed sweeper pilot I am, I transmit the tech and holovid data to Godspeed Earth. But with almost a 12-hour transmission turnaround and at least a normal two-month trip west to me, I'm not counting on a quick rescue from the *something really big*. Following emergency protocol, I also pop a copy to Godspeed's Martian research center—not that the Ares Lab monkeys have any ships to deploy—but they'll get the data a little earlier. Maybe some of the lab techs there can hand out some quick life-saving advice.

I spend some time trying to make sense of the senseless graviton wave readings, looking for some pattern—and finally set one of the analysis computers to search for periods of up to a thousand. How could these readings not repeat?

Briefly, I think about dodging around the *something really big*, but its energy and gravity scare me into running away. Since I'm already roughly heading toward Uranus, and Neptune's on the other side of the Sun, I plot a course East toward Uranus since it is the closest planet and more or less lined up with Earth and Mars. The two big giants, Saturn and Jupiter, are about 90 degrees out, so I only have the little gas giant to use as a gravity assist or maybe act as a shield from the *something really big*. Trouble is, Uranus lies halfway home and will take me a month to reach. I check the *something really big's* speed. I let out a sigh: it's steady at two thirds of mine and is probably being drawn toward Uranus, too.

Now there's nothing more I can do without more data, so I reconnect my audio alarms and put myself under for an 8-hour cycle.

As soon as I wake, I see the mail files streaming in. But the analysis computer is still chugging away—no results there.

I read the first mail file:

TO: SWEEPER TWO
FROM: BONNIEP@GODSPEED.ARESLAB1

HAIL NAOMI!

LONG TIME NO HEAR, SEE, OR READ.

ALL SIX OF US HERE AT ARES ARE WORKING THE DATA ROUND THE CLOCK. WE NOTIFIED UN AUTHORITIES AS PER PROTOCAL AND RETRANSMITTED YOUR INFO TO GODSPEED EARTH AND GODSPEED LUNA JUST IN CASE YOURS GETS DEFLECTED OR DISTORTED. AT LEAST THEY'LL KNOW WE ARE ALSO ANALYZING THE DATA.

WE SHOULD HAVE SOMETHING FOR YOU WITHIN THE HOUR.

BONNIE JUL 14 2097: 2313 ARES LAB TIME

It was just too incredible! When did Bonnie Perez come back to work for Godspeed? I guess three years of her femme fatale fling were enough for her—but signed on with the Ares Lab monkeys? That didn't sound like the Bonnie who swore off Godspeed forever. But at least there's somebody I can trust. Somebody who might not put Godspeed's image and profits before my well being.

The second and third files are long news vids with no mention of the *something really big*. I delete them after a quick scan. The fourth file is a bare acknowledgment from Godspeed Earth. They received my data—oh, how wonderful! The bastards.

I transmit a short thank you to Bonnie, using my pet name for her, "Bon-Bon." But don't get me wrong; we never really had a romance going like most sweeper mates. Just a little hugging and kissing whenever monotony and melancholy got to be too much. When you're both missing most of your reproductive gear, sex is more a juicy memory than the juiced intensity of sweaty body electricity. At least it was that way for us. If she'd been a man, my body might have risen to the occasion even so.

Not that I didn't fantasize about Bonnie a little, especially after she ran her stash of homemade holovid porn for me. Naturally, I laughed (and lost my breath a few times) at her wickedly scornful narration, but mentally I was participating in her holovid adventures and imagining she was doing the same with me.

But it never happened. She was just the only warm, fleshy body besides mine, for millions of kilometers.

In reality, I usually daydreamed about men with thick hairy forearms, high IQs, and other above-the-norm necessaries. Musings I shared with Bonnie. Along with so many feelings, secrets, and follies during the 18 months we were so up close and personal. Point is: we loved each other, but we were not lovers. Nothing sexual haunted us—no erotic undertows, jealousies, or resentments to distort our close connection. So, I trusted her completely.

Whatever she told me to do, I'd do without question. Well, almost without question. I might have a few quibbles about life and death issues.

Bonnie is back:

TO: SWEEPER TWO

FROM: BONNIEP@GODSPEED.ARESLAB1

WELL NAOMI, YOU'RE NOT GOING TO BELIEVE THIS, BUT ALL OUR "MONKEY ANALYSIS" (REMEMBER WHAT WE USED TO CALL THESE GUYS?) SHOWS THAT A BIG FAT BLACK HOLE IS ON YOUR TAIL.

FOR NOW, JUST KEEP HEADING EAST TOWARD US. START DOING NAVIGATION COMPS TOWARD UMBRIEL. YOU MAY NEED TO SWITCH RIDES. NOT SURE YET. OH YEAH, SPEED UP A LITTLE, IF YOU CAN.

ALL HOPES WITH YOU.

BONNIE JUL 15 2097: 0016 ARES LAB TIME

Whoa! A goddamned black hole about to chew my ass!

I run some calculations. Then quickly, I wop the aft gun again for almost a minute and widen the magsail to the limit. Old Sweeper Two slams a little faster toward Uranus and its darkest moon, Umbriel. Accelerating a little too suddenly, I feel a brief wave of nausea as the dampening field kicks in much harder this time. No crushing sense of pressure, just the woozy undulating sluggishness of moving underwater or swimming inside a giant gelpak.

I stop the analysis computer's fruitless attempt to make sense of the chaotic readings and set it to project the path of the black hole.

Then I reread Bonnie's message. Two parts really bother me: "You may need to switch rides" and "All hopes with you." What the hell do they mean?

"All hopes with you" sounds like doom or they're counting on me to do something about the black hole. Attempt to save the solar system or something equally foolhardy. Air blows out of my mouth sarcastically at the thought.

And how in Christ's name am I supposed to switch rides? Does she mean routes? Or is some other sweeper ship coming to rescue me? Not likely.

While I'm pondering these mysteries, the computer bleeps and displays the black hole's trajectory. Actually, five trajectories.

For minutes, my mouth hangs open, silently screaming just like my aft monitor yesterday. Slowly, my overheated haywire brain cools down and reorders itself. I force myself to think objectively.

The good news is that two of the five paths show the black hole careening close to Uranus, and then heading out Wild, Wild West into deep space. Unfortunately, in the other three, Uranus actually boosts it East toward the Sun, brushing Mars a little tidally. But the worst is that it then captures the Earth and Luna—swallowing them for lunch or dragging them along for a snack later as it sweeps out West past the Sun.

Serenely, I determine that such results may be very bad for Godspeed's business image. All my retirement stock, for example, will be worth less than the aneurysm that's probably forming now in my brain.

Calmly, I scream, "YOU STUPID BASTARDS!" Referring, of course, to the bubble heads at Godspeed.

My first impulse is to send the projections to Bonnie and the other monkeys at Ares Lab. And so's my second impulse. I let them fly.

I switch off my nutrient implant and decide to pull a real meal from cold storage. My mind flitters east and West and all around the solar system a few times as I prepare something billed as "Hungarian goulash." Mentally, I keep repeating: *Maybe it isn't a black hole. Maybe the trajectories are all wrong.*

Now that the meal is over and my under-used digestive system is rumbling with surprise at something a little more solid to process than water, my mind seizes on Umbriel. What's there—a secret base? I know Bonnie's itching to share some big mystery. But she's not giving me more than a hint.

As though answering my thought, a transmission shows as incoming. I grab it for the main screen.

TO: SWEEPER TWO

FROM: BONNIEP@GODSPEED.ARESLAB1

NAOMI, JUST PASSING ON A HOLOVID I THOUGHT YOU'D LIKE TO LOOK AT. I DON'T LOOK MY BEST BUT I THOUGHT YOU'D LIKE TO SEE HOW THE ARES LAB LOOKS NOW.

BONNIE JUL 15 2097: 0139 ARES LAB TIME: FILE ATTACHED

I prompt the holovid file to play. Suddenly, the view from a handheld swoops around an ordinary lab from strange face to strange face, and all the chatter teases a tall man, who looks 40, about his retirement. High-pitched squeals and noises fill up the brief silences between catcalls and laughter. Then the focus lands on Bonnie. "You look too good to retire," she says with a laugh and then the holovid abruptly ends.

"What the hell was that?!" I yell. But, of course, I know.

Her message is full of "look" and "looks." Since I've never been to the Ares Lab, how it "looks" now is part of Bonnie's obvious signal to me to look for a hidden message. The high pitched noises probably carry what I need.

I pull the holovid file over to an analysis computer, and, within seconds, the embedded message appears:

NAOMI,

THANKS FOR FINDING THIS SECRET-SPY MESSAGE, BUT WE CAN'T TAKE THE CHANCE THAT GODSPEED EARTH OR UN UNITS MIGHT BE MONITORING. UNFORTUNATELY, EVERYONE HERE CONCURS WITH YOUR TRAJECTORIES OF THE BLACK HOLE—WITH MOST FAVORING THE WORST-CASE ONES.

HOWEVER, THE SURPRISE FOR YOU IS THAT SWEEPER SIX, WHICH IS EMERGENCY STORED ON UMBRIEL, HAS A FUNCTIONAL Q-DRIVE ALONG WITH SOME SPECIAL MONITORS. A FEW FUEL PACKS, PIECES OF EQUIPMENT, AND DATA UPDATES FROM SWEEPER TWO AND THE SHIP WILL BE AS GOOD AS NEW.

BECAUSE SWEEPER SIX HAS BEEN IN STORAGE SO MUCH LONGER THAN EXPECTED, IT WILL TAKE A MONTH TO OVERHAUL.

YOU'LL HAVE LESS THAN 23 DAYS. SINCE YOU'RE ALREADY ON COURSE FOR URANUS AND YOU ARE THE BEST MECHANIC/ELECTRONIC REPAIR EXPERT IN THE SOLAR SYSTEM, THIS DUTY FALLS TO YOU. BESIDES, ALL Q-DRIVE SHIPS ARE DEPLOYED WILD, WILD WEST AND NONE ARE DUE BACK FOR MONTHS.

SORRY, NAOMI, BUT YOU'RE LITERALLY THE ONLY ONE TO DO THIS.

HERE'S OUR ARES MONKEY PLAN:

1. YOU GET SWEEPER TWO'S MHD FISSION DRIVE ONLINE, GO COLD SLEEP, AND MAKE HASTE EAST FOR UMBRIEL.

2. LAND YOUR SWEEPER AS CLOSE TO SWEEPER SIX AS POSSIBLE IN THE FLUORESCENT CHEERIO CRATER.

3. INSPECT AND INVENTORY SWEEPER SIX. STRIP SWEEPER TWO OF ANYTHING SWEEPER SIX NEEDS TO BECOME OPERATIONAL.

4. THEN IN SWEEPER SIX, HEAD WEST TOWARD THE BLACK HOLE AND TRY TO CREATE RIFTS WITH THE Q-DRIVE—RIFTS THROUGH WHICH THE BLACK HOLE CAN ESCAPE TO ANOTHER UNIVERSE. SWEEPER SIX'S SPECIAL MONITORS WILL HELP.

5. RETURN EAST TO MARS AND THROW YOURSELF ON THE MERCY OF THE UN. WE WILL TAKE FULL RESPONSIBILITY HERE, BUT THAT WON'T TECHNICALLY GET YOU OFF. AS YOU KNOW, A Q-DRIVE CRIME IS A CAPITAL CRIME. HOWEVER, YOUR HAVING JUST SAVED EARTH AND MOST OF THE CIVILIZED SOLAR SYSTEM SHOULD HELP YOUR DEFENSE MAGNIFICENTLY—AND PERHAPS LEAD TO A SLIGHTLY EARLIER RETIREMENT.

WE'RE COUNTING ON YOU.

AFTER ACKNOWLEDGING THIS MESSAGE INDIRECTLY, TAKE COMMUNICATIONS OFFLINE UNTIL END OF MISSION TO AVOID UN OR GODSPEED COUNTER-ORDERS.

BONNIE

P.S. YOU MAY ALSO WIN A NOBEL PRIZE FOR HAVING DISCOVERED THE FIRST "TRAVELING" BLACK HOLE—WOULDN'T THAT BE SOMETHING?

"NO!" I scream at the top of my lungs. "I can't do it!"

I *need* the MHD fission drive and cold sleep to return east to Earth at my retirement in ten months. About the same time that my replacement will be heading out West from Earth or Luna in cold sleep.

The magsail and the particle beam propulsion system are fine for cruising the Q-drive lanes and sealing spacetime holes. But when you're 39 AUs West, the MHD fission drive is the only serious non-FTL way to move east. Because of UN regs, the sweeper's MHD fission drive has what is called "a limited-range fission reactor." It carries only enough fissionable fuel and propellant for four "burns"—once to get here Out West and then decelerate and then once East to Earth with deceleration. And I don't want to waste my last two burns on some sorry ass Ares monkey plan to save the free solar system.

On the other hand, what choice do I have? If Mars is tidally stressed and destroyed and Earth and Luna get dragged along with the black hole, I have nowhere to go anyway—except the miserably hot penitentiary communities on Venus, where retro-viruses rule.

At my present speed, I'll reach the orbit of Uranus and hook up with Umbriel in less than a month with the black hole maybe a week behind me. Being twenty-three days ahead of it, by using the MHD fission burn instead, is a little better for doing the impossible. What's the old joke? The difficult, we do right away, but the impossible takes a little longer.

I transmit a thank-you message to Bonnie about the holovid being a real "eye-opener," and tell her that I hope to see her months earlier than I previously expected. I also add that I'll be shutting down communications for repair. Just enough to let her know that I read the embedded message and will follow the monkey plan.

After taking communications off line, I spend a few hours triple checking that the navigation, fission burn, and cold sleep calculations are all correct. Next, I follow the online procedures to fire up the fission reactor.

Then I prepare the cold sleep box, which will protect me from the stresses of acceleration when the sweeper's dampening field shuts down and from any leakage of hard radiation. Once inside the box, I trigger the burn and cold sleep simultaneously.

While the cold sleep system checks me physically and prepares all the plug-ins, I call up holovid and data files about Umbriel on my little cold box monitor. I try to process the info as an electro-chemical wave the size of the Pacific Ocean pushes me deep into the dark oblivion of cold sleep.

I awake screaming. But I'm not the only screamer. The ship's alarm system is shrieking, too. I stare at the cold box monitor, trying to focus my eyes. But all I can see is dark gray. The fore monitor must be out. Then I think again. No, that's the dull, gloomy face of Umbriel. Something's wrong with deceleration or the navigational computer.

I emergency eject from the cold box and pull myself forward, slamming into my control chair. Umbriel's dark, ancient cratered image fills the main screen completely. I'm seconds from crashing. Hairs stand frozen on the back of my neck. I swallow hard and tense my muscles to suppress shivering spasms. A cold sweat soaks my body, which to my addled brain smells like stale beer.

I don't know if the MHD fission drive is still engaged, but panicking, I cut its power anyway. I fire all three particle guns aiming fore and, simultaneously, spread a magsail aft. The dampening field is still offline, so my head jerks forward rattling the teeth in my jaw as the ship pounds backward hard. Then as the magsail catches the blowback particles, I almost black out in the second brain-numbing jolt.

Through my black-and-red brain fog, I focus on the main screen. Umbriel still fills up the monitor, but the shadowy craters look smaller. I fire the guns fore again. Now, I'm definitely out of danger, so I engage the dampening field and try to get my bearings. But the dampening field won't go online.

Once the entire sphere of the moon shows on the monitor, I reverse and accelerate slowly back toward its most prominent feature, the "fluorescent cheerio," a frost-white ring of ice lining the bottom of a 140-kilometer-wide crater. From my partial pre-cold sleep briefing, I know Umbriel is a dark frozen mix of rock, water, and methane—though its designation as "unexplored" means that precise data is not available.

But Godspeed must know something if at least two pilots landed two vehicles—Sweeper Six for storage and some other craft to return the pilots East. Somehow, Godspeed has kept Umbriel's dark mystery hidden. And since sweeper ships are not designed to land on anything, Umbriel is now a double mystery.

I'm not a bad pilot, but my ship looks like a giant silver metal spider that has lost half its legs. So, I initiate an emergency landing procedure for a slow collision with Umbriel, and aim for the middle of the ice-lined crater.

A few seconds into my descent, I finally get a reading for Sweeper Six and begin correcting to come within a half kilometer of its landing site. For a long moment, I hold my breath as my ship meanders slowly out of my control and falls obliquely toward a crater wall. I struggle with the stiff controls and begin to brace for a slow-motion crash that will probably kill me. But with only meters to spare, I manage to right the ship, and the crashing part of my crash landing is minimal. Nevertheless, I black out with impact.

I have a hammering left temple and some upper back pain, but nothing is broken. I press the analgesic button on my forearm, and let the chemical relief wash throughout my body. The beer odor evaporates.

Then I assess the damage.

The rear magsail array and the aft holovids are offline, but as long as Sweeper Six can lift off, I don't care. Everything else checks out okay.

I close my eyes for a minute and think about sending an "okay" message to Bonnie, but then recall that I'm remaining incommunicado until (or if) the black hole is exported elsewhere. No one has deliberately punched holes in the spacetime continuum before, so I will be the first. Lucky me.

From spare quilted insulation and some vacuum bags, I fashion a large white Santa Claus bag full of tools, fuel cells, gelpaks, electronics, and diagnostic modules that I hope won't be destroyed by the moon's airless, cold-hearted surface. Then I suit up and push the bag with gentle kicks of my boot to the port airlock and cycle through.

Outside, I feel like I'm pulling along a large party balloon without a string. In the distance, I see the white ice that rings the bottom two-thirds of the giant crater. With each footfall into the starry darkness, I sense the hard crunch of dark ice-gravel beneath my thick boots. A wave of utter loneliness almost doubles me over, down to the black alien surface. I shiver and feel unbearably naked without the cozy bulkheads and lights of the ship wrapped around me.

Umbriel's mass is about three-one hundredths of Earth's—about a fifth of Luna's. Even with the suit, my weight feels less than two kilograms.

Suddenly, a reckless terror urges me to jump so high that I will fall off the moon and drift toward the merciless stars forever. My shivering only increases the pull—though I know the sensation is an illusion. I swallow hard and switch on a light, aiming it at the dark pockmarked surface, and avoid staring at the frozen dome of beckoning stars overhead or the distant ice ring of the crater wall.

Checking for Sweeper Six with a finder, I note very few obstructions and push forward with a hopping gait and a forward lean to counter the slight backward drag of my Santa Claus bundle. I fix my eyes on the darkly cratered and rilled surface.

I used to love the open stars. Twelve years ago during spring break, I had fun going outside on Luna for a few hours at time. Once, a group of us got tanked, hopped wildly to a partially fallen mountain peak and lay back, lost in the multihued blaze of millions of stars. Their overwhelming beauty made us sob, so we were still weeping when a rescue team came to "save" us. Then we all laughed hysterically because we felt invulnerable.

I don't feel that way now. One slip, one tear in my suit, and death will come in seconds. Hopping too high, my mass and the mass of my bundle could break my ankles or damage my suit if I landed the wrong way. Then I might have to crawl back inside Sweeper Two and sit out the gravitational avalanche of the black hole that's falling toward Uranus. Umbriel could even get pulled along for the ride.

Since no rescue team will come for me, I yell with false bravado, "I am the rescue team for the entire solar system!" I laugh softly and check the finder, which tells me I am getting a little closer to Sweeper Six.

Now, I hop for distance but also to avoid all the small craters and rills. My hopping rhythm soon gets me to Sweeper Six, and I play the light over its surface. Instead of being all silver like my sweeper, it is painted white with Godspeed's insignia in blue: Jove using his powerful breath to scatter stars like pollen in the wind—and the number "6" in orange near the airlock. But looked at against the ice ring, it is virtually invisible.

With no air to cycle and no power, I manually work the airlock. In minutes, I am inside with my bundle. Inside one of the darkest holes in the solar system. A little spooked, I wave the light around in wide arcs to prove to myself that I really am inside a sweeper, just one without air or power. Dragging the bundle behind me, I slowly hop toward the command cabin.

Scanning with the light, I suddenly see in full yellow vacuum suit a pilot lying face-down on the floor of the cabin. Startled, I yell and let go of the bundle. It barely misses bumping my leg as it slowly drops like a drifting balloon. I want to leave the sweeper immediately and hop back to the safety of Sweeper Two. I make myself stay. I know that this corpse has been lying here in the cold dark for a long time.

Nausea almost doubles me over as I realize what I must do. Slowly, I move toward the pilot. Then I turn the body over to read the name tag: "R. Arnsdale." The vacuum suit has no handle or strap, so I grip the body like a drowning victim and hop backwards toward the airlock. Once outside, I lay the body gently down. I should find out who R. Arnsdale is. But the only way to do that is to restore power.

I go to work.

Countless quick trips back and forth and several days later, I have the power partially restored, at least enough to use some of the ship's own internal lights and maintain a breathable, though musty, atmosphere. Now, I feel less like a spooked spelunker. Slowly, I hop back to Sweeper Two and allow myself a short glimpse at the stars. I also see aqua-blue Uranus and a few moons to my far left, just above the dark crater ridge. If I weren't so tired and scared, I would sit and stare for an hour or two. Even so, I force myself to make a few high jumps and tumbles just to show I am not afraid, careful to land on all fours each time.

Back inside Sweeper Two, I download system upgrades, all sorts of software, and navigational data to a series of thirty-six gelpaks. While the computers take care of that, I put myself under for six hours and dream about how Bonnie and I are transporting some diplomat to Pluto. I keep telling him Pluto and the five researchers are gone, but he won't listen. Instead, he begins kissing me all over. Bonnie is jealous, and then I awake.

I take inventory of myself. I still have several weeks on the nutrient implant, but I jettison it anyway and give myself a 90-day supply. Water is a bigger problem. If Sweeper Six's recycler is defective and I cannibalize Sweeper Two recklessly and lose all its water to vacuum, I might die of thirst after my suit runs dry. So, I pump water from the environmental system into spare tanks as a back-up plan. I pray that I don't wind up carrying them to Sweeper Six.

I restock my O2, grab the gelpaks and a few more gizmos, and hop my way to Sweeper Six. Uranus hangs like a blue giant's head in the black starry sky.

Grimly, I say good morning to the yellow-suited corpse of Arnsdale as I shine my light on the orange 6 of the airlock.

After working nearly four hours on the ship's main computer, I realize I have a hardware problem and a software problem. More than a decade of unrelenting icy vacuum has leached away all the gelpaks, which is why I brought new ones. But the old hardware can't communicate with the new gelpaks. Short of transporting the computer from Sweeper Two to Sweeper Six, I've got to fabricate an interface device or rig something else. I hope Bonnie's twenty-three-day estimate included time for solving intractable problems, but I doubt it.

I already know what the solution is: transmit the complicated code directly from Sweeper Two's computer to Sweeper Six's. But I can't use normal means of transmission because of interference from the Uranian system's energy fluctuations. Only fiber optic cable can work precisely enough here, running a land line between the two ships.

My rough calculation is that I'm already behind schedule by at least three days. Running the cable will probably add two more days. But what can I do? I have to keep going. To gain some time, I decide not to take regular sleep breaks—but only nap when I can.

Measure twice and cut once would be great if I had a half kilometer of cable to roll out. Instead, I have to cannibalize meters and meters of vid and comm line and splice it all together. I waste a whole day carefully laying cable over Umbriel's dark, craggy surface. In the brutal cold of Umbriel, the brittle line snaps twice before I perfect my technique. How ironic that Umbriel gets a land line ahead of all the moons except Luna.

While the data streams from one computer to the other, I doze in Sweeper Two, letting my last working holovid camera and the computer monitor the line and the transmission. Twenty minutes into my nap, shock waves and alarms toss me awake. The line looks broken in at least several places and I access camera memory to see what's happened. All it shows is a suddenly shaking picture. "Moonquake?" I say aloud and suit up.

After tedious hours of repair, the cable is transmitting again. I doze once more and hope for a peaceful sleep without quakes or tremors—just long enough to transmit. I am pleasantly bleeped awake and all the parameters check. Suiting up, I head for Sweeper Six to finally get that ship's computer running, all the lights and vid cameras working—and then test the magsail, Q-drive, particle guns, and environmental subsystems. As I hop, I avoid touching the cable so I can check at least once more from Sweeper Six.

Just as I reach the airlock and open it, I see in my reflected light a yellow blur on my right and am grasped suddenly around the arms of my suit in a bear hug, except Umbriel has no bears. A jolt of electric terror makes me crouch down and then high jump toward the stars, but my assailant doesn't loosen his grip.

Arnsdale flashes through my head, but it can't be him. On one of the darkest and loneliest moons in the solar system, almost 3 billion kilometers from Earth, I'm being attacked.

Just as we start falling, without thinking I bicycle-kick backward, making contact against my assailant's suited legs, and tuck my head under, drawing my knees toward my chest. Slowly, I tumble forward and float free, landing on all fours. My assailant topples backward and hits the surface a microsecond or two after me, probably with yellow legs and arms writhing clumsily in the dark. I don't care if he's torn his suit, cracked his helmet, or damaged his environment pack—and is dying now or is already as dead as Arnsdale. Without looking, I propel myself into the airlock and cycle through, locking it down.

Shivering and breathing rapidly, I sit in the comfort of the thick, well-lit airlock walls without taking off my suit. I replay the nightmare like a vid in my head.

More minutes pass. Gradually, I remove the suit and force myself to ignore the menace outside.

Still shaking from adrenaline, I concentrate on rapidly getting the main computer and holovid cameras back online. I echo some signals back and forth to Sweeper Two's computer—and everything looks good. Once everything is humming, I focus lights and vid cameras on the outside of the airlock.

Only Arnsdale's yellow-suited corpse remains lying forever immobile among the dark rocks and icy sand immediately around the airlock. My assailant, assuming I didn't imagine the whole attack, is gone. Vacuum suits have a max capacity of 12 hours, so he can't last too long outside. Where could he go—except back where he came from? And where is that? And where is he now?

As if responding to my questions, gibberish begins to appear on the main screen, streaming in from the fiber optic cable.

My assailant is in Sweeper Two.

I enter, "Who are you?"

Gibberish.

"Don't understand you. Try changing the parameters."

Eventually, the text decrypts itself: "I am Leonid Baglinsov, your relief. Are you getting this transmission?"

"Yes, what are you doing here ten months early? And why did you attack me like some lunatic?"

The pun is not wasted on Leonid; he replies with "Lunatic. Ha, ha." Then he continues: "Colonel Priestly and I were sent by the UN and Godspeed Luna to stop you from using the Q-drive. I did not mean to startle you, but I was told that you had gone crazy and had to be restrained. Priestly was killed when we both woke up from cold sleep just seconds before we crashed. I ejected from cold sleep and secured myself. Priestly ejected at the moment of impact."

I have no sympathy for the UN Security assassin.

I enter: "Yeah, there's some glitch in navigation when it comes to this moon. Maybe it's deliberate, now that I think about it. I can assure you that I am rational. Take a look at my holovid records."

"Okay, will do," he answers tersely.

I spend maybe thirty minutes checking the transferred programs and updates. For a change, everything works and none of the computers crash. Unfortunately, I discover that the recycler has almost no water. I start checking for breaks in the lines.

"Captain, are you there?" appears on my screen.

"Yes," I reply. "Let's switch from text to voice, okay? I'm sure you can find the menu to do that."

Twenty seconds pass.

"Okay. This makes more sense. Communication speed should triple now," he says in a moderately deep voice that has just the hint of a French accent. His voice fascinates me.

"Are you French?" I blurt out.

"No, Russian. But my parents joined Godspeed in Belgium when I was nine, so I speak French as well as any native."

"So, what do you think after seeing the records?"

He laughs. "You are not the only crazy one. The Ares Lab people are also quite insane to have one old ship with a Q-drive divert a black hole."

"But you believe them and me?"

"Yes."

"Will you help me ready the ship?"

"Yes."

I love to hear him say "Yes," but I can't think of more questions to keep getting yeses.

"No tricks and no more attacks, right?" He answers swiftly, "Of course not! You have my word. Naturally, if Colonel Priestly were alive, he might still insist that you be taken into custody or—"

"Killed?"

"Yes, my sweeper had UN armaments, and Priestly carried several guns himself. The threat of causing a rift even this far from Mars panicked everyone, which is why we were dispatched so quickly."

Involuntarily, I blow air from my mouth. "What about the black hole? Didn't anyone consider that a major threat? Jesus!"

"Before now, I hadn't seen the evidence. I was told you had fabricated the whole black hole story. As we launched, I heard that the UN was arresting everyone at Ares Lab, but heard no details—no connection was made to you. I am so sorry for grabbing you. I must have scared you."

"Okay, Leonid—"

"Call me 'Leo,' okay?"

"Okay, Leo. I am going to trust you—but not so much that I won't put unbreakable passcodes on everything in this ship. If something happens to me, you will join Arnsdale."

"Arnsdale?"

"Yes, the corpse by the airlock—that Arnsdale," I say a little sarcastically.

He laughs. "Oh, yes, Captain. I know of him. He was part of my Umbriel briefing."

"You can call me 'Naomi,' instead of 'Captain.' And you can tell me all about Arnsdale later."

"Ah, maybe Captain Naomi then?"

My turn to laugh. "Okay, Leo. Your first assignment is to replenish your suit and maybe replace your nutrient implant. Next, you've got to get me a few hundred liters of water. I've stored most of it in tanks on Sweeper Two."

"Aye, aye," he says, which sounds almost as cute as "yes."

"Let me know when you're on your way. And don't go near the cable. It breaks if you stare at it too hard."

He agrees and I start replacing seals and fixing conduits on the water recycler. Hours go by and I wonder if Leo is hatching some new surprise attack. Putting the paranoia out of my head, I nod out.

"Naomi! Naomi!" someone is shouting. I look at the screen. A dozen white ships with Godspeed's blue insignia are landing on Umbriel's surface all around me. I know they are going to kill me. I scream and try to power up my ship, but I remember that I haven't checked the power cells for the particle guns.

"No!" I shout. "This can't be happening!"

"Naomi, what's wrong?" says Leo's melodious voice.

No invading ships show on the screen. "Nothing, Leo. I guess I was dreaming. Are you ready with the tanks?"

"Sorry, Captain Naomi. These tanks won't work very well."

"What do you mean?"

"They're aluminized plastic—just thin internal storage tanks," he says.

Suddenly, I recognize the trouble. The storage tanks couldn't be used outside the ship's interior, not in space and not even briefly on surface of Umbriel. Quickly freezing water in a vacuum would probably burst their seams explosively. And even if they didn't explode, melting ice in leaky tanks would create a mess once inside Sweeper Six. Some water might even boil off before Leo got it in the ship. Another intractable problem.

My mind races. "Maybe, we can take some ice from the crater wall."

"That ice is contaminated with methane, microparticles, and who knows what else. I already thought of mining it for water—too much trouble. But I've got a better idea."

"Yes?"

"A vacuum suit," he says enthusiastically.

"Leo, suits only hold a few liters at a time. We'd need a hundred trips to get enough water."

"No, we can fill a whole vacuum suit with water. The environmental controls can keep the water from freezing. And even if it does freeze, a suit is flexible and will expand, instead of bursting. Several trips and we'll have all the water we need."

"Leo, you are a genius! It would have taken me days to think of that."

"We did stuff like that on Luna all the time," he says, suddenly reminding me of how much I miss that world of shops, parks, nightclubs, and heated swimming pools.

While Leo fills up Bonnie's spare suit, I do another rough calculation. The black hole will enter the Uranian system in roughly two weeks. So, if I create a large enough spacetime rift with the Q-drive, it's got to be *before* it gets this far. Otherwise, we might lose a few moons or Uranus itself. That means we've got ten days, tops.

And I haven't even met Leo face-to-face yet.

Ten minutes after Leo signals he's leaving Sweeper Two, I pull the holovid port side view over to the main screen. In the harsh exterior lights around the airlock, I see three suited creatures in brilliant yellow, blazing against Umbriel's night of shadows and starlight. One is Arnsdale, a frozen corpse. Another is Leo, who dances and bounces up and down like a boxer on Luna. And the last one is a slightly bloated manikin, made entirely of water, floating behind and tethered to Leo's shoulder.

I unlock the airlock and hope that my paranoid vision of Colonel Priestly hiding inside that floating yellow suit turns out to be a pure fear fantasy. As Leo cycles through, I begin to panic and frantically search among my tools for something that I can use as a weapon. I grab a laser fuser and hold it tightly in my left hand behind my back. Close up, it can make a nasty burn.

"Captain Naomi honey, I'm home!" Leo's voice rings melodiously through to me. I hear him laughing. Suddenly, a handsome, unshaven man, who looks around 35 garbed in a UN dress blue uniform, appears before me.

He quickly notices that my eyes are bugging out at the uniform. Smiling, he says, "Don't worry about the uniform. I was only conscripted for this mission—something Priestly insisted on. I'm really a Godspeed pilot, just like you, Naomi."

"But your height and your face. . ." I blurt out.

"Oh, yeah. Sorry. I *am* a little big for sweeper pilot. And I didn't have time to undergo any modifications."

"So, you still have your beard and—and all the rest?"

He laughs. "Yes, I'm quite intact reproductively, too. The launch was done in a rush. My modifications weren't scheduled for several months."

He pauses and says to himself, "Why not?"

Then he turns around, undoes his dress pants, bends forward, and shows me the cheeks of his butt. "Can you zee zem?" he asks, comically exaggerating his French accent.

"Is this how you greet people when you come to visit?" I ask, teasing. Of course, I can see the twin infinity signs in bright blue, one on each cheek—standard tattoos for Godspeed pilots. Both Bonnie and I have the same ones.

He pulls up his pants and turns around smiling.

Reflexively, I smile, and hold up the laser fuser. "See this?" I say. "I was going to use this on you, if you tried to trick me. But no UN officer would get a Godspeed tattoo just to fool me." I toss the fuser back in my Santa bag, and pray I am right.

Leo bursts out laughing again, and I join him. If he really is a UN Security assassin, then I will at least die laughing.

After adding the suit full of water to the recycler, we spend almost two hours refining a plan to meet the ten-day deadline. Then we go to work like space demons. At least seven times, Leo returns to the wreck of his ship to cannibalize parts.

☸

Then finally after nine frantic, almost sleepless days, Sweeper Six is ready. Unfortunately, with all our lugging and hopping around, the air smells faintly like unwashed socks. And it's not the fault of the environmental system. We just stink. Occasionally, Leo rubs his nose, but says nothing. But I know what he's thinking.

"Okay, Leo," I say. "We have enough water for a quick shower. So, let's heat some up."

Before I know it, we are lathering up in the most luxurious hot shower I can recall. And before long, we are lathering each other. Waves of hot water transport us far away from Umbriel, and slowly, tentatively we progress toward lovemaking. Leo doesn't seem deterred by my tomboy appearance, and the ravenous lust that his large naked, hairy body ignites in me catches me completely by ecstatic surprise.

Almost breathlessly, we fall asleep together for a full nine hours. I awake to see Leo leaning over me, dressed in his formal blue uniform. "Captain Naomi, by the power vested in me by the authority of the UN, I am placing you in my protective custody."

He smiles.

"Not funny, Leo," I say and swat at his head.

"But I'm really serious," he says. "Why don't you return to Sweeper Two? Only one pilot is needed for this insane mission. And if the black hole captures me, you'll have a chance to make it to Venus."

I make a face. "What chance is that, Leo? We've gutted Sweeper Two."

"Ah, yes. But together with my wrecked ship, surely you could—"

"Forget it, Leo. This is *my* mission. If you want to take your chances in Sweeper Two, you are welcome."

"No, no! It's just that this is so dangerous."

"Well, unless you are staying, then we're both going, right?"

"*Oui*, yes, both."

Sweeper Six launches awkwardly, but within hours we are heading West toward the probable path of the black hole. The special spacetime monitors that Bonnie mentioned bring tears of anger and frustration to our eyes. The three monitors take normal holovid camera images and show the stresses and strains—the swirling fractal-like fabric of spacetime. Our old monitors only show actual rifts—these show weak areas in spacetime. Why weren't sweepers equipped with these more sophisticated monitors?

"We work for criminals, Naomi," Leo announces. "Godspeed wanted to pretend that the spacetime rifts appeared anomalously, as an occasional byproduct of faster than light speed. So, sweepers had only monitors that detected actual rifts—not ones that show degraded spacetime from each Q-drive launch."

What can I say. We both know that if data from these monitors got out, then the UN and space environmentalists might have tried to stop FTL travel altogether—or at least forced Godspeed to use the Q-drive just East or even West of the Kuiper Belt. But all along, Q-pilots could have avoided stressed parts of space using these monitors. Just as we can use them now to know where to keep using the Q-drive. Once the shock of Godspeed's machinations lessen, I ask about Arnsdale.

Leo shakes his head. "They are truly bastards, Naomi." Then he tells me Godspeed's brilliant emergency plan, which he's pieced together from Godspeed's official briefing and several stories from retired pilots.

Fifteen years ago, a Godspeed ship's Q-drive failed on a non-cold sleep ship. Two UN Security Councilors were aboard, stuck, after over two months travel, about 40 AUs West of Earth. Godspeed had no provision for rescuing them—and they spent two months griping on their return to Mars. Reparations were embarrassing and costly.

So, Godspeed execs invented "The Plan." Secretly, a sweeper ship with a Q-drive needed to be stored somewhere safe, stable, and close enough to the launching area of Pluto's old orbit—and yet not impossibly far from Mars. Moons of Saturn or Jupiter were the most likely candidates. But those systems were still too dynamic and regularly explored by geologists and astronomers to safely and inconspicuously hide a sweeper for the four or five years they wanted. Umbriel with its millions of years of stability and its fluorescent cheerio marker was perfect. And it was one of the last moons anyone would want to explore.

To preserve secrecy, Godspeed also needed a willing suicide. Some pilot who'd land Sweeper Six and die. That was R. Arnsdale. Even so, word eventually got out about a pilot suffering from a terminal disease, who'd been willing to sacrifice his last months of life for permanent financial security for his family. As Arnsdale headed West in cold sleep, supposedly Godspeed faked his death on Luna. The UN knew nothing—or pretended not to know an unregulated Q-ship was illegally stored far beyond its control.

Colonel Priestly got a more dramatic version of "The Plan": a criminal faction in Godspeed had supposedly stored the sweeper—unknown to Godspeed execs—for some smuggling operation that fell through. And now I knew why the Ares monkeys and Bonnie had been arrested. Some members of that team must have worked on part of "The Plan"—and knew where the sweeper was stored. Godspeed shifted blame to them. If we pulled this off, I'd have to do something to stop their executions.

Ironically, Leo was sent not just to stop me, but to bring Sweeper Six back to Mars, where some Godspeed execs probably waited to take a sudden trip Wild Wild West while the black hole swept through the solar system, destroying any evidence of their malfeasance.

I guess they didn't believe in our monkey plan.

About fifty-million kilometers from Uranus is where we want to "cut" spacetime. But we're not Q-drive pilots, so once we reach that point, we stall—constantly rechecking and reprogramming the Q-drive to buy some time. Then feeling like a diver jumping off a cliff into a cold lake, I push the launch initiator.

Now, my body is being snapped, displaced forward and then back a hundred eighty degrees, faster and faster until suddenly I break into little hard marbles that swarm up and crash explosively against some unyielding metal barrier, bounce back and reform into me again. The process repeats endlessly. Whether as a displacing whole or as crashing hard marbles, I scream with all my being, partly in pain, partly in frustration, but mostly because I have no choice. My whole identity is in the scream. And suddenly, the screaming stops.

Leo is swearing in long and colorful strings of insults made from three languages. He goes on so long and so profanely that I break into hysterical laughter. He ends with, "I PISS ON THEM ALL—THOSE BASTARDS!" and then breaks into uproarious laughter himself. Now I am laughing so hard that tears drown my cheeks, and I struggle to breathe.

Once I catch my breath, I do my impression of a Godspeed promotional holovid: "Passengers may experience some momentary discomfort as the Q-drive engages."

"Yes, if being diced into little pieces and slammed against a wall is your idea of a little discomfort," Leo says, shaking his head.

"Add it to the list," I say, laughing again—referring to our running list of Godspeed's crimes.

We try to relax because the Q-drive is about to bring us back from a quarter light year away to where we started our "cut." The agony does not lessen, but Leo's swearing has less English this time, and so I laugh less hysterically.

The new monitors show just what we hoped—fraying fractals of spacetime, partial disconnects in the swirl. We repeat the trip to nowhere and back seven times. By the third time, the rift is so large that we have to avoid falling into it ourselves. With each use of the Q-drive the rift gets massively, geometrically bigger. When it is about five times larger than our estimate of the black hole, we stop. Frazzled from Q-drive trips, we use the magsail and the particle guns to move toward the black hole. Then with the alarms set, we both go under for a few hours.

Smashed into little pieces, I *become* screaming again. Screaming is everywhere, and I feel I am launching the Q-drive. But I'm not. I am only waking from a nightmare. The alarms, Leo, and I are all screaming at once. I force myself to stop and Leo stops, too. Only the alarm continues until Leo hits the reset.

The black hole is dead ahead. Graviton and X-ray readings explode whirling rockets across the main screen.

Head on, the black hole is a gigantic maw of chaotic hell. I imagine that millions of black, nearly invisible teeth are gnashing under a glimmering darkness that smudges out the rest of the universe. Such a dark hypnotic mouth cannot be satisfied, eating everything until it explodes in a new Big Bang or spirals down and winks out of existence.

Then I hit myself in the head. "Leo!" I cry. "We've got to transmit this to Earth, Mars—everywhere. Even if we fail, Bonnie and the Ares lab monkeys shouldn't spend their last month locked up."

Together, we slowly maneuver the ship and pan the holovid cameras so that astronomers can get an easy fix on the stars. Godspeed, Inc. might downplay our vids as fakes, but the millions of professional and amateur astronomers will vindicate us.

For close to 30 minutes, we transmit the images on several commercial channels—as well as official Godspeed frequencies. Then we cut off communications again.

We need to shadow the black hole to make sure it enters the rift, but we cannot get so close that we lose ourselves to either. "Scylla and Charybdis," I say aloud.

"What?" Leo asks.

"Nothing, Leo." I smile, and add, "Just remembering Odysseus in similar straits with two monsters."

Leo wants to station the sweeper a few million kilometers from the rift and use instruments to track the black hole's disappearance into the rift before we swoop in to close it. But I need a closer look. We settle on 800,000 kilometers, more than twice the distance between Earth and Luna.

Several hours later, we are holoviding the black hole's slow push through the fabric of spacetime and begin transmitting the images toward Earth and Mars again. A few seconds before the black hole disappears, an urgent aud message bypasses our security filters and blasts our ears: "DEPLOY MAGSAIL AFT! FIRE ALL PARTICLE GUNS FORE! FIRE

ALL PARTICLE GUNS FORE! NOW!" At first, I think the voice is Bonnie's—familiar all right, but no, not Bonnie's.

Just as I switch on my aud to reply, the rift implodes and then expands again—only the dampening field keeps us from having our heads torn off as the ship lurches forward, accelerating recklessly toward the rift. Somehow the implosion acts as a graviton lens for the black hole, snagging the ship. Now, both monsters may swallow us, first the rift and then the black hole, one after the other.

Fortunately, I have my lines all ready: "DEPLOY MAGSAIL AFT! FIRE ALL PARTICLE GUNS FORE! FIRE ALL PARTICLE GUNS FORE! NOW!"

While Leo spreads the magsail behind us, I start firing the particle guns. Neither seems to have any effect, but I keep firing. Waves of gravitons are hitting us in long pulses now, but the dampening field stops us from being rattled around like beans in a glass jar. Still, we can feel each pulse.

"Get the Q-drive back online!" I order. Leo has no time to program it, but any Q-drive trip has to be better than piercing spacetime, only to become a meal for a black hole.

As the dampening field kicks in harder and harder against the pulsing acceleration, my vision begins to blur. We must be less than a minute away from the rift. So, I yell for Leo to launch the Q-drive initiator while I keep firing the particle guns.

Leo is yelling something back, but I cannot hear him. He grabs my head and kisses me hard on the mouth. I push him away to keep firing. "You crazy Russian! What are you doing?!" I scream at him.

"You've done it, Naomi. Look at the monitors." Now I can see that my firings are mending the swirls of spacetime and that the ship is starting to pull backward. The black hole and its pulsing waves of gravitons and X-ray pandemonium blink out.

I let out a whoop and kiss Leo back.

We spend almost four hours mending spacetime. While we realign the swirls, I ask Leo about the urgent message to deploy the magsail and fire the guns fore—my own voice transmitting orders to us seconds before I spoke them. "What was that?"

"An echo," he says simply.

"How can that be, Leo? I gave those orders *after* we heard the message."

"A time echo. Everything goes mad around a black hole. Or maybe another Captain Naomi on the other side of the rift gave the order."

Then we shoot a vid that makes us celebrities.

We include everything we can think of—"The Plan," Leo's orders, as well as the criminal nature of Godspeed's execs—and transmit it everywhere.

Passing through the Uranian system again a few days later, we get a vid from Bonnie. She is back in the lab, which is decorated festively. She looks ravishing and reminds me of my own body restoration plans.

Quickly, she says, "We're getting ready for a party here, Naomi. Partly to celebrate our release from jail, and partly to celebrate you and Leo as heroes. The images of the black hole, especially disappearing in that rift, have made you and Leo famous. See the banner?"

The holovid camera pans to her left. Gigantic holovid images of us from our vid play in a short loop on a huge banner that reads, "Naomi and Leo, Godspeed Employees of the Millennium."

When the camera focuses back on her lovely face, she continues: "And your vid just blew away the UN and Godspeed's Board of Directors. The Board acted quickly to replace the president, five vice-presidents, and about a dozen directors, especially since they're all in UN custody now. Word is that the Board will honor you and Leo with big bonuses and promotions. The UN will probably give you medals, a parade, or something, too. Anyway, have fun on the trip home."

We could rig up the ship for cold sleep and get the MHD fission drive online. But Leo and I want to enjoy a quiet month or so together. I wonder whether he'll like me better when I'm not a tomboy anymore, but I don't ask him. I'll make it a surprise.

Night Is My House

Night is my house and I am her king.
She answers my summons when we are apart;
Until death we are bound by a black velvet string.
Day's widow submits under my silken wing.
Succumb she does sweetly to my gentle art.
Night is my house and I am her king.

Alone in my chambers of mist, she will sing;
With a touch of my hand does our dark anthem start.
Until death we are we bound by a black velvet string.
All fear her shadow, but to me she is evening;
The stars are her eyes, the moon is her heart.
Night is my house and I am her king.

Round my finger her soul is wrought like a ring.
But when daylight returns, she will smile and depart.
Night is my house and I am her king.
Until death are we bound by a black velvet string.

—Christopher Vera

Metamorphoses in Amber
by Tony Pi

Darkness was my cloak, and the sounds of nighttime London masked the whispers of my trespass. I knelt by the skylight and used my trick-shadowbox to tap into the townhouse's security system. The *Chrysalis V* was nigh impossible to crack . . . unless, of course, you designed it in the first place. In a former body I had been Rafe Sali, security guru and inventor of the *Chrysalis* system, and I had embedded a backdoor deep in the code for just such an opportunity. It was a cinch with the algorithms in the handheld shadowbox to override the alarm, unlock the skylight, and disarm the sensor-web in the library below.

The scent of myrrh teased me from the open skylight like a pitcher plant seducing a fly. We Elect were fascinated with all things insectoid, and I had gambled on the *Chrysalis* name to pique the interest of my ancient rival Mantis. Still, I wouldn't put it past her to lure me to London with tips of a lost Fabergé. Mantis was cunning and resourceful. Just as I knew her weaknesses, she knew mine. One thing remained a constant in our ancient feud, true since the days when she had been Nottingham and I, Little John: my love of stealing her ill-gotten treasures.

I pulled out my pendant, holding the virgin amber between my fingers. It was electric to the touch. In the moonlight, I could barely make out its leafhopper inclusion. The insect's metamorphic energy, caught and distilled in the amber for millions of years, roiled within. We called it Lightning.

I meditated on the gem, imprinting my current sense of self, my instar, onto the outer matrix of the amber. I tucked the necklace back, snug against my chest. The Lightning prickled my bare skin, a minor irritation. If I got injured, I would use the pendant or the backup piece in my pocket to restore my shape as art dealer Felix Lea. However, I was loathe to activate the metamorphoses needlessly. Any change, whether a total moult or minor maintenance, carried risks: unintentional morphs, hidden medical time bombs, and even death. Though I was a skilled shifter, I preferred to rely on a single body until age, injury or plot forced me into another moult.

The shadowbox showed no guards in view of surveillance cameras, but hardly proof that the house was empty. I divided the shadowbox unit into two, leaving half connected to the security system but taking the remote.

I rappelled into the library and scanned the room for potential escape routes before unhooking the line. One door and two grand windows that gave spectacular views of the other multi-million pound townhouses on Cheyne Row.

My penlight revealed the decor to be Victorian with a dash of rococo. The books lining the shelves shimmered silver and gold, with volumes ranging from Shakespeare through Machiavelli to Nietzsche.

Mantis had *been* Machiavelli, once, before *he* became *she*.

Another Elect, Antlion, owed me a favour and repaid me with the location of the Fabergé, supposedly in Mantis's library safe. I stole across the room, knelt in front of the mock fireplace, and pressed the trick brick, left back corner, fourth down. The back façade slid up to reveal the safe. My hacks tricked the timed lock and retrieved the combination with an algorithm. Child's play.

However, it seemed too easy, this heist, my centuries of experience and technological tricks notwithstanding. Dread flowed through my veins; the kind that plagued every burglar in the history of time yet thrilled us nonetheless. I took a deep breath and opened the safe door.

No poisoned darts or hissing gas. Good. My penlight revealed the treasure within, resting on a red silk pillow: golden heraldic lions supporting an egg enameled white and blue. I smiled. The jeweler marks confirmed it to be the 1903 Danish Jubilee Imperial Easter Egg, lost since the Russian Revolution.

I hooked the shadowbox remote onto my belt and took my gloves off to better handle the fragile Egg. I didn't care if I left fingerprints; it would take a mere spark of Lightning to scramble them. I sealed the Fabergé inside the air-tight and armoured shoulder case, letting the smart-foam cradle the treasure. As a final gesture, I flicked a calling card, a plain white business card emblazoned with an emerald woodcut print of a stylized flea, into the empty safe.

As I slung the case over my shoulder, the door slammed open. Having no intention to be caught like a fly in honey, I grabbed a poker and tumbled towards the nearest window, confident I would survive the three-storey fall.

But before I could smash the windows, a bullet flew past my ear and shattered a pane of glass. "Next shot's through the heart," said a man in a Polish accent, perhaps ten steps behind me. Probably Mantis's henchman Nicodem Walczak, an ex-military operative whom I knew by reputation only. "Drop the poker and turn around."

I lowered the poker in my right hand but surreptitiously pressed my left thumb against the shadowbox's touchpad, letting it scan my print and activate a silent countdown.

Three. Two. One. The charge inside the other half of the trick-shadowbox, still attached to the security system on the roof, detonated. The minor explosion provided the distraction I needed. With the shadowbox no longer blocking the system, all hell broke loose. When the alarm shrieked, I swung the poker to shatter the window's remaining glass panels before hurling myself from the building.

Shards of glass cut into my flesh and I fell three storeys. I had built this instar with the reflexes of an acrobat, and I relied upon them now to save me. I cushioned my fall as best I could, but the jarring impact broke my left shinbone. I stifled a cry and focused on the amber against my chest, filtering a measure of Lightning through my imprint of self. My skin tingled, my sinews burned. The power stitched my cuts closed and knitted my bones back together, fitting my body to the blueprint of the lithe Felix Lea.

I pulled myself up. Hoping that the poor lighting would hide me, I sprinted down Cheyne Row towards the Thames, ignoring the stares of passers-by. As I raced across the last boulevard towards my speedboat at Cadogan Pier, pain exploded in my upper back and knocked the wind out of me.

I had been shot.

I stumbled to the edge of the Embankment and fell into the river. The gunshot wound and the chill of the Thames water nearly overwhelmed my senses, but I fought to keep my wits about me. This bullet had pierced my right lung. I had to stop the bleeding, fast. I unleashed the Lightning in the amber, electrifying my body. My regenerating flesh forced out fragments of lead, repairing my lung while burst blood vessels and torn muscles stitched back together.

But one piece of amber wasn't enough. I had been shapeshifting at an extraordinary rate, costing more Lightning than a slow, controlled moult would require. I had burnt off some of the pendant's stored power when I fixed my leg, and now the gunshot wound demanded even more. I grabbed the spare amber in my pocket. With no time to prime it, I sucked the power straight from its heart. To draw upon Lightning without an instar imprint was as deadly as juggling live grenades blind, but I had no choice. I chained the raw power to the current metamorphosis and willed it to heal me.

While the wound ousted the bullet fragments before it closed, I was running out of air. I shed my shoes and my heavier gear but kept the shoulder case, swimming as far away from shore as I could before surfacing to gulp down air. I swam for the south bank, glad to have escaped Mantis's trap with another of her treasures. I had won another battle . . . or so I thought.

Shivering, I hid in the shadows at Battersea Park, wrung out my clothes and activated the homing device hidden inside the shoulder case. Five long minutes later, an innocuous blue Volkswagen Beetle pulled up near my hiding spot. My partner-in-crime, Thomas Thickett, rolled down his window. "What's the word, guv?"

The password was our routine security measure to confirm my identity even if I took a new face. "*Enkidu*, Thicks."

"Right. Get in, Felix." Thicks drove while I toweled myself dry and struggled with a fresh set of clothes in the tight confines of the car. My partner was a 'fixer' without equal: he could fence anything, find anything, and cover his tracks with aplomb. For someone like me, who might need a new identity fast, Thicks was a godsend. Although he wasn't Elect and hadn't the talent, I trusted him with my life, or more accurately, lives. "Back to Hathersage Mews, then?" he asked.

I grunted. "Yeah, I hurt like hell. Take care of the Egg for me, will you?"

" 'Course. You keeping it?" He adjusted his rear-view mirror.

"No." I patted the Fabergé's carrying case. I rarely kept what I stole. I suspected Mantis could care less about the Fabergé, as her true goal had been to capture or kill me. I could sell the Egg to a private collector and donate the profits to charity, as I often did, but I wanted to goad Mantis by putting the item back into the public eye. "Have it mysteriously appear at the British Museum. Let them take the credit."

"Will do."

Even after Thicks dropped me off, I was still shivering. My head was pounding and I hurt all over, but I shrugged it off as a consequence of my recent shapeshift and bloody-cold swim. I ditched my clothes and stumbled into the shower, letting the bliss of hot water cascade over me. Only after I had washed away the stink of the Thames did I first notice the rash on my arms.

I dried off and inspected the rest of my body with a mirror, wondering if more of the rash hid under the mat of dark hair on my chest or on my back. As far as I could tell, it hadn't spread beyond my forearms, but my lymph nodes were swollen. A thermometer confirmed I was running a high fever. Something had gone quite wrong.

I slumped into the leather chair in my cedar-and-emerald den and gazed at the painting of Sherwood Forest. We Elect rarely got sick. Each time we made a new body, Lightning made our immune system stronger. My first thought was poison: had Walczak laced the bullets with a toxin? My attention had been on physical injuries. But on further reflection, I realized when I had seen these symptoms before. The same illness had befallen Mantis a century ago. The Widowing.

Only a small group of humans could tap the Lightning inside amber, moulting old bodies like a cicada shed its shell. We called ourselves the Elect, after the Greek word for amber: *electron*. We could re-design our bodies to our whims, even reverse the aging process. However, biological sex could not be changed beyond deliberately induced hormonal imbalances.

With one odd exception. A strange disease sometimes afflicted male members of the Elect: an uncontrollable and irreversible transformation from man to woman. Curiously, the female Elect seemed immune to a sex change. Since the earliest days, this transformation had been called the Widowing, so named because it meant the death of the man and new life for the woman he had become. It struck without warning and had no known cure.

Trembling, I poured myself a glass of brandy. I did not want to be a woman. I had been born male, raised as a boy, lived centuries as a man's man. Though I had nothing but enlightened attitudes towards women, it was antithetical to my very being to even imagine that I would become female.

I remembered when Mantis Widowed. Once, he had been a man who inspired dark legends in every age. Now Widowed, she seemed content with her amber mining empire. While I did not bemoan the seeming retirement of such a formidable rival, I couldn't decide whether the Widowing softened Mantis, or if she had simply become subtler in her methods.

I tossed back the brandy and pulled out the two pieces of amber. Both had gone dark, their energies spent. Did I bring this disaster on myself by tapping the second amber raw? Had my luck simply run out?

Someone among the Elect must know how to stop the Widowing, but who? Cicada? Probably still underground. Scarab? A mind as old as Egypt and an ego to match, but he rarely divulged his secrets without exacting a devilish price.

That left beautiful, spectacular Spider. She was one of the oldest among us, the most beautiful woman in each generation since the days of Babylon. She had been Nefertiti, Helen of Troy, Guinevere, and others. Clever and irresistible, Spider's knowledge of history was also unrivaled, and the secrets entrusted to her innumerable. I smiled, remembering our one wild night of passion in Venice. Last I heard, Spider was spending an instar as Professor Ariana Strand, a paleoentomologist at NYU, but I wouldn't find Spider in New York this weekend. Like Mantis, she would be at the *Fourth World Congress on Amber and Its Inclusions* in Saint Petersburg.

I speed-dialed Thicks's number as I was opening the safe behind the Sherwood painting. When Thicks answered, I used the next password on our list. "It's me again. *Kato*."

A pause. "Felix? I almost didn't recognize your voice."

Was the Widowing starting to affect my pitch? I cleared my throat. "Never mind that. I have to go to Saint Petersburg. Call the airport and ready my jet, will you?"

" 'Course, guv. When will you be back?"

"Honestly, I don't know." I grabbed the right passport from a tall, neat stack and a fresh piece of amber from my collection. "I'm not even sure what I'll look like next."

"Not again." Thicks sighed. "Stick with cloak-and-dagger passwords, then?"

"Right. Trust the password, not the face or voice." I pondered whether I should warn him that I might be a different gender the next time we met, but decided against it. Why concede defeat so soon? "Take care, Thicks."

"You too, guv."

I hung up. I unhooked the expended amber pendant from my chain and replaced it with a new piece. I was about to toss the two darkened ambers into the safe but thought better of it. Perhaps the gems could tell Spider why I was Widowing. I tried to imprint the new amber with my Felix Lea construct, but the persona failed to crystallize, meaning any energy I drain from the amber would be raw. In any case, I didn't know if tapping more Lightning would be wise.

I slid open the mirrored closet door, pulling out a dark green long-sleeved shirt. As I changed, I examined my reflection. The hair on my chest was growing lighter, while my five o'clock shadow had faded to peach fuzz. The rash was starting to spread up my arms. I cursed and grabbed the keys to my Ferrari. I only hoped I could reach Spider in time.

❀

On the plane to Saint Petersburg, I called the Grand Hotel Europe, the venue of the Amber Conference, via satellite phone. Spider was registered under her alias, but the concierge was holding her calls. I left a message in Russian for her to contact me as soon as possible. "It's Felix Lea, regarding the health of Bernstein's widow. Tell her she needs to call before it's too late. I'll be in town in four hours." Spider ought to catch my use of the German word for amber, *Bernstein*.

I barely cleared Customs at Pulkovo Airport with my current passport, and if I had sweated any more they might have thrown me into quarantine. *That* would have been disastrous, but it would have been interesting to see what they'd do when they found a woman in the cell.

Painkillers eased my migraine, and caffeine pills kept me awake. Sleep was the surest thing to speed a metamorphosis, and I couldn't risk falling asleep and waking up forever Widowed. Even so, my legs felt shorter while my torso lengthened, fitting me closer to a woman's proportions. My once scruffy appearance softened to a more boyish look, stealing my edge from me.

My phone played a snippet of the William Tell overture, alerting me to a missed message. Spider had called ten minutes ago. "Flea, it's Spider." A mellifluous, contralto voice. "In trouble again? Meet me in front of the Catherine Palace, five after ten."

I checked my watch, now loose around my thinner wrist: nine a.m. I hailed a cab, and headed for the palace. It was no surprise that Spider chose the Catherine Palace for our rendezvous. The palace was famous for its magnificent suites, the Golden Enfilade, especially the Amber Room, recently recreated meticulously from existing records and photographs. I sat on the front steps waiting for Spider, smiling at a few passing tourists, but my mind was elsewhen: the first time I met Spider at the Battle of Agincourt, then our fleeting encounters across Europe throughout the Renaissance, culminating that magical evening at the opera in seventeenth century Venice. Alas, the last time we met, in eighteenth century Edo, it had been on platonic terms. I wondered what she looked like now.

At the appointed time, a dark-skinned, statuesque beauty in a white dress and summer hat sauntered down the path towards me. She had a certain *je-ne-sais-quoi*, and her every movement was laced with grace. "Hello, Flea."

It must be Spider . . . or was it? How could I be sure she *was* Spider? Could Mantis have intercepted my message and changed her shape to trick me? Maybe it was the fever making me paranoid, but I had to confirm her identity.

I greeted her in Italian, one of dozens of languages I picked up over the centuries. "You're as radiant as that night at the opera. Remember *The Return of Ulysses* at the *Teatro San Cassiano*? That sensuous kiss we shared during intermission?"

Spider crossed her arms. "I'm appalled you don't remember, Flea. It was a private performance of *Orfeo* without an intermission, and a slap, not a kiss."

"There were plenty of kisses much later." I managed a weak smile. "So it is you, Spider." I descended the steps, took her right hand and kissed it, catching the scent of lily upon her skin. She wore three silver rings on each hand, set with an individual amber gem.

A wave of shudders overtook me when I touched her. My once light skin darkened a shade, and my chest ached as my ribcage constricted. Did my touch shift my shape closer to hers?

"Just like you, Flea," Spider said, switching to English. "Always trying to be a gentleman and failing miserably."

"I'm hoping you could keep me a gentleman."

"I'll try. Shall we?" Spider gestured at the doors.

"I thought you'd never ask." Arm in arm, we entered the Catherine Palace. At the Grand Staircase, a museum guide asked us to don slippers to avoid scuffing the floors. My dress shoes came off with disturbing ease. My feet had shrunk a size.

Spider surprised me, leading me to the right, away from the Amber Room. Instead, we passed through the Knight's Dining Room and entered a hall of golden resplendence.

Great windows framed by gold let sunlight into the hall, and in between were mirrors reflecting the sunlight many-fold to swathe the room with brilliance. On the ceiling was a grand mural, a *trompe l'oeil* that gave the illusion of colonnades and blue sky above. Beneath our feet, the smooth, almost slippery floor was inlaid with crisscross patterns of dark and light oak.

"The Great Hall, also called the Light Gallery. Such celebrations we had here!" Spider reminisced. In this light she seemed a goddess of burnished gold come to life. "Magnificent."

I drank in the majesty of it all. "A man caught in amber might see the world in this slant of light."

Spider lowered her voice. "Show me your rash."

I rolled up my left sleeve, showing her the purplish spots. They had already spread to my upper body. "Is it bad, Doc?"

"Petechial eruptions under the skin," Spider said.

"Remind me what that means? It's been a while since I graduated from medical school," I said. 1878, to be exact.

"Perfectly round, purplish-red, pinpoint spots. Nothing you can't live through," Spider said. She touched my forehead. "Fever. I've never seen you looking more delicate, Flea. You tend to go for the tough look. I guess the feminine characteristics are catching."

I eased away from her touch. "I can't accept that. How do I reverse it?" I asked.

"Best you can do is slow its progress." Spider tugged on the chain around my neck until the amber showed. "First, this must go." She exchanged my necklace for a new pendant of amber from her purse, one without an insects caught within. "Amber's a natural reservoir for metamorphic energies. Pieces without inclusions are perfect matrices to drain off excess Lightning."

As soon as I touched the new amber, my fingertips became numb, but my headache subsided a little. The amber fluoresced faintly blue under the golden sunlight streaming through the windows. "Do I need to imprint it?" I asked. "Earlier, I couldn't crystallize my persona."

"I'm not surprised. The Widowing has already changed you beyond what's possible with a classic moult," Spider said. She tucked the pendant back under my shirt and patted it through the cotton. "Your mental self-image is at odds with your changing body. You need to leech away the tainted power. Since you're merely letting the amber siphon power out, skin contact should suffice. The siphoning will only buy you some time, but won't halt the Widowing. It's like drinking water to dilute a poison, but it's no antidote."

"Thanks." I stroked my chin. How I missed the roughness of my beard! "Could Mantis have done this to me intentionally?"

"Mantis?" Spider paused. "Highly improbable. The cause of your

Widowing is almost certainly the amber you used. The insect within must have been infected with ancient bacteria."

"Bacteria." This was news to me. "What do you mean?"

"Modern science has allowed us greater insight into Elect physiology," Spider said. "I have been studying the causes of Widowing in Elect men for decades, and we're much closer to understanding part of the mechanisms behind our metamorphoses."

"You're saying science actually explains what we do?" I furrowed my brow. "Isn't it just magic?"

"In a way, magic is mostly undiscovered science. Haven't the centuries shown us that?" Spider said.

"Ah. Clarke's Third Law." *Any sufficiently advanced technology is indistinguishable from magic.* In the past, many Elect hoarded scientific knowledge from one part of the world and passed it off as sorcery in another.

"Right." We paused at the eastern windows, where Spider drew my attention to the butterflies flittering from bloom to bloom in the park. "Insects generate metamorphic energy naturally, using it to moult between instars, changing from larva to pupa to adult. When an insect dies, its death will leave a fleeting psychic imprint on its corpse. Left to decay, that energy will dissipate."

I pressed my hand against the glass. "But it becomes Lightning when caught in amber?"

"Right. Millions of years ago, resin from ancient trees caught and killed prehistoric insects, but it also preserved the insect's trace metamorphic energy. The residual power is distilled and magnified by the fossilization of amber, making Lightning." Spider gestured at the Light Gallery around us. "See how the mirrors boost illumination in this room? Something similar happens inside the amber during those million years."

I caught my reflection in one of the mirrors. My blue eyes had grown hazel like Spider's. "So how does that explain the Widowing?"

"If Lightning can be magnified in amber, then so can other kinds of energy," Spider said. She took a handkerchief from her handbag and touched the sweat from my forehead. "Come. I want to see the Amber Room."

"I think touching makes it worse. My body seems to be mimicking you." I showed her my darkened hands. My index fingers had grown longer, like hers.

"Ah. The mirroring effect. I'll keep my distance." Spider drew her hand back and took a step away.

"Thank you." I followed her back through the door we came in. "You're saying there's a tainted power inside the amber."

"Exactly. Have you heard of the *Wolbachia* bacterium?"

I shook my head.

"It infects insects and other invertebrates like spiders and mites, and is in the same family as the microorganisms that cause typhus and Rocky Mountain spotted fever."

I was beginning to understand. "The same symptoms I have."

Spider nodded. "Curiously, the bacterium changes the reproductive mechanisms of its host. *Wolbachia* has been known to selectively kill off males, changing males into sexually functioning females, even inducing parthenogenesis: eggs developing into females without fertilization."

"Sex change *and* immaculate conception? I had no idea insects could do that. Why?" I asked.

"To ensure its own survival. *Wolbachia* travels in their hosts' eggs, infecting new offspring. But if the microbe ends up in a male, sperm cannot transmit the parasites to the host's children, unless. . . ."

"Unless it's able to change the male host into a female." I produced the two burnt-out gems and held them to the light in the Grand Staircase. "So these microbes tainted the Lightning?"

Spider took the ambers from me and examined them. "The organism infected invertebrates as long ago as 100 million years, and insects, 50 million years. Most of our amber falls well within that timeframe. Over the centuries, I've collected dozens of ambers from Widowed Elect. Once the technology became available, I extracted DNA from them. The ones they used before the Widowing were clean of *Wolbachia*, while the ones that triggered the sex change were infected."

We continued through the north wing towards the Amber Room. "So we've been playing a game of Russian roulette aeons in the making? Couldn't I just cure it with Lightning, like any other illness? That's how I survived the Black Plague."

"That's the worst thing you can do for the Widowing. Others before you have tried and failed. The Lightning in your typical piece of amber won't be enough to undo the sex change."

I ground my teeth. "There must be *some* way."

Spider led me through the next door into the Amber Room. My muscle pains subsided immediately when I crossed the threshold. If the Light Gallery had been golden sunrise caught in a glass mirage, then the

Amber Room was crystal dusk shattered and re-imagined as mosaic. Gilded cherubs smiled coyly from above, as though they knew the current panels were replicas. The originals had been taken from the Catherine Palace in 1941 and sent to Koenigsberg on Hitler's orders, as the dictator had been ordered by his doctors to seek the curative powers of amber. But when the Russians searched Koenigsberg Castle in 1945, the panels were nowhere to be found.

"A valiant copy, but it does not compare to the real thing," I commented. "The original is always best."

"I don't know," Spider said. "Much of the Catherine Palace we see today is restoration. World War Two destroyed much of it, but artisans were able to recreate, if not improve upon, the original design."

I examined the countless pieces of amber precisely fitted into the walls. The thirteen shades of amber ran the gamut from whiskey-yellow to blood-red, but when I brushed my index finger against one, the orange stone flickered electric blue. "You said *typical* amber. What aren't you telling me, Spider?"

Spider sighed. "There *might* be a way to fight the Widowing, but it's not mine to offer."

"Whose, then?"

"Mantis."

The feeling of dread spread from my stomach like a swarm of locusts. "So that's why you wouldn't tell me."

"I know of your feud. Don't get your hopes up, Flea. The piece of amber in Mantis's possession is unique and its power boundless, yet no one has yet conquered it. You will more likely die than master its power. Even I fear it."

"Sounds intriguing," I said. "What is it?"

Spider shook her head. "Talk to Mantis. Don't you think it's time to put aside your quarrel with her, Flea?"

"There's too much bad blood between us. Centuries worth."

"She's changed," Spider said. "How about negotiating a temporary truce? You want something she has. Is there anything you could offer her?"

I let my gaze drift over the contents of the amber-paneled room around us, thinking. I knew Mantis's fatal flaws: greed and envy. There *was* something I stole years ago that might tempt her. Slowly, I nodded. "I think there is."

We exited the Amber Room together, but as soon as we left the vicinity of the amber panels, sharp pains assailed me and my world spun. I tried to steady myself against Spider, but I had little traction in these slippers. I slipped on the smooth wooden floor and hit my head hard. My world went black.

❁

I dreamt of ancient and colossal trees, the scent of pine and fissures in the bark deep and full of glistening sap. I floated between the living towers, their images caught in swirling hexagonal crystals in my field of vision. A nymph's gnarled wood-grained face grew on the trunk of the tree ahead. I pulled a steep turn to fly away, but other dryads showed their faces and laughed. There was nowhere to run. Something invisible caught me and held me in place. A web?

"Felix," called a woman's sweet voice. There it was again, the fragrance of lilies. "Flea. It's Spider. Can you hear me?" She wasn't a part of the dream. I mumbled and pulled the covers over my eyes.

"Wake up, Little John, before you become a Jane."

Groaning, I pulled off the covers off my face. I was in a soft bed. Spider hovered over me, taking a piece of blue amber from my forehead and daubing the sweat off my brow. I felt sore all over. "No one has called me that in years," I said. My voice was tenor, no longer baritone.

"How are you feeling?" Spider asked, caressing my hand. I drew it back sharply, aware how much slimmer my fingers had become.

"Like I've been flayed, trepanned and leeched. Again." The suite was decorated in the turn-of-the-century style—the twentieth century, not the twenty-first—with anachronistic touches clashing with the antiques, like the shaded lamps and the hotel phone. The light from outside told me it was still day. "How long have I been out?"

"Six hours. The high concentration of stones in the Amber Room likely dampened your Widowing even without physical contact. When you left the curative field, the Widowing hit you twice as hard," Spider conjectured. "After you fell, the museum personnel wanted to take you to the hospital, but I greased a few palms to have you brought back to my suite. I've gone through five good pieces of amber slowing your Widowing."

"Hey, they're worth more blue," I joked.

"They won't stay blue long," Spider said. She dropped the blue amber into her purse. "It's easier to make popcorn from kernels than the other way around. The distilled Lightning inside the amber is diamond-like, structured perfectly. By comparison, Lightning already in the body is coal, and saturates amber fast. Blueness means the stone has reached its absorption limit, but it will return to its natural color."

"So much for making profit out of my predicament." I ran checked my body for further changes that might have infected me during sleep. My athletic body hadn't lost its muscularity or definition, but my chest hair had thinned to nothingness. My pecs became fuller, rounder. My hips were wider and my arms shorter, but at least the rash on my arms was fading. I sat up and examined my reflection in the mirror opposite the bed. The colour black had won the war against my hair's original chestnut shade. While my face still bore elements of my original design, the brow was less pronounced and my features finer, almost androgynous. I didn't want to think about what was changing *down there*. "How long do I have?"

Spider tossed me the amber. "You're not dying, Flea. Stop talking like you are."

"But I *am*." I grabbed my shirt off a bedside chair.

"I fail to see how it's different from any of your other metamorphoses," Spider said. She helped me with the buttons on my shirt. "You've taken different sizes, changed the color of your skin, and lived the seven ages of Man. You experimented with our ability to transform, even reveled in the changes. Why would a new sex frighten you so?"

Good question. "It's a matter of control. When I first learned I was Elect, I designed the new life I would have, the body I would wear. But this Widowing robs me of that choice. My crusade's always been against tyranny, and this is no different than what Mantis did for centuries. I won't let some parasitic microbe from a million years ago control me!"

"The Widowing is a far different beast than the Sheriff of Nottingham, Little John. Disease does not discriminate," Spider said. "We all have aspects of the masculine and feminine, the animus and the anima. The Widowing is only bringing to the fore a part of you that has always been there."

I shook my head. "Being in touch with my feminine side isn't the same as being forced into a sex change. You can't know how I feel." Or could she? "Were you ever . . . ?"

She handed me an old-fashioned thermometer. "Does it matter?" she said, her face inscrutable.

I stuck the thermometer under my tongue and thought about her question. It shouldn't. She was older than any Elect, and we all acknowledged her as the paradigm of a woman. Would any of that change, if she had in fact been a Widow?

When she indicated that the time was up, I gave her the thermometer back. "I'm just curious."

Spider smirked. "Every woman has her secrets." She read the mercury. "Your fever's subsiding, as are your other symptoms. The Widowing has entered its second stage. Your body has already started to moult its male parts and will continue until you are completely biologically female."

"Not if I can help it." I refused to let the disease conquer me, even if it meant I would have to grovel at Mantis's feet. "Very well. A man's gotta do what he's gotta do," I said, aware of the irony of my statement. "Call Mantis. Give her time to set up another trap."

"Stop being so paranoid," Spider said.

"Force of habit." I pulled on my pants under the covers, but they fitted too loose. "I hide, he seeks. I flee, he chases. It's been our way for centuries."

"The old *he*. Not the new *she*." Spider opened a musical jewelry box—playing the aria *Possente spirito* from Monteverdi's *Orfeo*—and plucked out an amber ring for me. I slipped it on my right ring finger with the gemstone facing in. If I needed its soothing touch, I could form a fist and press the amber to my palm. "Besides, you're forgetting one thing. This time, I'll be there to protect you." Spider grinned.

Spider and I arrived early at the Caviar Bar and Restaurant on the Mezzanine Level. Marble and mirrors were the theme of the Caviar Bar décor. We took a table in a quiet corner and sampled luxury vodkas and caviars while waiting for Mantis. A few conference attendees came into the restaurant and greeted Spider, but left us in peace.

A thirtyish-looking woman with short auburn hair and fierce green eyes entered the restaurant. She wore red amber earrings and a custom-tailored woman's suit, a black leather portfolio under her arm. You wouldn't call her striking or sensuous, but she had the presence of a lioness. It was Mantis all right, or in her present incarnation, Morgan Grandin, president of the Adamantis Mining Corporation.

The *maitre-d'hotel* escorted Mantis to our table and held the seat for her, but she waved him away. "Good evening, Spider. Flea," said Mantis in English. She tossed a British newspaper on the table. The headline read, *LOST FABERGÉ RESURFACES, BRITISH MUSEUM BAFFLED*. "You wouldn't happen to know anything about that, would you?"

"You know it was me," I replied icily. "You steal something from the people, I liberate it and give it back."

Mantis appraised me. "The Widowing is *very* becoming of you. Why, with a little blush and some fashion tips, you'll be racking up wolf-whistles in no time."

I rolled my eyes. "Payback?"

Mantis smiled. "I seem to recall someone taunting me the same way when I Widowed."

"Guilty, as charged," I said. "But you deserved it."

Spider shook her head. "Play nice, children."

"I was merely remarking on Flea's inhibitions," Mantis said. She picked up a delicate silver spoon and polished it. "He's always had gender issues."

"That's not true," I said, drumming my fingers on the table.

"You say that, but I only have to cite one thing to prove otherwise. Marian."

I shook my head. "That's different. *You* started the whole Marian fiasco as a personal attack against me."

"Now I'm curious. What Marian fiasco?" asked Spider.

Mantis placed a napkin in her lap. "He's mad that I invented Maid Marian in the late sixteenth century."

"There never was a real Marian," I said. "The original Merry Men were just that. Men." That wasn't what we were really called, but the name stuck. "Mantis perverted the Robin Hood legend just to spite me."

"I thought the story became more romantic with my revisions," Mantis said. "The King of Thieves must have his Queen. I did more to keep the legend alive than you ever did, Flea, but you obsess on Marian and not the liberties I took with other parts of the legend, like the time period or the location. It's almost as if you're jealous of a fictional character."

"I am not!" I said, but Spider and Mantis only exchanged glances, as though they knew something I didn't. "Look. I'm here because Spider said you have something that might cure me."

"Did she now?" Mantis frowned at Spider.

Spider dismissed Mantis's accusing stare with a wave. "Trust me, Mantis, I wouldn't have told Flea if he wasn't the ideal candidate. He's a perfect test subject."

Mantis put her elbows on the table and folded her hands together as though in prayer. I tensed. That was her tell when she held a good hand. Mantis might really have something that could cure the Widowing! But if so, why hadn't she used it to change herself back into a man?

"Enough," I said. "What's so special about this mysterious amber of yours?"

"That information will cost you," Mantis said. "But what could you possibly have that I might want?"

"Oh, you might be surprised. Something extraordinary that you've lusted after for a long time," I said, leaving her imagination to fill in the blanks.

"Tell him, or I will," Spider said. "You owe it to Mayfly and Hawkmoth."

Now Spider made me even more curious. "Spill it, Mantis. Trust me, I will make it worth your while," I said.

"You damn well better." Mantis unlaced her fingers. "My mines are under explicit instructions to deliver the best amber inclusions to our headquarters in Gdansk. The nominal reason is that an insect trapped in the amber might be an undiscovered species, but in reality I keep the best samples for sale to the Elect. Metamorphic amber is, for all practical purposes, a non-renewable resource. Six months ago, a mine in Kaliningrad discovered an extraordinary piece of amber with an unknown specimen and sent it to me. As soon as I laid my eyes on it, I knew it was no ordinary amber. A gem the size of a hen's egg, it was the most perfect piece of amber I had ever seen. Although amber is normally warm to the touch, being a poor conductor of heat, this gem was hot."

"Could it be the Lightning inside?" I asked.

Mantis shrugged. "Could be. Even my assistants who weren't Elect could feel its heat. I could sense that there was an immense store of Lightning in the amber, but it felt *wrong*. The inclusion was a curled tadpole-like worm roughly eight centimeters long, but I did not recognize the species. Neither did Mayfly, a young Elect biologist training under my tutelage."

"No one told him the name's cursed?" Every Elect took the name of a critter, often embodying the traits of our namesake or changed to fit. No one named Mayfly ever lived past a year.

Mantis lowered her head. "You've anticipated his tragic end. When Mayfly tried to imprint the amber, he suddenly burst into flames. Although the sprinklers eventually doused the fire, it was too late to save him. All that remained of Mayfly was wet ash. The amber egg remained intact."

I winced. "Spontaneous human combustion? Ouch."

A nod. "I could scarcely believe it myself. Hawkmoth, a senior scientist on my staff, tried as well. She managed to use the fire amber to reverse the Widowing for a few seconds, before being consumed by flames."

She still used people like food-tasters. I rose and grabbed Mantis by the collar across the table, sending a vodka glass tumbling. It broke against the tiled floor. "Do you ever face the risk yourself?"

I felt the tines of a fork pressed against my stomach. Her reflexes hadn't dulled any. "Hawkmoth volunteered," Mantis insisted.

Being so close to her sent a shiver of change through my body. My lips trembled and curled to match her sneer, while my chest strained the buttons on my shirt.

"Put her down, Flea. People are staring," Spider said. "She didn't have to tell you any of this."

I supposed she didn't. She could have told me that the fire amber was safe even if it wasn't. But was she being truthful only because Spider was mediating? I took a long, deep breath and let go of Mantis, and glared around the room. The other restaurant patrons tore their gazes away and pretended they hadn't seen anything at all.

I sat back down. "Go on."

Mantis straightened her shirt. "The fire amber was too dangerous to use and too powerful to leave a riddle. I knew I was out of my league, so I asked for Spider's help." A waiter came by to sweep away the glass fragments while another brought a replacement.

"I was intrigued," Spider said. She stole a spoonful of caviar from Mantis. "I flew to Gdansk to head up research on this fascinating fire amber. I exposed the gem to various tests. It floats in salt water like amber would, and the surface does not react with alcohol to become tacky, as it would if it was copal. However, when exposed to ultraviolet light, it doesn't glow green or blue, but red."

"That doesn't sound like amber. You sure it wasn't red kryptonite?" I joked. Spider smiled, but Mantis didn't. On a more serious note, something had been bothering me. "Amber can't survive heat over 300 degrees Celsius, and by your description of their immolation, I'd expect a blaze as hot as 1,200 degrees, at least. How could it survive the fire?"

"Strange, isn't it?" Spider said. "The fire amber is flame-resistant, but if you chip away a piece and expose it to fire, it will soften, blacken, and burn with amber's characteristic incense-like scent. I concluded that it was the inclusion that made the fire amber unique."

"What have you discovered about the worm?" I asked.

Spider exchanged glances with Mantis. "It would be best if you saw the fire amber for yourself. Mantis?"

Mantis ran a finger idly around the rim of her vodka glass. "Not until I know what you offer."

Spider turned to me. "She's kept her end of the deal."

She was right. The fire amber could indeed be my salvation, if I could master it. "Then I offer you the Amber Room, Mantis."

Mantis laughed. "You plan to rob the Catherine Palace?"

An interesting thought, but I pushed it aside before I could be distracted by the intricacies of such a heist. "The original panels, all twenty-seven crates of them. All except the *Touch and Smell* panel that got away." That one, stolen by a German soldier before my heist, was back in Saint Petersburg.

The expression of surprise on Mantis's face was well worth the sixty-odd years wait, while the look of understanding and admiration on Spider's was a pleasant bonus. "Bastard. I've been searching for the Amber Room for decades, and all along you had it," Mantis said. "How?"

"We all have our trade secrets," I said, leaning back in my chair. "Let's just say that it took a lot of ingenuity, planning, and luck to steal six tons worth of amber from the Germans."

"I'd have thought you sold them piecemeal," Mantis said.

"Never. The Room is an exquisite masterpiece of amber art with much history," I said. "So much blood and sweat went into its construction I couldn't simply smash it up for the amber."

Mantis narrowed her eyes. "Even if you still have them, the amber's surely damaged over the years."

"I'm scandalized that you think I'd leave them to degrade. I restored the damaged panels and spared no expense to protect them from discolouration. A controlled microclimate keeps them safe from oxygen and water vapour. Do we have a deal?"

Mantis spread a smidgen of caviar on a blini and cut a piece from it slowly, mulling over my offer. She savoured the caviar and daubed her lips. "I want it."

"Half now. The rest after I try this amber of yours."

"And if you don't survive?" Mantis asked.

"It's in your best interest to see that I do," I said.

"Very well." She opened her portfolio and took out a business card. "Have it sent to my castle in Poland. That's where we're heading as well, if you intend to see the fire amber."

"I'll call to arrange it," I said.

Mantis lifted a tumbler of vodka. "To truce."

Spider and I lifted our own glasses. "*Na zdorovje!*"

I downed my vodka. I wonder who was getting the better deal: Mantis, with the Amber Room, or me, with a potential cure for this disease. On the other hand, if the cure was as dangerous as they intimated, perhaps Mantis was hoping to be rid of me once and for all.

"Let's go, then," I said. I was eager to know if this amber could indeed cure me.

"Soon." Mantis spread more caviar on her *blini*. "I never let good Sevruga go to waste."

After I phoned Thicks in London to arrange the amber delivery, Mantis, Spider and I boarded my jet for Gdansk. I would need new forged documents soon. Any more changes to my face and I wouldn't be able to use my current passport.

Mantis sat across from Spider and me, sipping a Grasshopper martini. Likely she designed her body for a high tolerance of alcohol as I did, a standard body-trick among the Elect. Still, it wouldn't hurt to try loosening her tongue with a cocktail or two. "So, Mantis. If I figure out how to use this thing, would you go back to being a man?"

"Believe it or not, Flea, I've embraced my new self," Mantis said. "I consider it a privilege to have experienced life as both men and women. There are unexpected advantages that a woman enjoys." She touched her left earring, which had a mite trapped inside, and *changed*. Her eyes became as blue as the sky, her cheekbones more angular and her hair white gold.

"Such flagrant waste of Lightning," Spider said, and I agreed. She stood. "Excuse me for a moment, darlings. I must call the university." She took a seat in the rear of the plane to use the satellite phone, leaving me alone with Mantis.

Mantis shrugged. "Ignore her. As men we used ambers reluctantly, fearing that the curse of Widowing might make us less than we were. Women have no such cares. We may moult as the mood strikes us, goddesses of a thousand shapes." Her eyes flickered brown, then violet, then green again. "When such power is mine, why would I have any desire to revisit the past?"

"Bollocks!" I said. "You were never able to resist fame. At heart you're still Mordred. Nottingham. Machiavelli. Moriarty! When you were a man, you let nothing stand in your way. What legends have you inspired lately, *madame*?"

"Still envious of my legacy, Flea? How well have *you* fared? People only remember you as a sidekick: Little John. Sancho Panza. Friday. Whenever you try to be a hero, you always fail miserably. Face it: when your balls shrivel up and fall off, you'll lose your last chance to prove yourself a man's man." She stabbed an olive and popped it into her mouth.

I shrugged at the notion. "I've little use for personal glory. If I helped any man to better himself and in turn the world, then let *him* be remembered, not me."

"But Flea, you're so convinced that masculinity and fraternity equal strength that you've subconsciously dismissed the female sex as weaker. That couldn't be farther from the truth. Think of insects in nature: queens among bees, termites and ants. Female mantises and black widows sometimes bite off the heads of the males after mating. Who's the stronger sex?"

"Nice try, but I'm not convinced." I leaned forward and stared into her eyes. "Look at the alias you chose. Why take an ambiguous name like Morgan and not something distinctly feminine? You're still looking for a way to change back. That's why you're desperate to unlock the fire amber's power."

Mantis said nothing. She shifted back to her Morgan shape and nursed her Grasshopper martini the rest of the flight.

The sun was setting when we landed at Lech Walesa Airport, roughly two hours after take-off. Gdansk on the Baltic Sea had long been a center for amber craftsmanship. In fact, the Amber Room was commissioned by the King of Prussia and first designed in this city. It was no surprise that Mantis had chosen this area of Poland to set up her amber industry headquarters.

Prorok Castle, Mantis's current residence, was some forty kilometers southeast of Gdansk; we would take Mantis's helicopter from the airport to save travel time. At the helipad, Mantis's pilot greeted us. I scowled when I recognized his voice: Nicodem. He was tall and stringy with curly brown hair, a handlebar moustache, and eyes like pits of darkness. He must have flown to Poland from London after our encounter. Nicodem never did see my face, and I doubted he recognized me in my current shape, though Mantis was sure to tell him who I was.

"Nicodem Walczak, my Chief of Security," shouted Mantis over the noise of the propellers.

I knew it would be risky, this visit to Mantis's castle. I had entertained the notion of stealing the fire amber, but with Nicodem here, the chances of theft had just halved and the risk of death doubled. Still, there was no turning back.

We arrived shortly at Prorok and landed inside the castle courtyard. Typical of Mantis, she had renamed the place for the Polish word for *prophet*, a play on the meaning of the word *mantis* in Latin. The little-known castle, built in the fifteenth century by Teutonic knights, had been converted into her private residence. If I wanted a fortress of my own, I could: like most of the Elect, I had made careful, long-term investments that had made me ridiculously rich. Mantis led us into her castle, and I watched for any potential escape routes.

"Nicodem, show our guests to their rooms," Mantis said.

Nicodem bowed and picked up our luggage. "This way, ladies." *Ladies*? Had the sum of my body's changes crossed the great gender divide? I needed a mirror, bad.

"I'll take that myself, kid," I said, taking my suitcase from him. Spider and I followed Nicodem up the stairs to the third floor. He showed us our adjacent rooms and placed Spider's luggage in her room. "If you need anything, just dial zero," said Nicodem, and departed.

"I have gifts for you, Flea." Spider opened her handbag and took out her music box and a worn paperback. It was a copy of *Orlando* by Virginia Woolf. She pressed them into my hands. "These ambers should give you some comfort in the meantime."

"Thank you. And the book?"

"It's about an Elizabethan lord, born a man but transformed mysteriously into a woman," Spider said. "He embraced his new sex quite matter-of-factly and lived for centuries. A fitting tale, don't you think?"

I flipped through the pages. "Spider, I appreciate what you're trying to do, but if the fire amber works, the point's moot."

"Read it," Spider insisted.

I shrugged. "I suppose there's no harm. See you soon." I took the gifts into my room and shut the door. The tight, once-medieval guest room had been modernized for comfort, as though small elements of all centuries I had lived through had been incorporated into its decor. The window, barely large enough to climb through, overlooked the inner courtyard. I tossed my suitcase on the bed. It would be difficult to escape Prorok, given what I'd seen of the castle and the region. I needed a quick way to leave, but I would have to get a message to Thicks.

I popped a scanner out of a secret compartment in my suitcase and started sweeping the room for bugs. There were two: one in the potted plant by the window and one in the base of the porcelain figurine of Leda and the Swan on the table.

Looking out the window and toying with the potted plant, I made a call to Thickett. "Thicks. Password *Lancelot*."

"You've gone falsetto! Having fun storming the castle?"

"Loads," I said. "You should see my room. Great view of the courtyard, though I would have preferred one nearer the corners instead of dead center. As it is, the sun will wake me too early. When can I expect the first shipment?"

"Within the hour. Best I could do on such short notice."

"You always exceed my expectations, Thicks. Think you can top the Milan job?" I hoped he caught the reference. "There's an extra set of wheels in it for you if you do. Send half as soon as you can, but not the rest until I call again."

A pause. "The Milan job, eh? Tough act to follow, but I'll give it a shot. Godspeed."

Forty minutes later, a crate of amber panels arrived by helicopter, airlifted to Prorok. I hurried downstairs to greet the chopper, but Spider, Mantis, and Nicodem beat me to it.

"You promised me half the panels," Mantis said.

"More will come. It takes time to move sixteen tons of amber safely," I reminded her. "This is the fastest I could arrange for a shipment to arrive from the nearest location. Is it enough collateral to buy me a peek at the fire amber?"

"Let's have a look." Mantis snapped her fingers and instructed her guards to move the crate to the West Wing. While her men struggled with the flatbed, we preceded them to the New Amber Room on the ground floor.

The room where Mantis intended to mount the panels was much larger than I expected. One side was a set of great windows designed to catch the morning sunlight. The original Amber Room panels were made for a small palace room in Berlin, and when they were transplanted to the larger room in the Catherine Palace in 1755, amber wallpaper, mirrors, and gilded frames were added to give the illusion of more amber than was actually present. It looked like Mantis imagined this bare room to exceed even the Amber Room's current incarnation in Russia.

"I've been saving this room for a day when I would find the Amber Room," Mantis said. "Did you know that I spent an instar as an artisan on the original panels? I know my own work, so these better be genuine, Flea."

"They are," I assured her.

Spider walked the perimeter of the room, trailing her hand along the wall. "How will you fill the gaps? Same tricks as the Catherine Palace?"

Laughter. "I am the queen of amber," Mantis reminded Spider. "I will encrust this room with my personal grand designs made from the ambers of the world, a merging of new and old."

Setting the crate down gently, Mantis's guards pried the lid open and eased the first panel out of the box. A dark Prussian eagle was set into the amber mosaic.

Mantis ran her fingers along the raised circle of amber that framed the symbol of Prussia. "It is genuine. You are a man of your word, Flea."

"That's the hope," I said.

"Nicodem, inspect the panels as they come in. Let me know if any are damaged or missing," Mantis said.

"Yes, ma'am."

Mantis motioned for us to follow, and took us to the end of the hall where a gleaming steel sliding door was set incongruously into the castle wall. Mantis touched an earring with a finger on her left hand, then pressed her right hand to the palm scanner. Tricky, that. Given that she could shapeshift at will, she didn't need to use her natural palm-print as the key to the door. She only needed to change her palm to the proper shape when she needed to unlock the lab. It made breaking and entering this room all the more difficult.

The lab door slid open. "After you," she said.

After seeing the true strength of her security system, I was now positive that last night's Fabergé caper had been a trap. Mantis might have changed, but at the core of it, the bitch was still a cunning bastard.

We entered a pristine suite of labs installed with the latest medical and chemical equipment. The door slid shut behind us. Mantis went to a wall and unlocked a safe with another palm-print, donned a pair of gloves and took a piece of amber the shape and size of a chicken egg from the cushion within. With small, cautious steps, she carried the fire amber to a lab table, placed it on a stainless steel stand, and shone white light on the jewel.

The golden amber was rough and vaguely egg-shaped. I had never seen a piece of amber so free of air bubbles. The most interesting thing about it, though, was the inclusion: a semi-transparent worm with a large head and a long tail.

"May I touch it?" I asked.

Mantis nodded. "Sense the power within, but don't try to imprint it. Mayfly and Hawkmoth tried and failed."

"I'll be careful." I touched the fire amber with a finger. As Mantis claimed, the amber was hot, brimming with a primordial power. It was obvious why Mantis wanted to master this gem.

Spider tapped a few keys on a nearby computer and projected a few enlarged images onto a white screen. The inclusion was a curled tadpole-like worm roughly eight centimeters long, but I did not recognize the species. I could make out two black dots in the head, and even rudimentary organs.

"It isn't an insect or a worm," Spider said. "It's not in the same phylum as invertebrates at all. See the tail? No segmentation. The creature has a nervous system, a notochord, which makes it a chordate like mammals, fish, and birds. The closest fauna it resembles is the larval form of a tunicate."

My zoology wasn't that good. "What's a tunicate?"

"Tunicates, or *tunicata*, are more commonly called sea squirts," answered Spider. "They're jellyfish-like but sessile filter feeders like coral. Most tunicates are hermaphroditic, carrying both egg and sperm. However, the inclusion doesn't resemble any modern *tunicata*. For one thing, it has no gills, which means it might not be adapted for aquatic life."

Strange that a tadpole-like larva could even exist outside water. How could this specimen even get caught in tree sap? I adjusted the light and held a magnifying glass over the amber for a better look. "Could you extract DNA from it to find out what it is?" I asked.

Spider shook her head. "In my experiments to find the cause of the Widowing, I discovered that the Lightning would be lost if the structure of the amber is compromised. There's no way to get a needle in there and keep the power intact. But as I said, I have a hypothesis about its true nature."

"Don't tell me just yet. I'd like to take a stab at it, if you don't mind." I thought about what I knew about the creature inside the fire amber. It wasn't a worm but a non-aquatic chordate in larval form. What would it metamorphose into? What would explain the amber exuding heat, and why would Mayfly and Hawkmoth be burnt to ash? I recalled my earlier conversation with Spider about science and magic.

Could the life-form within be a creature of myth?

"Blimey. It's a bloody phoenix in there, isn't it?" I said, excited by the possibility.

Spider smiled. "It was the only logical conclusion."

Mantis peered at the critter inside the amber. "It looks nothing like a phoenix. All I see's a worm."

"In the legends, the phoenix lived for five hundred years, give or take a few centuries depending on the source," I said, putting the magnifying glass aside. "When it was ready to die, it would build a pyre and immolate itself. It was said that a worm would crawl out of the ashes and become the phoenix reborn."

"There's truth in every myth," Spider agreed. She tapped a key and called up a map of the world. "The legend of the phoenix can be found in many cultures around the world. The Russian firebird, the Egyptian *benu*, the Chinese *fenghuang*, the Japanese *hou-ou*. In Central America, the old Mayan sun god Kinich Ahau was portrayed as a phoenix. Even the Malay Garuda is a phoenix." She pointed to each named region with a laser pointer, then overlaid the slide with a map of the world's amber. "Phoenix myths and amber deposits match worldwide."

I thought about the implications. "You think those myths were based on sightings of real phoenixes? But amber is millions of years old. Why would the phoenixes stick around the same place? Migratory routes?"

Spider shook her head. "I think there were more phoenix larvae caught in amber. Those ancient sightings might have been the phoenixes escaping from their eggs. Don't ask me where they are now, if they still exist."

I picked up the fire amber. After hundreds of millions of years inside this amber tomb, this creature was still alive? "You can't be serious."

"Why not? The phoenix's supposed to be immortal."

I put the gem back on the stand. "How on Earth does a sea squirt turn into a phoenix?" I asked.

"Modern science might not be able to explain it, but magic might. Birds have been around since the Jurassic, millions of years older than the first amber deposits. What if the phoenix larva was originally a simple chordate like the tunicate, but somehow learned to *evolve* into a bird using metamorphic energy?" Spider suggested. "What are we but highly-evolved chordates?"

"Still doesn't explain why a phoenix larva would get caught in the amber," I said.

"Could be any number of ways," Spider said. "Caught in a windstorm and blown into the resin. Part of a phoenix's lifecycle that we don't yet understand. Legend also claims that after the new phoenix is born, it gathers the ashes of the old phoenix into an egg of myrrh. What is myrrh but tree resin, just like amber was millennia ago?"

"I couldn't care less what it is," Mantis said, her eyes aglitter. "Think of the power! Look at what we can already do with dead insects in amber. This thing's *alive*. We have an inexhaustible source of living Lightning, and all we have to do is to figure out how to control it."

"All I have to do." If we were right, then this amber was the philosopher's stone: the ultimate source of metamorphic energy. If our standard insect inclusions were batteries of power, then the fire amber was a pocket fusion reactor. All the more reason to take this time-bomb out of Mantis's hands. "Why do you think I'll succeed where others failed, Spider?"

"You're different from Mayfly and Hawkmoth. For one, you're more experienced than those neonates. For another, you're in the middle of the Widowing, itself an ancient and powerful metamorphosis. If you direct the phoenix's energy against the Widowing, their energies might cancel out, or at least weaken enough for you to seize control."

"Or I might just die from double the infections."

"That's the risk," admitted Spider. She logged off the computer. "How far are you willing to go, Flea? Is preserving your sex worth your life?"

Spider was right. It could be suicidal. Two people already died. Life was more precious than controlling my own sex. Still, I had a chance, however small, of living through the experience and mastering the phoenix's power. If I gave up this opportunity now, I had zero chance of beating this Widowing. It was a gamble with long odds, but I had never let that stop me before. Besides, if I didn't try, Mantis might find someone else who might unlock the phoenix's secrets, and I couldn't have that power falling into her hands.

"All my life I have played the outlaw, risking my life so that others might live a better life," I told them. "I've faced death more times than I can remember, suffered through countless tortures and lived. I survived because of my will. I will survive this too. I'm ready." I reached for the fire amber again.

"Not so fast," Mantis said, snatching the gem before I could. She stepped back from the table. "I haven't gotten my Amber Room yet."

I shook my head. "I can't wait that long. Sooner or later I would need to sleep again, and I won't risk the Widowing changing more of me while I'm dead to the world."

"Then give me your next password, in case you die," Mantis said. "Then I can be sure your crony will deliver the rest."

As I expected, Mantis *had* been listening in on my call. "No way. You'll find a way to kill me and use the password to get to the amber. Let Spider be the intermediary," I offered. "She's always stayed neutral in the disputes of the Elect."

Mantis caressed the amber egg. "Very well. Tell her."

I pulled Spider aside and whispered into her ear. I couldn't resist giving her earlobe a quick nibble while I was at it, changes be damned. "*Aguecheek.*" Spider chuckled.

Mantis gestured at a hospital bed on the other side of a glass wall, next to an array of medical equipment. "Strip and lie down, so we can monitor your vitals."

I hesitated. I was reluctant to let anyone see how the Widowing had ravaged my body, least of all myself.

Spider put a hand gently on my shoulder. "It's all right, Flea. There's nothing we haven't seen before."

I walked over to the bed and took off my shirt. My pecs had grown so full they resembled breasts. Even now, I felt my neck lengthen and slim to match Spider's. I quickly dropped my pants but left the boxer briefs on. My hips were fuller, stretching the elastic, and my 'boys' had jumped up inside my body. I pulled the covers off the bed in one smooth stroke and wrapped it around my waist, cursing in twelve languages as I lay down.

Mantis stood by with the amber egg in one hand, a fire extinguisher in the other. Spider placed four electrodes on my chest, turned on the EKG, and positioned an infra-red camera to conduct a thermo-imaging scan of my body temperature. "Ready?"

I cupped my hands over my stomach. "Let me have it."

Mantis pressed the fire amber into my hands. Any hotter and the stone would burn me like coal. I closed my eyes. If I was going to survive this, I needed a self-image that was most familiar to me. I invoked my oldest memory: seven feet tall, tree-trunk legs, hairy arms, and the hefty build of a grizzly bear. I would become Little John of Hathersage again.

I folded my hands over the fire amber and primed the jewel with the pattern of my first body. At first, the amber matrix resisted the imprint, but I took my time. Likely the two who died rushed the process. Slowly, the Little John imprint took.

The fiery energy inside the amber pulsed against my psychic imprint. I opened the floodgates and the power poured into me.

My world caught fire.

The moment I tapped into the fire amber, my imprint fractured from the sheer force of the liberated Lightning. The pattern of Little John burned itself into my body haphazardly: my gums bled, while my bones were growing faster than my muscles, tearing them. Worst of all, patches of third-degree burns erupted on my skin. I screamed.

"Incredible," Mantis said. "Your internal temperature's reached a hundred degrees Celsius! How are you still alive?"

"Your heartbeat's erratic, but I can't keep these on you," Spider said, ripping the electrodes off my chest. "They're going to melt. Come on, Flea, you can beat this!"

"Thanks for your vote," I managed between breaths, "of confidence." I tasted blood in my mouth. The Lightning from the amber continued to flow, but now it was fighting against the tainted Widowing power. Pulled in two directions, my body didn't know whether to return to male or complete the change to female. I was the rope in a tug of war between two powers, strained near the breaking point.

"Flea, let go," Mantis said, trying to pry the amber out of my hands, but I couldn't will my hands open. *Something* forced me to grip the fire amber.

Flames flickered out of my pores, burning away hair. I could smell burnt flesh and old pine. My underwear and bed sheets caught on fire. Mantis raised the fire extinguisher and sprayed foam on me, quenching the flames. "Keep it up, Flea. You're doing a lot better than Mayfly or Hawkmoth."

"No, it's worse," I said, struggling to my feet. Foam slid off my body. The energy was building up inside me. Like trapped steam, the more the pressure built, the more dangerous it got. When Mayfly and Hawkmoth tapped into the amber, they could only hold a sliver of the phoenix energy before it consumed them. "If I don't control this power, I'll explode and take this castle with me!"

"Don't you dare!" Mantis said, tossing the empty fire extinguisher clattering across the floor.

Spider unhooked her necklace, a clear amber, and hung it around my neck. "Does this help?"

The pain eased some, but it was small relief. "We need a lot more amber than this!" I said. I remembered the calming effects of the Amber Room at Catherine Palace. "The amber panels! What if we built a temporary cocoon around me? Will that dampen the shapeshift?"

"It might, if we seal you in," Spider said.

"But will the panels survive?" Mantis asked.

"This is no time to worry about your treasures!" I shouted. "You'll lose it all if I die!" Hands stuck together, I stumbled from the smouldering bed, ran for the lab door in my misshapen body and slammed the door switch. The door slid open. Another wave of flickering flame pulsed from my ankles up to my scalp, burning away more of what made me a man.

"Stop!" Mantis screamed, but I ignored her. Bare-naked, I raced down the hall towards the New Amber Room, with Mantis and Spider close on my heels. Every step sent a jolt through my body. When I got there, Nicodem stood in my way. His eyes widened in surprise when he saw my nude, hermaphroditic body. He tried to tackle me, but I sidestepped his attack. Though my hands were stubbornly clasped around the fire amber against my will, I could still swing my arms. I wound up for a two-handed haymaker and slammed Nicodem in the jaw. He reeled and fell to the floor. *Damn* that felt good!

The New Amber Room was deserted. The panels had been removed from the crate and now lay on the castle floor. I turned to Spider and Mantis, who had caught up with me. "I can't do this on my own. Please, help me."

"But the amber!" protested Mantis.

I winced. "There's much more to come, but you'll want to be alive when you gloat about it." I laid down on my back on one of the large tiles. The panel turned blue when I touched it, and the amber against me soothed me. I was no longer sparking flames. "Please, build a triangular cocoon around me."

Spider started to lift one of the panels, but Mantis stopped her. "We need to do this carefully." She took her walkie-talkie and instructed for her guards to hurry to the Amber Room. After they arrived with due haste, Mantis told them how to set up the amber panels carefully around me.

"My million-dollar coffin," I joked.

"This is only a loan, Flea," Mantis said.

Spider kissed me. "Come back safe, John Little."

"You might want to evacuate, just in case," I said.

"And leave you alone with the fire amber? Not a chance." Mantis rose and took two steps back.

"I'm not going anywhere either," Spider said.

"Suit yourselves." The guards sealed the ends of the triangular tube. Inside my *Chrysalis*, the amber walls crackled and sparked sapphire-blue. The war of powers inside me slowed, but I also sensed something becoming *aware* of me.

The larva wasn't just alive. It was *sentient*.

I knew now why I couldn't let go of the fire amber. The phoenix had been controlling my hands. What did it want? If I wanted to live, I had to understand what I was up against.

Warily, I touched the mind of the phoenix. Strange images and sounds began assailing my mind.

. . .soaring through the air, diving steep towards a jungle of giant ferns, chasing feathered dinosaurs gliding over green waters. Strange cries echoed from vale to vale in the morning light, and the earth trembled as great beasts stampeded over stony terrain. . .

. . .in darkness, I made flames dance in waves from wingtip to wingtip, drawing moths and flies close enough to snatch with my beak. Elsewhere under the canopy of sweet-scented trees, others like me play the same burning game. . .

. . .drenched by a torrential rain, strutting in a circle with others of my kind, ruby and sapphire feathers spread. I chirped a crisp melody while the other phoenixes sang in harmony. When the clouds broke and the sun shone, we summoned the heat within to dry our plumes. . .

. . .tired wings brought me to a hollow near the top of a great coniferous tree, the scent of sweet resin in the evening air, I sang a lament and set myself afire, lighting the wood-pyre around me as I burned and changed. . . .

I was seeing its world through its eyes, hearing the ancient past through its avian ears, and *lived* those moments of its lives. I fought the urge to drown myself in more wonders of that Age. I had never dealt with Lightning controlled by an intelligence before. How could I fight it for dominance?

Maybe these memories of the past were its attempts to imprint its sense of self on *me*! I fought back, focusing on my Little John memories in hopes of bending the phoenix to my will.

. . .milking cows and putting them to pasture as a boy of thirteen, already taller than the men in the village. . .

. . .my first meeting with Robin atop a log spanning a creek in Barnsdale Forest, neither of us willing to yield the path. The ruffian in muddied green barked a challenge: duel by quarterstaff. Smiling, I swung my oaken rod. . .

. . .tied up before the Sheriff of Nottingham, who raised his whip to lash me again and again. A pendant of amber hung from the Sheriff's neck. He laughed at my pain and taunted me, telling me that I was only bait, and that he would keep me alive to see him skin the other outlaws . . .

. . .I held my beloved Robin in my arms, knowing he was at the end of his life and that I could do nothing to save him, not even with the power of the magical amber I ripped from Nottingham's throat. Robin asked one last thing: to fetch his bow and arrow for one last shot, so that I could bury him where the arrow fell. . . .

The phoenix and I were at an impasse: we both demanded the other to submit, but neither of us would yield. The longer we fought, the weaker we became. I had thought the phoenix would have overwhelmed me with its power by now, but why hadn't it?

The *Wolbachia*. I had almost forgotten the third force in the struggle. Did the tainted Lightning inside me infect the phoenix larva somehow? Spider had said that *Wolbachia* behaved differently depending on the species it infects, sometimes changing gender, other times killing them. What if it killed phoenixes? If the phoenix was fighting both me and the *Wolbachia*, then it would likely weaken under the double assault.

By now, I had taken much of the fire amber's energies into me. What would happen if the phoenix larva died from the *Wolbachia* infection? I didn't know, but I had a suspicion that it could be disastrous for me. Even if I died and the fire amber survived the resulting inferno, the *Wolbachia* would still kill the phoenix. I had to find a way to save us both, but I was swiftly running out of options.

I had to face my fear. What if I nullified the *Wolbachia* energy not by fighting the Widowing, but *completing* the transformation? I had been resisting the sex-change, which only made it worse. If I encouraged the metamorphosis instead, perhaps the tainted energy would be consumed in process. For this strategy to work, not only would I have to accept life as a woman, but also win the phoenix's cooperation. It would have to help me channel the *Wolbachia* energy out of itself and into me.

I reconsidered my reluctance to become a woman. I had fought so hard to stay a man, but why? Was Mantis right that I wanted to prove myself as great a hero as Robin? Throughout my lives, I had chosen to recreate that first fraternity, the brotherhood of outlaws with our lofty dreams. However, only I had survived to rebuild that legacy, and I did a lousy job of it. After Mantis invented Maid Marian, the tale had changed so much that the real Robin was forgotten in favor of an idealized version. All I was able to do to honour my fallen comrades was to be the faithful companion, a part I played so well. Somehow, in trying to be the hero that Robin was, I had convinced myself that I could only do that in the mould of man.

But I had known strong women, like Jeanne D'Arc, like Elizabeth the First, like Spider.

Strength and honour did not belong to a single sex.

Spider had been right, back at the Catherine Palace. The recreations were as beautiful as the original, and no less worthy of admiration. The vision of the artist, the true essence of any masterpiece, lived on even if the original materials were gone. I would still be me even if my sex had changed. I might not like it, but at least I could continue to live, love . . . and scheme. And who knows? Maybe one day, I'd find a different way to regain my manhood.

But how could I communicate my plan to the phoenix larva? How could two minds, separated by species and millions of years, even begin to understand each other?

If the phoenix could not understand human language, perhaps it understood the basic instincts all living things knew: hunger, pain, birth and death. I projected my thoughts as images, praying it would understand our common ground.

. . . a man struggles with a phoenix, ants crawling over them both. They plummet off a cliff and drown in the river below . . .

. . . a woman holding the legs of a phoenix, coated with fire ants, jumping off the cliff but in cooperation, gliding to safety on the other side of the river where the woman picked the ants off the phoenix's feathers . . .

The phoenix mind sent an image of flame in response. Did that mean understanding? I hoped so. It guided the *Wolbachia* energy towards me, and I opened myself to receive the Widowing. The tainted power of the Widowing power eagerly left the phoenix larva, rushing into me. I stripped away my physical memory of the Little John body and fortified the sum of my personality and memories, letting the Widowing sculpt my body into a woman's but keeping the essence of who I was. Sparks cascaded from my head to my toes, cannibalizing my fondest parts to build new curves and unfamiliar organs.

Yet our battle had greatly weakened the phoenix. What would become of it, when my metamorphosis was complete? Mantis would exploit its fragility and enslave it. I couldn't allow that, but how could I steal the fire amber from Mantis? Even if the phoenix had been at full strength, and I freed it from the amber, would it survive the modern world?

A wild idea occurred to me, a theft so outrageous that if I succeeded, I would inspire my first legend as a woman.

I communicated my idea to the phoenix, hoping it would understand freedom versus slavery; death and rebirth; trust and friendship. It might not comprehend all those concepts, but I hoped it could sense that I had the best of intentions.

The phoenix crafted another image of flame.

I took a deep breath and drained every spark of Lightning from the fire amber, channeling the power to complete the final alterations to my body. Stimulated, my follicles grew new hair, while the myriad changes finally coalesced into a well-proportioned female form.

At last, my hands were free to move. I held the amber egg in one hand and flexed my new fingers. The electric-blue amber tiles around me dimmed, leaving me in deepening shadow. I banged on the tiles. "Let me out!" I shouted. My voice had gone soprano.

My coffin was gently taken apart by Mantis's men. Spider rushed over to help me sit up. I winced when she touched me, as my new skin was still tender. She looked me over, an apology in her eyes. "Oh, Flea. I'm afraid the Widowing's won."

I nodded sadly and held up the amber egg. It had turned so darkly red that it almost seemed black.

Mantis snatched the dead amber from me. "What happened?"

"I'm sorry," I said. "The Widowing was too strong. It murdered who I was and killed the larva, corrupting the energy. There never was a way to conquer the phoenix's power." I touched my face. Beardless and delicate.

"No." Mantis buried her face in her hands.

"You honored our deal, Mantis, so I will fulfill my part of the bargain. The Amber Room is rightfully yours." I kissed Spider on the cheek. "Thank you, Spider, for all you've done for me. I'm a better woman for it."

Spider helped me up and wrapped a blanket around me. "Come on, let's go back to your room."

"Thank you." We left Mantis in the New Amber Room to cry over her burnt-out amber.

❁

Spider opened the door to my room for me. "Will you be all right?" she asked.

"I think so," I said, hobbling over to my bed. "This body feels strange, but I think just I need to get used to it."

"Trust me. It's not so bad being a woman," Spider said. She leaned against the doorframe. "You survived the phoenix's touch, and I'm glad."

In the mirror, I saw my new body for the first time: a slim woman with shoulder-length black hair and hazel eyes. Like Mantis, I had a heart-shaped face, but the curves to my figure must have been lifted from Spider.

I sighed. "I suppose I could grow accustomed to this . . . in time."

Spider smiled. "Would you like to try on some clothes? I think I have something in your size."

"Maybe tomorrow. I need some time alone."

"I understand. Sweet dreams." She closed the door.

Grabbing a t-shirt and baggy shorts from my suitcase, I dressed. I dialed Thickett's number on my satellite phone. "Thicks, it's me again. *Aguecheek*."

"It's gotten worse, hasn't it?" Thicks said.

"Like you wouldn't believe. I'm done here. You can send the rest of the panels in the morning."

"Your wish is my command."

I hung up, picked up Spider's copy of *Orlando*, and pulled a chair up to the window. Putting the potted plant aside, I opened the window and gazed into the night sky.

The phoenix wanted to live, but I knew it couldn't survive long in the modern world. I ought to thank Spider for telling me about parthenogenesis. It gave me the idea to give the phoenix a new, healthy body to host its mind. I offered it a choice, and it chose life. Soon, I would be far from here, the phoenix-child safe within my womb, free from Mantis's lust for power. My sudden motherhood was beyond frightening, but it was a fear I would strive to conquer. I would cherish my phoenix daughter, my Firefly, and protect her with my life.

I leaned back in the chair and began to read *Orlando*.

An hour later, a black rope lowered from the sky in front of the window. I stashed the book in a small bag of necessities and left one of my calling cards leaning against the Leda statuette. I squeezed through the window, grabbed the rope and climbed. At the top, Thicks helped me into the gondola of the black hot-air balloon. We floated up and away in the night, and soon Prorok Castle vanished beneath a bank of rolling fog.

Maybe I should have said good-bye to Spider, but that wouldn't have been me. "I'm glad you remembered Milan," I said.

"Hard to forget a midnight getaway in a bloody balloon," Thicks said. "A car will meet us downwind." He took off his night-vision goggles and looked me up and down. "Man, this is different, Felix. Er, should I still call you that, guv?"

"I suppose not. I'll need a new passport."

"Gotcha. Under what name?"

"Marian. Marian Robinson." I smiled. The world would come to know a new legend.

Flea, *Queen* of Thieves.

City of Beautiful Nonsense
by Justin Howe

It was night in the train yards, and all the ghosts had crept out of their cars. The nine-forty local, the uptown line, the husks of metronauts wandered under the arc lights. Impervious to the cold, each sang an identical song:

Slow magic, time sorcery—equal parts alchemy and pathology. Do it twice a day, do it everyday. Ride the under-roads of the City Beautiful—low roads, twice steel, reeking of sewage, lipstick and bubblegum.

Down the tiled halls, along the grease-stained platforms through miles of endless tunnels, captivated by a beauty larger than ideas. Impressions birthed the City. Memory served as the scaffolding. We, the architects and the masons, designed the City Beautiful stone by stone. When the mortar dried, the City had vanished—carried away by time. Lost on familiar street corners, the bakery is gone. There's a shoe store there instead.

We sought security, and with its idea in mind each morning we kissed our loved ones goodbye. It worked like magic—the dark, the steel, engine brakes and municipal mops—all elements combined.

Slow magic, pathological. Go east and catch a glimpse of yourself going west on a different line.

Down the steps, into the dark where the rats danced with the bubblegum, and the smiles looked like grease. Often no place to stand, pushed along, straight on, for as long as we can. Dodging crisscrossing trajectories, awash amid vectors, bumping and colliding, the scent of perfume and the instant of music from a pair of bargain speakers. Up the stairs, down the passage, endless, endlessly on—the City pulled us apart.

Time sorcery—do it everyday, but watch how you go.

Kiss the wife and say goodbye, but remember to take your time. Transfer too often, and you'll pass yourself going the other way. Red lights of the train shrinking down the dark of the tunnel—shrinking down, down, down, with and without you.

So sing the metronauts, their lives lost somewhere on subway lines.

New Spectacles
by Will McIntosh

"I can't believe it's really over."

Shocked, Tristan glanced at his grandfather, taking his eye off the road for a second. It was the most genuine thing his grandfather had ever said. Tristan didn't know how to respond. His grandfather stared straight ahead, his big head bobbing a palsied rhythm as it had for the last twenty years. His fat, crooked Irish nose was unaltered by the weight loss, but skin dangled loosely from his neck. Sixty pounds in five months. Christ, it had been an ordeal. But it was almost over now.

"You've had a good life. Eighty-five years," Tristan said.

His grandfather grunted, looked out the side window at telephone poles whisking by in the rain.

This was probably Tristan's last chance to say whatever he wanted to say to the old guy while he was still lucid. But what would that be? I love you? That seemed an awkward, unimaginable leap, and not one his grandfather would particularly appreciate.

Tristan programmed a fragrance from the vehicle's menu. An old time comfort smell. The car filled with the aroma of old wood furniture, a hint of corned beef and cabbage cooking in a distant kitchen. Cut grass. And something else Tristan couldn't quite place. His grandfather leaned his head on the headrest, closed his eyes.

The hospital came into view, blurry then clear as the wipers swept the windshield. He pulled up to the front doors.

"Pop, we're here. Wait here while I get a wheelchair."

Hand trembling, his grandfather struggled with the seatbelt. "I don't need no damned wheelchair," he said in his brusque Irish brogue. "I can walk." Tristan knew better than to argue.

Taking old-man steps and gasping for air, Grandpa bulled his way through the stark fluorescent halls to his room. As soon as he was settled,

Tristan left, saying he had to get to work, that mom would come soon. His grandfather nodded, heaved a sigh.

That's the last time he'll ever walk, Tristan thought.

The Poly-Layer Voice Analysis glasses sat on the edge of Tristan's mahogany desk in their cushioned black box, looking like any other pair of specs. Tristan took off his regular pair, laid them on the blotter, put on the PLVA's. Grabbing his notes, he headed to his first interrogation of the day.

"Hi Tris," Mike Miller said, passing in the hall. He put his hand to his throat and pointed dramatically. "Aaugh! You've got *the glasses* on! And I spoke! You've seen into my soul, you—you know I'm in love with you. I'm still speaking! You're seeing even deeper. I have to shut up!"

"You'd better, the PLVA's just told me you've got six dead bodies stuffed under your bed," Tristan shot back. Mike screamed again, holding his hands over his ears as he raced around the corner and out of sight.

Actually, the PLVA's readouts indicated that Mike was tired, amused, at ease. The readouts that lit up in Tristan's peripheral vision would be meaningless to an untrained eye, but Tristan picked up the patterns with the practiced ease of a chess master appraising a game-board.

"Hi Becky," Tristan said as he passed the department's secretary and headed into the interview room.

"Hi Dr. Sanders, your first interview is waiting."

"Got it, thanks," he said, closing the door behind him. Becky didn't like him much; it registered consistently on the PLVA. Tristan had no idea why.

A tall, stocky man with short brown hair and a goatee stood as Tristan entered. "Dr. Sanders? Roy Regan." Regan moved in the smooth, hyper-confident way that was common among the CEO's and CFO's Tristan dealt with as an investigator in the white collar crime division.

They shook hands and sat down facing each other. Regan sat forward, elbows propped on knees.

Tristan gave him the standard spiel—he wanted to ask some questions about potential irregularities, blah, blah, blah.

"Shoot," Regan said confidently. He leaned back, crossed one leg, and jiggled his foot.

Three questions in, Tristan could tell Regan was lying. He pulled off the glasses, wiped them on his shirt sleeve. "Mr. Regan, have you ever heard of Poly-Layer Voice Analysis? PLVA?"

"No, I don't think so."

"PLVA analyzes 8000 algorithms to measure 129 aspects of a person's speech, and can deduce everything from anxiety to boredom to sexual excitement . . . to truthfulness. And it does so reliably. If PLVA technology ever gets cheap enough to market commercially, nothing will ever be the same."

"So?" he said. His anxiety level was sky high. You'd never know it from his outwardly calm, reasonable tone, but the PLVA was not fooled.

"Here," Tristan said, handing the glasses to Regan, "put these on." Regan took them like he had been handed a dead Chihuahua. Tristan nodded encouragement. Reluctantly Regan put them on.

"My name is Tristan Sanders, I have a wife," Tristan said. "Both of those things are true, and mundane. Notice the readouts in the periphery?" Regan nodded uncertainly.

"Good, now I'll say something true, but not mundane. My grandfather is in the hospital, dying . . . notice the difference? I know you can't interpret the readout, but can you see the difference in pattern?"

Regan nodded. Droplets of sweat had formed on his forehead. Tristan had never seen anyone begin to sweat so abruptly.

"Now, I'll tell a lie. My grandfather and I have always been close. Notice the difference?

Regan didn't nod. He pulled a handkerchief from his back pocket, dabbed his forehead. He was a good looking man, actually. Studious and square-jawed—kind of a puffy Clark Kent. Tristan held out his hand, and Regan returned the glasses. He followed the path of the glasses intently as Tristan cradled them back onto the bridge of his nose.

"Now," Tristan continued, "explain exactly what aspects of your business are fraudulent."

Tristan dropped his notes on the desk, grabbed his jacket from the back of the chair. He was not looking forward to returning to the hospital. He'd probably taken some of his dread out on Mr. Regan. He'd been pretty rough on the guy.

As he walked through the metal detectors, out of the building and across the mostly-empty parking lot to his Volvo, Tristan was vaguely aware he had forgotten to take off the PLVA glasses. If security had noticed the glasses and stopped him, Tristan would have chided himself for his absentmindedness and trotted back to his office to swap them for his regular glasses, which were still sitting on his desk. He may have even believed the forgetfulness excuse himself. But security mostly focused on who was going in, not who was coming out, and Tristan had been working there for years.

By the time he stepped into the hospital room, his heart was pounding and he was fully aware he was still wearing them. His mom was sitting by the hospital bed. Grandpa was sleeping. He wasn't wearing his dentures, and his face looked mummified. His chest rose and fell in violent fits as he labored to take liquid breaths. The room was filled with the scent of a spring meadow, but the stink of hospital—urine, antiseptic, infection—lay just underneath. Light music drifted from hidden speakers.

"How's he doing?" Tristan whispered.

"New glasses," mom said, smiling. "They're nice—simple and basic."

Tristan just smiled.

"He's okay," his mom said. "He keeps asking for water, but the doctors say he can only have eight ounces an hour because of the medication they're giving him."

Emotional distress registered high on the PLVA, but otherwise there was nothing out of the ordinary. Tristan grasped the frame of the glasses, nearly pulled them off, then left them on.

"What sort of medication?"

Mom shook her head. "Something to fight the cancer. I'm not sure what it is."

"But isn't he dying?"

"I know, I don't understand it either," mom said, in a low, conspiratorial tone.

Grandpa's breath hitched. He coughed weakly, opened his eyes, looked at mom, then at Tristan with bewildered eyes.

"How are you doing?" Tristan said.

Grandpa nodded. "Okay," he said.

"Are you in pain?"

"No pain," Grandpa said, shaking his head. He was telling the truth.

His grandfather had never felt pain. Once Tristan had seen him snare his thumb with a fishhook and tear the hook right back out, unflinching, cursing at the annoyance and seemingly more worried about the hook than the ragged, bloody mess he'd made of his thumb.

His grandfather smacked puckered lips. "Get me a drink of water, will you? I'm so thirsty."

Tristan grabbed the plastic bottle from the table and put the straw between his grandfather's lips. It was a shock to see the man so helpless. Grandpa did not radiate the resentment at having to be helped that Tristan expected from the sour old man. He pulled furiously on the straw, his sunken eyes filled with gratitude.

"That's enough, Pop . . . don't give him too much," mom said. Reluctantly Tristan took the cup away. Grandpa let out a satisfied gasp, just like he used to do after taking a swig of beer.

Lana appeared in the doorway, with grandma hanging onto her arm. She knocked on the doorframe. Even after a year of marriage, Tristan still lit up at the sight of Lana. Her long, dramatic red hair and light-blue eyes gave her an unearthly beauty, like some faerie or pixie made real.

"Hello? You've got a visitor." Lana led Grandma to a cushioned sofa chair next to the bed; grandma's ruined hip forced her to take hobbled, uneven steps, as if she was perpetually walking up stairs. Lana gave Tristan a quick kiss on the cheek, took a half step out of the circle of family.

"Hello Frankie," Grandma said, her lilting Irish accent still thick seventy year removed from Ireland. The PLVA indicated embarrassment, fairly high SOS (how badly you don't want to say something), and sadness.

Grandpa turned to look at her; Tristan was astonished by how much his face looked like a skull under the low fluorescent light.

"Hello Mam," he said. "I'm going fast." The PLVA monitors went wild. Tristan could hardly believe the cacophony of indicators that were red-lining. Anger, SOS, emotional stress, even some deception. Tristan was stunned. He waited for his grandfather to speak to his grandmother again, unwilling to believe the reading.

"How are you feeling?" Grandma asked. "You look good, you look much better."

"Well, I don't feel very good," Grandpa said evenly.

The readout went nuts again. Suddenly Tristan wished he wasn't wearing the glasses. He'd always interpreted his grandfather's short, impatient way with grandma as a gruff facade masking an old-style, pragmatic love. According to the readout, his grandfather hated his grandmother, truly hated her.

"Are you warm enough?" Grandma said. Grandpa ignored the question, looked at Tristan. "Tristan, boy, I'm counting on you to take care of old Ginger. Your grandmam's too old to do it, and Ginger's always liked you." The PLVA registered sadness, emotional distress, but none of the vitriol of a moment before.

"Sure, I'd be happy to." He looked at his grandmother. "I'll bring her over for visits so she won't miss you too much." Grandma smiled sadly, said nothing.

"How are you holding up?" Lana asked Tristan, wrapping her arm around his waist as they headed out the hospital's big electric doors, into fresh air. Actually, the air stank of city—black exhaust, wafts of rotting trash—but after the death-smell of the hospital it was like fresh-cut flowers to Tristan. He did not like hospitals.

"I'm good," he said. "Where you want to eat?" They had an hour for dinner, then they were back on point while the next shift ate.

"How 'bout Mackelwees?" The suggestion was nearly drowned out by a honking yellow cab.

Tristan smiled. An Irish pub, a fitting tribute to the old man. "Maybe I'll have a little taste while we're there—me first one today," he said in a bad Irish accent. Lana had only been around for a year, but she'd already picked up on the family in-jokes.

She laughed and punched him playfully in the side. "He's *dying*. You're supposed to be nice to people who are dying." Unwittingly she hit the pocket of his jacket where he'd stashed the PLVA specs on his way out of the room. He flinched, but didn't think she'd done any harm. Everyone had liked his new glasses.

"I actually like the old guy okay. He's cold, kind of mean, a bigot. He called me a sissy once when I was little—"

Lana gasped. "Oh, that's awful! When you were *little?* Why? Did he catch you playing dress-up?"

"No," Tristan said, laughing, "I wasn't playing dress-up. It was back when I was afraid to fall asleep. I told you about that, remember?"

Lana nodded. "Your parents thought you were afraid of the dark because you were watching too many monster movies. You didn't have the vocabulary to explain it was existential angst. Sleep freaked you out because it felt like temporary death."

"Damn. You listen to me *way* more carefully than I listen to you."

Lana laughed. "Very funny."

They turned in under the green awning, entered Mackelwees. Making their way through crowds of happy-hour revelers, they found a booth toward the back. Tristan could just barely hear "Danny Boy" over the rumble and laughter of the crowd.

"So," Lana prodded when they got settled.

"Okay, so it's Christmas Eve. My parents want to go to a party, and I'm freaking out that they're leaving me alone to struggle with my existential falling-asleep angst. My grandparents are visiting, and mom explains the whole thing to grandpa, who agrees to stay up with me as late as I want. As soon as the folks are out the door, grandpa gets up, turns off the TV, and says 'I'm going to bed.' I start crying, saying he promised to stay up with me. He wheels around and says 'You're nothing but a sissy,' and launches into a tirade about how my parents are too soft on me, and how I'll never be a man."

"Oh!" Lana said. She reached over and rubbed the top of Tristan's hand. "That's rotten! How old were you?"

"About seven. But you know, I think in his own ignorant way he thought he was doing me a favor."

Lana nodded, considering. "That's a nice way to look at it."

The waitress came to take their order. Lana ordered a Guiness in a damned good fake Irish accent, surprising Tristan. Tristan could barely keep a straight face when it was his turn to order.

When the waitress left, they sat in silence for a moment. Tristan bobbed his head in time to a drinking song he didn't recognize.

"He's colorful," Tristan said. "One of those larger-than-life characters. It's hard to hate him." He flinched, reminded of what he'd learned from the PLVA.

"It's sad," he said. "I don't think there's much love between my grandmother and grandfather. He doesn't even seem to *like* her much."

Lana nodded thoughtfully. "They're so repressed. Who knows what's going on inside them?"

The beers arrived. Tristan hefted his pint, the cardboard coaster sticking to the bottom of the damp glass, and took a swig.

"One thing's for sure," Lana said, "the old man isn't going to tell your grandma or anyone else how he feels, so he'll take the truth to his grave."

"Kara will be in college soon," Tristan's mom was saying when they returned. She was talking loudly to his dad and sister Sarah. Sarah had just flown in from Seattle. Tristan gave her an awkward one-armed sideways hug and disengaged. They were a pretty reserved family. Tristan looked at his grandfather, staring at the ceiling, and his grandmother, sitting stiffly at his bedside staring out the window, and wondered how far back through the generations the dead spot rippled. He had inherited it a bit more than Sarah, but it was in her, too—he'd felt her stiffen slightly at his touch. But he knew it was nothing personal.

"The Mets won today," dad said, venturing into the desperate search for safe conversation.

"Did you hear that, dad?" mom said. "The Mets won. I wonder if they'll make it to the World Series?"

"I'm not going to see the World Series," he muttered. "I don't care. Jesus, this is miserable. Can I have a drink of water? I'm so thirsty."

"He's not supposed to have any more water for an hour, the nurse said he shouldn't," mom said to no one in particular. Sarah and Lana were standing by the window, talking in whispers. Grandma sat in her chair.

"Somebody give me a drink of water," Grandpa repeated.

Tristan retrieved the water cup, let his grandfather drink his fill. He caught Sarah's eye; she nodded tacit approval. When Grandpa finally stopped drinking, he let out a satisfied gasp, closed his eyes.

"I want to go to heaven. This is miserable," he said.

"Daddy, do you remember when we used to take the girls to Coney Island?" Grandma asked.

A grunt from Grandpa.

"They'd have their little pails and shovels, and we'd buy ice cream from the man on the boardwalk." Tristan didn't really need the PLVA's to tell him grandma's casual tone masked agitation, but he had them on, and they confirmed it. The talk of death and heaven made her uncomfortable. She found talk of skin rashes too revealing.

Grandma carried on with her story. When grandpa interrupted to repeat that he wanted to go to heaven, grandma kept talking, turning to look at Tristan's dad, as if she had been telling the story to him alone all along.

Tristan wanted to get the hell out of there. He tried to think of some excuse for why he and Lana might need to get home, but knew that wasn't fair. Everyone in the room wanted to go home.

It occurred to him for the second time that this was his last chance to tie up any loose ends with the old man. Problem was, there wasn't any particular glaring event that needed to be resolved between them. Sure, he'd like his grandfather to apologize for calling him a sissy when he was little, but his grandfather probably didn't even remember that particular incident among a lifetime of calling people nasty names.

Tristan pulled up a metal chair, sat next to the old man.

"Is there anything I can do for you?" The words sounded forced to his ears. He wondered what he would see if the PLVA registered the wearer's voice, and not just the voices of others.

"Hold me hand," his grandfather said, sounding scared.

Hold his hand? Tristan was stunned, and a little repulsed. He took his grandfather's huge, calloused hand, weathered by thirty years of unloading trucks for the A&P Supermarket on the night shift. As far as he could remember it was the first time he had ever touched the old man's hand. Maybe when he was very young his grandfather had taken his hand when they crossed busy streets, Tristan wasn't sure.

For a moment the scene before him flickered, took on a surreal hyper-focus. "You're really dying, I can't believe it," Tristan heard himself say. The light seemed to dim, then rise again, then everything was back to normal. Except he was still holding his grandfather's hand. He caught Lana's eye. She smiled encouragement.

"I'm dying," grandpa repeated. His breathing was more labored now; a howling squeal accompanied each inhale. The PLVA indicated that he was eager to talk about dying.

Sarah sat on the opposite side of the bed, took grandpa's other hand in hers.

"I love you, grandpa," Sarah said. It was mostly a lie, and she was dragging it out of herself with great effort, but Tristan was proud of her for saying it.

"I know you do," grandpa said. SOS through the roof. Even now, it was too much for him. "All of you, too," he muttered, and closed his eyes, locking out the intimacy as if it were blinding sunlight.

Light classical music continued to play in the background. Tristan guessed some researcher had found it to be the most soothing sound for terminal patients. Of course, that research might fall into the magic twenty-two percent. Tristan felt a surge of irrational anger. Letting go of his grandfather's hand, he went and reprogrammed the room's environmental unit. 'Irish Rover' replaced a reed flute version of the Brandenburg Concerto. The scent of wisteria in early bloom was replaced by spilled beer, cigarette smoke, and pub grub. Everyone in the room smiled except his grandmother, who nattered on, scowling slightly, pretending not to notice. Tristan returned to his grandfather's side, took his hand again. Grandpa appeared to be asleep.

He felt a tap on his shoulder, turned. His mom pointed emphatically toward the foot of the bed. His grandfather's big toe was bobbing in time with the music.

"Harry was a cutup," Grandpa mumbled.

"What's that?" Tristan prodded.

"Harry O'Donohue. Eddie Mahoney. Used to sing this one."

"Yup, yup. Those were good times, at the beach," Grandma said loudly. Her words registered embarrassment, agitation. Grandpa was talking about bars, about drinking. Grandma had always been horribly embarrassed by his drinking, by how boisterous and outgoing he got when he drank. Tristan had only seen his grandfather drunk a few times—grandma had kept him on a tight rein in his later years—but he'd thought it was a marked improvement. It was the only time the old man looked happy, had any light in his eyes.

Maybe that was why his grandfather hated her. Grandma had stifled him, took away his greatest joy—partying with his friends. Slapping backs and singing, downing shots of Jack Daniels. Now that he was dying, maybe he was regretting all the time he'd spent sitting in that antiseptic living room on the plastic-wrapped couch, saving money, having to sneak down to the pub for a couple of quick drinks before scampering back.

"I wanna go to heaven," his grandfather said loudly, opening his eyes widely.

"We know," mom soothed.

Grandpa closed his eyes, sank immediately into sleep. They all watched, saying nothing. His breathing became more labored, competing with the boisterous music. Tristan felt Lana's hand on his shoulder, covered it with his own.

Grandpa's chest rose so high with each gasp that it looked as if he was levitating above the bed. His hand was limp in Tristan's. Tristan stared at the rippled patterns formed by the white sheets, and for some reason thought about how he used to run Matchbox cars between the ripples of his sheets when he was little, pretending they were hills and roads.

Grandpa stopped breathing. No one moved. Tristan stared into the darkness of his grandfather's open mouth. Suddenly, long after it seemed possible, grandpa took another heaving breath. It turned out to be his last.

Grandma cried. "Goodbye, Frankie. I love you," she said. She was mostly telling the truth. Why hadn't she said it an hour ago? He heard sniffling, glanced toward his mom, who had her face buried in dad's shoulder.

"He was a good father," she said. Her voice sounded sad, but the PLVA registered relief.

"He had a good life," Sarah said. Relief. Tristan realized he was also relieved, and not particularly sad.

Mom went to find a nurse. Dad sat and held grandma's hand, patting her shoulder as she cried. Tristan went and stood with Sarah and Lana.

"Isn't it sad that we aren't sadder?" he whispered.

At the funeral people cried again. Tristan brought the glasses, but left them in his pocket. He already knew that the sadness, the platitudes, were as hollow as the rationalizations of the medical research cheats. As hollow as his own sadness as he stood at his grandfather's grave and listened to the minister read from a book.

His Aunt June caught his eye, and gave him a sympathetic look. She probably thought he looked so sad because his grandpa was dead, but that wasn't why he looked sad. He was sad because his grandfather had lived a pallid, empty life, with a woman he couldn't stand. And because everyone was lying, and he was lying too.

He felt Lana's hand touch his; he laced his fingers in hers, felt her squeeze. He squeezed back.

When he pulled the glasses from his suit pocket on the way back to the car, he knew he was doing it, but couldn't have explained why. He slipped them on, watched the soothing patterns of Lana's speech as they made idle conversation.

"New glasses?" She said, glancing at him.

"Yeah," he said.

"They look good." She registered as relaxed, truthful. Free of SOS. God, he loved this woman. Such a difference from his first marriage.

"I love you," Tristan said. He didn't say it often enough.

"I love you, too," Lana said.

A jolt ripped through Tristan like barbed wire pulled through his spine.

"What did you say?" He asked.

"I said, I love you, too," Lana repeated.

The tips of Tristan's fingers began to tingle. His feet felt far away, so far away he wasn't sure how they kept moving. They reached the car.

"You okay?" Lana asked, looking at him over the hood as they opened the doors.

"Yeah," he said, not able to meet her eye. He took off the glasses, put them back in his pocket.

He tried to keep a conversation going as they drove, but he was far away, preoccupied with thoughts of the PLVA readout.

"Hey," Lana finally said when they got home. "What's the matter? It's me, tell me what's going on."

"I'm just bummed about the whole grandpa thing," he said. He sat on the couch, turned on the TV. It gave him an excuse not to look at her. Lana sat down next to him, reached up and massaged his neck. It felt good; his neck felt like a rusted hinge. He kept his eyes on the TV, scanned the channels till he found the Mets game.

"Hey!" Lana said. "What's the matter with you? Did I do something?"

"No," Tristan said, "I just—" He started to cry.

Lana wrapped her arms around him, rocked him. "My God, what's the matter?"

He told her. When he got to the part about wearing the glasses in the hospital room, she let go of him and leaned back, stared at him in disbelief. He plowed on. When he got to the part about wearing them while walking to the car, Lana stood up.

"You bastard," she said.

"I know it was wrong—"

"Wrong? You *shit.*" She sputtered for words, shaking her head slowly. Speechless, she spun, looked around until she spotted her purse on the kitchen table, yanked the purse off the table and headed for the door.

"Lana, I'm sorry. I'm so sorry. Please come and talk to me."

"Let me tell you something," she said, stabbing a finger at him. "And you don't need those *damned* glasses to interpret this. You'll be lucky if I ever talk to you again! You're a selfish, manipulative little shit." She wrenched the door open. "Why don't you dig up your grandfather and try apologizing to *him.*" The door slammed.

Tristan stared at the carpet. The Mets' announcer cut through the silence, shouting "Base hit!" Tristan retrieved the remote and turned off the TV. He stared at an old stain on the carpet. After a while he pulled off his shoes and lay down on the couch. He stared at the ceiling, unable to muster the energy to move. The spackled finish swam sickly.

When the door finally opened, his heart twisted, tripled in speed from one beat to the next. He sat up, searched Lana's face as she dropped her purse on the table by the door, went into the kitchen, poured herself a glass of wine, all without looking at him.

She carried the glass into the living room, sat across from him.

"I'm so, so sorry," Tristan said. "Please don't hate me."

Lana stared at the carpet for a long time, one slender hand wrapped around the wine glass.

Finally, she started to speak, aborted, sighed heavily, tried again. "I know your intentions weren't malicious. Once I cooled off I saw that."

Tristan nodded. "I wasn't trying to catch you in a lie," he said, "I think I just wanted to balance all the bad things I'd learned. I wanted to reassure myself that it wasn't all bad."

"That doesn't make it right."

"No, I know that," Tristan said quickly.

Lana sipped her wine, looking over Tristan's shoulder. Her eyes were bloodshot. Tristan wished she would look at him.

"Did the glasses tell you I was lying completely?" She asked.

"No," Tristan said. "It's not really either/or. It signaled you weren't being completely honest."

"No, I guess I wasn't. I didn't see any reason to tell you, but no, I've never felt that spark with you. I can't honestly say I love you. In a way I did. I mean I do."

Tristan's cell phone rang. He made no move to answer it.

"Go ahead, it could be your folks, or your grandmother," Lana said. Her voice was gentle. Tristan felt grateful for the little kindness; he so desperately needed it right now.

"Tris!" It was Mike. He sounded excited, or scared. "Jesus, you're not gonna believe this. Somebody leaked our findings to CNN! The shit's about to hit the fan!"

"Oh, Jeeze," Tris whispered.

"I know. Rich wants you here by 6 a.m. You ready to be on TV?"

"I guess so," Tristan said. "Look," he cut Mike off before he could continue, "can I call you back in a while?" He arranged to call Mike back, then set the phone back on the end table.

"My faith in science has been shattered," Tristan said. "Everyone is relieved that my grandfather is dead, including me. And you don't love me. My world is collapsing around me."

"No it isn't," Lana said. She shrugged. "Nothing's changed. You're just aware of it now." She looked at him, finally. "Put on the glasses."

He gaped at her.

"Go ahead."

He put them on.

"I am happy being married to you," Lana said deliberately. "I have no second thoughts. What I feel for you is enough for me." She looked at Tristan levelly. "Well?"

Tristan nodded. "All true."

"Is it enough?"

He took off the glasses, folded them up. He nodded. "It's enough."

He wondered what the glasses would have revealed about that one. Was it the truth? He honestly didn't know.

The Devil You Know
by Heidi Kneale

"May I join you for breakfast?" the Devil asked with a flourished bow. Then he eyed her young figure up and down.

Mrs. Timmor, sitting on her verandah, tea cup halfway to her lips, stared at the handsomely dressed figure before her. Why couldn't he wear the traditional horns and tail? If Mr. Timmor saw him as he was . . .

The Devil didn't wait for an answer but settled in Mr. Timmor's chair. Mrs. Timmor's eyes darted nervously from side to side. She wasn't supposed to have guests, especially of the male persuasion.

"How about some tea?" he asked her as he poured himself some. "Two sugar? Don't mind if I do." Plop, plop.

"My husband will be here any minute!" she whispered.

The Devil didn't care. "He won't show up as long as I'm here," he assured her.

That didn't stop her from listening for the slightest footstep, the sharp intake of breath that presaged another beating.

"You know, those muffins look delicious."

For once, she looked at him directly, eyebrow raised. "You really think so? I baked them fresh this morning." Carefully she lifted the platter and offered it to him.

He took two and shoved them in his mouth. "Fankth," and blew crumbs across the table.

He washed them down with tea and crammed more in. Mrs. Timmor lifted a hand to protest, but it was too late. He had scoffed the lot, leaving none for her husband. Oh, she worried to herself, he will be so angry when he finds out . . . Oh well. She would have to bake some more special muffins tomorrow; she could endure one more beating until then.

The Devil grew still, the last muffin half-chewed in his mouth. He coughed, spitting chewed muffin all over the table, spluttered as his eyes grew wide and his skin turned a mottled purple. Clawing at his own throat, he fell face-forward into the cream jug, the cream spreading across the table to fall onto the floor drip by drip.

Mrs. Timmor didn't move. She stared at the body lying across her table, her ears pricked the whole time for those dreaded footsteps.

They never came. The birds twittered and the sun moved across the sky. Afternoon came and with it the afternoon breeze. But no Mr. Timmor. The Devil had said that as long as he was there Mr. Timmor would not show up.

His body had started to bloat in the heat. Oh dear. He would smell soon. If she buried him under the verandah, would his promise still hold?

Dear Yourself

You do not have to carry your story alone,
However you write it, or others read it.
There is the wind your sister, whose paths are never paths.
There is the sun your lamp, and its attendants the clouds,
Tracing that forever arc in its yellow youth.
There are the stars your jewels, and their stitchery
Of past light and mingled aeons.
These too are your stories, swept by the galaxy's wheeling mass.
These too will carry the fingerprint whorls of your words.
You do not have to carry your story alone.
I am here, thinking of how your story will intersect mine
In the weave of days, the sieve of years.
There are so many ways of marking time, the notches, the scratched moments.
There are so many ways of mapping your way through the world.
Your shadow flies through the continuum upon time's arrow.
There is gravity your anchor, and the weight of narrative.
There are beginnings and ends, the egg unvoiding.
There is the microwave whisper. Listen. It knows your name.

—Yoon Ha Lee

Nomad
by Karl Bunker

Whatever she said, it must have been pretty harsh. The man jerked his head back, his eyebrows raised. His face hardened with anger and he opened his mouth to say something, but then turned and walked away. It was the third time Jack had watched a man approach that woman and then slink away.

This was usually the sort of bar where a woman could sit alone without being sniffed out by every dog in town. She was pretty enough, in a no-frills way: brown skin, short hair, a strong face with African features. It was the UNSA uniform that was the draw, Jack was sure. A real bona fide spacer girl had quite an air of exoticism, in this town at least. But this woman was on a mission and she wasn't interested in distractions. She was here to drink. There was something grim and mechanical about the way she emptied each glass and asked for another with a little gesture. He could see she was tired of the taste of it, tired of drinking, tired of being here and tired of being hit on, but she stayed and she drank.

"Jack!" A familiar voice pulled Jack's attention away from the woman. "Can it be? Jack Birch, sitting in a bar? With a beverage of alcoholic nature in front of him? I'm bowled over, Jack. This is the first time I've seen you outside of work in months. I was beginning to wonder if you had a keyboard permanently grafted to your fingers."

"Hello Mr. Herzfeld," Jack said. "How are you?"

Herzfeld ignored the question. "I see you're celebrating the end of your project," he said with a smile. "Cutting loose and going wild out here in the land of the living. Well good for you. You deserve it. I know I already said this Jack, but you did a wonderful job." He turned to the elegantly dressed woman standing behind him. "Janey, you've met Jack, haven't you?"

The woman smiled uncertainly. Herzfeld grinned. "No, of course you haven't!" Then to Jack: "Because you never come to the company barbeques, do you, you antisocial bastard!" He thumped Jack on the shoulder with his palm. "Jack, this is my lovely wife Janey. Janey, this is Jack, our star software engineer. Jack just finished up the orbital navigation software for the scooper ships that will be going to Jupiter in a few months. Tell Janey about the scooper ships, Jack."

"Um, they're the ships that will gather fuel for the *Nomad*," Jack said, making fleeting eye contact with Janey. She was an attractive woman of about fifty, groomed and dressed in that exquisite balance of opposites that says 'very wealthy but tasteful'.

Her eyes widened at the mention of *Nomad*. "Oh, you're working on the starship project?"

"Only peripherally," said Jack. His lips had a little trouble with 'peripherally' and he realized he was slightly drunk. "The scooper ships will orbit Jupiter, dip into the atmosphere with each orbit and gather Deuterium and Helium 3. They, um, liquefy those gasses and store them to be transferred to *Nomad* later."

"And it's Jack's software that will keep those suckers from flipping ass-frontward somersaults when they're surfing through the cyclones of Jupiter. Ahead of schedule, and fully tested and verified by UNSA. A terrific job, Jack, just terrific."

Jack smiled. "Thanks, Mr. Herzfeld."

"Well, we'll leave you to your celebration. . ." Herzfeld paused, looking concerned. Jack couldn't tell if he was feigning it for comic effect. "You look a little dopey Jack; are you okay?"

"I'm fine. Just tired and happy. Something I made is going to Jupiter. So it's like a part of me is going to Jupiter. That's pretty cool." He was smiling broadly and realized that he probably did look dopey.

Finally Herzfeld and his wife left.

Musicians mounted the small stage. The music started; loud and fast and louder and faster, a driving, passionate, coordinated assault of sound. Jack grinned and let it wash over and pound into him. After too many days and endless hours of grueling mental labor, the physical energy of this music was paradoxically relaxing. Jack closed his eyes and conjured up the image of the scoop orbiters. This music could be their theme song. He imagined them screaming through Jupiter's atmosphere at the perigee of their orbit, howling like frenzied monsters as the gaping mouth at their bows swallowed ton after ton of atmosphere to be processed and stored in their bellies.

Jack smiled at the image, at the sheer beauty of it. A part of me is going to Jupiter. His mental picture changed; now he saw the scooper ships as incarnations of himself. His oversized nose and sharp cheekbones over the wide-open mouth at the bow. His arms held tight to the body of the ship for aerodynamic efficiency. His blue eyes wide and wild as he flew high over Jupiter, exulting in his own speed and power. He laughed aloud at the image, feeling safe and hidden by the deafening roar of the music.

He looked back at the spacer woman, curious if she would show any reaction to the music. If anything, she looked more depressed. Her head was bent over her glass as if she was looking for something in it. Her eyes were almost closed. Jack felt a flash of anger at the bartender; this woman should have been shut off long ago.

Jack nursed his own drink, then another. The live music ended, recorded music came on, couples danced, cute little holo-projected animation creatures scampered and danced on the walls and ceiling. Jack got up to leave, looking over to where the spacer woman had been sitting. She was gone now.

In the parking lot, a low shape on the ground caught Jack's attention. It was the spacer woman, lying on the pavement. The blue uniform was hard to see in the darkness. Jack squatted beside her. She was snoring, on her side with one arm pillowing her head. The front of her blouse was wet and she smelled of alcohol-vomit. "Hey," said Jack. "You can't lie here, you'll get run over." He shook her shoulder gently, then harder. "Hey. C'mon. Wake up." Without opening her eyes she made a whining sound and swatted at his hand.

Next Jack tried to get her to sit up. She came awake enough to push him hard, tipping him off balance. While he was recovering she started crawling away, mumbling something unintelligible. Sitting on his haunches, Jack watched her for a few moments. She was headed toward the center of the parking lot. She stopped, still on her hands and knees. Her back arched spasmodically and she vomited onto the asphalt. She started crawling again. A string of spittle hung from her mouth and caught a flash of light from a street lamp. Then Jack heard a new sound and saw her shoulders shaking. She was crying.

He walked to her and squatted at her side again. "Honey," he said, and instantly was embarrassed at the word. "Woman, I know a little about UNSA. It is going to be very bad for your career if the cops find you passed out drunk in a parking lot. And that's assuming you don't get killed by a car first." No response. "Oh fuck it," he said. He took her arm over his shoulders and stood, pulling her up with him. "Can you tell me where you live? Where you're staying? If I put you in my car, can you try not to puke any more?" She said nothing. Jack couldn't tell if this was because she was too far gone to understand him, or just some drunken, sullen stubbornness.

She seemed barely conscious by the time he got to his car. He folded her onto the back seat and started driving home. *Shit*, he thought. *This is insane. She could wake up at any second and start screaming, I'll be surrounded by cops and charged with kidnapping and attempted rape. Or if I take her home she could wake up in the middle of the night and run off to the cops and tell them I'm a kidnapper. Or wait—better still, she could wake up, decide I'm a kidnapper, rapist and murderer, and kill me in my sleep.* "Shit, shit, shit," he said aloud.

He arrived home at his condo and half carried, half walked her inside. As he did this he talked to her: "I'm going to let you sleep at my place, okay? That's all. Just sleep. I'll be in another room. You can leave whenever you want, okay?" She was standing on her own now, but her eyes were almost closed. Jack held her by both shoulders and shouted. "Do? You? Un-der-stand?"

"Yeah, yeah, yeah, okay, jus' lemme go to sleep" she said, frowning. Then she made a visible effort to focus her eyes on his face "Y'know, you're kinda cute," she said without much conviction.

Jack helped her to lie down on the carpet, rolled her over onto her stomach and covered her with a blanket. It all felt very clinical until he lifted her head to put a folded towel under her as a pillow. Feeling the skin of her face against his hand sent a chill of emotion through him; a feeling of tenderness like the jolt of a suddenly awakened memory. He stroked the side of her head, barely touching her. Then he went to bed.

He woke up a few hours later to the sound of a whispered voice. "Hey. Hey pal. Can I lie on the bed? I'm okay now, I'm done throwing up."

"Um, yeah, okay." He said foggily, shimmying to the far side of the bed.

"I washed myself off too."

"Mm." A moment later he was fully awake and his eyes snapped open. Trying not to jostle the bed, he slid out from under the sheet, took his pillow and lay down on the floor beside the bed. Eventually he went back to sleep.

It was nearly dawn when he was awoken again. He sat up and looked at the figure on his bed. She was asleep, but making a sound—a long, high-pitched keening. The sleep-paralyzed version of a scream. "Hey, wake up." He reached over and shook her. "Wake up!"

With a ragged gasp she sat up. In the dim light Jack saw she was naked, at least to the waist. "It's okay," he whispered. "You're okay. You were dreaming." She grunted and sat for a while, breathing hard, her forearms resting on her raised knees. Her dark skin was shining with sweat. From where Jack sat she was silhouetted by a dim light from a window behind her. A long ribbon of silver traced her profile: down the straight line of her forehead, the curve of her nose, over the fullness of her lips, around her chin and back to the long line of her neck, and finally the perfect parabola of the upper side of her breast, ending at her nipple. Jack stared, feeling guilty, but feeling also that only a fool would look away from something so beautiful. Her breathing slowed. She rubbed her face and lay back down, covering herself.

Jack got up and sat reading from his hand held computer. Not sure why he was doing it, he turned his chair so that it faced the bed. At odd intervals he stopped reading and watched the woman as she slept. Hours passed.

When it was light, the woman stirred, groaning slightly as she woke up. She was facing Jack when she opened her eyes. They looked at each other for a few seconds. "Good morning," Jack said, tilting his head to one side. "Do you know where you are?" She nodded, barely moving her head, then closed her eyes again and seemed to fall back asleep. Jack got up to shower and dress.

When he came back, she was sitting up in bed, making no attempt to hide her breasts. "Good morning," she said.

"Hi. Good morning. Again. Um . . . how are you?"

She smiled, her eyes narrow and pinched. "I'd laugh at that question, only I think my head will explode if I laugh."

Jack fetched a couple of pills and water. "Here. This should help. My name's Jack, by the way."

"Thank you Jack. I'm Madi. Madior, actually, but I let people who pick my vomit-soaked corpse up out of the gutter call me Madi."

"Well, technically, it wasn't a gutter. Just a parking lot."

She smiled again. "I remember, Jack. I seem to remember everything—no blackouts. You were very kind."

While Madi showered, Jack put her clothes in his washer. He gave her a bathrobe to wear and they ate breakfast, Madi nibbling on toast.

"You said something about knowing UNSA," she said.

"Yes, the company I work for contracts for them."

"Ah. And you are in software, a programmer?"

"Um, yes. How did you know?" he asked.

"'Not a gutter, but a parking lot,'" she quoted. "It's my experience that people who are that literal are usually software engineers."

Jack laughed. He talked a little about his work on the scoop orbiters and other UNSA projects. There was a lull, and Madi stared into her mug of tea. "I was on the Iliad," she said.

Jack started. "Oh. Oh. I'm . . . I'm sorry. . ."

"We . . . the survivors, just got back to Earth orbit a few days ago. Yesterday was my first day surface-side. I came here to Portland to see the wife of one of the men who died. I was good friends with both of them. She was in rough shape . . . angry . . . said some very angry things . . . So anyway, after that, getting drunk seemed like a good idea, so I did."

"Did it help?"

"Well, it wasn't any worse than the damn post-trauma therapy UNSA's been shoving down my throat."

"I'm sorry. . ." Jack said. "It was a terrible accident."

"There have been worse. Yes. It was terrible."

"So you're on the *Nomad* project," she said a few moments later. "That is so exciting. God, a starship. It still seems unreal to me."

"Well, it is sort of unreal, isn't it? Between the seventy six years it will take to reach Epsilon Eridani, and another ten years before their report is received here . . . You and I will be dead before anything is heard from them, before it's known if the ship made it, or if the crew survived the cryo-sleep, or what they found, or whether they decided to head back to Earth or to go on to Tau Ceti . . . There's something very unreal about the whole thing."

"Perhaps there is," said Madi. "But it's something that has to be done."

"Has to?" Jack was looking at her eyes. Her irises were such a dark brown they seemed almost black. *Obsidian*, he thought, smiling to himself. *Polished obsidian.*

"Yes, absolutely. It sounds melodramatic, but I really believe starships are necessary for human survival. And not because the sun is going to burn out in a couple of billion years. I mean much shorter term than that. We can't sit around forever hoping that some day we'll come up with some magical way of traveling faster than light. Because while we sit here, the human race is rotting away. People are spending more and more time and energy and money on entertainment—on VR immersives and games and movies and holos and all the other sensory junk foods—and they're losing interest in the real world. The solar system isn't enough of a *frontier*. Most people see it as a bunch of places that are too hostile, too alien, to get excited about. We need planets humans could live on, planets with life, to get people excited about space. To get people interested in the real universe again. And we need it soon, before we turn into a race of jellyfish that can only sit and be entertained and is incapable of getting off its ass and doing anything. I say thank *God* for *Nomad*. I cried like a baby when I heard that project was approved." She stopped, took a breath. "Sorry. I get a little carried away on that subject. You're smiling; you must think I'm just doing my silly spacer-fanatic thing. . ."

"No!" said Jack. "No. I'm smiling because I think you're magnificent." Then he blushed. "Oh, um, I don't think I meant to say that out loud."

Madi put her head back and laughed. "Thank you, Jack. That's quite a compliment. Hey, I laughed and my head didn't explode. Those meds must be working. I actually feel okay."

When they finished their breakfast, Madi said, "Well, I should go." She got dressed. Jack stood, put his hands in his pockets, took them out. He opened his mouth to say something, changed his mind, closed his mouth. She went to his door, he followed her.

"Thank you again, Jack," she said, putting her hand on his shoulder. "Thank you for everything."

"Madi, um, you don't need to thank me . . . it was my pleasure . . . it was an honor . . . I mean, I enjoyed meeting you. Um, very much . . . and I . . . um, hope—"

"I brushed my teeth, Jack."

"What?"

"You didn't have any mouthwash, so I put some toothpaste on my finger and brushed my teeth. See?" She brought her face very close to his and huffed a breath at him. It smelled of toothpaste. "Nice and fresh."

"Um, that's nice. . ."

"Jack?"

"Yes?"

"Could you stop saying 'um'?"

A pause. Then: "Yes. Yes I can." And he kissed her.

Later that morning, Madi asked to go to a park. "A big one, with trees, grass, birds," she said.

They went to a park and walked. "I have two week's leave," Madi said, "more, if I want it. After that I'm under orders from my shrink to only take short assignments for a while—just Earth-orbit hops. So we'll be able to spend some time together, if you want."

"I want," said Jack. "I want."

They stopped and sat under a tree. "Oh, god," Madi said, inhaling deeply. She lay down, first on her back, then rolling over onto her stomach and pressing her cheek and opening her palms to the grassy ground. She closed her eyes. "Oh god, oh god, oh god. It's good to be home."

Jack watched as tears leaked out of one closed eye, then the other. He put his hand on her back, stroking her. She started sobbing quietly, and Jack lay beside her and pulled her close and ran his hand over her short bristly hair and kissed the side of her face again and again. Soon she was quiet, and soon after that she fell asleep.

She dozed for only a few minutes, then rolled over and opened her eyes. Jack was sitting, looking down at her. She smiled. "And there you are," she said. "My own personal angel, watching over me as I sleep."

And the next morning, when Madi awoke in Jack's bed she saw he was already awake, sitting in the half-light, reading and watching her. "Okay," she said with a laugh. "I can see this is going to be a habit."

"I like watching you sleep," Jack said. "It makes me happy. It feels like . . . It feels like that's where I belong."

"Okay, my love. As long as you know you belong other places too." She held the sheets open for him.

When Jack came home Madi was sitting at the same table where they had shared their first breakfast five months ago. She was staring at her folded hands, and was slow to look up when he came in. "What's wrong?" he asked.

She stood up, and somehow that frightened Jack. It made her look military, hard, ready to do what she had to do, regardless of the consequences.

"I've been accepted for an assignment, Jack."

He waited.

"It's something I volunteered for. A while ago. I didn't think they'd accept me, but they did. And I have to go, Jack."

"What are you saying? What assignment? How long?"

"It's for the *Nomad*, Jack. I'm going to be part of the crew."

For a moment Jack felt like he was falling. "No," he said. *I am not falling*, he thought.

"Jack, I—"

"No."

Madi was silent.

"You can't. Madi . . . Madi. . ." He stopped, and stood looking at her. "Okay," he said finally.

The next day Jack went to see Herzfeld. He sat in the CEO's elegantly decorated office and stared down at his own feet. "I need you to put me on another project," he said. "I want to . . . I have to work on the *Nomad* MIR's."

"What?" Herzfeld said blankly.

"The software for the *Nomad* MIRs—the bots—I have to be on that project."

"But Raj is heading that project, and he has been for months. You know that Jack; what are you talking about?"

"I'm sorry, Mr. Herzfeld. I don't like asking this, but I have to. I don't have to be chief engineer. I'll take anything, as long as it's on that project. If you can't do this for me then I'm resigning. Quitting. Now."

Herzfeld took a slow breath, then spoke with a deliberate calmness. "Listen to me Jack. You know the kind of security we have on these UNSA projects. I can't let you—I can't let anyone—come charging into my office and bully his way onto a project like this. Not unless I know *exactly* what the hell it's all about. I know you don't want to Jack, but you're going to have to talk to me. You're going to have to tell me why you want this."

Jack stood up and paced around the office. After a few moments he started talking. He explained as well as he could. He talked about Madi, about her being accepted to the *Nomad* crew. At times he stumbled over his words, or sentences trailed off unfinished, at times his face burned with embarrassment, but he explained what he wanted.

When he was finished both men were silent for a while. Then Herzfeld said "Alright Jack. Raj has been wanting to do something more managerial anyway. You're chief engineer of the MIR project."

A little over a year later the *Nomad* left Earth orbit with Madi aboard.

There were thousands of systems aboard the *Nomad*, each one built with redundancy upon redundancy. It carried an army of self-testing and repair mechanisms that would, in theory, keep the ship intact and on course, keep the crew preserved in cryo-sleep, keep the dormant systems of the ship ready to function when they would be needed, decades in the future. Most of the ship's self-maintenance happened quietly, invisibly, behind panels, under the decks and within the walls. Every circuit and electronic component had redundant twins, and every mechanical system had a way to replace its own parts. But apart and independent from all this were the Mobile Inspection and Repair units, commonly called the bots. Wheeled and legged, these semiautonomous mechanicals would roam the decks of the *Nomad*, looking for signs of damage or wear or malfunction that the ship's other sensors might miss.

In all of the byzantine maze of systems on board the *Nomad*, the MIRs were the one that Jack knew he wanted to work on.

And when the *Nomad* left on its journey, and for the rest of Jack's life, he could close his eyes and imagine the bots. He could see them in his mind's eye, walking the corridors of the silent ship, walking past the coffin-like cryonic enclosures where the crew slept. And he knew that a part of these lifeless mechanicals was his; a small part of him was going with them. He could see them quietly inspecting, testing, measuring. Watching, watching, for year after year, for centuries even, he would be watching over Madi as she slept.

Stories of the Alien Invasion
by Manek Mistry

1. Arrival

They came in small ships—small but numerous, shaped like objects from our houses, familiar and strange: a flying toaster, an easy chair that hovered, a lampshade dropping gently down from orbit. The ships landed on roads, rooftops, and parking lots; they landed in parks, fields, and forests; they landed everywhere, and then they opened and unfolded in complicated ways, revealing interiors of shiny chrome, and delivering the aliens. The creatures themselves resembled small piles of sticks—like the beginning of a campfire, before it's lit, before it acquires the weight of heavy logs that will turn to glowing coals—small piles of sticks that marched across the roads, rooftops, parking lots, through the parks, fields and forests, to our doorsteps.

The twig-piles spoke to us in raspy English, in Spanish, in Japanese, in Hindi, in a hundred other languages. They spoke to each other with clicking sounds, and with vibrations that we felt as compressions deep in our chests.

"Greetings, Earthlings," they said. "We come in peace." Then they laughed—the recognizable sound of human laughter, familiar but incomprehensible. "Take me to your leader," they said, but refused to follow. "Take me to your leader," they repeated, and laughed some more.

They invaded our lives, disrupting traffic, interrupting broadcasts, justifying absence from work, from school, from home. They overwhelmed small towns, gathering in prodigious numbers, clicking at each other, laughing at us. And we watched them, speculating, guessing. They were opaque to our questions, answering in riddles: "Where are you from?" drew the response "Home," or maybe "Heaven," or sometimes "Oz," or "Narnia," or "Wonderland."

And always laughter. Some of us became sensitive and angry; others became bored, and left the aliens alone. But most of us were drawn to them, and tried to engage, to understand, to communicate.

They did not care. They spoke to each other, they spoke to cows, in long, lowing "mooooos," they spoke to the air, to the grass, to cars and trucks, to empty buildings. They spoke to us, yes, but also to themselves, mumbling long strings of words, words that used to mean something.

2. Close Encounter

Nick came to the coffee shop every afternoon before work, hoping for a few words with the barista. Hoping to flirt, without coming across as needy, which was how he felt. Sometimes she would smile at him, but mostly she would make his coffee and then move on, cleaning out the machine or wiping the counter.

Today, when he walked in, there were aliens.

He had seen them before, from a distance, but today, after he sat at the counter, one came and perched on the stool next to him. Its companions remained clustered on a table near the door, watching.

"Smite me," said the alien.

Nick glanced over at the barista, who was steaming milk for a latte, then looked back at the small pile of sticks at his side. "What?"

"Smite me," repeated the creature. It sounded like a smoker, hoarse from shouting, its voice rough. "Smite me with your . . . with this." It pointed to Nick's hand, extending one of its stick-like arms.

"Hand," said Nick. He had large anvil hands; even as a kid, he'd been able to pick up a basketball in one palm.

"Yes," said the alien, grinding its harsh voice into the air. "Smite me with your hand, closed like a rock."

Nick made a fist, held it up.

"Yes. With that."

Nick paused, glanced again at the barista as she handed him his latte. Did the alien really know what it was asking? Would it be insulted if he refused? And that word—smite. They wouldn't have picked that up from TV or radio—it must be mistaken. He tried to think of other things it might want with a fist.

The alien watched him with one eye; the other eyestick poked across the counter toward the barista, who slapped at it. "Keep that thing away from me," she said to Nick.

Nick shifted uncomfortably on his stool. She shouldn't do that, he thought. "Where do you want me to hit you?" he asked.

It lifted a stick, bent, and pointed delicately at itself. "Here," it said.

Nick tapped it with his knuckles; the sticks shifted and shuffled against each other, then resumed their previous configuration.

"No," rasped the alien. "Hard. With . . . gusto."

With gusto. Ok, Nick thought. I guess there's no misunderstanding. There was a feeling he had—he'd heard other people describe it this way too—a feeling like he'd just lost an argument with the alien, and that he had to comply, even though he didn't want to. He pulled back and punched the pile of sticks; they scattered and fell, and the alien's eyes bounced on the floor and rolled under a table; the other aliens laughed and clicked at each other, and Nick felt the compressions in his chest that he'd heard about, the compressions that meant they were talking to each other.

"What the hell did you do that for?" asked the barista. She brushed sticks off the counter.

"It asked me to," Nick said. His hands shook, and he clutched the counter to steady himself as the other aliens opened the door and shuffled out, chuckling. Had he killed it? They wouldn't just leave it if it were dead, would they?

"You shouldn't listen to those things," the barista said.

Nick leaned over to look at the broken twigs, inert on the floor, then straightened, his hands still shaking. "How are we going to understand if we don't listen?"

She shrugged, finished wiping the counter, and looked at his drink. "There's crap in your latte—you want another?"

He nodded.

She drew two shots, steamed the milk, and handed him the warm mug. "It's on the house," she said, winking. "We humans have to stick together, right?"

He nodded, looked at her, then looked away. She wasn't Julie. I guess it's too soon, he thought. "Can I have that to go?" he asked.

3. Comfort

Julie arrived early at the doctor's but they still made her wait. She flipped through an old issue of Newsweek—early pictures of the invasion. They had seemed so strange, then, these visitors from—where? No one knew, still.

"Julie?"

She looked up, but the summons was for someone else—a girl, nine or ten, whose thin frame and sunken eyes suggested a poor prognosis. Julie smiled sadly at the girl, and then thought about her own son: My son will grow up in a world where aliens are ordinary, she thought. She got up for a drink of water, returned to her seat, flipped through the magazine a second time.

"Julie?"

At last. She followed the nurse into the back hallway, where he took her temperature, blood pressure and pulse. Finally, he settled her in a room. "Doc'll be in here in a minute," he said.

But it wasn't a minute, it was twenty. She paced around the room, looked out in the hallway, sat down, stood up, looked out the window, read the charts on the wall—about smoking, about prostate cancer, about the circulatory system.

When the doctor came, he had two aliens with him, riding an inflatable ball that rolled beneath them as they walked backwards on top. "Our guests would like to observe. Is that ok?" the doctor asked.

Guests, she thought. They weren't exactly guests, were they? They hadn't been invited. She shrugged her assent, feeling the uncomfortable pressure that was a combination of guilt and a desire to please; she'd experienced it before. The aliens rolled their ball against the wall and hopped onto the examination table near her.

She let the doctor feel the lump; he pressed it and poked at it, and she sat still, trying to read his face.

"Is this a sexual encounter?" asked one of the aliens, its voice like gravel.

"No," said the doctor. "A medical exam."

"It is the same, though?" asked the alien.

The doctor shook his head, still prodding her. "Similar, but very different in how we both feel about this touching."

The aliens both inched closer. She heard their clicks, felt the compression in her chest as they spoke to each other.

"Feelings are so important," said one. "May I?" It extended a stick toward her.

She hesitated. This is private, she thought. "Ok," she said, reluctantly. The stick arm touched her, a rough poke on her side. Then she felt it, a gray rumbling somewhere in the back of her mind. Her own emotions—fear, hope, sadness—diminished as she shared them with the alien. The second alien touched the first, and she felt an echo of the rumble, and her feelings diminished further. Maybe this way is best, she thought.

"Ok," said the doctor. "Here's what we'll do." He stripped off his plastic gloves, threw them in a box marked 'biohazard.'

Biohazard. Those are just garbage, she thought; there's nothing hazardous about them. She wondered where biohazard went. Was it buried? Burned?

"We'll take a biopsy to confirm it's malignant, and then—assuming it is—we'll do a scan-and-destroy, to see how far it's spread and to wipe out as much as we can, ok?" He left the room without waiting for an answer.

She looked at the aliens, then turned away. Malignant.

The doctor returned with an enormous syringe. Her fear spiked, and then it faded, replaced by the alien rumble.

"This won't hurt," said the doctor. He pushed the needle into her breast, feeling the lump with one hand as he drew on the syringe with the other. "That's it," he said, pulling the needle out. "I'll have the lab check this, and they'll synthesize some nano for the scan-and-destroy based on what they find." He left the room again.

She glanced at the closer alien, who withdrew its sticklike arm. Her feelings flooded back, and she started to shake. "Touch me again," she said. "Please."

The stick arm returned, and she relaxed a little, taking a deep breath as rumble replaced fear.

"You are afraid," said the alien.

"Yes," she said. "Very."

Then clicks and the chest compression. "I was explaining to my friend," said the alien. "It does not speak English."

She nodded. "What are your names?" she asked, wondering how long it would be before the doctor returned.

"My name is Comfort," said the alien. "And it—" pointing with another stick appendage—"it is Mother Teresa."

Julie closed her eyes and leaned back against the wall. Scan-and-destroy. The success rate for the nano treatment would depend on how far the cancer had spread. I might die. She thought of her son—growing up in a world with aliens, but maybe without a mother.

"You want to be healthy?" asked the alien. "You want to live?"

"Yes," she whispered. She started to cry.

The alien lifted a twig to her face; she felt it touch her gently, then felt a warm and affectionate sadness wash over her, hold her, comfort her.

4. Visitation

Nick saw his son every weekend, from Friday at six until Sunday at six. It was almost too much time, but he never allowed himself to say that out loud. On Sunday afternoons he loaded up the bag, put Aiden in the stroller, and walked over to Julie's. She wasn't unfriendly, but it was better if he left quickly. And he always needed Sunday evenings to unwind after the full-time weekend stress of being a father. Sometimes he dropped in at the bar for a drink; other times he strolled around the little lake on his way home.

He worried that he wasn't a good father. Julie was always so confident; motherhood seemed to come naturally to her. He thought maybe he'd have an easier time when Aiden learned to talk—which was coming late, but he'd been told not to worry—when Aiden finally learned to talk, they could interact more meaningfully, he thought, although he didn't really know what that would look like. Sometimes being a parent just felt so boring.

One Sunday in September the temperature dropped unexpectedly to below freezing. Nick bundled Aiden up, worried about the cold. Julie had the car seat, though—he never took it, because he always walked, with Aiden in the jogger. Probably not a good idea in this weather, though. Aiden fussed while Nick hesitated. "Hush, it's okay," said Nick. He carried Aiden out to the carport, started the car, then went back inside. "It's okay." Shit it's cold outside, he thought. He put on a hat and looked for a pair of gloves. Aiden cried when they went outside. Nick thought about seat-belting his son in the back seat, but decided instead it would be safer to hold him on his lap. He backed out of his driveway, and drove slowly over to Julie's, watching the traffic carefully, paying more attention than usual, his hazard lights flashing. "It's okay," he repeated as he drove.

At Julie's, he carried Aiden to the front door. "He's a little fussy," he said, handing him to Julie.

"He must be cold," she said. "Poor little bug—are you cold?"

"I forgot his bag," said Nick. "I'll drop it by later." He looked at her face; watched her watching his son. Julie.

She nodded. "Bye," she said, and shut the door.

He walked back to the car and pulled away from the curb. He drove around the lake instead of heading straight back home. There was a fire burning on the hill near the lake, and he heard sirens.

An alien by the side of the road caught his attention. It waved to him and he stopped the car and rolled down the window. "Will you drive me to the fire?" it asked.

He shrugged. "Ok," he said. "Hop in."

The alien climbed the side of the car, came in the through his window, clambered over him to the passenger seat. "Thank you," it said.

"Why do you want to go to the fire?" Nick asked.

"To see," said the alien. "Also, I am cold."

"Isn't your house warm?" He had never been inside the messy-looking alien structures on the south side of town, but he'd always assumed they were at least heated.

"I am not at my house," said the alien.

Nick drove up the hill and parked on a side street away from the fire. "I'll walk over with you," he said.

The alien sat on his shoulder as he made his way to the fire. A single-wide was engulfed in flames; black and gray smoke filled the air, climbing toward the sky, while firefighters methodically prepared their equipment. Clusters of neighbors stood nearby watching; a family wrapped in blankets huddled near the fire trucks.

"What do you want to see?" asked Nick.

"The drama," it said. It turned its eyes toward him. "Thank you again." It jumped down from his shoulder and moved to join a group of other aliens watching the fire.

Nick strolled over to a firefighter standing with a radio to her ear. "Need any help?" he asked.

"Just stay back," she said. "And keep them back, too," she added, nodding toward the aliens.

Nick went to stand over near the aliens. He recognized the alien named Comfort, who had started wearing a pink ribbon tied to one of its eyestalks. He had met Comfort at Julie's the month before, and had seen the alien a few other times at her house since then. The other aliens were indistinguishable; he couldn't even tell which one had been in his car. As they watched the fire together, his cell phone rang; he looked at it, saw it was Julie, and answered.

"Did you drive over here without the car seat?"

He swallowed. "I was worried he'd be cold, in this weather," he said. "I was very careful."

"Don't you *ever* do that again," she said. "Don't you ever! You could have called me; I would have come."

"I didn't think of that," he said.

"Idiot!" She hung up.

He put his cell phone in his pocket and watched the fire with the aliens. He heard one of the firefighters say "Total loss." They still hadn't hooked their hose up, and Nick realized there wasn't a fire hydrant nearby; they'd have to pump icy water from the lake, down at the bottom of the hill. He looked at the family hunched in their light blue blankets—there was a woman crying, holding two children to her side, and a man in a wheelchair. "*Everything's* in there!" the woman wailed. "Everything we own!"

Nick heard the clicks of alien conversation, felt compression in his chest, then saw three of the creatures dart into the burning trailer. "Shit!" he said.

"Keep them back!" shouted the firefighter he'd spoken to earlier.

"Stay here," he said to the remaining aliens.

They didn't answer, but he heard more clicks.

"What are they doing?" he asked Comfort.

"Helping," came the reply.

He watched one of the aliens come out, dragging a chair. It pulled the chair away from the fire, then turned and went back in as the other two came out with a table. Just then, the whole trailer collapsed, and flames soared upwards; he heard shouts from the firefighters over the roaring crackle of the fire, as they stepped back. A small bundle of burning twigs stumbled from the flames, staggered a few feet, and collapsed, blazing quickly down to a pile of ashes. The two aliens who had rescued the table rejoined the group.

"I'm sorry," said Nick.

Comfort turned one eye toward him. "Why?" it asked. Like all of them, its voice was low and raspy, but Comfort sounded less like a machine and more like a person from another culture.

"I'm sorry for your friend, because it's dead," said Nick. He wondered if they believed in an afterlife. Or maybe they didn't die when their bodies did—maybe there was some kind of mental energy transferred to the others. He thought he'd heard something about that, maybe—or was he imagining he had?—but then, who understood them, really?

"Yes, it is dead," said Comfort. "But why does it matter?"

The others turned their eyes from the fire as well, and edged closer, until they crowded around Nick and Comfort.

"Explain to us," said Comfort. "Explain to us why life and death are so important, and why it matters so much if a person lives or dies."

Nick sighed. The question was like many others he had tried, inarticulately, to answer—about the meaning of art, music or literature, or how watching a sad movie might make a person cry. "Because," he said, "because the person is no longer there to talk to and to spend time with."

"But there are other people," said Comfort. "Billions of them; more than you could ever meet in your lifetime."

"Yes," said Nick, "but each person is unique, and their passing is a loss."

"No one is unique," said the alien. "Your people are all the same—two arms, two legs, a head, with a collection of memories and psychic scars. I am the same as all my siblings—a set of appendages," it moved some of its sticks, "with eyes, curiosity, and a certain way of speaking. If I die, you could interact with my neighbor and not notice the difference."

That was true, Nick reflected. They all seemed alike, to him—or what differences there were didn't register. "But each person is related to others, and the death of a relative is a sad event." He felt himself struggling, faltering, and knew there were better explanations. He thought of his mother, who had overdosed when he was fourteen, and his father, who had left when he was five.

The alien shook its eye-stalk. "Relatives die all the time, without affecting their kin—we have seen it happen, repeatedly. To say someone is related does not explain this sadness about death."

He told them about Julie, about how he loved her, despite their fights, despite the fact that she had left him for someone else; he told them about the ache he felt when he thought of her, and the sadness he felt in her presence, when she spoke to him, and how the air around her, the smell of her made his heart pound, even after almost two years of separation. "If she died," he said, "I'd fall apart . . . I love her; she's important to me."

The aliens considered this, and Nick heard clicks and felt compression in his chest. Then Comfort turned back to him. "But you are already sad, and she is alive," it said. "If she died, perhaps you would move on, find someone else important to you—another woman, perhaps—and if this other woman died you would find yet another person."

"But she's the mother of my child," said Nick, and realized with guilt that he hadn't thought of Aiden's death; had thought only of Julie. "And if my child died. . ." he said half-heartedly, and trailed off. He felt, for his son's sake, that he must, he *must* persuade them, make them understand why it would be sad if Aiden died. "If my son died, I'd be heartbroken."

The alien's eye-stalks rose an inch. "You are still fertile," it said. "You could have another child, with another woman. Perhaps you would love this second child even more than the first . . . and the other woman as much as Julie?"

No, thought Nick. Maybe another child, but never another woman. He sighed. "I love my son," he said. "He's important to me; if he died, I'd be sad—devastated, and I could never replace him with another child." He said these words, but thought of Julie; sweet, beautiful, irreplaceable Julie; Julie who was already gone forever.

5. Departure

It was not a departure so much as a migration and an extinction. The alien slums grew larger, then spread thin and shrank as aliens died from contagious diseases or wandered back to the orbiter, drifting away from the harsh conditions.

Comfort stayed. "I am stubborn," it said. "And there is more to explore; more to discover; more to learn. I am curious, like a child."

Nick sat across from the alien, reading a reprint from a medical journal. He looked up. "But you're at risk," he said. "You might die."

"I know," said Comfort, then launched into a speech, imitating the style of a preacher who had spoken on TV the day before. "And I have come to fear death; to dread the reaper and his formidable scythe." The alien shifted on its ball, and gestured with an appendage. "But against that fear, I weigh all the things I have never known—things like joy, or excitement." Comfort paused, and resumed its normal speech pattern. "I will never understand these things if I go now. The other day I saw a leaf falling from a tree into the river, and it was so beautiful. I think I have grasped beauty, and I am hungry for the rest."

Nick nodded. "I want to tell you something," he said. Talking to Comfort was easier, sometimes, than talking to people. "Aiden has autism—a disease. He was just diagnosed." He stood up, went to the refrigerator, looked inside, then returned to his chair. "I think it's because I'm a bad father."

Comfort turned both eyestalks toward Nick.

"I don't know what to do," said Nick. "I feel like I'm letting him down."

"Julie was a good mother," said the alien.

"She was," said Nick.

"She would have known what to do."

"Yes," said Nick.

"Think what she would have done," said Comfort. "And then do it."

Nick nodded.

Several days later, Nick, Aiden, and Comfort went to a nearby field to watch a small band of aliens crowd into a rundown ship, preparing to return to the orbiter. The craft resembled an old sofa, its fabric shredded in spots as though scratched by a cat.

"Doesn't look safe," said Nick. He watched Aiden sitting on the grass, holding a stone. "Not that I know much about the technology."

"They do not know to be afraid," said Comfort. "They might die, or they might not. They do not understand the difference."

Nick watched as Aiden raised his stone, lowered it to the ground, raised it again. "But if they're so indifferent to their fate, why are they bothering to leave?"

Comfort shrugged, lifting sticks and dropping them again. "They are bored of what they are experiencing now, and curious about what life would be like on the orbiter, or on the next planet. They lack the staying power to investigate this experience. To really live it."

The small craft rocketed upward, quickly disappearing from sight, leaving only a wispy trail of blue vapor and the scent of lavender.

"Well," said Nick. "That's that." He picked Aiden up, and the three of them returned to the car. "Are you sad at all? Lonely?"

"No," said Comfort. It helped Nick fasten Aiden into the car seat. "I have friends."

Nick started the car and they drove home.

That night, after Aiden was asleep, Comfort went down into the crawlspace below the house and puttered around, working on the nest it was building. Nick sat at the kitchen table with a glass of milk, and thought about the arc of his own loneliness. He'd been devastated when Julie left, and his grief had worsened over the years they lived apart. But now that she was gone, the intensity of his unhappiness was subsiding.

Although he didn't believe in God, or an afterlife, he liked to imagine Julie looking down on Aiden, watching to make sure their child was safe. He took a sip of milk, and wondered if she ever saw him when she looked down from above. Then he thought about the orbiter, up there in space with Julie, getting ready to move on to another planet.

He finished his milk and stood up. As he walked to put the glass in the sink he heard Comfort bang on something beneath the floor. Aiden made a noise in his crib, and then was quiet. Nick realized, for the first time in a long while, that he didn't feel lonely at that moment. He stood by the sink, the empty glass in his hand, looking out the kitchen window into the darkness, the unlonely feeling settling in his heart

A Clockwork Break
by Shawn Scarber

Last night Angie dreamed her heart had turned to a metal box with broken gears.

She pulled the lifter and positioned the sleeve under the presser footer. In one smooth motion, she guided the garment across the cloth plate. She did this for every piece of clothing, and had for the past four autumns. The sewing machine had become a part of her.

As the needle bar glided up and down, she considered her younger brother's latest letter. Thomas promised her, after his graduation in spring, train fare from Lowell to Boston.

The city offered an easier life, he wrote. Her arduous hours, pricked fingers and watering eyes had paid for his education. Now it seemed he wished to return her favor with a respectable home, employment as his children's governess and a furnished room where she could live out her life as a spinster.

Angie handed the garment to her left, to Susana Ward, a dirty-looking girl from Kansas. She attached the pearl buttons with some care not to soil the sleeves.

An older woman to her right handed Angie the next sleeve. Work continued that way for hours.

Then the equipment clogged. A leather engine belt had caught fire. Bruce, the machinist, had to attach another.

Angie focused her gaze toward her sewing as he worked. Another woman might catch her glancing in his direction. While he lifted the engine parts, and the muscles on his arms tightened, and his back and chest swelled with the exertion, she wondered how his black beard might feel against her bare neck and shoulders, prickly like twined hemp or yielding like a sheep's fleece.

He repaired it quickly, as he did with all things mechanical. Angie thought again about her dreams of clockwork hearts. The equipment bustled. She pushed another sleeve through her Wilcox-Gibbs and then handed it to Susana.

In mid-September the days brought cool breezes, and the bosses left the factory windows open. Compared to most supervisors, Angie's were pleasant. They allowed the doffers, the youngest girls who replaced empty bobbins and swept the floors, to stare at the nearby woods and river during breaks.

When the girls laughed aloud, many of the women, including Angie, turned to see what had attracted their attention. For a second, Angie believed a large butterfly, or some type of clumsy beetle had flown through the window.

It fluttered toward her, and she recognized its shape as a sparrow's, but she hadn't seen a bird colored silver before. It landed on her sewing machine's spool pin with tiny tick-tick sounds. It hopped about and cocked its head to the side.

Angie scarcely believed what perched near her. Someone, for a reason she could not fathom, had constructed a bird made from tin. Her first impulse told her to shoo it away and continue her work, but she didn't listen. She reached for the mechanical bird. It moved in a natural manner, like the motion God built into his own creations. It jumped back a step from her fingers.

Angie stood and gazed over the factory floor. The machines no longer whirled. Everyone gawked at her and the toy.

When it chirped, the women seated near her startled and scurried a few steps back.

Angie again reached out, this time with her hands held together as a bowl. It eased into her hold. She expected the bird to weigh more, perhaps as much as a man's pocket watch, but it weighed the same as a child's cotton sleeve.

While it lay in her hands the clockwork inside ticked like a heartbeat, fast and steady similar to a genuine sparrow's. Upon closer examination she understood why its initial flight had seemed erratic. One of its metallic feathers hung loose between two others, stuck in a wing joint. The bird attempted to reach the feather, but its creator had not made it well enough for the feat.

Angie turned toward the window to find Bruce standing two polite steps behind her. The sweat from his earlier labors still clung to his shirt. He looked at the toy and held his hands together in a cup.

She placed her hands in his. Her knuckles rubbed against his callused palms. She held her hands there a moment longer than needed, so the warmth of his touch might reside on her skin. He cradled the sparrow in one hand. With the middle finger of his other he stroked along the errant feather's edge until it slid into place with a click.

The clockwork sparrow flapped its wings, but didn't fly away.

Bruce nodded to Angie and smiled. A glistening row of pearl button teeth showed through his cracked lips and black beard. She couldn't help but return a smile.

She tenderly scooped the bird in her hands and walked toward the window. It opened wide to a denim blue sky and stretching pines. The doffers angled like wide-eyed puppies to get a last look of this marvel.

Angie held it low for the girls to see and they thanked her with delighted gasps, giggles and ooohs.

She raised the tin sparrow toward the open window and as quick as a needle breaks it shot to the sky.

Angie turned to a silent factory. One of the bosses set down his clipboard and clapped. The machine operators clapped and all the women and the doffers joined. The room roared with applause.

She made a modest curtsey, though she didn't believe anyone clapped for her, maybe for the bird's freedom or Bruce's skill, but what had she done to deserve attention?

Maybe they clapped in appreciation of a moment, she thought. A moment she had accepted as a gift from an unlikely bird. A moment different than any they had shared, or would ever share again.

They had all stopped clapping by the time Angie returned to her station. She reached for the next sleeve to push across her cloth plate as the machines breathed to life. She gazed on Bruce without reservation as he oiled the generator, and she thought of his strong hands sliding the gears of her heart gently into place with a click.

The Knife
by Jason L. Corner

The rays of the noontime sun glinted through the diamond prism leaf Jessica Chen held in her hand as she stood outside the house. The light entered the transparent, paper-thin leaf and split into a six-pointed wheel of single-colored beams. Jessica grew them in her house; they weren't native to this part of the planet Esef, and to grow them here took immense diligence, care, and specialized equipment. There were jungles in the north, apparently, where they grew in great numbers and different varieties. They were some of the most fascinating plants in the universe as far as Jessica knew, and she had come here with her family to study them.

She hadn't planned on living here.

And the light shot through the leaf, and struck beneath her son Bobby's bed, and revealed a small stone knife. Jessica looked around a little nervously, then picked it up. It had jagged edges, like an Indian arrowhead, and was about half again the length and width of her hand, There were three symbols on it, painted on it in red. She didn't recognize the symbols; she assumed that they were Eosfi, although she had learned the basic Eosfi alphabet and didn't recognize them.

"So the question is now," she said to herself, "is this something my son ought to have or not? And it looks like not. Because it's a knife, and because if it was something he ought to have, I'd know about it already." She had never talked to herself before, but the last two years had changed everybody.

Wouldn't she? She wondered. Bobby had put it under the bed to conceal it. But then how did she justify searching his room? She did it regularly, of course; she worried about Bobby, after all. But she guessed he didn't know that.

She would have to talk to Ziggaut about it, and wrote that into the Planner window on her handheld, right after 'check the garden,' which would have to be done right that moment.

Even though Jessica walked the tree branch from her back door to the garden three or four times a day every day, for the last two years, since the destruction of the Gate, she still put her arms out wide each time to balance herself. Even though the branch was twenty feet wide! For on rainy, nutrient-rich Esef, the trees grew huge, and the Eosfi built cities of interconnected tree houses, and the humans in the diaspora lived in them.

The purple irises (a human name) looked all right; she had trouble getting used to the taste and had started out just seasoning her food with them, but Bobby liked them, so they had been eating more and more. Satisfied, she bent down to inspect the meat-flowers, the large, thick fungus-like plants that provided most of their protein.

Jessica peeled open one of the smaller plants. The pure white inside was blotched and full of holes. A fat purple worm poked its head out of one of the holes.

With a muttered curse, she looked briefly through a couple others. All infested, all ruined. And Jessica knew the reason why. Her section of the tree bordered on the section of Dr. Hand, and he let his tree grow wild. Even here she could see just the edge of one of his branches; thick with overgrowth and wild plants, with a few larger branches shooting out at jagged angles from the wall of overgrowth. It looked like the underside of a giant hairy spider.

When you didn't keep your area pruned and clean, the wild plants attracted bugs and the bugs destroyed gardens, and not just your own. They had all decided at the last Human Neighborhood Association meeting that everyone would *voluntarily* take care of their areas. But Dr. Hand never came to meetings (he must have gotten the newsletter, though), and he didn't take care of his area, and he didn't, apparently, *care* at all.

Jessica reopened the Planner window on her handheld, and wrote down "Next meeting (tomorrow)—bring up tree care (Dr. Hand)." Sitting right there above the words, in her blocky scrawl? "See Ziggaut about knife."

Bobby had soccer after school. She didn't have to pick him up for another three hours. So in theory, she could go to Ziggaut's office now and talk to it, unless it rained of course.

She looked to the alien sky, hoping it looked like heavy rain. It didn't. So there was no putting it off. She put her arms out *very* carefully and walked down the tree.

"Hello, Chen-Jessica!" Ziggaut, the Earthling-Eosfi Liaison for Jessica's region, said as Jessica entered its office. "That is the proper name protocol for Chinese Earthlings, is it not? I have been reading about China."

"Yes, that would be right in China," Jessica said. "But Chen is my husband's name; *he* was Chinese. And he had never been there. His *great*-grandparents were born there."

Ziggaut was typical, in appearance, of its race, which is to say it looked (to Jessica) like a large red octopus with tusks and five tentacles (a pentapus? The word had not caught on). It sat on an Eosfi chair, which looked like a wicker chair with no back and a thin blanket instead of a cushion. Ziggaut's desk was shaped like a donut and the chair was in the center; a human would have been trapped but Ziggaut had its climbing bars on the roof.

Ziggaut fingered its tusk thoughtfully. "But . . . your name is Chen, also? So are you also Chinese?"

"No, it just means that Chen is my husband's name."

"But Amanda Abernathy? Her husband's name is Schwartz."

Jessica thought for a moment, framing her words carefully. Though it had been studying art history at Yale and was only home on vacation when the Gate was destroyed, and it was employed by the Eosfi government as liaison to the human community in this district for its knowledge, it still found itself stumped on what seemed (to Jessica) like the most obvious bits of knowledge, and she knew that it always appreciated her help. "It used to be tradition for wives—marriage partners with female gender—to take the names of their husbands when they got married. When females gained more political and economic equality, many—most, actually—gave up the custom."

"But you and your male marriage partner kept the tradition?"

"Yes. We both wanted to."

"Ah, then you are a conservative, Jessica Chen!" Ziggaut leapt up and grabbed the climbing bars on the roof by two tentacles, then wrapped two more around another bar and crawled away from its desk like a sloth. It dropped—gracefully—in another Eosfi chair near the door, motioning with a tentacle for Jessica to sit down in a nearby human chair.

"I am glad to hear this, Jessica Chen, for I am a conservative too, you know," Ziggaut said. "But perhaps I read from your face that you are surprised?"

Jessica had been thinking no such thing. But Earthlings and Eosfi were known, already, for their incompetence at reading each other's body language. Not wishing to provoke a discussion either way, she made a vague, noncommittal noise.

But nothing could ever stop Ziggaut from talking. "It is true that I am a conservative," Ziggaut continued. "Many of our liaisons between Earthlings and Eosfi are those that affect to be—apologies, I must translate the idiom—of all trees and none. Maybe there is an English equivalent?"

"Cosmopolitan."

"Thank you, Jessica Chen. Cosmopolitans. But I say no, I must be a liaison *because* I am a conservative. This is our planet and our civilization, worth preserving, and so also worth extending. On Earth—Earth is a great civilization also—if you are an Eosfi and you visit, you let the Earthlings extend their great civilization to you and you learn English and you get a driver's license. And on Esef you send your young to Eosfi schools and you do things this way. It is like your naming and reproductive partnership protocols." As an asexual species that reproduces by budding, the Eosfi were utterly confused by human marriage and family structure, but Ziggaut took it all as part of the job. "I will never understand it, but it's good that you have them."

"Ziggaut," Jessica said. "I need to ask you something." She took out her handheld and e-pen and quickly sketched a picture of the knife she had found. "I found this under my son Bobby's bed. And there were some characters—some letters—on it. Like this." She sketched those as well. "But they're not in the regular alphabet, are they?"

Ziggaut looked at the symbols and blinked. "No. They are archaic." It paused. "This is your child's ramos."

"His ramos? What's that? And why hasn't he told me anything about it?"

"Hroom, hroom, hroom!" Ziggaut made a kind of snorting noise, muffled by its tusks. This seemed to be an Eosfi equivalent of laughter, triggered by embarrassment. "It's not the kind of thing, hroom, that one *talks* about!" Ziggaut put its tentacles to its head and breathed deeply. "Apologies. Your child is how old?"

"He'll be fourteen next month."

"Yes, that's right. Well, on the first summer day, your son and some others will take these ramoses and our priests will blindfold them and lock them in a room with an angry zunder; you know the animals that roam the southwestern desert. When they kill it, they'll be let out and they will all be ramos-mates for the rest of their lives. This is the ramos-reed. We all do it."

There was absolute silence in the little building. Jessica contemplated Ziggaut's tusks. They were painted purple, with a few star-shaped flecks of gold. Ziggaut's tusks were always painted interesting colors, not like her neighbor Kupp, who wore the same green every day. It was very interesting to look at and kept her from having to think about what she had just heard.

"Jessica Chen?" Ziggaut said. "You understand, then? I am pleased you are not resistant as many humans have been."

"No, I'm sorry," Jessica said, snapping out of reverie. "I was just thinking that there must be something wrong with my hearing. Because I—believe me—thought you just said you were going to have my son blindfolded and sent to kill a wild animal with a bunch of other children."

Ziggaut breathed what might have been a sigh. "Not so wild. An old zunder, who has lived an easy, boring life, and is now showing signs of age. Believe me, it will be a favor to the animal."

Jessica felt, later, that perhaps this was another occasion for forming her words carefully. But it didn't work out, and she doubted, in the state of mind she (inevitably, necessarily) had been in, she could have done anything to curb what came out of her mouth, which was a torrent of obscene adverbs and adverbial phrases, all coming before the word 'crazy' and after the words 'you are.'

Nothing if not nonchalant, Ziggaut waited patiently for Jessica to finish, and then said, "I see you have some objections. Many of your fellow Earthlings, particularly the females, have had objections, but all have agreed in the end. Let me present the arguments that have convinced them. First, the Zunder is tame and generally toothless; only two per cent of ramos-mates are ever injured, and far less are killed. Second, adults will kill the Zunder very quickly and painlessly once the fatal blow has been scored by one of the children. Furthermore —"

"Stop. No, no. Just stop. Stop." Jessica did not say these things to communicate information; she was using words as a buckler to ward off blows. The world had gone quite mad, and was lashing out at her. Well, she was lashing back.

"Do you think," she said, "that you're convincing me of anything? Do you know that you just said there was a one in fifty chance of my son getting killed?"

"Seriously injured," Ziggaut said. "Fatality is really quite rare. You have driven cars and flown in airplanes, have you not? The risk is similar. Look, look," Ziggaut raised two of its tentacles and waved them around. "Do you see this?"

Jessica stopped protesting just long enough to see a long purple scar on the underside of its tentacle. "You see this? Even injury to this extent is rare. And I treasure it as I treasure my own life.

"Look here," it continued, reaching into its desk and taking out a photograph. It showed five Eosfi; strikingly, they were touching each other, which adults never did. The five of them, their tusks dyed in jaunty stripes of bright green and blue, had their tentacles draped across each other, and one of them, she was pretty sure, was Ziggaut, although she wasn't positive; Ziggaut must have been younger. One of the Eosfi had an eye patch.

"Apologies. I become sentimental. But you must understand. These are my ramos-mates, Zaddut, Ettaro, Chima, and Mett. I was with them when those terrorists attacked, on this side of the Gate, in my home, our reunion, trapping us all here. Never go back to Earth. I like Earth, but this is my home; only at home can I live. So you see, they have saved my life again. Only a ramos-mate could. How many times can I thank them? Jessica Chen, would you spare your child this?"

Jessica had come to Esef to study the plant life. She was not uninterested in this planet. And she knew that Ziggaut was genuinely emotional, that this was, for it, intended to be a touching moment. But only part of her mind knew that; on the whole, she could only understand that Ziggaut wanted to kill her son.

"How did you get that scar?" She was throwing words now, as a monkey hurls its own feces to defend its territory. "Was it the Zunder? Or could it be that blindfolded children with knives make mistakes? Maybe you put your blood brother's eye out?"

Ziggaut slammed all its tentacles down at once, quivering with what had to be rage in any species. "Are you so short in the tusk that you can say such things? *Lakk*!"

The two sat there silent for a minute. Finally, Ziggaut said, "Do you really plan this little revolution? Don't you know that you will be alone; that all the other parents, thus far, have agreed?"

"If all your friends jumped out of the tree," Jessica started to say, and then laughed. "I'm sorry. I just felt like I was talking to my son for a minute. But no. My son's life and safety are not at the mercy of your primitive—your whatever." She stood up. "I think I'd better go now."

"Go now," Ziggaut repeated. "There are consequences. You will be contacted later. But go now."

Both Bobby's soccer team and the opposing one were equal mixes of human and Eosfi, which was good, because although the Eosfi made excellent goalies, they simply weren't very good on the field. Too slow. They whipped any humans that played against them in their tree-hanging and vine-swinging games, but on the ground they didn't move very fast.

So, for reasons of fairness, Jessica and a majority of the members of the Earthling-Eosfi parents council decided that each team would an equal mix of both species, which had seemed very important to Jessica once. Now, she felt a little out of place, wandering from knot to knot of onlookers. Some Eosfi parents were there—maybe one for every three or four children on the team; they just weren't as involved—but Jessica felt shaky as she neared them, even friends like Mizzov and Kupp. *We have never really known our hosts*, she thought, and the thought was the push you give to a billiard ball on a slightly tilted table, and she floated, almost unconsciously, to Amanda Abernathy and a small circle of human parents standing off to the side.

"Jessica!" Amanda said, breaking from the circle, her hands fluttering up like little birds. "I just *have* to talk to you."

Ziggaut had said that all the parents had agreed to the ramos-reed. So now, Jessica reasoned, Amanda—strangely Amanda, who for all her leadership in the Human Neighborhood Council didn't, as far as Jessica could tell, really *like* the Eosfi—had been sent as an emissary to try to persuade her again.

Jessica shrugged as Amanda cantered over to her. "Sure," she said. "Let's talk. Over there." They walked away from the open field, over to a nearby tree. Only faint glints of sunlight darted through the leaves overhead, so a string of lamps (although it was midday) hung from the branches over the field. The lights gave Amanda's face a harsh, surreal, horror-movie pale gleam. It hurt Jessica's eyes and made her tired. She leaned against the tree.

"Well," Amanda said. "I presume you've spoken with Ziggaut."

"Yeah, I did," Jessica said, closing her eyes. The glare from Amanda's face had given her a headache. "And I really hope you know that my decision's final. I'm not going to be talked out of it."

"Well, that is just. . ." Amanda looked like she didn't have words bad enough. "Of all the irresponsible . . . I'm very surprised, Jessica Chen."

"I'm surprised at you too, you know," Jessica said. "But I'm not going to get my panties in a wringer over it." Amanda gave a small gasp, a thimbleful of distressed air. "And you can tell Ziggaut that too," Jessica continued. "Tell Ziggaut my child's life is more important to me than what everybody else is doing. And that's final."

The effect on Amanda was dramatic; a melting in the shoulders, like steel rods into pudding. "Oh dear, Jessica. Oh dear me. You're laboring under something of a misapprehension, aren't you? Jessica. Do you think my Kirsten is going into that awful room?"

Jessica opened her eyes. "You're not going to let your daughter do it either? But—Ziggaut told me all the parents had agreed to it."

"Did Ziggaut say that? Well, it's not true. Ziggaut's a politician, dear Jessie, and it's a liar. So far as I can tell, the split in this community is about fifty-fifty, and I figure Ziggaut's been telling all the undecided parents that to get them in line. It's downright authoritarian and we of the diaspora aren't going to stand for those kinds of pressure tactics.

"Now listen, Jessica," Amanda continued, stepping closer to the tree and placing her hand on Jessica's arm. "I'm going to need your support on this at the meeting tomorrow."

Jessica laughed, and Amanda backed a bit away, giving her a confused look. "Forgive me, Amanda. It's just that . . . the meeting tomorrow. I was going to take up the question of Dr. Hand's tree-care. You see, he's attracting bugs. Bugs!"

"Yes, er, that does seem like a less important problem now." Amanda was nonplussed, having been taken away from her subject. "Now, listen. I need you on my side at the meeting tomorrow, because —"

"Forgive me again, Amanda," Jessica said. "But *why* do you *need* me on your side at the *meeting*? I've taken my son's *ramos* away. And I wouldn't advise anyone else to do it. But I don't think it's any public issue, is it?"

"Oh, but Jessica, don't you know? Didn't Ziggaut tell you? *They're* making it a public issue. Apparently, if we don't comply, our children—and we too—will all be deprived of citizenship. And they want to move us onto a Yorn reservation!" She chuckled mirthlessly.

"But . . . *can* we live with the Yorn? Does their religion allow that?"

Amanda snorted. "The government worked out some deal. *That's* why I need you on my side; we've got to resist." She looked up into the sky, northward, where the Gate used to orbit. "I hate them sometimes. Orphaning us here like this."

"So do I, Amanda." Jessica's husband had been on Earth when the Gate was destroyed by human supremacists. She knew about hate.

"No, I mean *really* hate them. Sometimes I go all day and feel nothing else." She stared at the sky for a moment, then shook herself. "Well. It looks like practice is over. Let's go get our little darlings home, safe and sound."

They walked back towards the field. Jessica asked, "So who is letting their kids do it? You said fifty-fifty."

"Oh," Amanda said, distractedly. "All *sorts* of people. Most of the single fathers, and that's not hard to believe. Because that's what men do with children, isn't it? They let them play with sharp objects and run around in the rain without a thought, and when they get cuts and catch cold, who takes care of them? And the Eosfi—they just let their children run wild; you've seen it. A whole planet of men."

Jessica heard none of this but nodded anyway. Bobby was coming up the hill from practice and she held out her arms to receive him. It had been a long time since she had felt her husband's absence so acutely; a long time since she had felt so strongly that Bobby was all she had left. As she hugged him, one thought filled her mind to overflowing:

You will be protected.

A ringing signaled that Ziggaut's branch-boat had arrived. Hurriedly, Jessica put the leaf in her pocket and walked to the boat. For long trips between forests, the Eosfi had built long wooden artificial branches that stretched for miles, and the boats traveled on top of them by electric current.

"Jessica Chen," Ziggaut, tusks painted a drab olive, said as she boarded.

"Hello," she said. "How are you today?"

About a minute passed before Ziggaut answered her in a quiet voice. "I am good," Ziggaut said. "And you?"

"My son hates me," she said. "I took away his ramos and he told me I was going to make him the most hated member of his school."

"He sounds wise, your child," Ziggaut said. They didn't converse for the rest of the trip, and since there were only two of them in the branch-boat, Jessica found herself fidgeting and looking out at the scenery quite a bit. They were passing over the Mondrott, one of the major rivers of the region, which separated the main forest village from the local Yorn reservation. Jessica knew little about them, save that they seemed equivalent to the Amish, more or less (they were definitely pacifists), and they were regarded with a mix of curiosity and revulsion by most Eosfi. There were a lot of jokes about them; Kupp had told her some once and Jessica hadn't understood them at all.

She looked over the side as the boat moved, and fingered the diamond-prism leaf in her pocket. She took it out to look at it, but her fingers weren't working properly and she gasped when the leaf almost fluttered out of her hands and she thrust it back into her pocket, terrified of losing it.

Her hands were clumsy because it had been a long night. Bobby had refused to give up the *ramos* at first, despite her explanations. She took the line that it was too dangerous at first, but Bobby pointed out (and his logic was, for a thirteen-year-old, trenchant) that none of his Eosfi friends seemed worried about it, nor did their parents. Changing her tack, Jessica said that what was appropriate for the Eosfi wasn't appropriate for Earthlings. (She had used this before, to keep Bobby from excessive branch-swinging—his lack of tentacles had made this argument pretty knockdown at the time.) But Bobby had anticipated this move and produced a thorough list of fellow humans whose parents were allowing them to engage in the ritual. Jessica said it was no secret that there were some dreadful parents in the world, but that didn't mean she had to be one of them; Bobby said he wished he *had* one of the dreadful parents for his mother, because none of them could be bad as her. The tone of the discussion degenerated from there. Bobby went into a massive sulk after Jessica simply took the *ramos* away; she had thought he would be feeling better by the morning, but in fact he was not speaking to her. So she had gotten maybe three hours of sleep the night before, and was just nodding off when she heard Ziggaut's voice announce: "We've arrived."

Jessica started and looked up. She had once had, in college, a roommate who went an entire semester without once doing the laundry or washing a dish. But that was nothing compared to what she saw. Dr. Hand's section of the tree was unruly, but this was sheer wilderness. There were no cleared paths, no real sign of civilization at all, nothing but thick masses of leaves and wild branches shooting out of every larger branch like porcupine bristles.

An Eosfi voice began singing, a strange, rhythmless melody. Another voice joined in, singing more or less the same tune, but starting at a different part and not bothering to try and catch up.

Two other voices joined in, and the resulting cacophony was like a John Cage piece. One of the voices dropped out—maybe the voice that had begun the song, maybe one of the ones that had joined in subsequently, Jessica couldn't tell—and the other three babbled for a while until each one dropped out, the final one quitting in, it seemed to Jessica, mid-syllable.

The last voice had sounded nearby, so Ziggaut called out a greeting the major Eosfi language. There was a rustling in the thick murk of the leaves, and then an Eosfi emerged into their presence.

It was smaller and scrawnier than Ziggaut, the size of an adolescent, but clearly an adult, judging by the size of the tusks. The tusks were unpainted, which in the regular Eosfi communities would have given the impression of being shamefully poor or else having just finished washing. The yorn stared at Jessica, started to raise a tentacle towards her, and then pulled it away. Without taking its eye off of Jessica, it spoke to Ziggaut in a few terse syllables of Eosfi. Ziggaut replied and then said to Jessica, "This is Yorn Atran. Yorn Atran is the yorn who deals with outsiders. It will be your guide in the community and show you the human area."

Jessica paused, wondering whether to trust Ziggaut or not, but finally decided she had no choice and said, "Tell Yorn Atran I am very thankful for its help today, and also thankful that its people are taking us in."

Ziggaut spoke to Yorn Atran in Eosfi. Yorn Atran turned away from Jessica and spoke sharply to Ziggaut, who immediately became pale and started wheezing.

"What is it?" Jessica asked. "What does it say?"

"Hroom, hroom, hroom," Ziggaut sounded like it was choking. "It says nothing—only a formality —"

"*Nik babbita-ramos! Nik babbita-ramos!*" Yorn Atran squeaked, slapping the branch underfoot with two tentacles.

Ziggaut took one, two, three deep breaths in and out, then turned to Jessica and said, "Yorn Atran says, hroom hroom, that the Yorn will always welcome those who are, hroom hroom, hroom hroom, not holders of the knife." Ziggaut sighed, looking exhausted from this exchange.

Yorn Atran placed its tentacles on an overhead branch that ran more or less along the same path as the branch they were standing on, and began moving into the growth. Ziggaut did the same, while Jessica walked behind them. Because of all the sub-branches and slippery moss growing out of the branch, Yorn Atran took it rather slowly, and Ziggaut, used to the cleanly pruned urban branches, was slower still. As Jessica walked slowly behind them, she saw an occasional head peeping out of the thick growth, then darting back, each with the same underfed, plain-tusked look as Yorn Atran. Every so often, the harmony-less, rhythm-less melody began again and minutes later it would just end, as if because of a distraction.

After about forty minutes, they stopped walking nowhere in particular. Yorn Atran spoke to Ziggaut, who turned to Jessica and said, "This is where the human settlement will be."

Jessica felt like she was going to cry.

"Historically, we have taken care of them because they were mystics in the old religion," Ziggaut explained as they boated back. "So even now we send them money, foodstuffs, building supplies. Every few years, the liberals on the council will say that they would be better off it they hung from their own five tentacles. And then we will cut off their funding for a while, and conditions will not improve, and the conservatives will reassert their historical prerogative and we will spend money on them again. It does not solve any problems either way, but it makes us feel good."

For Jessica, the idea was tantamount to living with a thousand Dr. Hands. She couldn't imagine building a house, raising a child, under such conditions—apparently, the Yorn didn't maintain any regular schooling for their children or do any real trade or commerce beyond gathering free-growing food. For a minute she started to waver, and Ziggaut, politician that it was, must have sensed it, for it extended a tentacle and said:

"It doesn't have to be that way, Jessica Chen," Ziggaut said. "Give your child his ramos and let him know true fellowship. Many in your community will be influenced by you."

She saw the long scar on its tentacle, and realized that could be Bobby's head. And once again, she felt that yawning gulf of space and stars between her and her husband, and she knew there was only one piece of him left that she could really get her hands on and that was Bobby. And she had made a silent promise to Bobby: *you will be protected.*

"Why can't we just live among you without it?" she said.

"Impossible," Ziggaut said. "And I, hroom hroom hroom, decline to discuss it further. If you would —"

Her handheld's communication line buzzed and she picked it up.

It was her babysitter. Bobby had run away.

It was raining when she got home, and so she didn't see Dr. Hand, leaning against her tree house.

"Your boy's in my yard somewhere," he said. She jumped. Then she jumped again when she saw him. He looked like a stick painted light gray, with milky blue eyes, a few strings of hair pushed down against his head by the rain, and a lump the size of a curled thumb jutting out of his forehead.

He must have noticed her staring, because he said, "It's cancer."

"*I wasn't looking!*" Jessica yelled, jerking away and knocking over a bottle. "Oh, God! I'm sorry, I'm sorry, you know? I'm just . . . I'm sorry."

"Yes," Dr. Hand said, with a little smirk. "I think it's something in the air here. I've heard of a few other people getting something similar; not many." He sounded as if he were discussing the price of soil.

"Have you seen him?" she asked.

Dr. Hand motioned vaguely in the direction of the tangle where he lived. "I saw him run in there an hour or so ago. I didn't see him come out."

Jessica trembled. Bobby could have easily gotten lost in there. But it wasn't that big, was it? The Eosfi had their Rip-Van-Winkle stories of being lost in a tree and finding one's way out only after a thousand years. But there was nothing else to do but keep looking. Drawing a deep breath, she started to walk in.

"Would you like some help?" Dr. Hand said, right as she stood at the border of the tangle.

"Yes," she said. "Oh, yes. You can't imagine what that would mean."

"Well, I didn't have much else to do. It's not as if I spend a lot of time gardening." He chuckled, then broke into a fit of coughing. He removed a small bottle from his pocket and put it to his lips. "Want some?" he asked. "You can make an all right whiskey from some of the roots here."

"Oh, hell yes," Jessica said, and took a quick swallow. Her mouth burned and she realized that Dr. Hand's standards of "all right" for whiskey were very different from hers. But it stilled the clamor of her nerves, and she handed the bottle back to Dr. Hand with a tiny smile and together they walked into the tangle that was his area. A branch sprang into her mouth as she took a careless step forward. It tasted sour and dry, and as she yanked it out, a thorn scraped the roof of her mouth and drew a thin trickle of blood. She looked back. Dr. Hand was right behind her, peering into the darkness.

"You may as well know," she said to him. "My son ran away from me because . . . there's this coming-of-age ritual that the Eosfi do and —"

"Sure," Dr. Hand said, still staring out. "The ramos-reed. I know all about it."

"Oh," she said. Then she turned away and yelled "*Bobby!*" into the blackness. Nothing but the bitter smell of roots and twigs, and the occasional rustle of the light wind.

"I guess," Dr. Hand said, following her as she walked, "that he doesn't want to do it. And you're trying to make him."

"No," Jessica said. "I won't let him. It's too dangerous. *Bobby!*" Nothing.

"Good for you," Dr. Hand said. "Keep him away from it."

Jessica's shoulders sagged with relief. "Oh, that is so right," she said. "I can't believe they let their own children do it. They're a modern people in so many ways, and this, this thing, it's just so dark ages."

Dr. Hand had the bottle to his lips, but he spat a burst of liquor out when Jessica said this. "Savage? Dark ages? That's awfully—I mean, that's really—that's sort of condescending, don't you think? I mean, have you thought about it? What do you know about it?"

Jessica muttered something noncommittal; she didn't want to talk about it anymore and was worried that Dr. Hand might be some sort of crank. She wandered off to the right and called Bobby's name again. But Dr. Hand stayed where he was and continued talking.

"Biology isn't destiny, but it certainly does a lot—destiny with blinders and a hand tied behind its back. All tied up in their reproductive pattern, it is. You can never tell whose spores fertilize who, so you never know who half your parents are, and the other half don't get *terribly* attached to their children either. There's enough maternal instinct to get the kids old enough to fend for themselves, but no *families*. So there's very little in the way of models for them of cooperation and group loyalty; very naturally individualistic. I mean, you see all that.

"That's what the ramos-mates do for them. Like fraternity initiations, or puberty rites. But more important for them. The ramos-reed keeps the whole society together."

It seemed to Jessica that Dr. Hand had been waiting a long time to say this to somebody. "I'm sure you're right," she said, her eyes darting. "But they cut each other up. Nobody cuts my son for any reason."

There was a noise, somewhere to the right. Jessica took off for it. Dr. Hand didn't move. She ran until she found a small animal rolling around, and she collapsed to her knees, calling Bobby's name over and over again. She had failed. All she wanted to do was protect him, was protect that last link to her husband, to Earth, and she had failed.

Dr. Hand caught up to her. "So," he continued. "You're quite sure that you don't want your son to do it?"

"Please stop," she said wearily. "I have to find my son. I have to find —"

"He's in my cottage," Dr. Hand said. "He's all right, you know. Just sleeping. He wore himself out running and I told him he could stay. I had to make sure that you weren't going to let him; it's important."

Jessica stood looking at Dr. Hand for a long time, at his skin stretched over his bones like too little paper on too large a present, at his tumor, jutting out of his head like a second nose.

"Take me to him now," she finally said. "Or I'll kill you."

Dr. Hand meekly led her back to the cottage, where she found Bobby lying on a mat on the ground, dead tired; he passively allowed his mother to awaken him.

"I don't know," she said to Dr. Hand, "whether to thank you or hit you. So I'm just going to go."

"Look at this." He motioned her to a small statue on the wall, one of an Eosfi with three bandaged tentacles. "This is Metto, a mythical ruler of theirs from the Keskilon-to period; this is how it's depicted in one of their greatest tragic dramas.

"The idea," Hand said, leaning in close to Jessica. He smelled like a brewery. "The *plot* is that Metto here lost three of his tentacles in his own ramos-reed. And he burns in anger over it. Of course, to express any kind of anger or resentment over such an injury is extremely taboo. But not only does Metto—who is quite noble in many ways, brave, intelligent, and decent—express his secret anger over it, he actually hunts down all its ramos-mates and kills them. It never finds out which one has done it, though, and that is Metto's most forbidden wandering of all. And, of course, the way the rite is structured, you're all blindfolded, you can't ever know. In the end the gods curse and destroy Metto. I had to see it, even though I skulked around in the back. So you see, the rite creates a center of guilt as well as loyalty; bottomless gulfs as well as shimmering rainbow peaks. You might say it creates their souls.

"Would they be better off eating hamburgers and listening to rock music? It's not as if the ramos-reed is entirely secure. Every year a larger minority wanted to opt out when we met up with them. We made it worse. The conservatives in their legislature have fought very hard on this issue, but the forces of cultural contamination are stronger than you can imagine.

"That's why I blew up the Gate.

"It wasn't easy, but it wasn't as hard as I thought; I had to deal with some unsavory people, human supremacists, but they needed somebody to work the other end of the Gate, so that two simultaneous nuclear explosions on opposite ends of a hyperspace tunnel would seal of the circuit and make further Gate-building impossible for light-months around both areas. Getting the bomb through customs, hiding it, making the announcement so the Gate would be evacuated—all tricky, to be sure, but actually easier than I thought. And now this planet is safe."

Jessica opened her mouth, but found nothing to say, as if a blanket had been thrown over her memory of words, utterly opaque.

"So don't undo it," Dr. Hand continued, in a voice both trembling and triumphant. "Take your boy to the Yorn colony and stay there. And discourage him from having any kids of his own." He cradled the empty bottle in his hands like an infant. "Protect them from us."

"I have to go now," Jessica said. It was all she could say.

Later, as Jessica was standing on her own front porch, she fished into her pocket and found (with Bobby tucked away in bed) the *ramos*, and the diamond-prism leaf she had been saving. A light gust of wind took the leaf from her hands and, with a microscopic gasp of panic, she tried to pluck it out of the air, but it escaped her, fluttering to and fro on tiny, abortive little quests as it danced.

She watched with a small tingle of fear, waiting for it to rip or for holes to appear. But it proved not so fragile.

Then, her mind wholly made up, she went into Bobby's room and woke him up.

"*Mom*," he whined. "I'm *sleeping*."

"Yes, I know. This will just be a minute." She opened up his small, strong hand and, covering it with her own, placed the ramos in it.

"Take this back," she said. "Take it and keep it and use it when the time comes, Bobby. We're going to stay here, and so I want you to do this."

Sleepily, Bobby stared at his hand, then looked at her and, his lip quivering, said, "Mom . . . thanks. I —"

"And for God's sake, Bobby," she said, squeezing his hand even harder, as if trying to keep hold of a keychain in a hurricane. "For God's sake, Bobby, be *careful*. Be *careful*." It was all she could say, as she let him go.

Hour by Hour
by Lindsey Duncan

Fate pooled at high tide around her and brought with it a taste of the future: cold streets, a slanted moon overhead, and a sense of loss, blindness six layers deep.

The priestess paused in mid-step, sucking in a long breath of apple-blossom air to remind herself where she was. Quiramene Telari, now known as Apex of the Hours, was accustomed to such premonitions—they were part of her calling—but never personal ones. She knew what it meant: her time as a priestess was almost at an end.

She fenced with the idea in her mind, but could not defeat it. Troubled, she wandered under the speckled shadows of the garden, rubbing at her face. She had to remain calm. The morning was still young, which meant one of her sisters—Leniya or Camuri, she was not sure of the exact time—could see her if they looked. As translator of the Hours, the Apex could not be seen to falter.

"Priestess?"

An initiate of Sielyn stood before her in colorless grey robes, fingers nervously twined. She mustered a smile for him. "What is it?"

"The High Canonite summons the Hours to the pearl chamber," he said. "The king of Alzhara needs a murder investigated."

Quiramene blinked in surprise. "He didn't tell the king that we're not the guard?" That each Hour could see anything that had happened within her time had never been meant as a tool. It took a great deal out of them, and with Sielyn's sanctuary on the borders of three major kingdoms, there was too much death and mayhem to trace even a fraction of it. She had railed against it, so long ago, but the Hours existed for one purpose: to steady the course of time and keep Fate in its banks. There were still moments when the chaos of possibility exploded, when anything could and did happen, but at least there was a rhythm to the floods.

"The king claims that the matter involves the future stability of his kingdom," the initiate answered. "And ah, the High Canonite believes that this is important enough to disrupt your devotions."

It was. Alzhara was on the fringe of the Principality, and it was the only buffer between the loose alliance of nations and the tyranny of the north. If it fell. . ." I'll summon them," she said. "Tell the king we will meet with him at noon."

The initiate bobbed his head and scurried away. Quiramene set out across the garden, looking for the afternoon Hours first—and Twilight, who could speak to the priestesses of the evening. The young Apex was a small woman, entirely unprepossessing, with tight cinnamon curls and almost no nose. Alone of those who had taken the oath of the Hours, she still spoke a language other than time. Had she removed the silver necklace into earpiece she wore and stepped out of the sanctuary, she might have been mistaken for anyone.

Camuri was performing her devotions in the chamber, and so she informed Leniya first. "Find Dawn," she said. "See if she can rouse the nights."

Within twenty minutes, only two of them were missing: one of the evenings who had contracted a cold, and Midnight, who had problems of her own. Quiramene checked the sundial; not a lot of time. After a brief hesitation, she sent Twilight to find the invalid. She went herself for Midnight, without a word to the others. She might not be able to translate the gap between them, but the darkest of the Hours needed a firm hand.

Polite knocking garnered no answer. She turned the handle to find the door locked. More hammering, finally calling her name. Midnight would understand the tone if not the words. Quiramene was about to send for the master key when the lock clicked. Midnight stood there, disheveled, dark blotches painted under her eyes, her hair parted in six different places and wrenched into deliberate knots.

Quiramene mimed, as she had learned to. She wondered how the other Hours endured this, losing their capacity for speech to the flow of time. She, as liaison, kept her own words while still being to talk to the daylight Hours. The lucky one.

Midnight nodded once and started down the hallway, no sign of surprise or curiosity in her manner. Quiramene hurried after her, protesting. She shaped a crown with her hands. Did Midnight understand they were going to confront royalty?

The darkest of the Hours paused and looked at her with flat eyes, no expression. Then she turned and continued up the hall.

Quiramene shook her head, trying not to feel like a lackey. Midnight had been in the sanctuary longer than she, and none of them, not even those Hours who had stepped aside to let others take their places, knew her real name or where she had come from.

Quiramene opened the doors to the pearl chamber and ushered them in, her head buzzing as each spoke. Degrees of separation determined who could understand who, the rest a tumult of words she tried to ignore. The Hours had a complex pecking order amongst themselves, or rather several, one in each bracket of comprehension. These were politics their visitor would never see.

"Send him in," she said to the herald.

King Yrrain of Alzhara was far from his prime and far from his dotage, a sharp man chiseled in silver hair and copper skin. For this meeting, he had eschewed the symbols of his office save for the single gold chain worn diagonal across his tunic. A man of metals, truly, and hard as that precious ore as he approached and bowed to the perfect circle of women around him.

"Hours of Sielyn," he said, "thank you for granting me this audience and your all-seeing eyes."

"Speak to me, your highness," Quiramene said with a bow of her head. "I must translate for my sisters." She paused, fumbling in her mind for the right words. Even as liaison, she was no stateswoman. She opted to come straight to the point. "How long ago was this murder?"

Yrrain grinned. It was a fierce expression; it took her a moment to see the amusement in it, as well. "Hasn't happened yet."

Quiramene blinked. "There are hundreds of days ahead of us," she said. "We can't hunt blindly."

The mornings and afternoons, who could understand her, studied her quizzically. Feet tapped and bodies tensed, but no one broke the silence.

"I know exactly what day it will happen," Yrrain said, "A seer told me, but he couldn't give me any other details."

He spoke as monarchs did, of the expectation that prophecy should be cut and dried for his convenience. Quiramene contained a sigh. "We can work with that," she said. "When? And whose murder?"

"The first of summer." The amusement fled. "The murder is mine."

Quiramene cried out in surprise, and the Hours jumped to a woman. Leniya leaned over to her, pulling on her sleeve. "What is it?"

"Is it gruesome? What is he asking us to do?" This from one of the afternoons.

Quiramene frowned at the man before him. After a moment, she saw the tides pooling about him. Low tide: he could not change his fate. "He wants us to find out who is going to murder him."

Her side of the chamber hummed with exclamations; then Twilight and Dawn turned to the nether side to interpret, and soon she had to shout for calm.

Midnight slid out of the passage behind the monarch, her expression still blank. A hardened soldier, he whirled to confront her. He started to sigh in relief when he saw it was one more woman in featureless grey, then stared in consternation at the figure herself.

"Shadows," he muttered. He turned to face Quiramene. "Is there something wrong with her?"

She suspected he might not have been so blunt had he thought he could be understood. "Do you know how many fearsome acts are committed in the dead of the night, your highness?"

He considered this for a moment. "I would rather not." He cleared his throat. "Is there anything you need me to do?"

Quiramene hesitated. "You do understand that, even if we discover the killer, that you can't change your fate?" It was terribly hard to frame the next words. She wished for a more compassionate way to say them, though she had no attachment to him. "The rivers of time run calm in their banks now, and you yourself are at low tide."

Yrrain chuckled. "I understand that very well. I also understand that, second to the Principality—who have no access to me, thank the guards who have risked their lives!—the most likely people to want me dead are my own heirs. If one of them was responsible, then I have to know that."

Quiramene found herself admiring the man, who could look his doom in the eye and concentrate on what had to be done. She wished she could be so clear-headed; her own private ending would not leave her be. "It will take some time to review that day," she said. "Even given a day and a place, there are hundreds of moments and images. Do you want to wait outside?"

It was not a question, but he treated it as such. "That's perfectly fine," he said. He folded himself on the ground like a much younger man, heedless of her dismay.

Quiramene swallowed hard, glancing around her. "We must search our memories of Alzhara's capital, on the first day of this coming summer," she said. "We look for the murder of king Yrrain."

Dawn flashed a pearly smile. "This may be surprisingly easy," she said. "When was the last time we had a living subject in front of us?"

Twilight frowned. "Don't be too confident. There may be no one simple answer."

"Let's hope there is," Quiramene said. "I'd hate for him to blame a backache on us." With that, and one last anxious look at the monarch, she closed her eyes and thought of that day. Around her, she could hear Twilight and Dawn directing the other half of the circle.

No one spoke to Midnight. No one ever did.

It started as whispers and murmurs in the back of her mind, fleeting trickles of light with no shape or substance, and the scent of smoke. It was the smoke that carried her, for it was scent that told the age of a thing, more than sight or sound or even touch. Noonday in the capital: a raucous clattering of silverware, the bustling of servants, and everywhere a sweltering heat she could almost feel.

She saw Yrrain conversing with his daughter—Tinhilde, named for her Kalbryde mother—in quips and turns of phrase, sometimes laughing outright as she bested him. His eldest son, an ebon-haired hound, pounding the table and declaring his intention to call some young man out on the honor of his lady love. Everywhere the aroma of exotic Alzhara spice as they reclined on cushions under the every-colored awnings of silk. The heat had not yet driven them inside.

The younger son absent, talked about—burrowed in his books and more wont to spark conversation with his absence than by anything he usually said. This was a family bent to destroy itself? Quiramene could not see it. True, a man nigh on thirty like Yrrain's elder son might indeed chafe at the bit, but...

News at the table, a servitor pale and grave. The Principality had made a successful incursion on the northern border. The older son who so freely tossed his honor about had not been there to lead his troops.

The daughter on her feet now, making an argument that seemed well-tracked in the dust. She could marry into the first family of the princes, surely win them some time.

"No daughter of mine is meat for their spit," Yrrain growled.

The elder son pasted a smile onto his harried face. "And where is your chosen son and his pet theories, eh?"

"They should not have risked crossing the border," the king said, with only a brief, absentminded scowl to his offspring. "Everything I know indicates—"

"I see something," Twilight said, jarring Quiramene back to the present.

She looked towards Yrrain, but could not tell how much time had passed by him: he looked as comfortable as ever, eyes slightly lidded. At the exclamation, though he could not understand it from a priestess who spoke time and nothing else, his eyes flew open and landed piercing on Quiramene.

She tried to smile, meaning to reassure him, but the expression was faint. "What do you see?"

"The garden. Sunset. Yrrain walking off the effects of the evening meal." Twilight's lips twitched with some passing amusement. "The man approaches him on a cross-path. Burly, dark-haired. Some family resemblance. A dagger in his hand. They greet each other, embrace heartily, and the blade goes between his ribs." Her tone was cool, composed, a recitation without emotion. Her eyes darted up to Quiramene's. "I don't think the matter is this simple."

She was used to Twilight's pessimism, but she had to be thorough. "What leads you to believe that?"

"Nothing I saw. Instinct."

Midnight's eyes flicked up, a sudden guttering of intensity. She seemed about to speak, then looked away.

Quiramene sighed inwardly and turned her attention to the monarch. "I have an answer for you," she said.

He arched a brow. "That was quick."

"At sunset on the day you indicated, your elder son—" she chewed on her lip "—puts a blade between your ribs. My sympathies are. . ." she hastened on.

"Wait!" Leniya cried.

Quiramene turned hastily to face her. "What is it?"

"The younger son, with the weaselly face." Though she tried to conceal it, Leniya flushed with pleasure at having something to contribute. New to the Hours, this was her first time seeking the future. "He poured something into his morning cup of heira."

She didn't want this complication. Perhaps if she just forgot about it . . . Yrrain wanted his successor to be innocent, but was any royal child? "Are you sure—" she paused, realizing if she did not choose her words carefully, she would give the truth away. "Might it have been meant to help? Sometimes even the most scoring insults can be intended as advice."

Leniya squinted at her, clearly unsure why the question had been phrased so. "No, it couldn't be," she said. "I'm an apothecary's daughter, and I know what poison looks like."

Quiramene schooled her features. "I see."

Yrrain frowned, glancing from one to the other. "What is it, priestess?"

She hesitated. "I. . ."And prepared or not, she could not lie to him. She sighed low in her throat. "You were also poisoned, your highness. I'm so sorry. It was—"

"Unless you were behind it," he said sharply, "there's no need for apologies. My younger son, I'd guess?"

Quiramene bowed her head. "Maybe it doesn't make a difference?" she offered. "The poison never had a chance to work."

"You could just as easily argue that my elder son's attack doesn't matter, because I was already effectively dead." Yrrain shook his head. His face was strained, emotion lined deep within it. "At least I still have a daughter." He closed his eyes, breathing deeply. A man who had been fighting on the fields of both war and politics for decades must have control more than she could possibly imagine, but some things could not be contained. "I love them all, you know."

"I can only imagine." Quiramene kept a close rein on a heart that wanted to break for him. Midnight made a sound like a hiss and turned as if to exit the chamber. She was stopped, without a word, by the Hours to either side of her. The gyrations forced the Apex to notice the whispering between the two Hours directly to Midnight's right. "I can only say—"

"Apex?" Dawn smiled ruefully. "I think there is one final piece in play."

Quiramene nodded once. "Tell me." She was somewhat troubled by the behavior of the darkest Hour, but even before her ascendance, Midnight had been surly and restless. Yrrain's inquiry was more important, even though there could be no good end to it . . . perhaps because there could be no good end to it.

Dawn spoke to the Hours, humming and smiling with every evidence of encouragement. "They say that in the early hours of the next morning, the raven-haired daughter met with a demon sorcerer from the Principality. She canceled his contract to kill her father."

Quiramene went white. Betrayed by all his children, the kingdom without a viable heir . . . it was a terrible choice she had to offer him. "Your highness."

"Priestess?" He looked at her in confusion that quickly faded to recognition, then resignation. "Tinhilde. No, don't tell me how. I already know I don't survive the first two attempts, and I want to remember my. . ." He held up a defensive hand as he rose. "You've answered all my questions more completely than I could have hoped."

The irony bit deeply. Quiramene rose before she could think about it, hurrying across the floor to him. "Your highness, can you not appoint a trusted general? An advisor?"

He shook his head. "My children were raised at the feet of my most trusted hands. Familiarity breeds contempt. If they could kill me, they would just as readily push us into civil war."

Quiramene made herself nod. "If there is anything I can do, in the name of Sielyn, please let me know."

Yrrain sighed in slow steps, the sound slow and controlled. He placed a light hand on her shoulder. "Priestess, you are only the messenger. Is there any chance that the tides might flood and my seer be wrong?"

She shook her head. "Not while the Hours keep Fate in trust, your highness."

His eyes darkened with weariness. "Then I have my answer." He reached up to touch her cheek. "Thank you for—"

An unholy screech filled the air, and a dark blur slammed into Yrrain, driving him backwards. Quiramene jumped back with a cry, shouting for the guards even as they broke down the door. Their weapons faltered, however, when they saw that the cause of the disturbance was Midnight, her chest heaving, her eyes staring at the king of Alzhara as she ranted, her voice as loud as a storm at sea now.

The evenings and the nights were on their feet just as quickly, shouting, almost drowning out their sister. Dawn and Twilight stood as well, speaking almost in unison. Quiramene stumbled back to her chair, her mind spinning, while the Alzharan monarch stood back with hands spread in reassuring fashion.

"He dwelt on it. One late night," Dawn said, her voice a whisper.

"Two," Twilight continued.

"Three."

"He found that though he had saved himself from the tides of Fate—"

"—he could not live with the crime he had committed." Dawn swallowed hard. "Apex, can't you see—" She swooned back into her chair.

Quiramene saw with terrible clarity. "Sielyn save," she whispered. "He's going to kill us."

They had seen it. His tide was low, the future was clear. Quiramene trembled wildly, realizing the import of her visions. The blindness was not that of retirement. Their deaths would set Fate free like a wild river, and he could change everything.

The guards moved in, the captain reaching for the king's arm with no gentleness. "The High Canonite will want to speak to you."

"Enough of this!" Yrrain barked. "Do you really think that I . . . would. . ." He looked around him, the words fading away.

"The Principality will win an overwhelming victory." Twilight spoke alone now. "It will become of paramount importance that the king keep his position or have an heir he can trust. We have left him with neither." She shot a quick look at Quiramene. "But that does not justify killing us!"

She turned to him. "If it was the only way you could save your kingdom?"

Yrrain was silent for a long time. Then he bowed his head. "A canny man would lie to that. I cannot countenance what that man would be forced to do."

Could one punish a man for a crime he had not yet committed? There was no question that this course of events would play out exactly as they had seen, but Quiramene could not make herself believe it. There had to be a way she could save her sisters, and keep this brave man on his course . . .

"Apex," Leniya said, bright and wondering, "I see you there."

The pieces fell into place.

"Wait." Quiramene rose, and was surprised when her soft voice brought the entire chamber to a halt. Even the ineffable Midnight, the raven who had brought this misfortune to light, watched her intently. "Your kingdom needs a strong ruler. What about one who has the blessing of a goddess?"

Yrrain's brows darted up. He apprehended the situation instantly, not even hesitating for confirmation. "My children were raised in devotion to our gods, it is true. But honestly, I don't see you as a ruler, whatever your visions have shown you, and whatever diplomacy you've had to utter in these halls."

"That's fair." She sucked in a breath. "Marry me to one of your generals, your advisors. My tide is high, your highness. If your fate cannot be changed, mine is very susceptible."

Dawn straightened, eyes wide. "Surely you can't be serious, Apex."

Yrrain took a step back and studied Quiramene skeptically. "You'd be willing to do that? To be a puppet, yet face the heat of Alzhara and the Principality alike?"

It was not a pun, and only the tension of the moment made her want to laugh. "I would, if you can trust me," she said. "Maybe as new possibilities show themselves, there won't be any need for this."

The chamber fell silent, a thing that never happened when so many voices spoke in round. The Hours stopped their whispering and watched.

"Or maybe there will, but I trust your vision more than I trust mine." Yrrain offered his hand, not as a courtier but a grip strong and firm. "Do you have a name other than Apex?"

"Quiramene Telari, your highness."

"Of the city-state of Vanhar?" He seemed surprised. "Your bloodlines do you credit."

Leniya flitted a quick, startled look to Dawn. "She's a noblewoman?" she squeaked.

"Heir in her own right," Twilight said with a small smile after one of the afternoons had translated for her. "You'd think she would have told us." The young Hour looked somewhat nettled.

"Lost in translation," Dawn said.

Quiramene turned her head then, more by chance than intention, and looked beyond the king of Alzhara to where Midnight stood. For the first time, the darkest of the Hours smiled.

Whatever she saw in the depths of a hundred nights, for once it gave her peace.

The Watchers
it's called the eye of the storm
for a reason

—Patricia Kelly

In the Season of Blue Storms
by Jude-Marie Green

In the four seasons since his naming, Naschi had built up herds of nutrient balloons rich in particulate density enhancing his own spectra - an intense bright oxygen blue. Now though, he was weak, slow in speed, pale in color, unable even to plant his foot on the planet's hot, restoring surface.

The blue storm was in trouble. He was on the outskirts of his storm family, ostracized and perhaps dying. His balloons needed nourishment. They were pale turquoise rather than the strong oxygen blue they should have been. The encounter with Coromell had worn him out. She had taken the largest part of his life force.

Coromell. He had strayed to the outskirts of his storm cluster. Other storm clusters smelled different from his group. Some smelled like salt, some of the bitter acids churned up from the planet's depths. His own storm cluster smelled of electrified oxygen and sported blue-shaded bands from crown to foot. He allowed his outer bands to touch the fingers of an anonymous green storm which swirled away from him and then he saw her.

She advanced on his bands then brushed into him. The brief contact generated long trails of sparks and cancelled some of his momentum.

Naschi swirled faster, inviting her closer. She ignored his advancing storm front and gusted away. Her droplets left behind a unique perfume of salt and electricity that he found irresistible. Her swirling bands of pink and peach mesmerized him. He followed as she twirled into his storm cluster.

She dived from her heights towards two lower storms. The juvenile blue storms shivered as she engulfed them.

They tried to separate from her. Her coriolis force caught at their edges and pulled them close. Their bands unraveled into her winds. The blue mineral threads wrapped her then melted into her. Her funnel swelled and spun even more fiercely. The young storms disappeared.

Naschi swirled, aghast at her actions. Juvenile storms were not strong enough to merge or even to share. He had met these younger brothers; they weren't even named yet. To get her attention, he threw a bolt of hot lightning at her.

"Who are you?" he said.

Her bands slowed as she tasted him then she twirled fast, spraying droplets. Her calm center expanded, forcing her bands up and out, tall and far. She shivered then split into double-funnels and danced around him.

Naschi screamed then threw himself at her.

She consumed him, her pink and peach bands of storm melding into his azure winds. Her winds shaded to purple and slowed.

She spat him out. He was much weaker, a pale washed blue. She had stolen from his herds and the ones that remained rumbled with electric hunger.

She snarled, "I am Coromell," then she swirled away.

Samma Jordan thought the survey ship's profile perfectly reflected the dual nature of its mission. The sleek cabin where she and Pachan Dao lived and worked and . . . did whatever they did while Versys wasn't looking . . . was married to a bulbous science bay that held the mission's precious cargo of probes and satellites.

Versys, the mining corporation, employed Pachan. He worked in the cabin, controlling probes and synthesizing data. The numbers might have been enough to keep Pachan fascinated—and employed—but Samma needed more to work with. HQ had leased her services to Versys to find life on the surveyed worlds. All the long-range reconnaissance had indicated that the planet should offer flora and fauna to categorize, distinct ecologies to study. Up close, though, Pachan's probes hadn't found a thing.

Video feeds of the storms swirling across the planet's surface had fascinated them both for a while, but now Samma was bored. She assigned herself to checking inventory in the science bay.

She gritted her teeth as always at the sight of HQ's trademark plastered across every surface. Joint mission. Right. Versys paid exorbitant prices for HQ's technology, and they figured that gave them the right to put pressure on her, too. Like she was just another piece of replaceable gear. She'd hoped for more from HQ, but their last relay had been terse—almost angry.

Samma ran her hand over the holographic HQ logo on the satellite probe in its cradle. The adamantine crystal rocked under her hands.

Circuitry traces filled the inside of the teardrop-shaped probe along the flaws threaded through the crystal. It looked a bit like an enormous Easter egg filled with smoke and foil.

She gave in to the urge to climb onto it. The probe rocked as she vaulted up but she kept her balance. She straddled it like a rocking horse then laid out full-length. The cold crystal tickled her cheek.

Her eyes were only closed for a few minutes before she smelled Pachan's deodorant soap. Seven years together in this small space and he still took pains to stay clean and smell nice.

"How long before it hatches?" he said.

She grinned and slid off the crystal.

"I thought perhaps we could send in another probe to replace number eight," she said. "Think you could program it?"

Pachan shook his head. "We don't need it. The other probes made groundfall. They're sending back consistent data. Another probe now would be a waste."

"Consistent," Samma said. "You mean no change. Blasted wind-battered ground and minimal ocean. No life. The verdict hasn't changed."

"We haven't processed all the data yet," Pachan said, "and we've only surveyed ten percent of the planet. Look, anything could be down there."

"Anything but life," Samma retorted. She took a deep breath then sighed. "I'm sorry. I'm just frustrated. We've been here a week and there's nothing I can use. All we've done is generate tons of meaningless chemistry reports. We haven't even played 'Name That Planet'."

"What do you think we should name this place?" Pachan said.

She smiled at this familiar game they'd played so many times before.

"Planet of Blue Storms?"

"That's a terrible effort," Pachan said. "You know the girdle of blue that snakes around the southern hemisphere? Your 'Blue Storms'? Those are storms contaminated with oxygen and cobalt. The storms change dominance over time. The blue ones subside and the orange ones strengthen. After a while the green belt overwhelms the others. For a while anyway. Has something to do with the axial tilt."

Samma considered. "Rainbow World? How rich are the iridium veins?"

"More than average. The planet must have suffered some serious meteor impacts once upon a time. Anyway, you're showing too much imagination! They never name the planet based on the planet. I just got the update from Versys. They've named it 'Wexless.'"

"Let me guess: another partner?"

Pachan snorted. "Nope, it's the new wife."

She laughed. "That makes, what, four planets named after partners and eight for wives?"

"Someday I'll name a world after you," Pachan said, not looking at her. "I just need enough time to make a partner bonus."

Samma kissed the top of his head; he turned his face up to meet her lips.

"I don't have very long," Samma said, pulling back. "I mean, before Versys gives up on finding life and sends in the mining team."

"What do you want me to do?" Pachan said, spinning his chair around to face her. "I mean, they can't be expected to care about some mystery indigenes who probably don't even exist. Seven years and you've never found life anywhere."

"You're saying my work is useless? Or just that I'm incompetent?"

He blinked up at her. "Of course not. No one can hold you responsible if there's nothing to find."

He turned back to the displays as if that had settled everything. "Too bad none of the probes passed through the big red storm. I wonder if it's carrying iron ore."

She snorted. "That's only the most interesting system on the planet. Couldn't you have aimed better?"

He spun back, annoyed. "I don't know what to say to you when you get like this."

"When I get like this? They're going to split us *up,* Pachan. Doesn't that mean anything?"

"Of course they won't. We'll find something," he said. "If not here, then on the next one. We can't be unlucky forever."

The crystal teardrop seared through Naschi's cloud bands, tunneling laterally. He noticed it just in time to catch it with a shift of winds. He twirled it with a tiny whirlwind then funneled the crystal teardrop to one of his remaining herds of balloons that lived in the skirt of his calm center and waited while they engulfed it.

Naschi recovered from the encounter with Coromell by burying himself in his storm cluster. He didn't dare touch his foot to the ground. He feared his storm would spin out and dissipate. He stayed near the Ancients, old storms who wouldn't steal from him. He spoke to them and sometimes they answered.

"Who is Coromell?" he said once. The Ancients groaned and sizzled and sparked huge amounts of ozone. Naschi thought they'd ignore him forever; he considered other questions.

One of the Ancients spoke. Tepec was a skinny deep blue storm reputed to own fewer herds than a first season juvenile, though each airbag held uncountable treasures and food from the planetary depths. He trailed sparks from his bands as he spoke.

"One who was separated and longs to return," he groaned.

"Forever apart, forever yearning," agreed Pecer, the oldest of the blue Ancients.

"Coromell, Coromell, return to the Father and be consumed," thundered Tehau the fat.

Naschi shuddered. Where the Ancients touched him, he felt sliced apart. The words rebounded through his calm center and fueled his bands to faster speeds.

"The Father? You mean the Great Red Father of All Storms?"

Naschi had heard of Vardarac, the Father. All juveniles heard the stories passed along by the parent storms. Long ago, they said, a giant from the above passed by our world. Out of boredom the giant kicked the world and the world twisted. Three times he threw mountains from the above and they struck the ground. Red Vardarac sprang from the heat and fire of the strikes and vowed to battle the giant. He circled the world, waking storms by his angry passage. Together Vardarac and his brothers caught the mountains and hurled them back at the giant. Three times they hit the giant and at last he broke into too many pieces to count. The sky rained stones from the above, fire-bright brothers that brought the balloons. That though was another story.

Not all believed the stories, though. Who had seen the Great Red Father of All Storms? Naschi scoffed; no one storm could be that powerful. The blue Ancients would know the truth.

"Tell me about Vardarac," he said.

The Ancients groaned in that way of old storms and stopped talking. After a time they gently shoved Naschi away.

Naschi had to get Coromell to return to him. She'd take the crystal teardrop, he was sure of it. He would buy back his herds and his strength from her. He would merge with her and they'd spin out strong storm children.

He pulled the crystal teardrop from his herds' keeping and held it high in his bands. It refracted rainbows onto his clouds and gleamed with light. He let his neighbors know that this was a gift for Coromell.

"See!" he said. "With this, she can bribe a place from Vardarac himself!" His neighbors laughed at him but obligingly passed the message through the ranks of storms.

He waited only a short time before he scented her again. Her salt and mineral perfume floated on a wave of electricity. She swirled into view, her strong pink and peach bands flashing with red bolts of lightning. He cowered back from her, remembering the damage she'd done to him, then he surged forward and touched her.

"Coromell," he crooned. "I long for you. Coromell, merge with me!"

"Where is the crystal teardrop?" she demanded. She twirled around him, caressing him from crown to foot. The full contact tingled and Naschi stuttered when he replied.

"Here and it is yours." He hid the crystal teardrop with his balloons. "Yours, once we merge."

Coromell poured herself into him.

Samma nibbled Pachan's chest as they clung together in the vertical hammock. He wrapped his arms around her, grabbed a handful of her short hair, and tugged.

"Stop that," he said. "No bite marks."

She grinned at him.

An alarm buzzed just inches from Pachan's ear. He winced and smacked the cutoff button. The display blinked blue text.

"What's up?" Samma said.

"Looks like number eight started up again. We're getting info from its satellite." He slid out of her arms and padded barefoot to the monitoring station.

"Samma! Come look at this."

He was too excited for it to be mail from Versys or HQ. She fought free of the hammock. "What do you have?"

"Organic data, just what you've been looking for!"

She stared at the video screen. "They look like floating sacs of mineral ores. They're mudballs." She chewed her lip. "But they're organic mudballs. Do we have any additional data on them from the other probes?"

"Nothing yet. I'll send a zap to refresh the probes." He punched a key that sped a signal from the ship to the satellite to the probe.

"Ah damn! The return signal from number eight flatlined." He sighed.

"You fried the line just as it was sending useful data." Samma smacked the back of his seat. "Can't you bring it back up?"

"We'll have to wait for the program to cycle," he said. "At least half an hour. But we know number eight isn't dead; if its signal came up once, it'll come back again."

Naschi felt a herd of his precious balloons die and cupped them in a pillow of wind. The withered balloons oozed dry minerals and fused metals. They had been closest to the crystal teardrop; he'd tasked them with keeping it safe. Perhaps something from the crystal teardrop had killed his balloons. Naschi tasted the crystal teardrop and smelled the burned ozone on the foreign object. He understood that it had somehow poisoned his balloons. He opened a tunnel to the ground far below and let the crystal teardrop fall. Now that he had Coromell he didn't need the lure any longer. He turned his attention to his other half, his beloved Coromell.

"We should have done this long ago," they said together. "We've never felt so strong! Now we can go to Vardarac and merge with him?"

"What?" they said.

Naschi said separately, "What? I don't want to lose myself in a dream."

"Vardarac is not a dream, he's real. I've seen him."

"Why do you want him? Stay with me."

Coromell cried, "He's all I've ever wanted! Vardarac wouldn't take me, he required a larger tribute than I had. Your herds with the crystal teardrop and mine together are more than enough to buy entry. Come with me, let Vardarac persuade you." She spun against him; sparks seared through them both.

He read the truth of Vardarac in her electricity and scents.

"Vardarac will consume you. You won't exist," he said. "I won't exist." He pulled himself apart from her.

She screamed and flung herself into him, trying to shred his winds. He fought to free himself but she clung to him. He remembered a childhood trick to win free: he caught up her tailwind and flipped. She spun out three times before she pulled her bands away from him.

"Oh, you gentle breeze," she sneered. "I'll go to Vardarac alone!"

"Go, then," he said. He felt tired. He felt like stopping.

"I have the crystal teardrop," she said. She tossed it near Naschi, ready to snatch it if he reached out. "You promised it to me and then you threw it away. But I saw where you dropped it and I grabbed it. I'll give it to Vardarac!" She spun away.

"Coromell! No! It's poison, Vardarac will punish you for a treacherous gift," he shouted, but she was gone. Her flavor dissipated. "Oh, Coromell," he sighed.

Versys finally responded to their regular status reports. Pachan opened his message and whooped in glee.

"Bonuses!" he shouted. "Bonuses for both of us and guaranteed future percentages. We are rich. Not quite partner level, but rich!"

Samma barely heard him. She stared at her own message from HQ and slumped in her chair.

"My new orders just arrived from HQ," she said. "When Versys gets here I'm going back to the training station. I'm to be an instructor. You're staying here to help Versys apportion the planet."

"HQ can't just break us up," Pachan said. "We've been together for seven years and a dozen missions."

"A dozen missions and we've never found indigenous life. They must believe we're a bad team."

Pachan crossed his arms. "We don't have to accept the new orders."

"Sure, we'll just homestead here," Samma said. "We'll become the indigenous life. HQ can put us under the protection they give other worlds with non-human life and Versys can share its profits with us."

"I'll go to the training station with you."

"HQ is sending out a new partner for you," she said.

Pachan said, "Huh. Wonder why they think they can break us up?" He reached for her but she shrugged away.

"There's no life here. Nothing here! All these worlds we've seen and always nothing." Tears slipped down her cheeks.

"We still have some time," Pachan said. He put his arms around her and this time she didn't turn away. "You never know what might come up. And I'm not leaving you."

He held her until her tears ran dry.

Naschi agitated his nearest neighbors.

"I need to get to Vardarac before Coromell does," he told them. "Sweep me forward."

"You'll need to cross three clusters at least," said his orange uncle. "The girls come and go at will but you'll have to pay tribute. You'll lose your herds."

"I don't care," Naschi said. "I have to stop her before she gives the poisonous crystal teardrop to Vardarac. He'll stop her winds, he'll obliterate her herds."

"You should have gone with her, boy," the orange storm rumbled. "Get ready."

The orange uncle attached himself to Naschi all along his height then heaved him forward.

Naschi flew, for the first time ever untethered from the nurturing rich ground and the protective cluster of his family's blue storms. He bounced into the next cluster but didn't put down his foot. The big green storm sank into him and snatched a portion of his herds. Naschi felt them cry as they passed through his outer bands into the opaque protection of the big green storm.

Naschi was tossed three more times, flying first, sinking into strange clusters, losing parts of his herds. Nearby clusters laughed and jeered as he passed.

He descended into the cluster nearest Vardarac. He had few herds left, and he'd lost a good portion of his electricity-generating spin. He sank his foot to the planet's depths and pulled up some fresh momentum from the ground heat.

"We know what you want. Vardarac is just there," said the gold storm that touched him now. "And so is the lovely Coromell."

Naschi could smell her through the soup of iron salts that flavored the atmosphere. She closed in on him then touched him.

"Vardarac will take me this time," she said, "because of your unique gift to me."

Naschi said, "Don't give it to him. It's poison! It killed a herd of my balloons; that's why I dropped it." He tried to catch at her winds but his foot was stuck in the ground and Coromell danced away. Then she pounced.

He didn't resist but he held himself separate. He felt her electric flavor through his entire self, felt her surprise at his depleted state, felt her mercy as she pushed portions of her own herds into him.

He felt her withdraw just as they spun even with Vardarac.

The wall of red winds curved as far as they could see in either direction. Vardarac's bands shaded from dark cinnabar through ferric red to a pale copper blush. His winds flew by faster than any storm Naschi had ever known. The shriek of Vardarac's movement tore at them and they clutched their own winds together with difficulty.

Vardarac smelled of everything red. Naschi couldn't even smell himself in the great storm's presence.

The idea of joining with Vardarac's storm pulled at Naschi. To join with the legend would make him part of the legend. Juvenile storms would hear stories about brave Naschi and huge Vardarac.

Naschi quelled the thoughts with difficulty. Juveniles would hear about Vardarac. Naschi's name would be lost, consumed into Vardarac's legend like his winds lost in Vardarac's storms. Naschi pulled himself a little apart from the Great Red Father of All Storms.

Coromell shouted, "Vardarac! Great Father, let me merge with you. See, I have a gift to pay my way." She pulled the crystal teardrop into her outer bands for his inspection.

Naschi screamed "No!" even as Vardarac said, "So? Come in, then, Coromell, and welcome."

Coromell slid into his red vastness with no hesitation. Not even a moment of color change marked her passage.

Naschi threw himself at the Great Red Father of All Storms. Vardarac laughed and threw him back.

"Why do you think the crystal teardrop is poison?" Vardarac said as he soothed Naschi's winds.

Naschi told him.

Vardarac mused, "What happens once may happen again. I don't need the gift but I need Coromell's strength and youth. You say the crystal teardrop came from the above?" Vardarac produced the object and tossed it like a plaything. "I'll return it there."

He tasked a section of his storm bigger than Naschi to handle the crystal teardrop. The wind spun ever faster, funneling higher than even Vardarac's head. Lightning sizzled from its foot to its crown and then it squeezed tight, collapsing beneath the crystal teardrop to spit it into the above with explosive force. They watched the object disappear into the above. It didn't return.

"Don't fret for Coromell," Vardarac said. "This is what she has always wanted: to be part of me.

"Travel with me a while. Coromell thinks well of your company." Vardarac boomed laughter and nearby storms cringed, including Naschi. "Gentle breeze indeed!"

❁

Pachan spotted the activity on the monitors.

"Samma, look at this," he breathed. "Number eight just launched out of the gravity well and into orbit! It's above its satellite."

"I don't believe you," she said. "The probe doesn't *have* that much propulsion."

"Believe it," he replied, rechecking the monitors. "The data keeps coming in."

Samma held back for a moment. "Wait. Play back the overhead visuals from the slave satellite. What happened before number eight came out?"

In double-speed motion the probe fell back into the planet's atmosphere. A narrow twirling tornado swallowed the probe; its winds slowed and melted into the big red storm.

"The *storm* spat it out?" Pachan scratched his chin, puzzled.

"The storm spat it out," Samma's eyes were wide. "Look at the pressure exerted on the probe. That was a contrived propulsion.

"Let's backtrack," she continued. "Where has it been for the last few days?"

The spotty recording showed number eight's haphazard trek in the body of a cobalt-and-gallium-laden storm across swaths of other storm systems. Then another storm, a blue oxygen storm, possessed the probe. They watched this storm, the one number eight had originally pierced, handle the probe.

"Number eight never went to ground," Pachan leaned back in his chair, stunned.

"No. That storm caught it," Samma said.

"That wasn't random movement," he said slowly.

"No, that was *intelligent* movement. . ."

They stared at each other for a long moment, their grins slowly widening.

"Contact Versys," Samma crowed. "Call *off* the miners."

"You'll have to build up a synopsis and send the data to HQ," Pachan said. "There's a lot of work to do here. But first," and he stood and pulled her from her chair, "we celebrate!"

They twirled around the tiny cabin until Samma broke into fits of giggles; Pachan retrieved bulbs of strawberry juice from the nearby galley and saluted her as he returned.

"You always knew we'd find something," he said, handing her the bulb.

"No." She shook her finger at him and he grabbed it, pulling her close. "I always knew *you'd* find something. Now all we have to do is make contact."

He kissed her forehead and smoothed back her hair. "But how are we supposed to communicate with *weather*?"

"I don't know," she answered, leaning up against him. "We'll think of something."

A Season With the Geese

Once when we
were young, we flew
to Europe with the geese.
Twined neck to neck
we sailed the Seine
chasing ripples and water bugs,
lost ourselves in Madrid
when sudden snow
veiled us, white on white,
nested in crumbling ramparts
overlooking Rome until
blossoms cracked
the frozen meadows,
reviving spring.

Our season ended
we flew home
clipped our wings
devoted ourselves
to grounded lives.
Now I watch
my window as geese
feather the moon
and long for
one more flight.

—Rachel Swirsky

Goddess
by Jon Hansen

From the instant the goddess walked in, Ben couldn't take his eyes off her. Where other customers tracked in dirty imprints of their snow boots, she trailed rose petals, curling pink on the dirty linoleum. Not that she even *wore* boots, of course; her feet were bare, as was the rest of her, save for a few spans of strategically placed white silk. She wasn't the first divine creature Ben had seen, of course; he must have served a half-dozen avatars and godlings this week alone, more since they started serving Jamaican Blue. But this one. Oh, this one had power, made all the more compelling by the grey January morning squatting outside.

Automatically Ben set a tall dark espresso on the counter. Without a word the goddess took it, sweetened it by swirling one long finger in it, then strolled to the table at the window. She didn't offer to pay. Ben didn't ask. Horatio, the owner, had told him not to. "If you don't give them an offering, they'll never come back," he said whenever someone asked why. He thought deities were good for business, especially after a fiery-eyed war god had cracked open the skull of a would-be robber one Tuesday night. Ben didn't see an advantage to non-paying customers, divine or not, but sometimes they performed a minor miracle in place of a tip.

After a few minutes the whole coffeehouse began to smell like oranges and spices, the rich odors mingling with the scent of coffee. The bleakness outside seemed to fall away, and Ben found himself smiling a wide, goofy smile. He wiped at the counter with more enthusiasm than usual, then went to bus the tables left cluttered by the morning crowd.

He had several cups clinking together in the busbucket when she spoke. The air rippled with the force of the divine: "You are happy in your work?" Ben's skin crawled at the small of his back. He stopped, forced himself to look over at her. She was smiling at him, face radiant and mysterious.

With an effort he kept smiling. "Content, really."

"Then what pleases you so?" She took a sip, eyes fixed on him.

A slow turn shuddered through his brain. Why was she talking to *him*? True, he was the only other person there, but still. Other deities had spoken to him at times, true. But the key emphasis was *to* him, as if issuing proclamations from a cloud chariot. No interaction required, no response needed except to say, "As you command."

The realization she was trying to engage him in small talk gripped him with terror. Every myth said that the divine caused serious trouble when they took an interest in mortals. He had an urge to make up something to deflect her interest, or just walk away, but knew it would be a mistake. Lying to a deity would be bad. Ignoring one would be worse. Much worse. He took a deep breath, then let it out with the words, "It's just having you here."

The goddess laughed, the sound ringing drops of crystal sun. "I am very pleased to hear that." She set the cup down and stood, muscles rippling in her near naked splendor. Ben inhaled, sharp. He stiffened in an instant, then felt himself blush.

She glided closer to lay a warm hand on his arm. All the hair on Ben's arm stood up, electrified by her closeness. He discovered he was staring down at her chest, two tanned and magnificent breasts barely hidden behind the thin silk. He closed his eyes and willed himself not to drop the busbucket.

She whispered, a soft breeze in his ear. "You are charming, mortal, and not unattractive. It would delight me to retire to some place more private with you, removed from the harshness of this world."

He knew what she meant. Steady breaths. Tell the truth. "I am extremely flattered, but I cannot. As I said, I am content."

"Are you quite certain?" Now her hand stroked up the side of his arm, trailing those long fingers of hers. His heart pounded in his chest, so loud he'd have thought it impossible, considering to where all the blood in his body had rushed. Another minute of this might kill him.

Another breath. "I am certain," said Ben. The touch left his arm. He stood still, concentrating on his breathing until finally, he opened his eyes.

She was gone. Her cup rested on the table. From the ceramic bottom a cluster of small blue flowers had sprouted. He set it beside the tip jar, then finished cleaning.

After a bit some new, mortal, customers walked in, and Ben began to feel her presence lessened a bit. At three he went home, riding his bike down the center of snowplowed streets, watching for cars not watching for him, breathing out small clouds as he pedaled. Fifteen minutes later he hoisted his bike onto his front porch. It was a rental by the campus, a little shotgun house, shabby but nice. He propped the bike against the porch rail, reasonably confident no bike thieves would be out in this weather, then went inside. He hung his coat and scarf and black knit hat on the hooks by the door, then looked into the living room.

Kathryn dozed on the couch, under the green and black checked wool blanket they had bought a couple years ago on a spring break trip to San Diego, before their wedding, before their transplanting to middle America and grad school and domestic existence.

Ben stood in the doorway, watching her. She was everything the goddess was not: small and winter-pale and a little flabby in her softer places. She opened her eyes then and smiled, long and lazy, making her look like a mischievous six year old. "Hey," she said.

"Hey yourself," he said, then smiled back, with more love in his heart for her than it ever held for the distant spring.

Quantum Semantics

Remember the electron
from high school chemistry?
Its orbit was a crisp affair
—at least pictorially.

Today it wanders here-to-there
without ensuing travel.
No rendering can render it.
All portraitures unravel.

We miss our things, Neils Bohr,
our fabled solid ground
—a place to rest our heads
that doesn't vanish and confound.
This quantum is a quagmire.
What pen can pin it down?
I penned this poem pinned on the hope
my ink might hold its ground.

—Norman Ball

When Maxwell's Demon Met Schrödinger's Cat
by Jack Hillman

I sat in the dining hall, nursing a cup of horrible coffee, as I surveyed my charges. I was the new staff psychologist for Trumbauer Station, brought on board by corporate management to try and improve the production rate of the personnel on the station, one personnel in particular.

"Mind if I drag up a chair?" a voice to my left said.

I looked up at Commander Joanne Patterson, a veteran of many assignments, but none quite like Trumbauer. Her short, graying hair framed a face lined by experience, both good and bad. The smooth play of muscles beneath her utilitarian coveralls told of a history of hard, physical labor and an effective effort to maintain that tone in a low-gravity environment.

"Sure, Jo, if you don't think being seen with the local head-shrinker will affect your authority," I answered.

Patterson pulled out a chair, twisting the frame with a practiced flip of the wrist to break the magnetic seal of the feet to the floor. She dropped down on the other side of the table from me and set her own coffee mug on the table. The mild magnetic field from the table grabbed the cup and pulled it the last quarter inch with a snap of metal on metal.

"Too late for that," Patterson answered. "These folks already think I'm an ogre and should be tossed out an airlock without a suit." She took a sip of her brew and couldn't fully disguise a grimace at the taste.

"Any chance you can teach the cook to make a decent cup of coffee?" I asked, taking a painful sip myself.

"He says the lack of gravity won't let the water perk through the grounds, and any type of pressure flow just makes the end result worse." Patterson scowled. "I hear Cookie and one of the engineers over on South Quadrant are rigging a centrifuge to hold a two-hundred gallon unit and spin it at one gravity. It will be interesting to taste the end result."

"I find it amazing what lengths humans will go to for a decent cup of coffee," I said, taking another sip. I grimaced again and set the cup down, far enough away to lessen the temptation to sample it again. "Anything new in the mail today?" I asked casually.

The corporate mail drop was a weekly event and some of the staff had a pool going to see which would be the next lab site to be shut down. Corporate kept careful account of the money spent on this asteroid out in the depths of space. Whenever one of the experiments began to cost more than their projected return, plus the expenses to date, the plug was pulled. The average was about one plug every three months. But for the past five months, everyone had been waiting for the announcement, with nothing coming from corporate. Even some of the scientists, who were notorious for being in their own worlds most of the time, had gotten in on the betting. It made for a welcome change to the daily routine.

"Trying to pump me for inside information?" Patterson asked with a smile.

"Of course," I replied. "It's my duty to be prepared for any psychological repercussions with the involved personnel and prevent any unacceptable events."

"And how much do *you* have in the pool?" The twinkle in her eyes showed Patterson was well aware of the answer.

"Ten credits, same as everyone else," I said. "But my interest is strictly professional."

"Right, and crystals can't grow in a vacuum," she grinned.

"Seriously, is there some hint about what corporate has in mind? Some of these scientists are on the edge right now. I don't want a repeat of Verazzi." I looked eye to eye with the commander and saw her nod of agreement.

Verazzi was an optics engineer who had plans to create a new medium for transmitting signals. The idea was to be able to use light transmission in underwater stations, increasing the communications effectiveness as well as the safety factors with the increased communication capabilities. When Corporate bean counters decided the research was costing more than they would get back in return and closed down Verazzi's lab, Verazzi had rigged the lab to explode and take the asteroid with it whenever the next person walked through the door, then walked out the outside airlock without a suit.

It took the maintenance staff a week and a half to defuse the bombs and the new patents they filed on some of the triggers Verazzi designed to make his last act memorable would have brought in enough capital to cover the remainder of his research without any problem.

Part of my job, the biggest part, was to make sure that didn't happen again. Corporate didn't want to lose the input of a scientist able to do what Verazzi had done before he took a walk. It cost the shareholders money and Corporate didn't want to lose money, the hard-hearted golems.

"Have you had occasion to speak to Stamford lately?" the commander asked.

"As a matter of fact, I'm meeting with him an about an hour," I said. "Why? Is there something I should know about?"

"Nothing you probably don't know already," Patterson answered. "Some of the personnel have stated he seems to be spending an inordinate amount of time in his lab, especially after that little mishap last week."

Stanford had an explosion in his lab that caused a fair amount of damage. Only the fact that he had followed every safety procedure to the letter, and made some improvements of his own on some of them, as well as monitoring the experiment closely, had kept the station intact. Everyone had been congratulating him whenever they saw him, which Stamford found as uncomfortable as the fact that his experiment didn't do what it was supposed to. Stamford was one of the reasons, perhaps the biggest reason, I was now stationed on Trumbauer.

"I'll see what I can do to get him out of his shell so he's at the party tonight," I glanced in the general direction of his lab.

"Make sure you do," Patterson looked down at the awful coffee rather than meet my eyes. "I've seen men like him work themselves to death just to keep away from people. I don't want that to happen on my station."

"No problem. By the time I get done with him he'll be doing a low-gee waltz with you around the mess hall." She looked up and I smiled.

"When pigs fly," she answered. "Just try to get him out of his shell and back to reality. He's too good a man to waste hiding in a lab."

"Not according to the company," I reminded her. "After all, that's why they sent him out here: so he'd have fewer distractions."

"And has he accomplished that much more?" Patterson asked.

"No, and that's why I'm trying to do exactly what you're suggesting," I replied. "He's been deadlocked on this project for six months. Corporate is looking for some way to break him loose and get some progress. If that doesn't happen soon, the plug gets pulled on his research. I think that would destroy him."

"Probably," Patterson agreed. "Keep me informed." She finished the last of her cup, grimacing theatrically. "I'm going to shoot the cook for putting this out and calling it coffee. See you later."

I triggered the access signal of Stamford's lab an hour later and looked through the view port set into the wall next to the lock. I saw him wave absently to for me come in. The unit cycled, equalizing the pressure before admitting me through the tiny lock. Stamford was engrossed in reviewing the results of his latest trial, scrolling through the computer readouts and shaking his head.

"Dr. Stamford?" I said, trying to gain a measure of his attention.

"This makes no sense," he stated, gesturing toward the readout and standing back.

Stamford was a tall man, taller than my six feet by three inches, and thick-built like a boxer. It was surprising he managed to maintain such a spare frame with the little exercise carrying equipment around the lab would give him. Having reviewed his personnel jacket, I knew he didn't spend time in the station gym or in the centrifuge chamber. Maybe the fact that he also didn't eat regular meals, tending to grab something when the hunger pains reminded him to eat, helped keep him from puffing up like a balloon. I envied him as I stroked the growing tire at my waist.

"And just what doesn't make sense?" I asked, trying to draw Stamford into a conversation.

"I'm getting three different sets of results that are mutually exclusive," Stamford began.

I wasn't certain he was answering my question so much as he was talking to himself.

"There is no reason this unit should be behaving in this manner." He began to pace the floor of his lab. "The energy output is carefully controlled from the source. If we're going to have an effective system for beaming power from one site to another, we have to be able to maintain the focus and limit any extraneous effects on the beam. Otherwise, the entire system takes more power to keep the beam together than is in the beam itself."

I listened as Stamford spoke. This was the reason he was here: trying to build an effective system to beam power from one site to another. If Stamford managed to come up with a way to accomplish this feat, the company would be able to put solar collector units in orbit and beam power to wherever they wanted, at a fraction the cost of other systems. Stamford had proposed a theoretical way to keep the power beam focused, but the technical aspects still needed to be worked out.

"The beam generates at seventeen gigajoules in this unit," Stamford said to himself. He stood in front of the large noteboard each lab had along the corridor wall. He was erasing specific sections of a maze of equations he had previously written, changing some values, deleting others entirely. "The focusing field, at minimum strength, is affected along the z-axis by the strength of the beam, the frequency of the input and the strength of the return signal. The gravity deviation is constant along the x-axis and helps maintain coherency by polarizing the output. The discrimination of the restraint field is charged to keep the higher state ions in place without degradation. What I can't figure. . ." His voice became unintelligible as he dropped into deep thought.

Stamford moved over to a clear section of the board and began writing like a fiend, building what was to me an amazing array of mathematical equations. As the doctor began to run down, making fewer and fewer notations on the board in between longer period of introspection, I decided to take a chance and interrupt.

"Dr. Stamford," I said, raising my voice slightly.

Stamford grunted in reply but was still focused on the board, one hand moving a stylus near the surface as he noted his thoughts.

"Dr. Stamford," I repeated, louder.

The scientist ignored me, still lost in thought.

I went over and set a hand on Stamford's shoulder, giving him a slight shake.

"What? Who? Oh, it's you, Doctor," Stamford said. "Did we have a meeting today?" He glanced down at his watch, a complex affair with an extensive calendar reminder system, that had a built-in tracer to let station personnel find anyone they needed, a necessity with scientists like Stamford.

"Yes, actually we did," I answered. "But I let myself in and waited. I didn't want to interrupt your train of thought."

"Hardly a train," Stamford answered. "Lately, it's more like a bicycle, and not a very fast one at that." He shook his head. "I'm beginning to think I need to close this experiment out and go back to Earth. I'm not having any luck here."

I shuddered inwardly. "Please be very careful with that line of thought, Dr. Stamford," I cautioned. "There are people that would take advantage of your intent to change your emphasis to use for their own advancement."

Stamford laughed, a whinnying sound similar to a horse's bray. "Let them try," he stated. "If anyone can make progress on this project without my input, they're a better scientist than I am."

"Look, doctor," I said, walking up to him and putting a hand on his shoulder. "You've been cooped up in this lab too long. If you don't get out and get some perspective, you're going to be no use to yourself or to anyone else." I waved a hand, encompassing the rest of the station. "Who knows, one of your associates may have the answer to your focusing problem."

"I could use some discussion time, to clear the air if nothing else," said Stamford. "Maybe I'm just overlooking the obvious."

"There you go, doctor." I clapped him on the shoulder, urging him toward the door. "Now go get changed for the party and be ready to indulge in human Brownian movement."

I guided Stamford through the lock and out of the lab. It was a step in the right direction, but I was worried about him. There was good chance the corporation *was* going to close him down, and I had no idea how he would react.

That evening, I sat at the corner of the dining area, watching the festivities. The station personnel, aided by the more gregarious of the scientific staff, had put on a real luau for Stamford. Someone had managed to browbeat the cook into forming processed meat into the shape of a pig, and placed a candied apple in its mouth as part of the main centerpiece of the food table. The maintenance technical staff had spiked the punchbowl with seventy-proof moonshine from the vacuum still they thought the commander didn't know about. As long as the end products of the still were kept below a reasonable production level, Patterson closed her eyes to the process. People on a place like Trumbauer needed a bit of a release, she agreed.

A couple of the shuttle pilots were shapely enough to make the fake grass skirts interesting as they did a extremely modified version of a hula dance, to the beat of improvised drums and tin whistles. The performance was energetic and highly appreciated, if not authentic. Stamford, as the guest of honor, was pulled up on the floor for thirty seconds of wild gyrations with the pilots, before he collapsed in a fit of laughter. The punch he had been given was barely flavored with fruit juice and the end result was good for his soul, if not for his liver.

Now, four hours into the celebration, Stamford sat in a circle with seven other scientists and a half dozen or so of the station staff. The discussion had degenerated into matters of scientific interest only and Stamford's project in specific.

"The idea is for the containment pattern to hold the energy flux inside, as well as bringing in any stray ions that happen by," Stamford was saying. "Sort of a semi-permeable membrane but in one direction only."

"Sounds like you're trying to build Maxwell's Demon," one of the other scientists stated, his words slurred by too many servings of punch.

"Why do you say that?" Stamford asked.

"Well, you're trying to build a system that will not only keep the energy flow within, but entrap similar particles from outside the system," the other scientist said. "You're trying to stop entropy. If that's not Maxwell's Demon, I don't know what is."

One of the station techs spoke up. "You want to bring the rest of us up to speed. What's Maxwell's Demon?"

"An engineer's pipedream," one of the other scientists offered. "Back in the dark ages of physics a scientist by the name of Maxwell postulated that since the second law of thermodynamics states 'entropy will always increase in any spontaneous process involving a highly complex system,' the only way to beat the system and keep reality from falling into chaos was to have a demon sit at a divider between the high and low energy state particles and open a door to let the high energy parts through to one side and the low energy parts through to the other. This would permit the system to maintain a high energy state and continue to function efficiently." The scientist laughed. "Maxwell's Demon has always been a bit of a joke among physicists."

"Not a joke," Stamford said, with careful clarity. The punch was catching up with him. "An unreachable dream, perhaps, but not a pipedream. We can build such a system."

"Right, doc," the tech stated. "And that's how you managed to make a new access to your lab last week, by stopping entropy from advancing."

The group laughed, all except Stamford and one other person.

I had been watching Dr. Elizabeth Connors during the course of the evening. She seemed to be taking more than a casual interest in Stamford. Another of those scientists Patterson was concerned about, Connors was, like Stamford, terminally shy. She was a cryonics expert, here to work on a possible process for suspended animation for deep space exploration. During the time I had been on station, I had spoken with her a total of three times, twice in my office, where she was required to attend "counseling" in order to determine her mental health in a deep space environment, and once in the mess hall, where she barely acknowledged my presence, staring at the floor as I spoke to her. She was one of the scientists I had tagged as a possible problem if her project was ever suspended.

She had been hanging on Stamford's every word all night. Wherever he was, she was nearby, listening in on the conversation without saying anything. At one point in the festivities, Conners had permitted herself to be forced into a slow dance with Stamford, keeping a mathematically precise one inch of space between them the entire time. Now, she was sitting on the floor at his feet, most of the chairs having been sequestered for the night to give floor space for dancing, gazing up at him with an expression I had last seen on the face of a teen-age girl looking at her current 3D video idol. Even in his present condition, Stamford had noticed the attention she was paying him. I could see the confusion in his eyes when he looked at her, unsure what to do next.

For the first time, Conners spoke up.

"Have you considered observational interference?" she asked Stamford.

He looked down at her, surprised by the question. "What do you mean?" he asked.

Conners looked around at the group, all attention focused on her. She was ready to crawl into a hole to escape the unwanted focus of her peers.

"I've, uh, noticed an additional error factor in my experiments that seems to occur only when I'm actually observing them. I wondered if that might be part of your control problem." She smiled timidly up at Stamford.

"I never thought of that," he stated, his mind already racing through myriad thoughts on the process, rapidly losing contact with the people he was with. A loud laugh brought him back to the group. The scientist who had mentioned Maxwell's demon was holding his sides in pain as he laughed even harder than before.

"Not only do we have Maxwell's Demon making an appearance, now we have Schrödinger's Cat here as well." He convulsed in laughter again, joined by snickers from some of the other engineering minded scientists and techs who understood the reference.

Conners turned bright red at the slur, trying to slide back out of the circle and make her escape. But she was at the edge of the room and the compartment wall was behind her. There was nowhere for her to go but through the middle of the circle, past all the laughing members of the staff. I saw what little self-confidence she had crumbling under the onslaught of the massed ridicule of her peers. Then a miracle happened. Her white knight appeared.

Stamford stood, looking down at the drunken scientist who made the disparaging comment. Even in his inebriated state, Stamford looked ready to do battle, short-lived though it might be.

"There are more things in heaven and earth, Horatio, than are dreamt of in your philosophy," he quoted to his hapless colleague. Then, turning to Conners, Stamford held out one hand to assist her to her feet. "Come, doctor," he enunciated carefully but imperiously. "I would like to hear more about your idea." He turned to the gathered throng. "Good night," Stamford said to the assemblage. The two slightly swaying scientists walked out like a royal couple.

There was a pregnant silence as Stamford and Connors left the room. As the door closed on them, one of the station techs turned to the deflated scientist and said, "Well, I guess he told you."

For some reason the crowd thought this was hilarious, confirming my impression of the general level of sobriety. Patterson and I looked at each other and exchanged smiles. From our point of view, this was a positive development for both Stamford and Conners. As for the rest of the staff, they continued talking and drinking for another hour before the party finally broke up.

The next day I had several appointments with some of the station scientists, trying to keep them on an even keel while they fretted about their own projects. By the time I was done with the counseling sessions, it was early afternoon. I decided to stop by Stamford's lab to see if there had been any changes.

There had been.

Dr. Conners was standing in the corridor, looking through the view port into the lab. As I came closer, she smiled.

"Nathan thinks he found the problem," she said to me. "He's trying another experiment to see if he can confirm the results."

I had to think for a moment before I remembered that Nathan was Stamford's first name. "Sounds good," I replied cautiously. "What's he doing differently this time?"

"He's watching it," Conners answered.

Before I could respond to such an obscure answer, Stamford's voice came over the intercom into the corridor.

"All right, ready to begin," Stamford said. "Lighting the torch."

Through the view port, we saw the beam of the power transfer unit begin to pulse. The argon laser surged within the containment field Stamford had created with a blue glow that reminded me of the sky of Earth on a clear day.

"Stepping up the containment field to full power," Stamford said.

There was movement inside the lab and I realized that Stamford was wearing not the lab coat I expected, but rather a fully plated space suit for heavy construction work. I turned to Conners.

"What is he doing in a suit inside his lab?" I asked.

"If we're right, he'll need it," was her only answer. She turned back toward the view port with a bright smile on her face.

Looking back inside the lab, I now realized that Stamford had rearranged the equipment inside. The power unit and containment field, which had originally been placed along the long axis of the room, was now oriented ninety degrees to the left and facing the outside wall of the station. I began to worry about station integrity.

"Beginning observation," Stamford said, his voice cheerful.

For five seconds the blue beam continued to glow as it had before. Then, suddenly, there was a flare that almost blinded us before the polarizers in the view port kicked in for three seconds. I heard the grating blare of the atmosphere klaxons reverberating in the corridor, matched by a loud whistling from inside the lab. Over the loudspeaker I could hear Stamford cheering over something as he moved toward the far wall of the lab. In his hands he held a steel plate, used for patching hull punctures on the shuttles when they received meteor damage. Stamford was moving toward a two-inch hole in the wall that was currently sucking the atmosphere out of the lab.

In the hard suit, with its augmented joints and powered limbs, Stamford had little trouble centering the plate over the hole and letting the pressure differential hold it in place, stopping the whirlwind in the lab. Beside me, Conners was bouncing up and down and clapping, looking as much like a cheerleader as was possible in coveralls and magnetic boots. The two scientists had obviously expected this outcome of the experiment, no matter how violent it seemed, and had taken proper precautions. I made a mental note to remind Patterson she needed to stress station security more with the scientists before they decided to blow a hole in the outside wall of the station.

"Okay, you knew that would happen," I said to Conners. "Tell me: just what *did* happen?"

"Oh, I can't spoil it for him," Conners stated, all smiles and bubbling happiness. "Nathan must tell you himself."

"Tell us what," Patterson demanded, appearing behind me in the corridor. A full damage control party clogged the passageway behind her.

Conners reply was cut off by the sound of the lock working to pass someone through. Conners turned as Stamford appeared in the opening. She was barely able to restrain herself until he removed the helmet of the suit before she planted a very loud, very thorough kiss on his smiling lips. He held her in one suited arm as he faced Patterson and the station personnel. He didn't seem to care that they were out for blood.

"It worked," Stamford stated, smiling broadly.

"What worked?" Patterson demanded. "And just why did you believe it necessary to burn another hole in my station, Doctor?"

"I apologize, Commander," Stamford said. "I didn't think it would be a problem, since the lab was sealed and I was ready with a patch. I needed to confirm my theory."

"WHAT theory?" Patterson demanded through clenched teeth. Her temper was stretched to its limit by Stamford's casual, uninformative responses.

The scientist began to strip out of the hardsuit, aided by Conners. "Well, it had to do with the conversation we were having last evening and something Hastings said to me." His explanation was halted for a moment as he removed the locking ring at the top of the hardsuit, permitting the rest of the suit to be sloughed off toward his feet. "While there was some truth to the comments about Maxwell's Demon and my attempt to limit the adverse effects of entropy, I believe I owe Dr. Hastings an apology for becoming so upset with his comments about Schrödinger's Cat. There was more truth to his offhand remark than he knew."

Patterson looked from Stamford to Conners and back again. She was still waiting for something to be said that explained another hole in her station. "*And*?" she prompted.

The green light went on over the door to Stamford's lab, signaling the atmosphere was back up to pressure inside. The klaxon cut off as the sensors registered the end of the emergency.

"Well, to be brief," Stamford said, "There was some truth to the assumption that my containment field was designed to maintain the coherency of the beam, to some degree like the analogy of Maxwell's Demon. But what Dr. Conners pointed out, and what I had not realized before, was that there was another factor operating on the beam that affected the results."

He grinned at Dr. Conners.

"And that was?" Patterson asked in clipped tones, ready to pull it out of Stamford by force if necessary.

"Why, the observational factor, Commander," Stamford said. "Haven't you noticed that there has been a much higher level of adverse results in the experiments run on this station? More so than any similar lab back on Earth?"

"For some of the scientists," Patterson agreed, her face relaxing a bit. "And how does that equate to your experiment?"

"Quite simply, the scientists have been influencing the results of their own experiments," Stamford said as he leaned against the observation wall's glass. "Unconsciously, I assure you. But there is a definite correlation between the direct observation of an experiment and the end result."

"Schrödinger's Cat," a voice in the back of the damage control group muttered.

"Exactly," Stamford agreed. "Here on Trumbauer Station, the gravity is greatly reduced from what we are used to on Earth. In addition, we are farther out in the solar system than any other lab has ever been placed before. While there is an influence of gravity on everyone here, it is much weaker than any of us have ever experienced before. This permits the minute ability of most humans to manipulate matter to make itself felt. The fact that we observe the experiment, and have some conscious or unconscious belief in the outcome, has an effect on the results."

"Are you trying to tell me you're telekinetic?" Patterson exploded. "You blew a hole in the wall of my station to prove you can move things with your *mind*?"

"In a manner of speaking, yes, Commander," Stamford said.

There was a murmur of disbelief and astonishment from the gathered personnel.

Patterson stared at him. "That's insane."

Stamford shrugged. "It was necessary to establish that my preconceived opinion on the outcome of the sub molecular interaction was establishing the parameters of the results."

"I think, therefore I flare," one of the scientists muttered.

"Exactly," Stamford said, his face beaming with approval of the simple explanation.

"Doctor, I have no doubt what you did made perfect sense to you, and I do plan to take up the matter of this type of experiment with the company before any more holes are shot in my walls, but I have to ask: did you think of the possibility that there may have been a shuttle on the other side of that wall when you let loose with your projector?" Patterson glared at Stamford like an angry mother.

Stamford's jaw bounced off the corridor floor, matched only by the look of horror on Conners' face.

"Oh, my god," Stamford said. "There wasn't one, I hope?"

"*No*, thank the stars," Patterson said, her fists on her hips, her lips a thin line. "But there easily could have been, given how close you are to the main boarding lock. I'd appreciate it if you and any of your associates would check with me before doing something like this again." She turned to glare at the rest of the gathered scientists.

"I certainly would," Stamford answered, "If I planned to be here any longer."

"And just what does that mean?" Patterson demanded. "You're not going to tell me you've solved all your problems with this little display of pyrotechnics."

"Oh, no," Stamford answered. "But I have managed to come up with a new set of parameters that must be reviewed with management before I proceed. I'll be heading back to Earth on the next shuttle to have a talk with them. Based on those discussions, I may or may not be returning."

"Well," Patterson said. She paused, then continued. "Whatever the outcome, please be more careful with your experiments, wherever you are, Doctor." She turned to the repair crew. "Go in and make sure of the seal and let me know if any additional repairs will be needed." To the others in the corridor she said, "All right folks. Show's over. Let's all go back to work now."

The crowd dispersed, although some of the scientists looked like they wanted to talk to Stamford about his discovery. Patterson waved away the most persistent of the lot and looked up at Stamford.

"Your comments implied some of the problems we're having on this station are the result of human intervention," she said. "I want a full report on your conclusions on my desk by the end of shift today."

"Certainly, Commander," Stamford said.

Patterson looked at him and Conners. “I’m not sure what’s happening here, but if it gives us results I’m all for it. The only thing I have to say,” she moved up until she was nose to chest with Stamford, looking up at him, “is that if you do come back to this station, and you ever pull another hare-brained stunt like this one, I will personally walk you out onto the surface of this rock and kick your ass so hard you’ll arrive on Earth *before* the shuttle. Do you understand me?”

Stamford stood with his head bowed, looking for all the world like a little boy caught with his hand in the candy jar. “Yes, ma’am,” he said.

Patterson continued to glower at him for a minute, then nodded at Stamford’s acceptance of her verdict, turned and walked down the corridor toward her office. I looked at the two scientists.

“So, you’re leaving us,” I said to Stamford.

“We both are,” he answered. “Elizabeth and I have a lot to talk about and the trip back to Earth should be just long enough to get to know each other.”

“Oh?” I smiled as I raised an eyebrow in question.

Stamford took both her hands in both of his, looking into her eyes. “We talked all night. I’ve never done that before with a woman. Elizabeth was the one who showed me what I was missing in my experiment. If it wasn’t for her I’d be going back to Earth in disgrace.” Dr. Conners grinned up at him with all the infatuation of a teenage crush.

“Now I can go back with the details of why my system, and probably a lot of other things the company is trying to do out here, won’t work until they do more research on the observational effect.” He turned to me. “I may not have solved my project’s problems, but the discovery of how Schrödinger’s Cat actually has an effect out here more than makes up for the difference. The company can find a thousand ways to exploit the observational effect for their benefit.”

“And what about Dr. Conners’ project?”’ I asked. “She hasn’t finished her research.”

“I finished three months ago,” Conners replied, still staring into Stamford’s eyes. “I just didn’t want to report my findings and be sent back to Earth. I was still looking for something here. I found it.” She stood on her toes and kissed Stamford lightly on the lips.

The physicist blushed bright red. He hugged Dr. Conners and she hugged him back.

“Well, looks like things are working out for you both,” I said. I watched the two of them for a moment, before clearing my throat. "Um, why don't you two go make plans for your trip back to Earth"

"An excellent suggestion," Stamford agreed. "Come, my dear." He offered Conners an arm.

"Thank you," she said to Stamford, linking her arm with his. "Goodbye," she added to me, looking back over her shoulder as they walked down the corridor, her feline grace an odd contrast to his careful gait.

I set off in the opposite direction, in search of a decent cup of centrifuge coffee. In more than one way, I felt like celebrating.

Fading Away
by Jay Lake

Aaron was sent to the park while the visiting nurse helped Momma. Momma coughed a lot more lately, but quieter, while Daddy prayed harder and harder over her. There was nothing Aaron could do but be in the way. Outside it was easier not to think about Momma—Aaron liked the hot Nevada summer days. Sometimes the other moms at the park were nice to him, too.

He saw the fat man sitting on the swing. The stranger had dark glasses, shaggy dark hair down over his ears, a white suit with spangles all over it, and a big cape like Superman's. Except the cape was white, and shorter. Aaron could see the park right through the fat man's white suit, kind of the same way he could see things when he walked around with his t-shirt over his head.

Aaron was a little afraid and a little curious all mixed together, so he went over to the swings. "Hey, mister, you gonna sit there all day?"

The fat man looked at Aaron, his eyes hidden behind the big dark glasses. He seemed surprised. "You can see me? Sorry, son. I'll move on." He gathered his weight and stood. The bottoms of his boots floated slightly above the ground. The fat man looked lost and lonely.

Aaron knew how that felt.

"You don't need to leave," Aaron blurted. "I don't mind you being here."

"That's mighty nice of you, son." The fat man had a rich voice, like listening to chocolate cake talk. He settled back on to the swing. "Is there anything I can do for you?"

Aaron knew the fat man was a ghost. He'd never seen one, but everyone knew you could see right through ghosts. He wasn't scared now—his Momma had become more of a ghost than this fat man. Aaron tried to remember what he'd heard about ghosts. "You're supposed to help someone before you can go to Heaven, right?"

The fat man looked disappointed, as if he'd expected Aaron to say something else. "That's not quite it, but near enough, I reckon."

Aaron imagined money, candy, Disneyland. "Cool. What can you do for me?"

"Not much, son. Show myself, sometimes. Talk." The fat man tried to smile, which made him look even sadder than before. "Sing."

That sounded so stupid to Aaron. "Sing? What good is that?"

The ghost glanced away from Aaron for a few moments before meeting his eye again. "Some folks love music, son. It lifts up their hearts."

"Momma loves music," Aaron blurted. She had, before she got sick.

The fat man smiled. "Who does she like?"

Aaron couldn't remember the names, but Momma had had albums everywhere. "Lots of people," he said, scuffing his shoe. "But she can't listen no more."

The ghost frowned. "Why not?"

"She's real sick." He scuffed his shoe again. "I'm not supposed to talk about it."

The fat man squatted down in front of Aaron, looking him face to face. "What's the matter with her, son?" He sounded like he really cared about Aaron and Momma.

Aaron's voice caught in his throat. "Got the cancer. In her belly. She can't get out of bed, she can't eat, she can't do nothing." His chest shuddered. "Nurse Simmons says Momma's lost her heart."

"Son. . ." The fat man's voice sounded like he was going to cry. He started to pat Aaron's shoulder, then pulled his hand back to smooth a wrinkle out of his white suit. "Let's go see her."

Aaron cut off his sob. The fat man seemed to mean it. Aaron figured Nurse Simmons was gone by now. "I ain't allowed visitors at the house. But if Daddy's out, I can get you in. Maybe your music can help Momma find her heart." Aaron didn't know how to help her, and it seemed no one else would.

They came in through the kitchen, past the old round-shouldered refrigerator. The house was quiet.

"Here," Aaron whispered to the fat man as he eased open the door to Momma's sick room. The nurse was gone. Everything smelled like pee and mold, not fresh and warm like Momma used to. Followed by the ghost, Aaron moved to the foot of the bed, clasping his hands behind his back so he wouldn't bother her. Aaron's eyes had that peppery about-to-cry sting they always got around Momma. The fat man touched him lightly on the shoulder, like the brush of a bird flying by in the woods, then moved to stand alongside the bed, where Daddy always sat.

In the dark room the fat man glowed, each little sparkle on his suit flashing like a star in the sky. He took off the glasses, which showed his glowing brown eyes. The fat man reached out and brushed Momma's lips with his fingertips.

"Frank?" Momma's voice was more of a gasp than a whisper.

"No, darlin'." The fat man's teeth glowed as he smiled in the dark. His chocolate cake voice was stronger. "It's me. You know who I am."

"The King." Momma sounded relieved, almost happy. "But you're gone. . ." She sighed. "It's really you, isn't it?"

The fat man looked down the bed at Aaron. "You sure you want me to do this? She needs to go on."

Aaron was so pleased Momma sounded happy, so pleased he had done something to help, that he couldn't bring himself to stop the fat man.

"No sir, go on. Sing to her. Please."

The fat man took Momma's hand and starting singing in a low, rich voice. He sang a song Aaron had never heard before, about how the fat man couldn't help falling in love with Momma. Momma cried—real small, quiet tears. Aaron wasn't sure why, but it made him happy to see Momma cry like that. It meant she forgot about hurting long enough to care about something.

After a while, Aaron realized the fat man wasn't singing any more. Aaron wiped his eyes. He could see Momma smiling in the glow from the fat man's suit.

"Why'd you stop, mister? You were helping her."

The fat man stared at Momma, and brushed his fingers over her lips one more time. "She's found her heart, son. Your Momma just needed someone to tell her it was okay to go on."

"Momma?" Aaron ran to the other side of the bed and picked up her hand. It felt like a bundle of sticks wrapped in tissue. He looked at her mouth real close, put his fingers near her lips. She wasn't breathing, not even a little bit. His heart seemed to fill his throat, so he couldn't breathe either. Aaron wanted to scream. He'd told the fat man to sing, and the fat man had killed her. "No, Momma. . ." he gasped.

Aaron felt a bird brush on his shoulder once again. But the fat man was still across the bed from him, now growing fainter. Aaron could see the dresser real clear right through the fat man, even in the dark, like he was less and less there.

"I'll watch over my boy for a spell now," said Momma from behind Aaron, her voice strong again.

Aaron's fear drained away like dishwater from the sink. He'd done Momma right by bringing the ghost to her. "Thank you," he whispered as the fat man faded away.

Then: "I love you, Momma."

The Man Behind the Curtain
by Joseph Paul Haines

I once heard someone say that we create our own reality. Even quantum physicists were jumping on board that bandwagon, talking about the nature of thoughts and the impact they had on the physical world. If it's true, I've never seen it.

Or maybe I just don't want to take credit for the reality I've created.

That's possible. That's very possible.

You'd think that if that was true though, some events in our life might match our expectations. Me? I was constantly being surprised. No. That's the wrong word. Disappointed is more accurate.

Only four of us made it, out of eight. Half. Half her children showed up for her funeral. When I heard that she died, I imagined a rainy day. Two score or so mourners stood around her open grave all dressed in black like a coven of dark acolytes gathering round an altar, waiting to sacrifice their troubled memories into the cold earth beside her. Instead, there was a brief ceremony in a small room at the back of the funeral home. Four of her children, the minister, and three old women from her church attended.

I didn't know the women, so I simply nodded my head when they offered their condolences. I hadn't seen Mother in about ten years. I lost contact with her and tried to find out where she was, but not too hard. I didn't want to find her, you see. I just wanted to have looked.

You really don't want to find your abuser, no matter how much you love them.

My wife, Monica, didn't want me to come to the funeral. We'd been having problems. They were my fault. When your world is cold and gray, you sometimes do stupid things to try to force the sun out from hiding. In the end, you only make it worse. We needed to spend a lot of time together if we were going to make it work. Instead, I came to the funeral and left her behind. I did it because I hoped that Suzi might be one of those acolytes gathered round Mother's grave. Had I been able to create my own reality, she would have been.

Suzi created her own reality instead.

In all the years since she left home with only a backpack and a handful of bruises, I'd never tried to find her.

Until now.

She had the magic, you see, and if I didn't want to end up in the ground with my mother, I needed to become a magician.

I can only tell you what I saw. It's up to you to believe it or not.

The last of the snow had melted and only infrequent patches of spring thaw mud left any clue that winter had ever existed. Blades of grass peeked out from barren patches of earth cautiously, like the groundhog, trying not to spook at the sight of their shadows. Honeysuckle from the bush under the dining room window bloomed and filled the house with spring. It was my seventh summer, and school would let out in a month or so. I'd gotten a new bike for Christmas—my first—and it seemed like anything was possible.

It wasn't a day for tragedy, but it came nonetheless. Suzi sat next to me on the piano bench while I struggled with "Ghost Riders in the Sky." The piano lessons were Suzi's gift to me when I turned five. She paid for them with the money she earned working behind the counter at a local pizza joint after school in the evenings.

When we moved into the house on West Washington Street we found the old piano sitting in the corner of the dining room. Our landlord's daughter used to play before she went off to college and instead of paying a mover to ship it to the new house, it was just left there. Mom threatened to make me give up the lessons every so often, saying that the money should be used for the whole family, not so that I could learn some silly skill that I'd never use but every time she brought it up, Suzi stood her ground. She said she'd quit working at all if Mom made me quit. As Suzi did chip in for household expenses, Mom didn't want to lose what money she did get. Sometimes I'd feel a little guilty about the whole thing. We didn't have much money since Dad died, and even though I loved my lessons I understood my Mother's point of view, even at seven.

But Suzi would have none of it. When I brought it up, she'd stoke my hair and say, "That's very sweet, Davey, but if you don't go to your lessons, I'll just be paying Mrs. Parker for nothing and that'd be an even bigger waste."

So I kept taking lessons. I had to practice while Mom was at work. She didn't like all the racket. She worked mornings and afternoons at the Congress Street Diner and said after spending all day at work the last thing she wanted to hear was bad piano playing when she came home. So when I heard the front door open, I knew it was time to stop for the day.

Suzi bit her lip and put her hand on my back. "You better go to your room," she said.

I almost argued, but there was something in her eyes that told me not to. So I took my lesson book with me and went into my bedroom.

I played with my toy garage and Matchbox cars for a while until the shouting started. There was nothing new about the fighting; it happened all the time. Mom and Suzi couldn't have been more different if they were broccoli and ice cream. They fought almost every day, skipping only the days when they didn't see each other. Once I listened in, but it made me feel really weird. I started to take Suzi's side in the argument and I didn't like the knot it put in my stomach. I loved them both, and I didn't want to be on anyone's side.

I just wanted them to stop fighting.

Their voices just kept growing louder so I started singing. I rolled a toy car into the elevator on the garage on cranked the wheel on the side until the elevator stopped at the top floor, the gate popped open, and the car sped down the long, curving ramp to the bottom. I pushed the car back into the elevator for another trip.

The floor shook with a loud thud. Suzi and Mom had stopped yelling.

I shot up and threw open my bedroom door. When I got to the living room, Mom was straddling Suzi, pinning her arms down to the ground.

Suzi screamed. Her cheek sported a bright red mark, just below her left eye. She fought with all her might to push Mom off of her but couldn't do it. "Stop!" she cried. "I'm sorry I'm sorry I'm sorry."

Mom leaned forward and spit on her face. "You're going to show me some respect, young lady," she said. Mom didn't yell, but the tone in her voice scared me even worse than the screaming.

It looked like Suzi was trying to cry, but she couldn't catch her breath enough to even sob.

I stood there and watched. I couldn't even speak. I'd seen them fight, but never like this. I wanted to throw up, but instead, I felt warmth fill the front of my pants and slide down my leg.

"No," Suzi stammered. "This isn't happening. This isn't happening."

I glanced down at the floor to the growing puddle of urine at my feet.

And then I got mad.

I grabbed Mom's arm and pulled with all my might. Mom glanced up, seeing me for the first time, and shoved me away. I stumbled backwards and tripped, slamming my back into the bookcase against the wall. It hurt, but my anger took away most of the pain.

Mom glanced over at me. "Get!" she yelled.

I didn't.

The sight of me sitting against the bookcase snapped Suzi out of it though. "I told you to get off of me, you bitch!" she said through clenched teeth.

Mom let go with her right hand and raised her fist.

And then, Suzi was no longer underneath her. She stood by the front door. Her backpack hung by a strap from her right hand. It was like someone has sucked all the air out of the room. We all stopped breathing—not holding your breath mind you—we just. Stopped. Breathing.

Suzi looked right into my eyes and smiled.

And then, like that, she was gone.

Mom finally managed to get to her feet. She chased Suzi down the street and out of sight.

She never did catch her. Somehow, Suzi had conjured up her magic and gotten free. No matter how bad the world was out there, it couldn't have been worse for her than here. As far as I know, the two of them never spoke again.

I haven't touched a piano since.

I spent the day after the funeral helping my sister Kate clear out Mom's apartment. Kate had dealt with the brunt of dealing with Mom in the last few years. The rest of us kids ignored Mother any way we could, but Mom had moved three blocks away from Kate's place so she didn't have much choice. The last time I'd seen Mom, she had been pulling her "I'm so lonely none of you kids ever visit I think I'll kill myself," guilt trip. I nodded my head and told her if it was really that bad, I'd buy her the gun myself. Not one of my best moments, but I'd had it at that point.

"Anything here you want?" Kate asked me. "The appliances are going to Jay, but pretty much anything else you can have.

"There's just a couple of pictures," I said.

"Nothing else?" she asked. "There's a bunch of jewelry in the—"

"Just the pictures."

She looked over at me and nodded her head. "They're in the scrapbook by the bedroom door."

The bedroom looked like the storage room for a thrift shop, odds-and-ends that no one would buy filled every available space. The bed had been disassembled and leaned against the far wall, the plastic still intact.

I found the scrapbook right where Kate said it would be. The decoupaged cover hung loose from two removable pins that allowed additional pages to be added and the pages slid around on top of one another like playing cards from a new deck. The pictures attached by a single, folded adhesive strip causing them to bounce around like jack-in-the-box heads atop worn springs. There were pictures of all of us kids: Old band photos, graduation pictures, a newspaper clipping from when we all built a fifteen foot snowman.

But the Superman picture was gone.

I pulled the most recent picture of Suzi I could find—her senior portrait—and walked back into the living room.

Kathy glanced up when I entered the room. "Find it?" she asked.

"It's gone," I said. The response was more to myself than to her.

Kathy turned her back. "What's gone?"

"You know. The picture of me in the Superman shirt jumping off the back stairs." It was a family joke. We talked about it all the time.

She kept her back to me. "I don't remember. . ."

"C'mon," I pleaded. "Suzi bought me that shirt. You know. . ." And then it hit me. "Someone took it."

She shrugged her shoulders

"Okay," I said. "Let's sit down for a minute." I put my arm around her and walked her to the couch. I pushed the pile of papers to one end and we squeezed onto the other. "Who's got it?" I asked.

She bit her bottom lip and stared me in the eye.

"It's very important to me, Kate. That day was special." I waited for her to say something. She crossed her arms and looked away. "Hey, really," I said. "Who has it?"

"I can't tell you," she said. "I promised."

I leaned back into the cushion and a broken spring bit into my back. "Who?" I asked.

She took my hand between hers. "Suzi," she said. "I promised Suzi."

I jumped up from the couch, tearing my hand from her grasp. "What?

When did you talk to Suzi! Where is she? Is she okay? Why didn't you tell me?"

"Stop!" she said, showing me both palms. "I said I promised."

I shook my head. "Uh-uh. This is one you're going to break. I haven't heard from her since the day she left the house. I was going to hire a detective to find her when I left here. If you know where she is—"

"I don't," she said. "Not exactly. I sent her the picture two years ago. I tried calling her for the funeral, but she either moved on or changed her number."

"Damn. I need to see her."

"Just to get the picture back? Is it really that important?"

"No," I said, sitting back down next to her. "I need her, Kate. I need to talk to her."

Kate took a deep breath, pursed her lips, and slowly exhaled through her nose. "She doesn't want to see you," she said.

She might as well have hit me. "Why?"

"She didn't say. Told me it wasn't really my business."

Suzi meant everything to me. "You know that picture?" I asked. "Well, it's more than just a picture."

She cocked her head to the side. "What do you mean?"

"Don't laugh," I said. "But I need to see it. I think I was really flying that day."

"What?"

"Just listen, okay?"

She nodded.

"Suzi bought me that shirt. She was always buying me little presents like that but this one was special. We'd been watching the old Superman television show every day after school. She gave me the shirt, made me put it on, then tied a towel around my neck and took me into the back yard." I put my arm on the back of the couch and leaned toward Kate. "We played for hours. She pretended to be Lois Lane stuck in another jam and I'd run to her rescue. I remember beating up the bad guys, swinging my fist into empty air, and Suzi'd clap for me and she laughed. She laughed herself silly, Kate.

"And then I climbed up on the porch stairs, hummed a few bars of the theme music and leapt out into the air with my fist outstretched. I did this three or four times, and then Suzi told me to go up higher. So I did. I climbed up higher and higher, my jumps going farther and farther away from the house. I remember it felt like I was really flying. Just when I thought that I'd gone as far as I possibly could with a jump, I'm keep my knees tucked up anyway and I just—swear to God I'm not making this up—I'd just float farther until I got scared and put my feet down. I was landing in the neighbor's yard, Kate, and I didn't think anything was strange about that at all."

Kate raised her eyebrows. "The neighbor's yard? That was a good fifty feet from the stairs. There's no way you were—"

"I was. It happened. I'm not making this up. When I got older, I looked at that distance and tried to convince myself it didn't happen. But no matter how hard I tried, I still remember it as clearly as if it happened yesterday." I leaned back in my chair. "I've got to see that picture again, Kate. Somehow Suzi made me fly, and I've got to figure out if it was real or not."

"I'm sorry," she said. "I wish I could but—"

The ring of my cell phone cut her off. I pulled it from my jacket pocket and checked the caller i.d. It was Monica, my wife.

I flipped open the phone. "Hey," I said.

"Hey," she replied. "How'd it go?"

"Weird, like everything else," I said. "Look, can I call you back? I'm in the middle of something with Kate right now."

There was a long silence on the other end. "Sorry to bother you," she said.

"No, Monica, it's just that—"

She hung up. No matter how hard I tried, I always ended up saying the wrong thing. I closed the phone and put it away.

Kate stared at me. She pulled an address book from her purse, tore out a piece of paper and scribbled down what looked like an address. "This is where she was," she said. "But you're not going to find any magic there. You should go home to your wife."

She handed me the slip of paper. I looked down to read the address.

The ink glowed on the paper, bright blue and purple and orange, swirling with a phosphorescence, the letters and numbers bouncing around on the page as if in a celebratory ritual dance. I blinked twice, and it was just black ink after all. The address was in Boston. "I'll go home when I find Suzi," I said. "And I think you're wrong."

"What?" Kate said.

I smiled and kissed her on the cheek. "When I find Suzi, I'll find magic."

❁

I'm not sure what I expected to find, but it wasn't this. The taxi dropped me off in front of the old tenement building and I asked the driver three times if this was the right address before I'd get out of the car. Hunks of plaster were missing from the walls. I tried not to look too closely as I was afraid I'd see bullet holes at their center. Ash gray paint clung to the sides of the three story building, giving it the pallor of the recently dead. I checked the address again, grimaced as I saw it was correct, and pushed through the gated front entrance.

A faded orange and brown couch occupied the center of the lobby, sitting atop a scratched hardwood floor pocked with poorly stained planks of woods to replace those that had broken over time. At the far end, near an elevator with a single wrought-iron gate, sat a single desk that appeared as if it might have come from straight from a third-grade classroom. The black man behind the desk typed on a pitch-black Underwood manual typewriter as big as his chest, his old hands shaking between key-strokes.. The lingering scent of pine cleaner hung in the air, mixed with the musk of unseen mold.

"Hello," I said, waiting for the old man to look up before continuing. "I'm looking for Susan James."

"You the police?"

"No, not even close," I said. "I'm her brother."

"You don't say." The old man smiled, pushed himself up from his seat with a great effort, then leaned across the desk with his hand outstretched. "You Davey?"

"Yeah," I said, slowly reaching out to take his hand. "How do you know—"

"Ah hell son," he said. "Suzi talked about you all the time. I'm Bernard."

"She talked about me all the time?" A chill ran down my spine.

"Yep. All the time, she did. 'My little man' this and 'my little man' that. A body would'a thought you were her very own."

I was, or at least might as well have been. "So she lives here then?"

"Used to. Pull up a seat," Bernard said, sitting back down. "There a folding chair behind the door over there. I hope you'll forgive me for not getting it myself, but the chemo's got me feelin' like whipped mutt. Hell, I bent over right now you could probably find the lash marks on my rear."

I pulled the chair over beside the desk and sat down. "Sorry to hear that," I said. "We can talk later if you are too tired."

Bernard smiled at me. "Nah, I'm okay. It's a bitch but the doc says we should know if it's working after just a few more sessions. Says about fifty-fifty, which means he don't got the slightest clue if it'll work or not, but the way I figure it, them's better odds than Vegas so what the hell."

I couldn't help but laugh. "So very true," I said.

"So you're a doctor, huh?" Bernard asked.

That stopped me. "No, where'd you get an idea like that?"

Bernard crossed his arms. "Suzi, of course. We were talking once about the cancer and she said that if 'my little man Davey were here, he'd be able to fix you.' Just assumed is all."

I didn't know what to say. "I'm not sure why she would have told you that. I'm sorry if—"

Bernard waved me off. "No, no," he said. "Just curious is all."

The sparkle in his eye faded a bit, I think. I wanted to change the subject. "So Suzi moved, huh?"

"Don't know if I'd say she moved so much as left," he said.

"What do you mean?"

Bernard shrugged. "Just packed up some personal things and was gone. She left her furniture behind, and most of her clothes. She never kept much anyway, but still. . ."

"She didn't say where she was going?"

He shook his head. "Not to me, she didn't. Just left a strange note behind."

"Strange?"

Bernard opened the center drawer on his desk, shuffled a few blank forms and produced a folded piece of purple notebook paper. The writing was in silver marker:

Bernard,

Hang tight. I'm off to see the wizard.

Suzi

I tried to hand back the slip of paper to Bernard, but he just shook his head. "Keep it," he said, smiling gently.

"Thank you." I folded up the note and slid it into my jacket pocket. "Is there anyone else she might have told where she was going?" I asked. "A boyfriend maybe?"

"Not unless she suddenly went straight and didn't tell me about. That would'a been enough to break an old man's heart."

I flinched. "Suzi's gay?"

"No, son," Bernard said. "She's a lesbian. Get the term right."

It clicked. Some of the most heated arguments I'd had with my mother growing up were about this very subject. My mother was obsessed with deriding anything that even hinted at homosexuality. I used to tell her that she'd probably do much better in life if she would start paying attention to who people were instead of who they slept with. But now I understood why she wouldn't listen. She felt like her daughter had betrayed her. Stupid woman. I wondered if that was why they fought like they did.

"Any girlfriends, then?"

Bernard shook his head. "Not since Nancy left. The two of them were together for years, then one day a couple of years back, they went on a trip and Nancy didn't come back. Suzi never said anything about it and I cared too much to ask."

Damn.

"She was kind'a friendly with the lady who lived next door to her, but not friendly like that if you take my meaning."

"She still live here?" I asked.

Bernard pulled the paper on which he'd been writing out of the typewriter. He turned the eviction notice to face me. "Not for very much longer, I'm afraid. Suzi used to help her with her rent, but stopped doing that a couple months back. Didn't have the money anymore. I waited as long as I could but there's a management company over my head, too."

"I understand," I said. "She still in her room?"

Bernard sighed. "Try Damon's tavern, down the block to the left. Don't tell her, okay? About the eviction notice?"

"No problem," I said. "What's her name?"

"Donna. Donna Price."

I stood up from the chair. "Thank you, Bernard."

"Want to repay me?" he asked.

"Name it."

He pushed himself up from the desk. "If you find Suzi, tell her the doctors are saying fifty-fifty."

"I will," I promised.

He took my hand, looked me straight in the eye and added, "Down from seventy-thirty."

❁

Sometimes a place takes on the characteristics of its inhabitants. While the other storefronts on the street had respectable street-level entrances, complete with enticing window displays and overstated signs proclaiming the name of the establishment, to get to Damon's you had to climb down a set of stairs from street level before you saw the name of the establishment hand-painted in blue letters on the front door. If I hadn't noticed the smell of stale beer creeping out of the stairwell, I'd have wandered around for hours trying to find it. I tried my best not to identify the stains on the cement stairs as I walked down them. Inside, scuffed dark-stained wood covered every wall. The dingy green hanging lights over each table shone against tabletops covered with too many layers of lacquer. Half the track lights pointing toward the bottles of liquor behind the bar were burnt out and display reminded me of a smile with missing teeth. You could tell it had once been a beautiful place, but now it just reminded me of the pretty girl from high school after two failed marriages and too many years of three pack a day smoking; there wasn't much left of the girl behind the years.

Like the customers, Damon's was lost and didn't really want to be found.

A well dressed couple occupied one of the booths, drinking what looked like margaritas from rocks glasses while they poured over a Frommer's guide. Two older men slouched over the bar at one end, while the woman at the other end arranged her collection of beer bottles and shot glasses in neat rows.

I sat down three spots to her right. When she glanced my way, I grinned and said, "Looks like I've got some catching up to do."

She pushed her hair back over her ear and leaned back on the barstool. "Good luck," she said, slurring the words. She blinked twice; long and slow and gifted me with a half-amused smile.

I ordered a scotch from the bartender and another beer and bump for the lady.

"Uh-oh Charlie, " she said to the bartender. "Looks like we've got ourselves a gentleman here." The bartender stared at me for a moment, scrunching his eyes and shaking his head side-to-side ever so slightly as to hide the gesture. "You got a name?" she asked. "Man buys me a drink and I like to know his name."

I handed the bartender a twenty and waved off the change. "Name's Davey."

She stared at me for a minute—almost an examination—and then looked back down to her empties. "Davey . . . Davey Jones . . . Davey Jones' locker, gonna drown me in beer and take me down to his locker. . ."

I could tell I didn't have much time. "And you?" I asked, loud enough to snap her attention back to the conversation.

"Donna," she said. She rocked in her chair slightly and grabbed the edge of the bar to steady herself.

I had to hurry. "So Donna, I understand you know my sister Suzi."

I might have well as slapped her. Her eyes opened wide and her jaw dropped. "Oh shit, you're *Davey*. Oh God, Oh God. . ."

I leaned in closer. The last thing I needed was for her to make a scene and draw the bartender's attention. "Yeah, it's okay," I whispered. "I just need to know where she went."

"You have to take me with you," she said. "Please take me with you. Suzi said I couldn't come with her. I wasn't ready. But you can make me ready. You're Davey."

"Shh, it's okay. Take you where?"

"There. The good place. You know." Tears formed in her eyes.

"I don't know what you're talking about," I said. "I can't take you anywhere. I just need to know where—"

"I'm ready!"

The bartender glanced over from down the bar. I pretended not to notice and said louder than necessary, "You've still got half a bottle left," then gave the bartender an amused shrug. He grabbed an ice bucket and disappeared into the back room. "I can't take you with me now," I said. "I have to find Suzi first. But I'll come back for you if you tell me where she went."

She stared into my eyes. "Really?"

I hated myself for saying it, but I did. "Really. Just tell me."

"But I'm ready now," she said. "I'll show you." Donna grabbed her beer bottle and held it between her hands. She closed her eyes for a moment, and just when I thought she might pass out, she opened them again and shoved the bottle at me. "Taste it."

"No, really, I don't like—"

"Taste it!"

I flinched and glanced down the bar, but the bartender hadn't returned. I took the bottle from her hands and took a sip.

It wasn't beer.

I don't know what it was, but there was honey and cardamom and clove in it. I tasted sunflower seed, parsley, licorice. It may have been the best thing I've ever had.

"How did you—"

"They wouldn't let me in," she said. She hooked her finger on a silver chain around her neck and pulled. A filigree skeleton key on the end of the chain popped out from beneath her blouse. "They said I didn't have the right key."

"Who said that?" I asked.

"You know," she said, getting irritated.

"Right, yeah, well it's not the right key, but if you give it to me and tell me where Suzi went, I'll fix it and give it to you when I come back. You don't just get the right key, you have to earn it."

She started to hand me the key. "Promise?"

I nodded.

Donna took my hand, slid the key into my palm and closed my fist around it. "Don't forget me, okay?"

"Okay."

"She went to see the wizard," she said.

I bit my bottom lip and sighed. "I know that," I said. "But where?"

She leaned back in her chair and smiled. "Where else would someone go to see the wizard?"

"Look, Donna, I need you to tell me."

She grinned. "Why, the Emerald City of course."

I caught the next flight to Seattle.

It could have been the altitude. I've always felt a little intoxicated when I flew, but it was never quite so pronounced before. I could still taste Donna's drink on my tongue and a pleasant warmth engulfed every inch of my body.

The flight left around three o'clock and as a result, the plane was only half-full. I had an aisle seat near the rear of the plane and there was no one within two rows of me. When the flight attendant passed, I stopped her and ordered a beer.

I'd called Monica from the airport before we left. I didn't explain it well, but even if I had I doubt she would have understood. Trust is a hard thing to rebuild, and it didn't help that I was disappearing for days without being able to give her a satisfactory explanation for gallivanting around the county looking for a sister I hadn't seen in years. From the tone in her voice, I could tell she didn't believe it was my sister I was looking for.

I couldn't really say she was wrong. I didn't know what I was looking for anymore. Did I really believe in magic or was I chasing boyhood fantasies? There were any number of explanations for the things that happened with Suzi when I was young. Even Donna's drink could have been a trick. It wasn't exactly like Donna had been a pillar of rationality after all. And here I was, jetting to the other side of the country on her word.

I couldn't even explain what I was doing to myself. I just knew that I'd tried everything else.

Rational hadn't worked.

I pulled the key Donna gave me from my pocket. What I had taken for silver was merely plastic. Some of the paint had even chipped off, exposing the dull gray surface below. It was a toy, the kind you'd find in any ninety-nine cent child's detective kit hanging from a peg in a dollar store.

I slipped it back into my pocket just in time for the flight attendant to drop off my beer.

I waited for her to walk away, raised the glass to my lips and then stopped.

Wrapping both hands around the bottle, I closed my eyes and remembered: Honeysuckle; strains of piano melodies; Suzi sitting next to me on the couch watching old television reruns.

When I opened my eyes, Donna sat in the seat across the aisle. The wrinkles were gone and her skin blossomed with daisies and carnations. Her tussled short hair framed her face like petals on a sunflower and her legs ended in cloven hooves. She raised a platinum gem-encrusted chalice in toast. I lifted my bottle in return and drank.

It was beer.

When I looked back across the aisle, Donna was gone.

And then, from nowhere, the faint taste of honey hit my tongue.

I set the beer down on the fold-down tray, leaned back my seat, and slept.

I'd need my strength when I got to Seattle. I had a wizard to find.

By the time my taxi got to Seattle from the airport, the sun had set and the lights of the skyline were just beginning to glow against the clear evening sky. I'd only seen it before in pictures, but now I understood where the city got its nickname. The buildings glowed a deep, emerald green. I'd been many places in my life, but I don't think I'd ever been anywhere quite so beautiful.

I checked into a hotel on Capitol Hill at the recommendation of the driver. I told him I was looking for the strangest neighborhood in the city and he drove me straight there without hesitation. He also told me that in addition to any and every type of person imaginable, the neighborhood was also the heart of the gay and lesbian community. It was as good a place to start as any.

I took a quick shower, changed clothes, grabbed Suzi's graduation picture from my suitcase and started walking down Broadway Avenue. I hadn't made it a block before I realized two things: I'd never been in a place like this before and my mother would have hated it.

Every telephone pole wore a second skin of fliers espousing everything from raves and concerts to any ideological point-of-view under the stars. The air carried curry and ginger and perfumed incense, pouring out of the little shops huddled together along each block. Men held hands walking down the street without looking over their shoulders. Teens, mostly in black, huddled in the doorways and entrances of eclectic shops and apartment buildings, some just smoking and watching the foot traffic while others actively panhandled. Two girls stood on a street-corner with an old, faded magician's top-hat held out in front of them while they sang:

If you want us to shut up, spare some change!

If you want us to shut up, spare some change!

If you want us to shut up,

And you think our singing sucks,

If you want us to shut up, spare some change!

One of the girls wore a black leather jacket with a pink tutu, black and white striped stockings and ballerina slippers. Her long black hair was tied off in pigtails from the top of her head. The other had short, spiked blonde hair, wore a black lace evening-dress and combat boots with orange laces. I didn't even try to count her piercings.

I added a couple ones to their collection, pulled a ten from my wallet and held up Suzi's picture. "Either of you seen her?" I asked. "Point me in the right direction and the ten is yours."

Boots looked over at Slippers and said, "The man wants to know if we've seen the girl. I think he's lost."

"Of course he's lost," Slippers replied. "Even though he thinks he knows exactly where he is. Should we help him?"

Boots bit down on her bottom lip. "I don't know," she said. "He is offering us money."

Slippers rolled her eyes. "Must you always think about money?"

"One of us has to," Boots said. "But I put it to you: Is ten enough to tell him where to find his sister? It's quite a conundrum, isn't it?"

I took a step toward them. "How do you know it's my sister?"

"I want to help him," Slippers said. "But I'm feeling crowded. Perhaps we should move on?"

"Sorry," I said, taking a quick step back. "Please, I need to find her."

Slippers crossed her arms and tapped her foot. "He is kind of cute, for an old guy anyway. And I think it's sweet that he's looking for his sister."

"You don't think she owes him money or something, do you?" Boots asked.

"It's not like that," I said. "I swear." I pulled another twenty from my wallet and added it to the ten in my hand.

"Now he's offering us thirty pieces of silver," Slippers said. "That can't be a good sign."

Boots sighed. "You really need to stop reading into things so much," she said. "I wonder if he knows how to foxtrot?"

"He could learn. But he'll need his energy. He should probably get a coffee."

I glanced down the street. The familiar green and white sign of a Starbucks hung from an awning not a block away. I pointed at the sign. "There?" I asked.

Boots chuckled. "Oh he really isn't in Kansas anymore, is he?" she asked.

"Give him a break," Slippers said. "He doesn't know that only tourists go there. He's probably never even heard of Vivace's."

"I haven't."

"I think he should pay us now," Boots said.

I dropped the two bills into their hat and they made a clink, like coins falling on coins.

The two of them turned their back and started to walk away. "I hope he finds her," Slippers said.

"I hope he knows what's he's looking for," Boots replied.

I found Vivace's a block further down. Two white lattice-topped steel tables sat in front of the coffee stand on the sidewalk underneath aqua umbrellas. The front of the shop had no door; the two male baristas stood behind a counter that opened right up to street access. Hot steam puffed out from the espresso machine like dragon's breath, billowing into the crowd of patrons waiting for service. To the right of the counter, separated by a common wall from the shop, a cement hallway reached back into the depths of the building. I peeked down the hallway as I approached and saw lit candles halfway down the passage, sitting on the floor next to the right wall beneath a painted mosaic of an elephant standing on one back leg. The candlelight flickered across the surface of the mosaic, making it look as if the elephant were swaying back in forth in dance.

I waited in line, pulling my jacket tight against the damp evening chill. No one else seemed to mind the temperature, wearing only light jackets at best, short skirts and sleeveless shirts at the worst. I couldn't have been more obviously a tourist had I tried.

Yet no one paid attention to me. People came and went all around me while I waited in line, but other than avoiding my space, they didn't so much as glance in my direction. It was as if I wasn't even there. I was a temporary passing—something to be avoided—like a non-descript car driving through the intersection in front of them; briefly encountered, certainly not remembered.

I reached the front of the line and unfolded Suzi's picture. "Just a regular coffee," I said to the barista. His spindly fingers danced over the cash register's keys as he repeated my order to his companion. "Have you seen this girl?" I asked.

He looked up briefly—just long enough for me to catch a glimpse of his bright gold contact lenses—and said, "No, sorry. I see a lot of people here. I barely remember the regulars."

"Damn," I said with a sigh. "Are you sure? A couple of girls down the street said I might find her here."

He didn't even look back up. "Sorry," he said again.

I felt myself being forced to the side by someone behind me, who ordered a soy mocha over my shoulder. I stepped directly in front of the interloper, giving no ground. I felt stupid asking the question, but I didn't have any other ideas. "One of the girls asked if I knew how to foxtrot. Does that mean anything to you?"

The barista stopped. He looked up at me and said, "Well, if you don't, you can learn right over there." He pointed to a spot on the sidewalk just beyond the tables.

"Where?" I asked.

"Near the street," he said. He handed me my coffee and I stepped out of line, pausing only long enough to add cream to my cup and securing it with a plastic lid. I walked over to the sidewalk where he had pointed. People passed by me in both directions. I scanned the shops on both side of the street looking for a dance studio or a street artist or something that would make sense and came up empty. I dipped my head to take a sip of my coffee when I saw it:

Inlaid in the cobblestones were brass footprints. Numbers were set into each step, with arrows pointing to other steps in succession. Near step number one was a square plate.

Foxtrot

Lesson 29.

I smiled, set my coffee down on the sidewalk, and took the first step. Then the second.

Someone brushed by me, almost causing me to lose my balance, but I spun and stepped backwards right onto plate number three. Then four. Invisible soft hands slipped into mine and we turned left with a glide to number five. Strains of "You Make me Feel so Young," filled my ears. Six. We spun, widdershins. I closed my eyes and breathed in soft perfume. The music grew louder, drowning out the sounds of traffic. Seven, eight, nine. I couldn't help it: I threw my head back and laughed. It was as if years of hiding to the side, afraid to stick my head out, never were, rushing out of existence with every laugh and turn and spin.

In that moment, life was earnest, not dutiful. It was everything my life to this point wasn't.

Too soon, the song ended. I opened my eyes.

I was no longer invisible. The customers sitting at the tables stood, applauding, shaking their heads while wide grins stretched their faces.

What could I do? I took a bow.

When I raised my head, I was alone. The street was empty. I turned, looking all around me. Not a single car drove down the street. Chairs around the table sat in their previous pulled-out positions, but with no one in them. Beside the counter, down the hallway, I heard Frank Sinatra still singing, but softer, as if from the single-speaker of a small radio.

I followed it. The Elephant on the mosaic waved his arm, beckoning me closer. When I reached the front of the mosaic, the outline of a door appeared in the wall, along with a keyhole right where a knob should have been. I took Donna's key from my pocket and slipped it in the lock.

The door opened, and I stepped across the threshold.

I stood in my hotel room and closed the latches on my suitcase. Check-out was at noon and the clock on the nightstand read eleven-thirty. It was time to go home. The foolishness of my dream the night before was just that; the deluded hopes of a man looking for something he could never find. Suzi was gone, and no amount of imagined tastes of honey or flights from the back stairs or evening dances with invisible partners could change that. My troubles were of my own making, and there was no savior out there to help me back on my path. There was no magic.

I picked up the suitcase and turned to go.

And stopped.

Beside the phone, a folded travel brochure sat on the nightstand. On the front was a picture on an elephant, balancing on one foot. The caption read, "Don't Forget!" I set down my luggage and opened the brochure. Inside it read, "Visit the Seattle Zoo!"

There was no good reason for it, but I picked up the phone and called the front desk. "I'll be staying another day," I said.

The pathways between exhibits at the Seattle Zoo are made of yellow brick. Any other day, I might have been amused. But I'd watched too many happy couples swinging their children between outstretched hands today. Too many images of what I didn't have taunted me. I'd left my cell phone behind in the room. I didn't want to talk to Monica today. I didn't want to hear the unspoken accusations. Hurting her was the last thing I'd wanted to do, but I didn't know if it was possible to fix our relationship anymore. Every time I tried, I just seemed to make matters worse. I'd start off great, and then say something stupid, almost as if I had intentionally tried to sabotage my own efforts. All it ended up doing was hurting Monica even more. I'd hold out the possibility of happiness, then snatch it away again for no good reason.

For the life of me, I couldn't figure out why.

I wandered the exhibits for over two hours, seemingly walking in circles. Just when I thought I'd seen everything there was to see, I spotted a glass enclosure directly ahead in my path. It sat quite a distance from the other exhibits, and as I approached I read the plaque on the front of the structure.

"Butterfly Exhibit," it read. And then in small letters, at the bottom, "Emerald City Structures."

A handful of small trees and bushes grew within the enclosure. Everywhere you looked, butterflies of every color bounced in the air or rested on branches. A single bench rested on the grass in the center of the structure, and on it, Suzi sat waiting for me. We were the only people there.

From an initial glance, it appeared that the years had been kind to her but as I approached, I looked into her eyes and saw otherwise.

"Hi," she said.

"Hey. You're a hard person to find." I sat down on the bench next to her. "This is a beautiful place," I said.

She nodded and looked around. "This is the last place I saw Nancy," she said. "I thought she might be here, but she's not."

"Is she the wizard you came looking for?" I asked.

She snapped her head around to look at me. She squinted her eyes. "No," she said. "You are."

"Me?"

"I thought you could help me, but I was wrong," she said. "A friend of mine from the Elephant Bar told me about last night."

It all came rushing back: I stepped over the threshold of the doorway and into another world. Inside, ogres conversed with manticores. A single dragon lounged around the outside of the cavernous room, its tail wrapping along the perimeter to rest not far from its head. Fairies danced on currents of air and at the doorway, a tall man with pointed ears stood guard. He put his hand on my chest, shook his head and said, "You're not ready," pushing me outside. I fell, but instead of landing on the cement floor, I started from my hotel bed. I was certain it'd been a dream.

"What made you think I was a wizard?" I asked.

"You saved me," Suzi said. "Mom had me pinned to the floor and then all of a sudden, I wasn't. You freed me from her."

I shook my head in disbelief. "Suzi," I said. "I didn't do anything of the sort. You did it. I came looking for you because you had the magic. You're the wizard. I convinced myself that it wasn't true over the years, but I had to find you and find out for certain."

She shook her head. "They pushed me out, too," she said. "I thought you could help me pass over. I can't help Bernard and Donna from this side. I didn't want to ask you, but I didn't have a choice."

"Why here?" I asked.

"This is where Nancy went over. I wanted to go with her, but they wouldn't let me. I'm so tired of living half-in and half-out of that world."

"I'm sorry, I can't help you."

Suzi nodded. "I know," she said. "I hated you for so many years I didn't even want to ask."

Sharp pain hit my chest. I felt my eyes begin to tear. "You hated me? Why?"

"You had the magic. I kept waiting for you to come save me. You saved me from Mom, so I thought you'd save me from everything else. When you didn't . . . well, I thought you just didn't care."

I shook my head. Now I understood. Every relationship I'd ever been in I'd ruined. Every woman I'd ever loved I hurt. Now I knew why. "I hated you too," I said.

"You did? But I loved you and took care of you. I protected you," she said.

"And then you left me," I said. "Behind. With her. You could make me fly and get away from Mom, but you left me there." I thought about Monica, waiting for me at home. "I didn't want to get hurt like that again, Suzi."

A single butterfly landed on her arm.

"I'm sorry," she said. "I couldn't take you with me."

"I know. I couldn't save you."

She reached in her handbag, pulled out a picture and handed it to me. It was the Superman picture. In it, I was forever suspended in mid-air above the back stairs, my cape flapping in the wind behind me. "You did fly," she said. "But I had nothing to do with it."

Another butterfly landed on her shoulder, emerald wings flittering. Suzi glanced down at the butterfly on her arm and smiled. "It's happening," she said.

And then, hundreds of butterflies filled the air, landing on every inch of Suzi's body. I saw her smile one last time before they covered her face, a chromatic silk skin replacing her own. "I'm sorry," she said. "I always loved you, even when I hated you."

"Me too."

"Come with me. I don't want to leave you behind again."

I shook my head and smiled. "You're not."

All at once, the butterflies scattered in every direction, leaving the bench where Suzi had sat empty beside me. I stood up from the bench and stared at the picture. "There's no place like home," I said.

I needed to get home to Monica. Maybe I could make things right with her, maybe I couldn't, but at least now I knew that it wasn't impossible.

Nothing was impossible.

I'd been to Oz, and it was time for the man behind the curtain to go home.

Ding dong. The wicked witch is dead.

God's Guitar
by Justin Stanchfield

The Angel of Rock appeared precisely at 7:14 A.M. on the second Sunday of November, and stood patiently beside Matt Torrence's bed, his scuffed leather jacket hanging open, the tips of his billowy wings brushing the floor. Matt opened a blurry eye, willing to believe the strange creature with the neon blue eyes was a by-product of too much beer and too little sleep.

"You'll find the guitar at Bruce's Pawn on Arizona Street." The angel's voice was sweet as a Strat with the tone rolled off.

"Who are you?"

The angel plucked a rumpled soft-pack of Camels out of his pocket and knocked one loose, pulling the cigarette free with his mouth. It flared, the tip cherry-red as he took a long drag, letting the smoke roll out his nostrils in wispy curls, and the scent was of incense, sandalwood and Turkish tobacco. Matt sat up a little higher, his mouth dry as cathedral dust, and tried again.

"Who are you?"

"You'll find the guitar," the angel repeated, "on Arizona Street."

He took a last drag off the Camel and snubbed it out against the nightstand. Butterflies rushed skyward where ashes might have been. The angel blew a smoke ring and stepped through it, fading out with just a trace of reverb. Matt lay in bed a long time, listening to the traffic and the church bells, wondering where in the hell he had dropped his mind.

His kidneys drove him where no angel could, across the apartment to the bathroom, pretending the visitation had been nothing more than an odd dream. Relieved, he wandered into the living room and flopped to the sofa, fumbling for the remote amid the scattered text-books, food wrappers and loose papers. Norman Kroft, his roommate, was thankfully asleep, snores muffled by the radio playing in the other, smaller bedroom. Matt finally located the remote beneath an empty CD case, a crack running diagonally across it, held together only by the faded red sticker proudly displaying the words, 'Bruce's Pawn, Butte's Best.' He snorted at the coincidence and clicked the television on.

"Oh, wonderful."

"If you need it," the unseen speaker announced, "Bruce's Pawn has it." The camera swept past long rows of hunting rifles and snowboards, slipping past a dozen guitars hanging from the wall. Matt quickly flipped channels. A commercial popped on, already in progress.

"If you need it. . ."

He shut the television off and sat for a very long time staring at the blank screen. He barely felt the telephone in his hand. It rang twice before a very sleepy, very female voice answered.

"Is Lonnie there?" he asked, suddenly sheepish for whatever he might be disturbing.

"'S for you," the girl mumbled. A moment later a man's voice picked up.

"Hello?"

"Hey, Lon. Matt here. I was wondering if you wanted to hit a couple pawn shops today?"

"Why?"

"I don't know." Matt paused, feeling very foolish. "I was thinking about maybe buying a guitar. Maybe. Figured you'd be the person to take along if I did."

"Who's coming?"

Matt glanced at Norman's door. "Just me." He waited a second longer. "Promise."

"All right. Pick me up around eleven, okay? Not ten. Eleven."

"Sure. See you in a bit." Matt hung up the phone, the scent of sandalwood and tobacco drifting in the morning air.

The car wouldn't start.

Battery dying, Matt surrendered and squirmed out of his battered Sentra and trudged back inside. He frowned, trying to place the ancient tune slowly demolishing his stereo. Norman nodded at the CD player.

"Cream, 'Sunshine of Your Love.' Great, isn't it?" He seemed on the verge of genuflecting. "It's from Disraeli Gears."

"Oh," Matt said, not wanting to pursue the topic. He checked his wristwatch, already hating himself. "How'd you like to give me a ride uptown?"

"Where to?"

"Well," Matt chewed on his lower lip, feeling like a traitor. "I'm supposed to pick up Lonnie Schmidt at eleven. We're going pawn-shopping."

"Okay." Norman popped the CD out of the tray and laid it gently in its paisley case. "What are you pawning?"

"Nothing." Matt's gaze drifting toward the flat-top Guild propped lovingly against the bookcase outside Norman's door. "I was thinking of getting a guitar."

"Cool!" Norman threw his coat on, an enormous blue parka, the quilted sides puffy as fresh marshmallows. "We can jam."

"Sure."

Norman had his coat on before Matt could change his mind, practically pushing him out the door into the brittle autumn wind. He glared at his traitorous Sentra, Norman's ancient Chevy truck purring to life without a hitch, tires crunching as they pulled onto the street. It was a short drive uptown, and far sooner than Matt might have wished, they pulled up beside a one-story house shadowed by a gnarled cottonwood. Norman started to get out, but Matt stopped him.

"I'll get Lonnie."

He stuffed his hands in his pocket and walked up the broken sidewalk. A pretty blond in a long gray coat let him in, smiling. At least, Matt thought sourly, Lonnie should be in a good mood about something. A tall man in his early twenties, tousled brown-black hair hanging just above his collar, stuck his head out of the kitchen.

"Hey, Matthew. I'll just be a second, okay?"

"No hurry." The glorious aroma of hot bacon hung in the air as Matt shuffled into the kitchen, his stomach rumbling, reminding him how long it had been since breakfast was anything more enticing than Mountain Dew and Pop-Tarts. On the refrigerator hung a cardboard sign, cheerful blue and red lettering proclaiming 'Albertson's Food Store, employee of the Month.' A Marshal amp with a torn vinyl case stood beside it.

"I'm running a little late, this morning," Lonnie said, elbow deep in suds. "I didn't go out to breakfast after the job last night."

"So I gathered." The girl's perfume mingled with the scent of bacon and dishwater. "Good crowd?"

"Kind of dead." Lonnie dried his hands. He had thick, crushing fingers, a workman's hands, not a musician's, but he was a wizard nonetheless, the sort of guitar player who could squeeze the strings until they screamed then turn around and coax notes from them gentle as a kitten searching for the tit. He threw on his faded Levi jacket. "Okay. Let's go."

His smile vanished at the first glimpse of Norman's pick-up idling in his driveway. Matt shrugged sheepishly.

"My car wouldn't start."

"Great." He glared at Matt "I knew things were going too fucking good today."

Matt prudently kept his mouth shut and slid in, his head brushing the cab. Lonnie crawled in after him and slammed the door.

The windows were filthy behind the steel bars, a layer of dust graying the crowded shelves while hand-printed price tags fluttered in the forced-air breeze. Bruce's Pawn felt rusty, as if the gears of commerce had finely ground to a halt behind its creaking door. Stale cigarettes, stale coffee, stale lives. A glowering man behind the counter glanced over his newspaper, grunted something that might have been a greeting, then forgot them. Lonnie blazed trail toward the far wall where a dozen guitars hung from pegs, a barricade of amplifiers and speaker cases standing sentinel beneath. Norman veered away, drawn irresistibly to the used CD bin.

"Eight pays ten he finds something awful," Lonnie muttered. "So, what kind of ax are you looking for?"

"Well," Matt admitted, "I'm really not sure. What's best?"

"Depends." Lonnie ran his fingers over the strings of a tobacco sunburst acoustic, the notes flat. "Can't they tune these sons a bitches?"

Perhaps Matt had expected trumpets from above, or a heavenly light to part the roof beams and spill over the guitar he was destined to find, but if a sign from above waited for him, he was obviously missing it. He took down a jet black electric missing the high E string. Lonnie shook his head.

"You don't want that one. It's got a bad neck. See?" He took it from Matt and hit the strings, pulling back on the neck, the notes rising uncomfortably. "How serious are you about learning? No sense spending three hundred bucks on something you won't play. But, you don't want to piss away good money for a piece of crap that you'll outgrow in a couple months, either." He paused. "What made you decide to buy a guitar in the first place? You always told me you hated music."

"I never said I hated it." Matt shrugged, hating to reveal his real reason. "Maybe I want some of those babes you always seem to wind up with."

"Yeah, like that's going to happen." Lonnie hung the guitar back on its peg, and moved down the line. He grabbed a bright red Strat copy. "Try this one. Ibanez builds knock-offs, but they're good ones." He played a fast riff, bending the last note with a flourish, then passed it into Matt's outstretched hands.

It felt as cold and dead as the first one, nothing but wood and sweat-grimed metal. If Matt had expected magic, he was disappointed. He fumbled with the guitar as he put it back on the wall, banging it harder against its neighbors than he intended. The fat man behind the counter lowered his paper, menace in his glare. Embarrassed, Matt grabbed the instruments, stopping their pendulum swing. His left hand brushed a pale, hideous pink guitar, the body curved into a deep cut-out where it met the neck. An electric ripple ran up his arm. From far away he thought he heard an angel cough.

"What about this one?"

"A Les Paul?" Lonnie shrugged. "Gibson's are nice. Damned nice. This one's pretty beat up, though." He fingered the price tag. "And, he's asking way too much for it. I mean, look at the paint job? Somebody's gone to a lot of trouble to hide the original color, and that usually means it's been damaged. I'd give it a pass."

"Oh." Matt started to put the battered Gibson back on the wall. The guitar seemed to grow heavier, an unendurable weight forcing him to miss the pegs. He tried again and failed. Hating to look weak as well as untalented, he pretended to study the control knobs. Around the edge of the broad, uncovered pick-ups faint traces of the original color remained, a bright sunburst lurking beneath the pink veneer. Norman sauntered closer, a pair of cassette tapes in hand. They fell to the floor, forgotten, the moment he saw the guitar.

"Jesus H . . . do you know what that looks like?"

"Yeah," Lonnie said. "It looks just like a piece of crap." He took the Gibson and hung it on the wall. Norman immediately took it down, his hands shaking.

"Buy this one."

"I don't know. . ."

"I do." Lonnie tried to take the guitar but Norman stopped him.

"Trust me on this, okay?" Norman stared in wonder at the Gibson, stroking it reverently. Tiny drops of sweat rolled down his face as he played the opening lick of 'Wonderful Tonight.'

"Don't do that," Lonnie said. "You don't know how."

Matt took the guitar from his roommate. The neck settled comfortably into his hand, vibrant and warm. Something about the ugly Gibson spoke to him, a rightness tickling his nerves. It faded as he caught a glimpse of the price tag.

"Shit, I don't have that much." Sadly, Matt lifted the guitar toward the pegs. Norman blocked his hand.

"Trust me," he repeated.

Lonnie rolled his eyes and looked away, disgusted. Norman edged closer, his eyes practically glowing. Feeling like a fool, Matt stumbled toward the counter. The fat man dropped the paper and raised an eyebrow. Matt set the Les Paul on the counter and cleared his throat, his chest suddenly tight. "Would you take three-fifty for this?"

The pawn-broker leaned closer. "Nope. Five hundred."

"Oh come on." Lonnie quietly pushed Matt aside. "Hell, it's not worth three-seventy-five."

The broker shrugged. "Five hundred."

Norman crowded up to the counter. "It's stolen you know?"

"Get the hell out of my store."

"Look. . ." Matt pried Norman's white knuckles of the counter and pushed him back. He took a deep breath. "How about four hundred?" The fat man scratched under his chin, looked at the guitar, then back at Matt. Finally, he nodded. Matt grabbed his wallet and started counting out the assorted bills inside. He turned toward Norman. "You got twenty bucks?"

Norman shook his head. Lonnie scowled. "Oh, for Christ's sake." He slapped a twenty on top of the pile. The pawn broker swept up the money, counted it, then slid the guitar toward them. Matt grabbed it by the neck and started toward the door, but Lonnie stopped him. "Hey? Isn't there a case?"

"Not for four hundred there ain't," the fat man said.

The door banged shut behind them, sunlight pouring down on the horrible pink Gibson. Lonnie laughed sourly. "What a pair of newbies."

Matt grabbed his roommate by the sleeve. "Mind telling me what the hell is so important about this guitar?" Norman nodded vigorously, grinning.

"That's a 1960 Sunburst. I think it was stolen."

"Oh, wonderful." Lonnie said. "Nice work, Matthew. You just blew your rent on a hot guitar."

"It was stolen," Norman continued, ignoring the outburst, "from Eric Clapton."

❁

The computer squealed onto the Internet, Norman's face pallid blue in the monitor glare. Matt set an unopened beer in front of Lonnie, currently trying to tune the pink Les Paul, then slumped onto the couch, his own beer cold in his hand, icy as the realization that he probably couldn't afford to drink another one until sometime next semester. Or the semester after that.

"How bad did I get screwed?"

"Not horribly. It's had some rough treatment, but it's not bad." Lonnie played a few bars of slow blues. "Not bad at all."

"It's worth a fortune," Norman muttered, his face pressed against the screen.

"This," Lonnie tapped the fret board, "is not a '60' Sunburst."

"The serial number says it is. And it's got Patent Applied For pick-ups."

"Big deal. Show me a Gibson that doesn't."

"I mean real ones." Norman clicked the mouse, the printer struggling sullenly to life. He snatched the paper out of the tray. "And look . . . The serial number isn't accounted for."

"Gee." Lonnie shrugged, unimpressed. "What were there, like fifty thousand of 'em made that year?"

"Less than seventeen hundred." Norman rushed to his neatly stacked collection of CD's and plucked one from near the bottom of the pile. "Scrape off the pink paint, and this is just like the Mayall sunburst."

Matt sat, beer in hand, lost in the unfamiliar language. "Somebody mind telling me what the hell you two are talking about?"

"Eric Clapton," Lonnie passed the CD across, "played a Cherry Sunburst Les Paul when he was with John Mayall's Bluesbreakers. It got swiped just after he joined Cream." He pointed at Norman. "Numb nuts over there thinks this is the missing ax."

The room wanted to spin. Matt dug his heels against the couch to stop it. "What . . . what do I do if this really is Eric Clapton's guitar."

"It isn't," Lonnie said. "But if it was, stick it on e-bay and start counting your money."

"Are you insane?" Norman's voice pitched higher. "That would be like . . . like selling the Holy Grail."

"What else are you going to do with it?" Lonnie said. "You can't prove it's *the* guitar. And even if you could, can you trace how it got here? Sell the damned thing to the next poor sucker, I say."

The beer in Matt's can had somehow vanished. He stood up, leaving his two friends arguing in the living room, and stumbled to the kitchen in search of another. The refrigerator door popped open, the cold scent of bologna past its prime rushing out, the final beer awaiting its fate beneath the flickering light. Matt grabbed it and popped the tab, then turned around.

"She needs to go home." The Angel took the beer from Matt's hand and drank, then wiped his mouth with the back of his hand. The Angel finished the can and crushed it into rose petals that drifted to the floor.

"I. . ." Matt stammered.

"She needs to go home," the Angel said softly, fading into the cheap yellow wallpaper. He smiled as went, his words lingering. "Take her home."

Matt stumbled back into the living room. Lonnie and Norman were still bickering, passing the pink Gibson back and forth between them. Lonnie shook the instrument for emphasis, his face growing redder.

"I don't give a rat's ass what Guitar Player magazine says. You can't prove it's Clapton's."

"Maybe, maybe not." Norman was just as adamant. "But I know one person who could, and he's in concert Tuesday night in Denver."

"You have his tour dates memorized?"

"Only the close ones."

"You're pathetic." Lonnie glanced up at Matt. "Jesus, man, you look like hell. You feeling all right?"

"She needs to go home," Matt said.

"Who needs to go home?" Lonnie stared at the Les Paul. "The guitar?"

Matt nodded. "It needs to go home." Gently, he took the battered Gibson. "Anybody know where Eric Clapton lives?"

"As a matter of fact," Norman's face lit up. "Day after tomorrow, he lives in Denver."

Flames raged in the dreamtime, pyrotechnic flashes of light and laser bursting in time to Ginger Baker's thunder from on high. Matt woke in a cold sweat, the clock beside his bed declaring the stroke of midnight, the walls rattling from the stereo blaring in Norman's room. He pulled on a pair of sweats and trudged through the darkness into the living room. Light poured out from under Norman's door. Matt rapped against it.

"Mind turning it down?"

"What?"

"I said . . . oh hell, never mind." He pushed the door open. Norman sat on the edge of his sagging mattress, a pair of headphones squeezing his temples white, the Les Paul perched on his knee. He saw Matt and blanched.

"Oh shit. . ." He quickly shut the stereo off then handed the guitar to Matt. "Sorry. I should have asked if I could play it."

"That's okay." Matt plucked the strings, the notes chaotic and not in the least musical. He handed it back to Norman. "Play all you want. Just turn the music down, okay? I've got classes in the morning."

"No problem." Norman dubbed his toe against the matted carpet. "Does that mean you're not going to Denver?"

"I don't know." Matt ran a hand through is hair. He needed a haircut. If he could afford one. "That's almost a thousand miles, and I don't know if my car is up to it. I don't know if I am either."

"But, this is the chance of a lifetime. You could be a part of rock and roll history."

"I'd rather pass my chemistry mid-terms." Matt looked around the cramped bedroom, open pipes and conduits running overhead, the single light nothing more than a porcelain fixture without the grace of either dome or shade. A poster dominated the wall behind the bed, a montage of Eric Clapton in concert, the words 'Clapton is God' across the top. "What is it with you and that guy?"

"I don't know. Something in his music just speaks to me. It's so pure, so intense." Norman fumbled for words. "Look, when I was twelve my parents got divorced. Really screwed me up for a while. My older brother had a copy of 'Derik and the Dominoes.' God, that's a great album. Eric Clapton, Duanne Allman. Ever hear a song called 'Bell Bottom Blues?'"

Matt shook his head.

"It's beautiful. Best song on the whole damn record. I used to play it over and over for hours. Guess it kind of pulled me through." He played a clumsy lick then set the guitar down. "Lonnie's right. There isn't any way in hell to prove this is Clapton's guitar, but, I know it is. Don't ask me why, I just feel it. It's like this is my chance to give something back. Sounds crazy, doesn't it?"

"A little." Matt started back to his room, then stopped. A cool breeze brushed his face, the distant sound of wings fluttering. He turned around. "Look, if you kick in for gas I'll go to Denver."

"Yeah?" Norman's face brightened. "Hey, we can take my truck, if you want."

"We'll talk about it in the morning. I'm going to bed."

He left the Les Paul with Norman, then, against his better judgment, grabbed the telephone and punched in Lonnie's number.

"Hey, Lon. It's Matt. Did I wake you up?"

"Oh shit no. Who the hell sleeps at twelve thirty at night."

"Sorry. I just wanted to tell you we're taking the guitar to Denver. Want to go?"

"I have to work all week," Lonnie finally said.

"So take a couple sick days? I promise, it won't cost you thing."

"Like it didn't cost me twenty bucks at the pawn shop?" Lonnie coughed, the noise loud in the receiver. "Look, I can't. They're breaking in a new assistant manager and need me to show him the ropes."

"Let somebody else worry about it. How often do you get a chance to meet Eric Clapton?"

"You're as crazy as your roommate."

"Does that mean you're going?"

"Good night, Matthew."

Matt grinned, the phone still pressed against his ear. "So, are you going?"

"Call me in the me morning." Lonnie hung up. Matt thumbed the phone off, crawled back to bed and fell asleep, blissfully dreamless.

Snow fell in the night, dusting the barrow pits, hiding the collected trash of a hundred thousand faceless drivers. Matt drove slowly as they topped the pass, the Chevy pick-up sliding under a cement overpass. A faded green sign announced they had just crossed the Continental Divide. He let the truck accelerate gently as they drifted down the other side, swinging in and out of tractor-trailers and mini-vans, the steering wheel unfamiliar in his hands. His Sentra had refused to start, and with daylight burning, had resigned himself to a long trip in the crowded pick-up. Lonnie Schmidt leaned against the passenger door, scowling, while Norman sat in the middle, bobbing his head in time with the music.

"Jesus," Lonnie said, "Don't you have anything that isn't Eric Clapton?"

"Uh, I've got some Jimi Hendrix and Jeff Beck's Greatest Hits."

"You know, there have been some guitar players since the fucking Yardbirds broke up."

"Name one as good as Clapton."

"Two words. Van Halen. No, wait, here's two more. Steve Vai. No, here's another. . ."

Matt grinned, tuning out the argument. The road leveled, mountains giving way to sage-brush hills, snow-capped peaks ringing the broad valley. Trucks passed them, hauling hay, hauling cattle, hauling crates and boxes and barrels, the lifeblood of the nation pouring down the snow-shrouded interstate. Matt checked the rearview mirror, craning his head to check the cargo. Lonnie had taken pity on him and stuffed the Les Paul inside a scuffed canvas gig-bag, refusing to let the guitar ride up front. It nestled between a beat up duffel bag and the spare tire, a fortune, if Norman could be trusted, covered in road-salt and slush from every passing vehicle. Matt clinked the turn indicator on at the next off-ramp.

"Anybody else have to piss? My teeth are floating."

They swung into a small truck-stop. Matt shut off the engine and stepped out. Norman followed, zipped his coat higher, and took up a position next to the cinder block building. "I'll stand guard until you guys get back." He nodded at the guitar hidden in the back of the truck.

Lonnie rolled his eyes. Matt shrugged and headed for the broad glass doors. He stepped aside for a girl in a dingy purple coat, her hands stuffed deep inside the pockets. An electric tingle ran up Matt's arm as they brushed. The girl turned and stared at him, her eyes wide. She was painfully thin, chestnut hair tucked under a knitted cap as ratty as her coat. Lonnie shoved Matt past the startled teenager.

"Forget it man. She's jailbait."

"Right." Matt tried to put her out of his mind, but her dark eyes followed him as he wandered toward the Men's Room. A bearded man in a brown canvas coat stood at the urinal. Matt hurried inside the nearest stall, not able to wait. He heard the trucker leave. Finished, he stepped toward the sink. His jaw dropped when he looked in the mirror.

"She's in trouble." The Angel lit a Camel and took a long, satisfying drag. "She needs to go home."

Matt blinked. The Angel was gone, incense-laced smoke curling toward the ceiling fan. Lonnie stepped into the bathroom, sniffing the air. "What kind of air-freshener are they using? Smells like a fucking yoga class in here."

"Yeah." Matt hurried outside, shivering. The girl stood near the soda fountains, staring at the slowly rotating rack of hotdogs. The bearded man from the men's room squeezed past her, managing to press his hand against her ass in passing. He whispering something in her ear. She smiled, but looked away. He wandered toward the counter, the girl, reluctantly, in tow.

"Here." Lonnie pressed a Styrofoam cup into Matt's hand, steam sifting out the tab in the plastic lid. Matt wrapped his fingers around the coffee cup, his eyes glued to the truck driver.

"Notice anything strange about that guy?"

"The one in the Carhart?" Lonnie took a cautious sip from his own cup. "What about him?"

"I don't know," Matt said. "That girl with him look okay to you?"

"As good as a meth head gets." Lonnie's eyebrows bunched together. "She did look a little young for the business, I'll admit."

"Business?" Matt stared. "She's a hooker?"

"Duh."

The bearded man pointed out the window at a bright blue Peterbuilt, then sauntered out the door. The girl loitered near the door, paper cup in hand. The angel's words rumbling in his mind, Matt saw his opening and walked over, utterly unsure what to do.

"Hi," Matt stammered.

"Hi." Her voice was high and pretty. Without thinking, Matt said the first thing that popped into his mind.

"I saw that guy put something in your cup."

"What?"

"That guy dropped something in your cup when you weren't looking." Matt felt his face redden, the lie already tangled in complications. "Uh, might have been like a powder or something. I don't know what it was. . ." He shrugged. "Just thought I should tell you."

The girl stared at her cup, then out the window. Without another word she walked away. Matt sighed, hoping the angel was listening. "Well, I tried."

He left the building, the cold cutting through his Levi jacket. Lonnie was already outside, arguing with Norman. Matt took a long, slow sip from his cup. The bitter liquid warmed him as the Peterbuilt swung past, black smoke churning out chrome stacks. Matt watched it go, the bearded man from the men's room behind the wheel. He tried to see the girl but couldn't. Feeling like a fool, he walked around the truck.

"You guys ready?"

"I've got to piss." Norman hurried into the store.

"How do you keep from killing that guy?" Lonnie asked.

"It's not easy." Matt watched the truck pull onto the blacktop, gears grinding as it gathered speed. He turned around. The girl in the purple coat stood outside the door, her knit cap pulled low, arms wrapped around her thin body. "Hang on a minute."

She backed up at his approach, her eyes wary, the building blocking any retreat. Matt tried to look unthreatening. "You need a lift?"

She stared suspiciously at the battered pick-up. "How many of you are there?"

"Three," Matt admitted.

"Going to be a little crowded, isn't it?"

"Yeah, I guess so. Sorry."

The door opened and Norman barged past, a bag of pork rinds crackling in his grip. He barely noticed the girl. "You ready? It's a long way to Denver you know." Matt shrugged and followed him to the truck, fumbling in his pocket for the keys. He set his coffee on the dashboard, steam fogging the windshield above it as a familiar figure stepped closer.

The girl tapped on the glass. "You guys are going to Denver?" She was shaking, her lips bright red against her pale skin. Matt rolled the window down.

"You guys are going to Denver?" she asked again, teeth chattering.

"Yeah," Matt said.

"Mind if I catch that ride?"

"Sure, if you don't mind sitting on a lap."

"I don't mind." She hurried around the front of the truck, shuffling foot to foot, waiting for the door to open, and settled against Lonnie. She fanned her fingers above the defroster vents. "Thanks. Fuck, it's cold." She smiled. "My name's Denise."

Matt backed away, Lonnie grunting as they trundled over the pot-holes, Denise's elbows jabbing him. Norman, perched in the middle, ripped the bag open with his teeth and smiled at the girl. "Pork rind?" The girl took one and bit down, crunching in time with the bass guitar blazing out the speakers.

Snow swirled in their wake as they headed east.

The road followed the river, the Yellowstone low, gravel banks and uprooted cottonwoods lining the banks. Limestone bluffs gave way to eroded hillsides as they crossed into Wyoming, long curtains of white hiding the Powder River Mountains. Matt drove, Lonnie and Norman argued, the girl dozed, her head against the door, snoring softly as the miles drifted past. Ahead, just visible around a long, sweeping curve, red and blue lights flashed, a wrecker flanked by patrol cars blocking the right lane. He slowed to a stop as a State Trooper waved them down.

"We'll just be a minute folks," the trooper said, bending low for a better look inside the cab. "You know you're supposed to have seat-belts on, right?"

"Yeah," Matt said, fumbling to find the belt-ends stuffed under the cushions. "Sorry."

The trooper waved them around the wreck, Matt's stomach dropping at the sight of the mangled semi trailer. Long sheets of twisted aluminum flapped in the wind, snow already covering the ruined boxes littering the ground. He coasted past the tractor, the once gleaming blue cab twisted past recognition, the chrome stacks snapped off. Broken bits of glass and plastic covered the road, a small red oval lying along the margin, 'Peterbuilt' still legible. Beside it lay a body shrouded in a green blanket, dark blood pooling beneath. He had no doubt it was the bearded man from the truck-stop. Denise gaped as they drove past, her face deathly white. Matt cleared the accident and sped up, anxious to put miles between them, certain he heard an angel whisper over his shoulder, 'I told you so.'

Highway song. Asphalt kisses rubber. Miles roll away, roll away while the sun traces westward, a bright spot in the snake gray clouds as morning bled into afternoon, dusk not far on the horizon. Matt leaned against the passenger door, eyes shut, trying to sleep before his next turn at the wheel. The girl, for her part, had not shut up since they passed the accident hours earlier, chattering incessantly, barely taking time to breathe before launching into another improbable subject.

"I've got a sister in Denver," she said for at least the tenth time. "She's got a job lined up for me. Like a receptionist or something, I'm not sure. But it beats McDonald's, right?"

His eyes drifted shut, her sweet voice blending into the endless stream of classic rock, trapped in a world forever spinning through abandoned airwaves. Matt slipped across the lonely border between awake and dead-ass exhausted, dreaming a Pentatonic dream in the key of A. Somewhere in the far distance he heard a man singing. Sang about the crossroads, and the devils waiting there.

Matt moaned softly, enjoying the floating, drifting motion. The song drifted across him, thick as the red dust that hung in the air. A flatbox guitar added counterpoint, and the notes slid serpentine beneath the bottleneck. It was a song of wanting and despair. A song of deals gone bad and hell holding the ticket.

Wyoming prairie shifted to Mississippi delta, hot as a potter's kiln, swirling with the ghosts of share-croppers and Model A's. The roads ran straight and true and vanished in the heat waves. Matt stood in the middle of the crossroad, feet chained, the shackles around his wrists chafing him to the bone. A figure walked through the haze, whistling off-key, a heavy Carhart jacket slung over his left shoulder. The bearded man stopped in front of Matt, grinning like a fool while sticky flies buzzed around his eyes. He laughed, his breath road-kill sour.

"They never tell you the price if you fail, do they kid?"

Matt bolted awake, shivering, cold air blowing through the gap in the weather-seal. The girl was still talking, the stereo still playing, snow still swirling across the interstate, ghostly snakes slithering towards the drifts on the shoulder. He sat up and punched the eject button. "Can't we listen to something besides Clapton for a while?"

"Yeah," the girl who called herself Denise chimed in. "What is it with you guys and all this old crap?"

Lonnie nearly choked laughing. Norman sputtered, torn between his devotion to the blues and his growing attraction to the girl whose ass was currently pressed warm against his thigh. Matt rubbed the sleep from his eyes, squinting into the gathering whiteness. "Where are we?"

"About twenty miles out of Caspar." Lonnie slowed down for a herd of antelope dashing across the blacktop. "You want my opinion, we should stop for the night."

"But, we're not even halfway," Norman protested.

"So what? The concert isn't until tomorrow night." Another trio of antelope darted across the highway. Lonnie tapped the brakes, the rear tires sliding. "Let's get a room and wait for the storm to blow out. These roads suck."

"No way." Norman's voice rose, sounding as if he might break into tears. "I can't afford a room."

Matt stared at the road ahead, the dead trucker's warning rumbling in the background. He felt the girl stiffen each time they mentioned stopping, no doubt wary about traveling with three strange men. Off to their left the lights of a distant ranch burned star-bright above the undulating ground blizzard. Matt made his decision.

"I'll pay for the room. Let's spend the night in Caspar."

The storm thickened as Lonnie pulled into a parking lot and shut off the truck, the engine back-firing. Denise sat in the truck, arms wrapped around herself while Matt jogged toward the office, head bent against the wind, Norman dogging in his tracks. The lobby was warm and dry, a blast-furnace compared to the November blizzard outside. He stomped the snow off his tennis shoes and walked to the desk. A mousy woman in a cheerful green vest looked up.

"You have any rooms left?"

"A few." She pulled an invoice up and started filling in the blanks. "How many of you are there?"

Before Matt could lie, Norman blurted, "Four of us."

"Okay." The girl spun the invoice around. "That will be ninety-six dollars."

Sick to his stomach, Matt counted out the last of his money, barely scraping enough to cover the charge. The woman behind the counter raised her eyebrows, but started counting. "I'll need a credit card number, too."

"I. . ."

Lonnie stepped inside, stomped his feet and pulled a visa card out of his wallet. "Put it on this."

"Thanks." Matt swept the cash off the counter and handed it to Lonnie. "I maxed my card out at the cash machine this morning."

"So I noticed." Lonnie stuffed the bills in his pocket then signed the invoice. Snow covered the sad luggage in the back of the truck by the time they found a parking spot, the guitar a pitiful lump of white. Cold, tired and hungry, they walked up the narrow stairs to the second floor hallway. Matt turned around, waiting for Denise. She stood at the bottom of the stairs, uncertainty in every movement.

"Look, I don't know what you're expecting, but I promise, nothing's going to happen, okay?"

She shrugged. "Maybe I'll just take off and see if I can get another ride."

"Suit yourself." He glanced out the glass door at the snow piling up against the rows of parked vehicles. "I don't think you're going to have much luck though." He waited, but she said nothing. Frustrated, he turned around. "If you change your mind, look us up."

Out the corner of his eye he saw her hesitate, glance once more at the storm, then start up the stairs behind him.

The ghost of pizza past hung in the air, the television tuned to an unremarkable football game. Matt sat on the edge of the bed nearest the door, bored, the guitar behind him. Lonnie stood up and stretched.

"Anybody up for a beer?"

"Sure." Matt grinned. "As long as you're buying. I'm broke."

Norman hesitated, staring covetously at Denise. "I think I'll pass."

She glanced at Matt, imploring him to do something. He grabbed Norman by the collar and herded him toward the door. "Come on. I don't trust you around my guitar."

The lobby was nearly empty, a handful of people clustered around the television, bored with the game. In the corner, a husband and wife duo was tuning up, programming their drum machine, waiting for a lull in the game before starting their first set. Lonnie stared at them.

"I can't believe they have music on a Monday night."

"Hey, not everyplace is as dead as Butte." Matt nodded at the band stand. "You going to sit in with them?"

"Thanks, but no thanks."

"Why not?" Norman said. "I was thinking about asking them if I could sit in for a while, myself."

"I don't think the world's quite ready for that." Lonnie drained his beer, his eyes drifting again toward the tiny dance floor. The pair was playing an Eagles cover, the amps barely audible above the television, not caring if anyone listened. Matt grinned as Lonnie's fingers played the solo note for note on his empty bottle. He pushed away from the table.

"Where are you going?" Lonnie asked.

"To get the guitar before you explode. I'll be back in a minute." He left the lobby, taking his time getting back to the room. He stopped beside a picture window, the fresh snow green-gold in the streetlight glare, the last lazy flakes sifting down. It was peaceful, a scene from a snow globe. He smiled, happy for the first time in days, satisfied that he was, for once, doing the right thing. His footsteps echoed as trudged up the stairs and found the room. The door popped open, the hinges sighing over the cheap beige carpet.

"What the hell?"

Denise spun around, coat and hat on, Lonnie's credit card in her palm. Quickly, she stuffed the card inside her pocket.

"You stinking little thief."

"I didn't take anything." She tried to brush past him, but he caught her arm and spun her around. She gasped, but he didn't loosen his grip.

"Let go of me or I'll scream."

"Go ahead. I'll knock you on your ass. If you're going to get the cops I'll give them a damn good reason." He shook with rage, angry at letting himself be tricked so easily. He wanted to hit her, wanted an excuse to do something awful. "This is how you pay somebody back for saving your life?"

"What the hell is that supposed to mean?"

"You saw that truck. If you'd stayed with that guy you'd be as dead as he is right now."

"Is that how you see it?" Denise's eyes narrowed. "That makes up for lying about him spiking my pop, right? I don't know what kind of games you weirdos are playing, but I don't want any part of them. I'm out of here."

"Not before you dump your pockets."

"Fine!" Denise emptied her coat pockets, throwing the credit card and the assorted change she had stolen on top of the nearest bed, then stormed out the door. Matt waited a few seconds, letting himself calm down. As mad as he was, he hated to see her run away again. He opened the door and stepped into the hallway, but the girl in the dirty purple coat was long, long gone.

Morning broke crystal bright, sharpened by knife-edged shadows cutting across the still white snow. Matt nursed his third cup of strong, black coffee, waiting for his head to clear. What had seemed so simple yesterday had become hopelessly tangled, the girl's departure casting a sour spell over everything. Finally ready, they set out, stopping for fuel at a gas station on the edge of town.

A familiar figure stood outside by the payphone, hands stuffed deep in her pocket, puffs of breath hiding her face.

"She's like a stray cat," Lonnie muttered. "You just can't get rid of her." He stepped out of the truck. Matt shut the engine off, leaving Norman to fill the tank, and walked toward her.

"Hi."

"Hi." Denise looked away.

"Thought you'd left last night?"

She shrugged, her boots stained by snow and road salt. "Thought I'd hang out here for a while."

He looked over his shoulder, making sure no one was within earshot. "I never said anything to the others, if that's what you were wondering."

"Thanks." Her lips trembled, slurring her speech.

"You still want that ride to Denver?"

She nodded and followed him back to the truck and climbed inside, no one saying a word about where she might have spent the night.

High prairie bled to grain fields, bled to suburbs, Wyoming gone, Colorado a reality. Ahead, the Denver skyline rose like watchtowers against the hazy blue sky, a mythical kingdom filled with cars hurtling breakneck in an unending parade of rubber and steel. Matt fought to keep up, knuckles white around the wheel. It had been ages since he had driven in real traffic and he had forgotten how much he hated it.

"Anybody know where the hell we're going?"

"The Filmore Theater," Norman said with authority.

"Nice." Matt swerved to avoid a blue sedan. "And where exactly is the Filmore Theater?"

Norman's face fell. "I don't know."

"Maybe," Lonnie said, "we should call Denise's sister and ask directions." If she caught the sarcasm in his voice, she said nothing, her face pressed to the window, hypnotized by the city's swirl and buzz. Matt dodged across lanes toward the nearest exit.

"This is crazy. I'm going to get some directions." A dingy convenience store waited in the shadow of the off-ramp. Matt opened the door, a gray-black chunk of ice breaking off the wheel-well, splattering against the oily rivulets running over the parking lot. Stepping through the slush, he headed toward the door, Norman and Lonnie following. Matt turned around, checking on Denise. "Keep an eye on the truck, okay?"

She nodded.

The bored attendant had no more idea where the Fillmore was than they did. Annoyed, he gave them a poorly printed street map and turned back to the television, leaving them to sort out a route to the concert. Matt wandered to the restroom, discovered it was locked, and went back outside, desperately needing to take a leak. He glanced at the truck, satisfied that Denise hadn't bolted, then walked around the corner of the flat-roofed building.

The snow was melting, slushy puddles shimmering in the breeze. Matt relieved himself behind an overfilled dumpster, and started back toward the truck, turning the corner in time to see a man in a gray sweatshirt grab the guitar.

"Why didn't you stop him!"

"Stop who?" Denise looked up, startled. Matt charged across the slick asphalt, gaining ground, the man in the sweatshirt hampered by the guitar. He turned around, saw Matt and ran harder, water splaying out as he crossed the street. Matt's right foot shot out from under him, dumping him face first in a ripe puddle.

"Shit!"

Soaking wet, he watched the man in the gray hood run away. Without warning, a lanky blur speed past him, Norman's skinny legs driving hard. Matt stared in utter amazement as Norman overtook the thief and grabbed him by the collar. Together, they careened into a lamppost, fell to the ground and rolled in the wet, dirty snow. By the time Lonnie and Matt arrived, the fight was over, the would-be thief vanishing into an alley. A trickle of blood seeped from the corner of Norman's lip. Beside him lay the gig-bag, the Les Paul nestled safely within.

Lonnie handed him a wad of Kleenex. "Remind me never to steal your guitar."

"Come on," Matt helped him to his feet. "Sooner we get out of this place, the better."

No one disagreed.

They wandered blind, precious time slipping away, the map in Lonnie's hand all but worthless. Pedestrians gawked, sullen people all, feet mired in the melting snow, their faces gray as the leafless trees. Matt drove on, wet and dejected, hating a universe that dropped a man like him in a city like this without so much as a star to steer by. Suddenly, Norman poked him in the shoulder and pointed left.

"There it is."

An ornate building stood across the street, an enormous billboard proudly displaying the magical letters 'Fillmore Theater.' They pulled around back, anxious to find a parking place, a crowd already gathered. A mud encrusted semi blocked the alley, tired roadies dragging heavy black cases through the open the stage doors as the sun vanished behind the uneven rows of buildings, twilight choking the last color from a cold gray world.

"So, this is it."

"Yep." Norman stared at the semi, eyes glazed, his glasses bent from the fight. No pilgrim had ever stared with such piety. "This is it."

"Come on." Lonnie opened his door. "Let's get this over with."

The guitar felt impossibly heavy in Matt's hand, the weight of years clinging to it. If it had burst into unearthly flame and told him to cast off his tennis shoes he wouldn't have been surprised. Across the lot they walked, four abreast, three men, a guitar and a half-grown girl, stragglers all, the journey come to an end. The roadies barely glanced at them, the chain of equipment slowing, the truck nearly empty, the thick double doors swinging shut. Matt took a deep breath and crossed the threshold.

"Hold on, buddy."

A tall man, broad shouldered and lean with a neatly trimmed beard put his hand on Matt's shoulder. An ominous bulge rested under the left armpit of his tour jacket, a plastic ID badge dangling over his pocket. Death swam in his eyes, an elemental power potent as the wind and twice as cold. "Nobody through this door."

"But," Norman stammered, "we have Eric Clapton's guitar."

The angel of death seemed unmoved. "You want to see E.C., buy a ticket." He tried to close the door, but Norman held his ground, too crushed to realize the danger he faced.

Struggling to stay calm, Matt unzipped the case, exposing the neck and the hideous pink paint-job. "He's not lying. We think this guitar was stolen from Mr. Clapton."

"Yeah? Send a letter to his manager." The security man tried again to close the door, but Norman jammed his foot inside. "Look, asshole, I'm trying real hard to be polite. No admittance, understand?"

"There a problem?" Another man appeared at the door, dapper in a gray silk suit and charcoal black shirt. He stared out at the guitar.

"No, sir. These people were just leaving."

"Look," Matt said, desperate to grab the man's attention. "I don't care if we go inside or not. But, I think we have one of Eric Clapton's guitars and thought he might want it back."

"When was it stolen?"

"It's the cherry sunburst he used with Mayall." Lonnie pulled Norman away from the door, then carefully took the guitar and let the bag fall open. "At least we think it might be." He offered it to the man in the suit.

"Hang on a minute." The man gave the guitar back to Lonnie and walked into the shadows while the security man blocked the entrance. A flock of pigeons fluttered overhead, turned and sped away, feathers drifting in the icy breeze. After a few minutes, the man in the suit returned. "Where did you get it?"

"A pawn shop in Montana."

The security man coughed, the corner of his grim lips curling up. The man in the suit nodded at the pink Les Paul. "Mind if I let one of the guitar techs have a look?"

"Go ahead." Matt passed the guitar back into his hands, the doors finally swinging shut. Norman seemed on the verge of fainting.

"What if he doesn't come back?"

"Get a life," Lonnie muttered. He turned his collar against the biting wind.

They huddled self-consciously near the door, the long line of concert goers moving, the gates open at last. Now and again the walls would shake, a fast drum roll or a sinewy blues lick, the sound-check thundering within. Lonnie stared at the bricks, his eyes far-away, a look of undeniable longing on his face. Matt nodded at the impenetrable wall.

"That should be you in there."

"Yeah, right."

"I'm serious." Matt moved closer. "You're wasting yourself back home."

"Easy for you to say." Lonnie kicked a snow clod away. It broke into a dozen grit stained pieces. "Trust me, it's harder than it looks to break in."

"Maybe. But I know one thing for damn sure . . . it's impossible if you don't try."

A sharp, metallic click ended the conversation as the stage doors swung open. Cigarette smoke and the heavenly aroma of hot food drifted out. The angel of death stood inside, the man in silk beside him. He nodded at Matt. "Eric's guitar guy said it might be the one." He scratched his nose, stalling. "Tell you what. I'm going to let one of you come backstage and talk to Eric." Again he paused. "Just one of you, understand?"

Nothing moved but the traffic and the split-splat of snow melting off the roof. Norman swallowed, the disappointment bitter. He stepped back from the door and smiled at his roommate. "It's your guitar."

Matt took a step forward, an electric tingle running over his body as he started through the door. He stopped in mid-step and turned around. "You go, Norm. You know more about this shit than I do."

"Are you sure?"

"Go."

"And don't leave us standing out here all night, huh?" Lonnie grinned. "It's colder than a witch's tit." The doors swung shut. Lonnie blew on his hands to warm them. "I'll give even odds he pisses his pants."

The door opened again, the man in the gray silk suit framed in smoke and shadow.

"Eric wants to know how much you're asking?"

Matt glanced at Lonnie, but he only shrugged. Denise slid behind him, hiding. He shut his eyes, visions of riches exploding in his mind, throwing him skyward. Just as quickly, he came back to the cold, sodden ground. "Four hundred, I guess. That's what I gave for it."

The man stared at him, head tipped down, deep gray eyes piercing to the bone. "You know what the guitar is worth?"

"Yeah." Matt said before he changed his mind. "I have a pretty good idea. We didn't come here to make a buck, if that's what you're thinking."

The man shook his head, pulled out a gleaning black wallet and counted four crisp bills into Matt's hand. He paused and counted out three more. "Call it a finder's fee, okay?" He started to close the door. "You guys might as well go. Your friend's going to hang out until after the show."

The door closed, leaving them alone in the alley.

"Now what?" Denise asked, her teeth chattering.

"Don't know about you guys, but I'm hungry." Matt pulled the first hundred off the top and gave it to Lonnie. "I still owe you twenty from the other day, okay?"

"You're crazy. You realize that, don't you?" Lonnie tucked the bill in his pocket. "I still think we should have put it up on eBay." They crawled into the truck, waited a few minutes for the heater to kick in, then drove off, looking for food and light and the thousand things that make life worth living.

The diner was quiet, the waitress slow, the burgers several degrees past wonderful. They lingered at the table, killing time until the concert would let out.. Lonnie studied a local ad-paper, folded open to 'Musicians Wanted.' He caught Matt watching him and flipped the flimsy newsprint shut.

"Got you thinking about it, didn't I?"

"Yeah, and thanks for nothing." Lonnie reached for his coffee and discovered it was empty. "Just what I want to do. Quit a good job and move down here to starve to death." He flipped the paper back open and circled several ads with a felt-tip pen. "I'm getting as crazy as you are."

Still grinning, Matt pushed away from the table and threaded toward the counter. He waited for the cashier. Absently, he reached toward a bowl of mints. A strong hand grabbed his wrist and pinned it to the counter.

"You're not there yet."

Matt spun around, recognizing the angel's voice, but he was alone at the counter. The hair along the back of his neck rose, the flesh around his wrist dented by fingertips that never were. His gaze drifted toward the table, Lonnie bent over his paper, Denise across from him, looking lost as she nursed her third Coke, a frightened teenager trying to bullshit her way through a world gone cold. Her hair was combed but greasy, the same blue blouse she had worn since they found her the day before still on her back. She could have been somebody's little sister. Too late, he realized, she probably was. Matt paid for the burgers then walked back to the table. "You okay here for a while?"

Lonnie glanced up, confused. "Sure. What's up?"

"I'll give Denise a ride to her sister's place." Matt watched her. Her face paled, but she said nothing as she followed him into the night. She sat, hands folded in her lap as they pulled into traffic. Matt drove left, vaguely recalling his destination as they had searched for the theater. A long, high set of doors beckoned ahead, the bays inside brightly lit. A flock of blue and silver buses rumbled inside the cavernous building. He parked across from the depot and shut off the engine.

"Time for the truth. Where are you from?"

"Why do you care?"

"Because I'm sending you back there."

Resolution far beyond her years roiled in her dark eyes. "No, you're not."

Matt recoiled, shocked by her grim determination. Whatever horrors had driven her away from home still waited for her if she went back. "Fine. So you don't go home. But, I'm not leaving you here. Not like this." He grasped for a resolution. "You said you have a sister. Is that bullshit, too?"

"No." Denise stared at the floorboard, her voice once again soft and small. "I have a sister."

"Where?."

"She lives in Cedar Rapids."

"Good enough." He opened the door and stepped out. Diesel fumes drifted hellfire strong as he took her by the wrist. "Let's go."

"Just give me the money and I'll buy my own ticket."

"Yeah, right." Together, they marched across the slushy street into the depot. Matt spotted a row of payphones, and dragged Denise toward them. "What's her number?"

"You're going to call her?"

"Damn straight I am." Resigned, she picked up a pencil stub lying under the dented phone and scrawled a number on the wall. Matt fed a string of quarters into the hungry phone and dialed, the buttons beeping off-key in the receiver. "What's her name?"

"Ginger. Ginger Alverez," Denise said sullenly. "Promise."

Someone answered on the fourth ring. "Hello?"

"Hi. Is this Ginger Alverez?"

"Yes."

"My name is Matthew Torrence, and I'm calling from Denver, Colorado. Do you have a sister named Denise?"

"Yes. . ." The woman was slow in answering, obviously suspicious. Matt took a deep breath and pressed on.

"Is she missing?"

"Oh, God. What's wrong? Please don't tell me she's dead."

"No," Matt said quickly, trying to reassure the woman. "She's right next to me, and she wants to go home. Is that okay? Can she come stay with you a while?"

"Oh, Jesus, yes." She sounded like she was crying. "Please tell her yes. Can I talk to her?" Matt handed the phone to Denise and backed away, giving her as much privacy as he dared. Denise was crying too by the time she put the phone back in his hand. Quickly, before the two minutes expired, Matt pressed the receiver to his ear.

"So, you'll be there to pick her up if I put her on a bus tonight?"

"Yes, oh God, yes. Thank you." The connection went dead, the quarters spent. Matt hung the phone up and started toward the ticket window. The man took his money, passed him a ticket and some change, and pointed at a bus three stalls down.

"Better hurry," he said. "It leaves in five minutes."

"Thanks." Ticket in one hand, Denise in the other, he led her to the idling bus. Blank, empty faces stared down from the dirty windows as they waited to board. He handed the ticket up to the driver, then turned to Denise. "The rest is up to you." He pressed two tens into her hand. "Should be enough to eat on until Iowa."

She stared up at him, the anger and resentment gone. "Why are you doing this?"

"To be honest, I haven't got a clue."

Matt waited until the Greyhound pulled out, then wandered back outside, hands stuffed in his pockets. The night was unusually quiet, not a single car in sight, nothing but the wind as it whistled down the long, empty street. He looked up, amazed to see stars shining brightly despite the city's glare. Far overhead a flight of wild geese passed southbound, honking mournfully on their endless journey. He turned around, not at all surprised to see a familiar figure leaned against a lamppost, wings brushing the dirty sidewalk. A Camel smoldered between his fingers.

"So, now what?" Matt asked.

The angel shrugged. "Now you go home."

"That's it?"

"What did you expect?" The angel took a long last drag off the butt and flicked it away. "A gold star for doing the right thing?"

Matt laughed softly and shook his head. When he turned back to the street lamp, the angel was gone. A silver Caddy with blacked out windows, rap music blaring, sped past. Slush sprayed his legs. Still laughing, Matt walked to Norman's truck, crawled in and turned the key.

It was going to be a long ride home.

Twelve Dancing Daughters

The Whatsis lived in the glove box
and the Widgets lived in the trunk;
between the two of them lived their offspring—
twelve celibate daughters.
The daughters were restless.
They wanted to gaze upon the stars,
to feel soft evening breezes,
to dance in the rain
wearing their sturdy floor mat slippers.
They wanted a moon roof.
They also wanted not to be celibate.

Although the four tribes of Isolationists
in the wheel wells,
(Thingajiggers and Thingabobbers
and two other fraternal Thingathings)
were timid,
they told the twelve daughters
that dwelling within the engine was a clan
of Doohickeys with sons awarded degrees
from MIT and Texas A & M.

The restless daughters set to work sending
promotional spam to the great infrastructure
of V6 and Cubic Inches of Displacement.

"Visit the Inland Hump"
"Conference Beneath the Dashboard"
"Utilize Your Intelligence"
"Up For A Challenge?"
"Looking for Girlz?"
"Hot Chicks!!1!"

"Exotic Foreign Brides Available"

The response was immediate and massive.
Soon, the Interior was overflowing with young men
with calculators and pocket protectors.
Tests were given, could they:
install a six speaker 54 Watt Music System,
untwist shoulder straps,
build bridges between bucket seats,
measure the depth of a kiss?

They could. They could.
Then, the final question:
could they design a moon roof
and oversee its construction?

They could. They could.
It would be a large job, but not an impossible job,
it would be the work of a lifetime,
and would twelve celibate girls
commit themselves
to twelve industrious engineers,
in the name of the project,
if not of love?

They would. They would.
It indeed seemed the work of a lifetime,
but, in the meantime,
the Doohickey boys
spoke with the tribe of people, Whois by name,
that controlled the electrical system,
and on special occasions,
like birthdays and anniversaries,
the windows were lowered
and the twelve sisters danced.

—Pam McNew

Unicorn's Rest
by Jill Knowles

"Jenna! Janek's been arrested," Devon yelled as she burst into the shop.

Again? Jenna sighed and wondered what new trouble her twin had caused.

Mama came from the back room, where she had been embroidering good luck symbols on a wedding dress. "What did you say, Devon?"

"Janek killed a deer on the Baron's property. One of the Baron's men caught him, and the rangers took him away."

"Go and find your father." Mama pushed her youngest daughter towards the door. "He's down at the inn getting the measurements for the new tablecloths."

"Wait." Jenna set her sewing aside and stood. "I'll go."

"Hurry, child, there's no time to spare." Mama leaned against the wall next to the door, placing one hand on her breast. "There's no telling what those awful rangers will do to him."

Jenna patted her mother's shoulder as she passed. "Everything will be all right, Mama, you'll see." She walked quickly along the cobblestone street, her worn boots making brisk tapping sounds on the smooth stones. *What is it* this *time*? Her twin brother spent his life in trouble, preparing to get into trouble, or recovering from trouble. Just last week, Alma, the local hedge witch, had come to the shop complaining that she'd caught Janek tying willow twigs to her cat's tail. Alma discovered this just as Janek was setting the twigs alight. Luckily for the cat, the willow was green, so the flame just smoldered and went out before any damage occurred.

Mama had given Alma two yards of handmade lace, and the hedge witch had agreed not to report the incident to the magistrate. And the family had eaten beans every night since then to make up for the lost sale. Janek had probably gone poaching in order to bring them fresh venison. He didn't seem to understand that it would make things worse.

Jenna arrived at the door of the Weary Unicorn, the town's best inn, which took its name from a local legend. On the north boundary of the town, two roads met beneath an ancient oak. Legend had it that sometimes, late at night, unicorns stopped there to sharpen their horns on the oak tree's rough bark before braving the dangers of the Chewaucan Forest. Jenna and her father were the only people who had actually seen a unicorn in this generation.

Janek hadn't seen the unicorn. He had spent the next few weeks alternately tormenting his twin and telling her how lucky she was. Jenna still sometimes dreamed of the ride—it was hers, something her twin hadn't shared and couldn't ruin.

Jenna smiled up at the unicorn on the sign and smoothed her long brown hair before pushing the door open. As she stepped inside, she stopped for a moment on the threshold, looking for her father's slight form. The innkeeper smiled at her and nodded toward the back of the room. Papa was bent over one of the tavern's larger tables, measuring the distance between the tabletop and the floor.

"Papa," Jenna called softly, going to him and kneeling beside him. "Janek was caught poaching on the Baron's land again."

Papa stood up with a groan, noting his measurements on a piece of parchment that rested on the polished oak table. "The fine will eat all the profits from the Southby wedding dress," he sighed and shook his head, "but there's no help for it." He tucked the parchment into his belt pouch. Pushing a strand of his shoulder length gray hair from his face, he said, "I'll be glad when your twin grows out of his penchant for mischief." He sat at the table, rubbing his temples.

"He's seventeen, Papa; he should have grown out of it years ago." Jenna stared into brown eyes so like her own, willing him to believe her.

"Nonsense, child. He'll stop this foolishness soon."

Jenna sighed and turned away. Movement in the far corner of the tavern caught her eye. It was Daschel, the trader who came to the village each season with magical goods. He sat his tankard down and nodded to her. She bobbed her head a bit in response, flustered.

Daschel had been coming to the village for the past ten years, yet no one really knew him. He would stroll into town, a heavily laden pack on his back, and go to the tavern. The innkeeper let Daschel use a table to sell his magical potions and amulets. People came from all the outlying farms and smaller villages just to buy his wares—and have a meal at the inn.

Half of the table in front of him was covered with delicate glass bottles filled with mysterious liquids. One the color of new leaves caught her eye. She leaned forward to look at it and smelled the faint scent of rosemary and lime. Lovely. The other half of the table held amulets suspended from silver chains. She saw several willow-knot good luck charms, wire-wrapped crystals of different colors, and a finely etched representation of Gwenna-of-the-Harvest.

"Anything in particular you're looking for?" He asked in a deep, musically accented voice.

Jenna smiled. She had spoken to him for the first time only yesterday. Her brother's antics kept the family far less prosperous than they would have been otherwise, so there was seldom any money for things like magic. The handsome trader had come into the shop just as she was putting out a new batch of lady's scarves. He'd examined them carefully, and finally purchased a narrow, black scarf that Jenna had stitched. He had been courteous, asking after her health and discussing the wonderful early spring weather. Jenna had been so nervous she had barely looked at him. Especially after he smiled. He had a lovely smile. The memory of it made her cheeks heat.

The tavern door opened with a crash. Two hard-faced rangers filled the doorway. With the boiled leather armor over the Baron's dark green livery, they made an imposing picture. Jenna unconsciously backed up, stopping next to Daschel.

"Baden Cromwell?" The taller of the two men spoke. It was Captain Tasdin, the Baron's youngest brother, the leader of the rangers.

"I'm Baden Cromwell," Papa said, stepping forward.

"Your son, one Janek Cromwell, was caught on Baron Tasdin's land, in possession of a nursing doe and her fawn."

That was serious. Janek's crimes just kept getting worse and worse. She wondered how long it would be before he did something unforgivable. Jenna bit her lip, listening to the unemotional voice of the ranger as he continued.

"Since this is Janek Cromwell's third and most serious offense, the Baron has sentenced him to six months in gaol, days to be spent laboring in the fields. Or he may pay a fine of fifty gold pieces." With that, the rangers turned and left the tavern.

Jenna sank onto the chair next to the trader. Her chest felt as if it was wrapped too tightly in her bodice. Fifty gold pieces. Her family didn't have that kind of money. In her most secret heart, she was glad. For once, her brother had found trouble he couldn't escape. Perhaps six months unpaid labor would cure him of his foolishness.

"Here, you look like you need this," Daschel's lilting accent was soothing after the harsh words of the ranger Captain. He held his goblet out to her.

Without stopping to think about it, she took a drink. The fiery liquid almost choked her. This wasn't the wine she'd had at village festivals; it was the dark, sweet whiskey the tavern keeper kept for his best customers. She sat the goblet down and blinked rapidly to clear her watering eyes, finally using the hem of her sleeve to blot away the excess moisture.

"My apologies. I didn't realize you weren't used to spirits."

She managed a small smile. "No harm done. I can breathe now, so it helped."

He gave her a quizzical look.

"Thank you," she said, meeting his eyes for the first time. They were blue-black, with golden flecks that sparkled mysteriously—like distant flames on a dark night. His dark auburn hair was pulled back in a loose ponytail that hung nearly to his waist. Jenna was pleased to see the scarf she'd made tied across his forehead. Daschel always wore a headband. Local gossip wavered between speculation that he was hiding a disfiguring scar, and the belief that it was a strange foreign custom that civilized people wouldn't understand.

A strangled sound from her father had her rushing to his side. Tears glittered in his eyes, and he looked far older than his years. "It's not so bad, Papa. You know the Baron won't mistreat him. We can visit him every sevenday."

"We can't let him stay there. He's just a child."

"He's seventeen, father. Most men his age are promised, if not already married." As she should have been. As she never would be without a proper dowry.

"A child, he's just a child," her father repeated. He pointed to the yellowed notice posted behind the bar. Years ago, Baron Tasdin had offered a one hundred gold piece bounty to anyone who could bring him a live unicorn. "This is our only hope."

"Oh, Papa," she said, laying her hand on his arm. When Jenna was a child, she and Janek had gone to play on the edge of the forest. He'd wandered off, leaving Jenna by herself. She followed a butterfly deep into the forest, becoming hopelessly lost. Before she could panic, she stumbled into a tiny meadow. A unicorn the color of a new copper coin stood in the center, munching on bright pink clover. She spent the next several hours petting it, talking to it, and weaving intricate braids into its mane and tail. Late that afternoon, it led her to where Papa had been searching for her on the forest's edge.

Her father flinched away from her touch. "You will lure the unicorn to you. When it lays its head in your lap, you will tie a white silk thread around the base of its horn. Then you will bring it to me. You will go to Unicorn's Rest tonight and every night until you catch one. Your brother must not go to gaol."

"Unicorns are not animals to be put in a menagerie. The Baron doesn't believe in them, but we *know* the truth. It's wrong. I won't do it."

He wouldn't look at her. "Janek comes first."

Jenna sat quietly at the crossroads, shivering as a cool breeze ruffled the hem of her skirt. The west road went into the heart of the Chewaucan Forest, where creatures of magic lived. The north road led north to the top of Mt. Pyre, where the mage called Firesoul practiced his arts. Neither road saw much use. The hard trunk of the ancient oak against her back gave her a measure of security; at least no one could sneak up on her. She started at every sound, imagining monsters roaming the darkness.

A yard of silken thread rested in her lap. How could such a fragile thing hold a creature of magic? No, not a creature. A person. She'd looked into the intelligent, compassionate eyes of the unicorn she'd met as a child. She knew it was as much a person as she was. And now she was to help imprison one of its kindred. For the first time in her life, she truly hated her brother. If the gods were just, Janek was as miserable as she was. She imagined him sitting alone in a cold, damp cell deep in the bowels of a dungeon. Not that the Baron *had* a dungeon, of course, but it made her feel better.

Musical hoof beats startled her. The thread in her hand felt heavy. She strained her ears, trying to gauge how close the sound was, but only heard the chirring of crickets and the faint rustle of leaves in the tree above her. It must have been her imagination. Jenna put her face in her hands and cried, soaking the silken thread with her tears.

A low whinny intruded on her misery. She looked up just as the unicorn knelt and laid its head in her lap. Without thinking, she tied the damp thread around the base of its horn. The unicorn groaned, but made no effort to stand.

"I'm sorry," she said, stroking the beast's neck. Powerful muscles rippled beneath the soft hair. "My father is the only son of an only son. If my brother doesn't marry and produce an heir, our family name will die out." The unicorn shook its head. She ran her fingers through the unicorn's silken mane. "I heard Mama and Papa talking once. Papa feels that he would be betraying his own father if he allows the family to fade away. Mama has miscarried several babies, and the healer has forbidden her to conceive more children. Janek will be my father's only son." The unicorn made a rude noise, somewhere between a snort and a whicker.

She talked all night, telling the unicorn of her brother's many sins, and of his virtues. How she loved him even when she hated him. Finally, the sun began its ascent. The dawn light was captured and made glorious by the unicorn's horn. Of the purest fire opal, the horn seemed to burn. Tears came to Jenna's eyes at the beauty of the creature whose head rested in her lap. The hair on the unicorn's body was copper-bright, and its mane and tail were the color of banked coals. Legend said that unicorns were white, with horns and hooves of pearl, but both unicorns she'd seen were sorrels.

She removed the silk thread from the unicorn's horn. "Go, quickly, before my father comes."

And so it went each night. Jenna talked of her brother, her family, and the hopes and dreams she'd forsaken. The unicorn listened patiently, answering her with soft sounds and urging her to lavish attention on it. Jenna loved the time they spent together, but the worry that her father would discover them haunted her. She knew she should warn the unicorn to stay away, but the thought of losing her only friend was too much.

"Whom have you been with?" Her father's harsh words awakened her.

"What?" She looked around, relieved not to see the unicorn anywhere near. Shaking fallen leaves and dew from her skirts, she stood.

"Ten nights. Today will be the eleventh day your brother has languished in gaol." Her father gave her a bone-rattling shake. "Who has taken your purity?"

"No one." Jenna had no more tears to cry. Her cheek still ached from the slap he'd given her yesterday evening—for daring to smile while her brother was gone.

Papa gave her one last shake before letting her go. "Tonight, Devon waits for the unicorn."

"Papa—" She flinched when he raised his hand. "I'll catch one tonight. Just give me a chance." She breathed a sigh of relief when he left, and sat, staring up through the tree's canopy at the rising sun. The shifting colors lulled her into a light doze. Too many nights spent talking to the unicorn, fearing every moment that her father would appear and capture it, had taken their toll. She slipped into a deep sleep.

The sensation of being watched awakened her. There was a dark human form bending over her. She froze, terrified. No one would hear her if she screamed, and she had no way to defend herself.

"So, Jenna Cromwell, have you captured many unicorns?" Daschel's lilting voice asked.

"No." She shivered, not at all certain she was safe with the handsome trader. Foreigners sometimes had strange ideas about right and wrong.

"I've heard it said that patience is a virtue."

"What are you doing here?" She stiffened as he sat next to her.

"Does a man need a reason to seek out a beautiful young woman?" He was still wearing the scarf she'd made.

Nervous laughter bubbled out of her chest. "I'm not beautiful."

His tone gentled. "Why aren't you married? You're an intelligent young woman, an accomplished seamstress, and you have a kind and generous heart."

His words filled her with a desperate, futile longing. "I have no dowry."

"Your parents own a successful shop."

"All our profits go to pay fines and damages for the mischief Janek causes." She bit her lip. It wasn't proper to tell a stranger the family's troubles.

He nodded. "I know. But surely there are young men in this town who are willing to look beyond that."

Blinking back tears, she looked down at her hands. "No one wants to be tied to my family." A tear escaped, trailing down her cheek.

A gentle hand tipped her head up. Daschel wiped away the tear with his thumb. "You're trapped by your brother's crimes. How can your father love one child so much that he abuses his other children?"

Jenna shook her head. "I don't know." She leaned into his hand. A small tear just above the cuff on his left sleeve caught her attention. Tracing her finger over the soft blue linen, she said, "Let me mend this for you." Her belt pouch held a variety of threads and several gauges of needles. She found some blue linen thread that was just a bit darker than Daschel's shirt, already threaded onto a needle. There was enough for this small job. "It won't take a moment."

She took his hand in both of hers, smiling as she felt the calluses on his fingers. Turning it over, she studied the tear, located just over the pulse point of his wrist. Carefully, she slid her fingers underneath the sleeve, holding it taut while she stitched. Under her fingertips, she could feel his heart beat speed up. "There," she said, tying the thread off and snipping the ends. "All done."

"Thank you." He stood, offering her his hand. "May I walk you home?"

"Yes." She let him pull her up and tuck her hand into his arm. As they walked, she wished he were a suitor, taking her walking in order to win her love.

"I'll be leaving tomorrow."

"Oh." Her heart sank. She couldn't think of anything more to say.

When they reached her parent's shop, he kissed her hand. "Good luck Jenna Cromwell. I hope you find happiness."

What an odd thing to say. "Thank you. Safe journey."

He bowed to her and strode toward the Inn. It was all she could do not to call after him and beg him to take her along on his travels.

"Goodbye, Daschel," she murmured before going into the shop.

Jenna bit her lip, alternately praying the unicorn would come, and hoping she never saw it again. Could she capture it, stealing its freedom to buy temporary freedom for her brother? Because it would be temporary, she knew. Janek wouldn't change, and eventually he'd do something even their father couldn't get him out of. And yet, her sister was innocent, only eight years old. Devon had done nothing to deserve being forced to sit the lonely, dangerous vigil at the crossroads.

It was a situation that had no fair ending. Jenna weighed all the different courses she could choose, trying to find the one that did the least damage. Finally, she made a decision. Steeling herself, she sent a prayer to Gwenna Tanglehair, asking forgiveness for what she must do.

The unicorn appeared not long before dawn, resting his head in her lap with a satisfied sigh. Jenna warmed her hands underneath his mane, absently plaiting the soft hairs. "I won't see you again. My sister will be here tomorrow night. Please, don't go to her. She doesn't understand that it would be wrong to steal your freedom. Promise me you won't trust her." Jenna would sneak out of the house each night and come here to watch over Devon.

Whickering what she hoped was agreement, the unicorn settled his head deeper in her lap. The tears she'd thought long gone made an appearance. "My brother deserves far worse than six months working in the Baron's fields. My father does as well. Maybe if Janek had been punished before now, he wouldn't have gone poaching." She wiped her eyes on her sleeve and stroked the unicorn's brow, just below the base of the horn. "I hope you will help me watch over my sister and keep her safe, but don't let her see you."

The unicorn stood, gazing down at her with dark, mysterious eyes. The air twisted and sparked, and Daschel was smiling down at her. Jenna scrambled to her feet, pressing her back against the tree. Her heart was trying to beat its way from her breast.

"My name is Daschel d'Pyre. It means 'Soul of Fire' in the unicorn tongue. Will you marry me?"

She let her eyes rest on the multi-faceted fire opal in the center of his forehead. "H-how is this possible?"

"Magic."

She pressed harder against the tree, willing it to keep her safe. "W-why would you want me?" Never in her wildest dreams had she imagined this. Jenna felt like a kettle about to boil over as fear and wonder bubbled inside her.

"Why wouldn't I?" He pointed north, at the mountain. "I have a cottage up there. You could see your sister when I bring my wares down each season." He knelt in front of her and held his hand out to her. A silver ring with a flame-colored opal set in its center rested in his palm. "Jenna Cromwell, will you consent to be my wife?"

She took the ring, holding it gingerly. The fire that sparkled inside it warmed her palm. "I'd travel with you?"

"I hope so."

"What about Devon?"

Daschel sighed. "Regardless of your answer, I'll pay your brother's fine—on the condition that your father never again buys Janek's way out of trouble. Your sister won't suffer for your brother's folly."

"My father might make such a bargain with you, but it would only last until my brother broke the law again." The words shamed her, but she owed him the truth.

"If your father gives me his oath, he won't be able to break it."

"You were the one that took me home that day, weren't you?"

He grinned at her, not at all confused by her words. "You were so unafraid, it intrigued me. Each time I came to the village, I heard tales of Janek's troubles. I watched you, and was charmed by your grace and kindness.

Jenna looked at him, considering. In her dreams, she married for love. She loved the unicorn. Could she love Daschel? Would she be happy traveling—and living—with him?

A faint smile played around his lips as he awaited her decision.

"I don't want you to pay Janek's fine. He deserves this punishment."

"What do you want?"

"My sister is in school right now. We can stop there on our way out of town and take her with us. If my parents want to suffer for Janek, they can. But I won't allow my sister to be sacrificed for my brother."

"Done." His smile widened into a grin.

Looking down at her dress, she chuckled ruefully. "You truly want a bride with no dowry—and nothing else except the clothes on her back?"

"I want *you*, Jenna."

She slid the ring onto her finger. "Yes."

The First Stranger

He was not claiming to be the messiah.
"Think of me as a door-to-door salesman,"
he said, "with things to offer—most of them
you do not need."

He smiled. His faded
jeans, wrinkled; his face,
shaved clean, reeked
of gasoline when he leaned closer.
I opened the door,
let him in.

He came from another place, insisted
that he could tweak our eyes so we could
see much better. I believed him;
he had brought my next-door neighbor
back to life.

"You are beautiful creatures," he went on,
"only limited. But I can help you with your vision,
make you see things beyond your visible range."

And he did. It only hurt when he grazed the optic nerves. He said that pain was all right, that it could not exist in the memory, that it was just there for the moment.

He told me to open my eyes, and all I saw
was darkness. "You blinded me,"
I said. "No," he said, chuckled.
"Look closely. There are certain colors
interspersed with the black."

Filmy, mottled swatches shifted
across the blackness.
All the colors were unfamiliar,
unnatural yet they looked as if
they had always existed.

And, oh, how the darkness sang.

—Kristine Ong Muslim

The Sea a Deeper Black
by Tim Pratt

"Hey, mister, want to buy a god?"

Charles looked up from the pebbly beach, squinting at the last blush of sunlight over the water. A skinny man in a pale blue jogging suit, wearing a huge black backpack, sat on a rock near the waterline, grinning at him. He was in his late twenties, perhaps, two decades younger than Charles.

Uncertain what to say, Charles stood still for a moment. This wasn't like the city, where you could push past odd people on the sidewalk, ignore them and disappear in the crowd on the next block. There was no one else here on this strip of sand, with water on one side and sea cliffs on the other, so how could Charles pretend he hadn't heard?

He decided to play it straight. "You're selling gods?"

"A god. And it's not really selling. And you don't get the god exactly, I mean, not to keep. Just an experience with the god, an encounter, like a revelation."

Like an hour with a prostitute, Charles thought, and liked it so much he said it aloud: "Like an hour with a prostitute."

The man frowned. "I've been with prostitutes, and I've never yet mistaken one for a god."

Charles shook his head. "No thanks. I'll pass." He started to walk on.

"Wait up!" the man said. "Really, this'll do you good. Once in a lifetime opportunity, I'm serious."

Charles crossed his arms, pleased to find himself annoyed; it was the first discernible emotion he'd experienced in days. He'd come to the beach to lose himself for a while, to look at the place where the water met the sky and be soothed, to count the stones in the sand and see how they outnumbered his troubles. He didn't need this. "What the hell kind of god is for *sale*, anyway?"

"An old, corroded one," the man said. "Mostly forgotten, greatly diminished. But still a god."

Charles snorted.

"Look, you're depressed, right?" the man said. "Life has no meaning, everything's falling apart, and what's worse, it doesn't seem like it's worth the trouble to keep it together. You're in the shadow of the valley of despair, abandoning all hope, am I right?"

"What make you think that? For all you know I'm on vacation."

"Look, I *know* you're a good prospect for this."

"How? How do you know?"

The man sighed and shifted on the rock. "Not that I expect this to improve my credibility . . . but the dog told me."

"The dog?"

"Over there." He waved toward the water, behind Charles, who turned and saw a very old but still majestic dog with a silver-white coat, standing in the shallows, water lapping at its paws. It gazed at the horizon and the diminishing sun.

"And is the dog the god you're talking about?"

"No, man, don't be silly. The dog used to be a priestess, a *long* time ago, and when I say a long time I don't mean the Sixties, you know? A long time. When her village was invaded, she called on the power of the god to transform her into a swift animal, a dog, so she could escape. But the invaders killed the whole village, all the god's followers died, except for the priestess there. So . . . it's like, if all the shareholders in a company dump their stock, right, and prices plummet, the company tanks. With all its believers gone, the god lost its power. Mostly, anyway. So the priestess couldn't ever change back. She's been a dog ever since. I met her in Vegas. I was really drunk, on a losing streak, passed out in an alley, some guys were gonna steal my shoes, and she scared them off. I stayed with her after that, and it didn't take me long to figure out she was more than just a dog. She'd been trying to get someone to take her seriously for just about forever, but I was the first one who did."

"You're insane," Charles said. That statement seemed inadequate. "*Very* insane," he amended.

"Ask her yourself!" the man said, and whistled. The dog looked up, then slowly loped over. She was a beautiful animal.

"Ask her what, exactly?" Charles said.

"Whatever! Ask her what you should do!"

This was only getting more surreal, but what of it? Life was pointless and absurd, and you took your laughs where you could. Charles looked at the dog. She looked back at him. "So, pup. Should I run away from your crazy friend here before he decides to eat my face or something?"

"You gotta be patient now," the man said, apparently unoffended. "It's kinda slow."

The dog began scratching in the packed sand with her paw, and after a few strokes, it was clear she was making letters.

Charles stared; suddenly his limbs were like rocks, his belly full of cold seawater, his mind blown open and filled with sky. The dog was *writing*.

In the failing light of dusk, Charles read "BE YOU NOT AFRAID."

"Oh, my," he said.

The man patted the dog's head. "You should've written 'Don't fear'," he said. "More economical." He looked at Charles. "She learned to write ages ago. She always sounds old-fashioned. It took her forever to tell me her story."

The dog lay down, giving the man what might have been an affectionately tolerant look, though it was hard to be sure. Charles was not adept at reading the facial expressions of dogs.

Charles sat on a rock beside the man. Hope was in him, cool and inviting, like a sea wind in summer. Maybe this was just a con man and an amazingly well-trained dog . . . but he thought not. Funny, how here at the end of the land, with the rational underpinning of his worldview just unraveled before his eyes, Charles felt like he was standing on solid ground for the first time in months. "I'm Charles," he said.

"I'm Jake. The dog's just dog, she says."

"Ah. So. What's the god's name?"

"Dunno. She won't write it down. Says that'd be profane."

"If I accept your offer . . . what will this revelation entail?" Charles kept looking at the dog. She closed her eyes and thumped her tail against the sand, seemingly content.

Jake laughed. "This shit's deep mystery, you know? I couldn't tell you. I've never seen the god."

"You haven't?" Charles couldn't be sure, in the disappearing light, but Jake's thin face looked sad.

"My soul's too thin," he said. "Shallow, stretched out, narrow, whatever. For a long time I haven't lived for anything but booze and cards and sometimes women. I don't have the inner resources necessary to call the god. But we're working on it." He spoke slowly, but with confidence. "I'm getting better, working out, getting my spirit in shape. We walked here, from Vegas, you know." He said this matter-of-factly, though the idea of such a journey staggered Charles. "That was . . . intense. But good for me. The trackless wilderness, and all that. It has purifying qualities, but I'm not there yet. I've got a long way to go. But you, she says you've got a deep soul, lots of caves and hollows. You're *copious*, robust, just worn out some, and dark. You've got what it takes to help bring the god."

"She told you all that about me? I haven't been walking on this beach for *that* long."

"We've got like a shorthand worked out. So. You wanna buy a god?"

That was the question, wasn't it? "What does it cost?"

"Everything you've got. Everything you've got *on* you, anyway. Wallet, clothes, jewelry, whatever. The god's old-fashioned, too, and doesn't really get the concept of land ownership and bank accounts and stuff like that, so you can keep those things, the god doesn't care."

""So you want me to strip naked?" Charles frowned.

"See, it's a sacrifice. You give up everything material, and get something spiritual in return. And it's best to go into it naked, stripped of pretense. Sacrifices give the god power, so it can appear, work its wonders, you know?" Jake grinned. "Besides, it's pretty much full dark, now, so I won't be able to see your naked ass."

Charles hesitated, then stood up. Why not do it, and see what happened? What did he have to lose? He'd seriously considered walking into the ocean this evening, letting the riptide take him away, letting all his pains wash into the darkness—free from the pain of the divorce, his children who never called, his bitter, never-ending job at the ad agency. Just . . . dissolving his consciousness into saltwater. He'd heard drowning was a remarkably pleasant way to die, though he had his doubts; who'd reported on the sensation?

When self-destruction was an attractive option, why hesitate to give your clothes and money to a stranger with a genius dog?

So Charles removed his wallet, watch, and wedding ring (which he'd never stopped wearing, though every time he looked at it, it hurt); slipped off his shoes, stripped off his slacks, shirt, undershirt, boxers, and socks, and piled them on the sand. The air was cool; night came quickly and cold to the coast of central California. Charles tried to remember the last time he'd been outside, under the sky, with no clothes on; probably not since childhood. His nudity didn't bother him now. Perhaps the obscuring darkness kept him from feeling shy about his middle-aged body; perhaps he was simply beyond that sort of embarrassment.

Jake slung off his backpack. Charles expected him to scoop up the clothes and put them in the pack, but instead Jake removed a fat plastic bottle. "Stand back," he said. He flipped the spout open on the bottle and sprayed the clothes. The sharp tang of lighter fluid filled the air, and Charles backed away, bemused. At least this proved Jake wasn't a con man out to abscond with his wallet.

Jake took a piece of paper out of his bag and, after several tries, set it aflame with a disposable lighter. Before the wind could blow it out, he threw the paper onto Charles's clothes, which ignited instantly. The dog barked, once, happily.

"Here's some rocks," Jake said, holding out a plastic baggie full of dark stones, also taken from his bag. "They're blessed. She blessed them."

Charles took the bag, then sniffed it. He frowned. "Did the blessing involve urination?"

"Don't ask. Let's just say, she's a dog now, she does doggy-type things. Call it marking the god's territory if you want; it's a little bag full of sacred ground."

"What do I do with it?"

""Walk down the beach a ways, find a nice spot, look at the water, toss the stones onto the ground. . ." He shrugged, his shadow in the firelight mimicking the motion on the sand. "Await revelation. Your sacrifice—giving up all your worldly goods, even if only sorta symbolically—and your need should be enough to bring the god. It'll draw strength from you. I wish I coulda done it . . . but I'm spiritually anemic. Not deep enough for that sort of thing yet." He shrugged.

Charles took the bag of stones, feeling faintly ridiculous, but also invigorated. The smoke from his burning clothes smelled surprisingly good, and he was glad he wore natural fibers. He walked a bit, until he found a nice place where the cliffs swooped in toward the water, and he sat in the shadow of the rock, looking at the ocean. Night was here in full now, and the sea was just a deeper black against the sky, untouched by moonlight, the stars clear and high.

He opened the baggie and shook out the stones. They fell to the sand with a series of quiet but distinct thumps.

Revelation. What would it be? How would it help him, reaffirm him, give him hope again?

Except he realized he already had hope. Just meeting Jake, and the dog, and hearing about the god, about Jake's struggle to make his soul stronger... that gave Charles hope, engaged his emotions in a way that nothing had for months. Maybe years, to be honest.

The wind picked up on the water, and a strange light grew in the water. Charles had gone to the Caribbean on his honeymoon, a long time ago, and seen phosphorescent fish; their eerie beauty had enchanted him. This was the same, only this light was vaster than any fish or school of fish; perhaps a pod of glowing whales could be this bright. Or a submerged god.

The dog ran into the water, splashing, streaking for the light, and Charles stood up to watch it. He glanced to his left, and saw Jake far off standing by the fire, watching the water, dancing in the sand. Charles grinned, looking at the sea again, at the imminence of the divine.

A figure walked from the waves, streaming water from long hair. It was a woman, and Charles looked, dumbfounded; Jake hadn't said it was a god*dess*.

But where was the dog?

The woman approached him, but the glow in the water remained. It began to drift slowly to the left, in the direction of Jake and the fire.

The woman stood facing Charles, naked. She was shorter than him, her hair white though she seemed young, her skin and eyes dark. "Hello," she said.

"You're not the god," Charles said, certain, but strangely not disappointed.

"I am the god's servant. Its priestess." She spread her hands. "Your sacrifice gave the god strength, and transformed me. I thank you."

"I'm... glad to help. But there was supposed to be a revelation..." He still wasn't disappointed. Her skin gleamed. He remembered how the first stirrings of love felt, like wings opening, like a long fall without fear of hitting bottom.

"The god considered your problems, and found it had nothing to say. You don't need the god, don't need to have your world broken apart and remade anew, don't need such a devotion to fuel your life. You... the god says you are lonely, and full of regret, and that if those things can be solved, you will be as healed as ever you can be."

Charles shook his head. "Just lonely? Is that it?"

"Don't say 'just'. Lonely is enough. I have been lonely for a long time, before Jake, and even with him, there is a deeper loneliness that cannot be touched."

Charles nodded slowly, then looked beyond her, to the sea. "Is the god going to Jake, now?"

"Yes. Jake will go into the water, and swim in the god's light. Jake's soul is not really so small; he has simply sealed the openings, made his soul into a tiny room, full of needless clamorings. I have been chipping away at those walls, but the god will knock them down in a rush, and fill Jake with light and meaning. You have no such problem. Your soul is deep already; only full of empty places, cold places, that need to see the sun."

"I don't know how to do that," he said. "If I did, I wouldn't be here, now, naked on the beach." Charles shivered and wrapped his arms around himself. "And it's getting colder."

"Then let me help you be warm," she said, and opened her arms.

—With thanks to Greg van Eekhout

Museum Beetles
by Simon Kewin

A scream rang then like a bell through the great halls, bouncing down gilded corridors and off stained-glass windows and ornately painted panels like a maddened fly trying to escape the place.

It was typical of Canto, of who he was and what he was, that he merely flinched at the sound. A single eyebrow was raised, a grey caterpillar amidst the larger, grey explosion of hair, but otherwise he might have been deaf to it. He continued with the meticulous analysis of the piece. In a great, blue, leather-bound ledger he wrote in tiny, neat letters, the ink black like the bodies of ants lying there in a variety of deaths. *Early clock. Gold, brass and steel. Quasi-astronomical symbols on the face. Simple escapement mechanism . . . .*

Only when the entry was properly completed did he set down his pen, push back his chair with a sharp grating sound, and, all wiry haste, run from the Hall of Clocks.

He was old now. The seventy-seventh and current Curator had been writing his neat ant-letters for nearly five decades. Still he moved quickly. Years of work with pieces large and small had kept him strong. He ran into the central hall. Giant skeletons filled the enormous space—long ladder-necks stretching up, up into hazy, golden light that streamed through the ring of small, high windows at the very top of the space. The bone-heads lost in the beautiful, airless glow. Once, a young boy, he had sat and stared up at these huge creatures, wondering about how they could have survived in life when the great hall was the only place big enough to hold them. Now, his mind was all cataloguing and categorization.

Another scream. *The Mammal Wing.* Canto ran across the great hall, weaving between the legs of the vast skeletons and into the oak-paneled splendour of the twenty-mile corridor. As a young boy he had ventured far, far down there too. Had explored perhaps halfway along, glimpsing new rooms, new wonders all the way, before his nerve had given way in the echoing dark.

This time he only went a short way down. A group of children were in the seventh Primate Room. Some he recognized; others were strangers to him, their clothes unfamiliar, from one of the northern or western tribes. They stood now in a silent circle around the stuffed body of one of the great apes that stood erect upon a low, dusty platform. *Pan Troglodytes*, catalogued long ago by the fourth or perhaps even the third curator. The head of the animal shifted a little, seemed to move and writhe as if the ape was trying to free a stiff neck after so many years holding the same pose, or as if trying to understand big, new ideas forming in its sawdust brain.

Canto looked closer, stepping through the ring of children. Insects were devouring the head, writhing in a seething ball that spilled out of the eye-sockets and nose and mouth. They burrowed ferociously, as if each was desperate to get to the center of the mass.

They were familiar. For a moment, he couldn't place them. He looked around the ring of faces, their expressions horrified, fascinated, shocked. At the back a young girl that he knew a little stood apart. She alone looked pensive. Her hair was long and rather tangled.

"Anya. The Great Beetle Colony. On the lower Coleoptery floor. They must be from there. Have you been that way recently?"

"No, Curator." She thought for a moment, her face very serious. "But that is only one floor down." She turned then and walked quickly away, clearly intent on going to see.

He smiled. He was getting old. Perhaps, he thought, as he followed the young girl, it was even time to decide who would become the seventy-eighth Curator.

They stood around the large, exquisite model palace that had housed the Great Beetle Colony for so many centuries. How many generations of the insects had lived and died inside the labyrinthine structure of gold and crystal?

The two of them walked around slowly, looking for holes. Then Anya spotted it—atop the highest dome, a small cupola with a ring of slits to let in the air. They watched as one of the shiny metallic beetles wriggled its way through.

"Fascinating. After so many years they suddenly find out they can escape. Why now, I wonder? Why now?"

"I don't know, Curator."

"Why did they suddenly discover they were living in a golden prison?" Canto spoke mainly to himself. "I must go and check in the archives. See if it has happened before. See if they are dangerous."

He hurried towards the door, then turned back.

"Thank you, Anya," he said.

The girl simply smiled.

The archive was a sacred, secret room that only the Curators entered. It housed the index, the records that made sense of everything else in the museum, that which gave all the objects their meanings.

The high walls were lined with bookshelves—leather cliff-faces, red for the journals of the Curators on one side, blue for the index itself on the other.

Anya sighed and put down the volume she'd been holding. The chair beneath her creaked in the still, dusty air. She was tired, feeling the aches of her age, her eyes prickling. She remembered that day more vividly than a great many that had come and gone since. It wasn't merely the first mention of herself. It was also the first mention of the escape of the Great Beetles. Strange that it should be the same day. Now, these decades later, it seemed as if the Beetles had always been everywhere, scurrying away wherever she went, turning up in every corner and niche—crawling, devouring, destroying. Almost, it seemed, exploring.

Anya had catalogued the Diaspora carefully, plotting their movements, trying to record what was being lost, trying to stay ahead of them. Now they filled all of the known halls and had probably spread out into some of the uncharted regions. Twenty years ago she had discovered the solar tower, its great, spiral staircase a single piece of polished brass. Doorways led to a whole series of unfamiliar rooms full of intricate, strange machinery. At the very top was a small chamber with a circular glass ceiling, reached after a full day of climbing and exploration. She had pushed open the green copper door and seen the Beetles scurrying away.

"Curator?" The voice at the door was quiet, respectful. But it must be something important for one of them to come and disturb her.

She sighed. More and more she liked to be here, amongst the reassuring rustle of the indexes, the smell of ages, and the calm. She was getting old. Everything seemed to make sense here. Out there so much was being destroyed. As fast as she could catalogue and re-catalogue, the objects were disappearing. The Beetles seemed to have worked their way into her consciousness too. She found it hard to concentrate. Whenever she sat down to work on a piece, there would be movement somewhere in the shadows of her vision. A scurrying that almost seemed to be a deliberate distraction.

And what had she found up there at the top of that staircase on that great day? It was, perhaps, the defining moment of her career, the event she would be remembered for. Now she found that she couldn't recall any of it. Her knowledge of those finds—glorious . . . dazzling—was fragmented, slipping away from her even as she tried to bring them to mind.

She arose and walked to the door. Her hand was on the familiar, rattling handle when she saw movement, tiny but unmistakable, on one of the shelves to her left, little more than a candle-shadow flicker.

"Curator? Are you there?"

It couldn't be true. They couldn't be here too. She moved slowly to the shelf, carefully lifted down one of the volumes. Ten years' work of the forty-seventh curator.

The pages were a filigree, just a lacework of tattered scraps. Where the Beetles had been, the words, the meaning, were gone.

In the end, after nearly a day of working themselves up to it, they had to break down the door to get to her. She lay on a carpet of shredded paper, pages from all the books she had hauled from the shelves.

They tried for a time to piece the scraps back together, but it was useless. So they made a pyre of the paper and, none of them speaking, set fire to their dead Curator's body.

The fires burned brightly in the central hall. The bones of the giants made huge, shifting patterns on the tall, shadowed walls around them. The Curator looked down, back into the fire, moving in a little closer to absorb as much as possible of the delicious warmth. The books burned well, but too quickly. He watched as red leather turn brighter and began to smolder, then reached behind him for another, ready to throw it on before the flames died.

The hunters had returned, again with little to show. Hungry, anxious eyes had glanced across at him as the people saw what had been brought back. Some small, pallid fish from the Turquoise Aquarium, a few dried-out fruit. It was not enough, never enough. They looked to him for answers, of course. But what answers could he give? Food was scarce; they had to forage further and further afield. And everywhere they went, the Beetles were there before them, devouring.

He was sure they were larger than they used to be. Sure that in the past, they hadn't fought back. When he was young, they hadn't used weapons ... had they?

Gun left the group of hunters and came and sat down next to him. They were silent for a while. She would be tired from the long hunt. She would speak when she found the words. Theirs was an awkward relationship. At some point, he couldn't say when, this fierce woman, her small eyes like knife-pricks, had replaced him as their leader. In such times, it seemed, they needed strength, not ancient wisdom.

"Curator, tell me," Gun said at last. "The books we burn for fuel. Are there many left? When I was young, I went into the archive, and it seemed that they were endless."

"There are not many left now, Gun, my friend."

The woman, her furs ragged and tattered, nodded her head as if she had expected as much. She was no fool either. Intelligent in her pragmatic way.

"But are there any answers there for us? All that knowledge. . . ." She trailed off; her weariness seemed to have come upon her.

The Curator looked into the flames. "The knowledge, the meaning of it all ... it crumbles away. There is little left now. I am sorry."

"Very well." She sighed, seeming to muster herself. "Then I have something to suggest to you."

The Curator said nothing; his authority was weak now; they no longer needed his assent to speak. He watched as a loose page from one of the books caught fire and burned. A thin line of angry red marched relentlessly across it, leaving behind a curled, crisp wafer of black. The ancient writing on it was destroyed—curious, angular letters, very small and precise. He watched as the words *Simple escapement mechanism* were consumed. He wondered about who had written them. About which ancient, forgotten Curator had laid them down with so much care and thought.

"Yesterday I climbed halfway up the neck of the tallest of these giants," said Gun.

They both knew this was forbidden. "Tell me why," he replied quietly.

"Curator, I sat here and watched as the day came; saw the light coming through those high windows. And I wondered where it was the light came from. I wondered what was . . . outside."

"And you thought that you, that we—" he paused, trying to understand these terrible new ideas— "that we could go there? That there is a place outside of those windows, outside of here, that we could actually go to?"

"Perhaps, Curator, yes. There is nothing here for us. We cling to life. It is forbidden by all our law, I know, but perhaps it is time to try. Who knows what is out there?"

"Who knows if there is an 'out there'?"

"I am willing to climb all the way up and see."

She was asking for his blessing, his assent at least, although she didn't really need it. They sat and stared together into the flames for long moments, watched as the books turned to smoldering cinders, shapes and faces appearing and disappearing in the shifting glow.

He imagined himself ascending that swaying column of bones, a precarious staircase leading up to the roof of their world. He looked up into the darkness and found himself wondering what might be up there. What might be out there.

"I don't know if I can."

"Out there we will need you again, Curator. There will be much that is new and dazzling."

"But is it possible? That outside. . . ." He spoke more to himself than to her.

"Curator, we used to have such knowledge, our lives were discovery and wonder. Perhaps we could be that again."

He didn't reply, but looked up into Gun's eyes, the fire bright in them. He looked around at the others, then back at Gun.

He nodded.

Far above his head, unseen, a fly crawled across one of the high windows. It came across a crack in the glass and crept through.

Outside, it paused for a moment before opening its wings.

four dimensional chess

I know you've beaten me
I just don't know when

—Robert Saunders

Wikihistory
by Desmond Warzel

International Association of Time Travelers: Members' Forum
Subforum: Europe—Twentieth Century—Second World War
Page 263

11/15/2104

At 14:52:28, FreedomFighter69 wrote:

Reporting my first temporal excursion since joining IATT: have just returned from 1936 Berlin, having taken the place of one of Leni Riefenstahl's cameramen and assassinated Adolf Hitler during the opening of the Olympic Games. Let a free world rejoice!

At 14:57:44, SilverFox316 wrote:

Back from 1936 Berlin; incapacitated FreedomFighter69 before he could pull his little stunt. Freedomfighter69, as you are a new member, please read IATT Bulletin 1147 regarding the killing of Hitler before your next excursion. Failure to do so may result in your expulsion per Bylaw 223.

At 18:06:59, BigChill wrote:

Take it easy on the kid, SilverFox316; everybody kills Hitler on their first trip. I did. It always gets fixed within a few minutes, what's the harm?

At 18:33:10, SilverFox316 wrote:

Easy for you to say, BigChill, since to my recollection you've never volunteered to go back and fix it. You think I've got nothing better to do?

11/16/2104

At 10:15:44, JudgeDoom wrote:

Good news! I just left a French battlefield in October 1916, where I shot dead a young Bavarian Army messenger named Adolf Hitler! Not bad for my first time, no? *Sic semper tyrannis!*

At 10:22:53, SilverFox316 wrote:
Back from 1916 France I come, having at the last possible second prevented Hitler's early demise at the hands of JudgeDoom and, incredibly, restrained myself from shooting JudgeDoom and sparing us all years of correcting his misguided antics. READ BULLETIN 1147, PEOPLE!

At 15:41:18, BarracksRoomLawyer wrote:
Point of order: issues related to Hitler's service in the Bavarian Army ought to go in the World War I forum.

11/21/2104
At 02:21:30, SneakyPete wrote:
Vienna, 1907: after numerous attempts, have infiltrated the Academy of Fine Arts and facilitated Adolf Hitler's admission to that institution. Goodbye, Hitler the dictator; hello, Hitler the modestly successful landscape artist! Brought back a few of his paintings as well, any buyers?

At 02:29:17, SilverFox316 wrote:
All right; that's it. Having just returned from 1907 Vienna where I secured the expulsion of Hitler from the Academy by means of an elaborate prank involving the Prefect, a goat, and a substantial quantity of olive oil, I now turn my attention to our newer brethren, who, despite rules to the contrary, seem to have no intention of reading Bulletin 1147 (nor its Addendum, Alternate Means of Subverting the Hitlerian Destiny, and here I'm looking at you, SneakyPete). Permit me to sum it up and save you the trouble: no Hitler means no Third Reich, no World War II, no rocketry programs, no electronics, no computers, no time travel. Get the picture?

At 02:29:49, SilverFox316 wrote:
PS to SneakyPete: your Hitler paintings aren't worth anything, schmuck, since you probably brought them directly here from 1907, which means the paint's still fresh. Freaking n00b.

At 07:55:03, BarracksRoomLawyer wrote:
Amen, SilverFox316. Although, point of order, issues relating to early 1900s Vienna should really go in that forum, not here. This has been a recurring problem on this forum.

11/26/2104
At 18:26:18, Jason440953 wrote:
SilverFox316, you seem to know a lot about the rules; what are your thoughts on traveling to, say, Braunau, Austria, in 1875 and killing Alois Hitler before he has a chance to father Adolf? Mind you, I'm asking out of curiosity alone, since I already went and did it.

At 18:42:55, SilverFox316 wrote:
Jason440953, see Bylaw 7, which states that all IATT rulings regarding historical persons apply to ancestors as well. I post this for the benefit of others, as I already made this clear to young Jason in person as I was dragging him back from 1875 by his hair. Got that? No ancestors. (Though if anyone were to go back to, say, Moline, Illinois, in, say, 2080 or so, and intercede to prevent Jason440953's conception, I could be persuaded to look the other way.)

At 21:19:17, BarracksRoomLawyer wrote:
Point of order: discussions of nineteenth-century Austria and twenty-first-century Illinois should be confined to their respective forums.

12/01/2104
At 15:56:41, AsianAvenger wrote:
FreedomFighter69, JudgeDoom, SneakyPete, Jason440953, you're nothing but a pack of racists. Let the light of righteousness shine upon your squalid little viper's nest!

At 16:40:17, BigTom44 wrote:
Well, here we frickin' go.

At 16:58:42, FreedomFighter69 wrote:
Racist? For killing Hitler? WTF?

At 17:12:52, SaucyAussie wrote:
AsianAvenger, you're not rehashing that whole Nagasaki issue again, are you? We just got everyone calmed down from last time.

At 17:22:37, LadyJustice wrote:
I'm with SaucyAussie. AsianAvenger, you're making even less sense than usual. What gives?

At 18:56:09, AsianAvenger wrote:
What gives is everyone's repeated insistence on a course of action which, even if successful, would only save a few million Europeans. It would be no more trouble to travel to Fuyuanshui, China, in 1814 and kill Hong Xiuquan, thus preventing the Taiping Rebellion of the mid–nineteenth century and saving fifty million lives in the process. But, hey, what are fifty million yellow devils more or less, right, guys? We've got Poles and Frenchmen to worry about.

At 19:01:38, LadyJustice wrote:
Well, what's stopping you from killing him, AsianAvenger?

At 19:11:43, AsianAvenger wrote:
Only to have SilverFox316 undo my work? What's the point?

At 19:59:23, SilverFox316 wrote:
Actually, it seems like a pretty good idea to me, AsianAvenger. No complications that I can see.

At 20:07:25, Big Chill wrote:
Go for it, man.

At 20:11:31, AsianAvenger wrote:
Very well. I shall return in mere moments, the savior of millions!

At 20:14:17, LadyJustice wrote:
Just checked the timeline; congrats on your success, AsianAvenger!

12/02/2104
At 10:52:53, LadyJustice wrote:
AsianAvenger?

At 11:41:40, SilverFox316 wrote:
AsianAvenger, we need your report, buddy.

At 17:15:32, SilverFox316 wrote:
Okay, apparently AsianAvenger was *descended* from Hong Xiuquan. Any volunteers to go back and stop him from negating his own existence?

12/10/2104
At 09:14:44, SilverFox316 wrote:
Anyone?

At 09:47:13, BarracksRoomLawyer wrote:
Point of order: this discussion belongs in the Qing Dynasty forum. We're adults; can we keep sight of what's important around here?

www.ingramcontent.com/pod-product-compliance
Lightning Source LLC
Chambersburg PA
CBHW061558100726
47898CB00002B/420